THE INFER?

COLD WARRIORS

He heard the mindless shriek of an animal slaughtered, the sound muted by the surrounding earth, and a second later he felt the splash of something warm and sticky against his cheek. A chicken, he guessed. Another symbolic death. The bird's blood trickled coppery into his open mouth, and he spat it out in disgust.

He tried to empty his mind of anything but Kate. The affectionate way she'd smiled at him when she thought he wasn't looking, the dimples that appeared in her cheeks when she did.

The poem kept coming back to him though, a couplet he'd forgotten earlier.

The grave's a fine and private place, but none I think do there embrace.

The grave's a fine and private place...

The line was still ringing in his head when they finally lowered the lid on the coffin and began to shovel soil on top of it. The sound of earth against wood rang hollowly inside his sudden darkness, until the lid was completely covered and he couldn't hear anything any more.

WWW.ABADDONBOOKS.COM

An Abaddon Books™ Publication
www.abaddonbooks.com
abaddon@rebellion.co.uk

First published in 2010 by Abaddon Books™, Rebellion Intellectual Property
Limited, Riverside House, Osney Mead, Oxford, OX2 OES, UK.

10 9 8 7 6 5 4 3 2 1

Editor: Jonathan Oliver
Cover: Pye Parr
Design: Simon Parr & Luke Preece
Marketing and PR: Keith Richardson
Creative Director and CEO: Jason Kingsley
Chief Technical Officer: Chris Kingsley
The Infernal Game™ created by Rebecca Levene

Copyright © 2010 Rebellion. All rights reserved.

The Infernal Game™, Abaddon Books and Abaddon Books logo are trademarks
owned or used exclusively by Rebellion Intellectual Property Limited. The
trademarks have been registered or protection sought in all member states of
the European Union and other countries around the world. All right reserved.

ISBN: 978-1-906735-36-4

Printed in Denmark by Norhaven A/S

No part of this publication may be reproduced, stored in a retrieval system,
or transmitted in any form or by any means, electronic, mechanical,
photocopying, recording or otherwise, without the prior permission of the
publishers.

This is a work of fiction. All the characters and events portrayed in this
book are fictional, and any resemblance to real people or incidents is purely
coincidental.

REBELLION

THE INFERNAL GAME

COLD WARRIORS

Rebecca Levene

Abaddon
Books

WWW.ABADDONBOOKS.COM

Dedicated to Anne Perry and Jared Shurin
for weird conversations, general enthusiasm
and a truly outstanding pig.

PROLOGUE

"Are you ready?" Nicholson asked.

Tomas shrugged, because really, how could you ever be ready for this? He looked at the soberly suited crowd, heads hunched against the fine, chill drizzle, but all the eyes that had been fixed on him darted away, embarrassed. Hidden behind gathering clouds, the sun was beginning to set, day fading into twilight around them. They'd already told him this was when it needed to be done. He'd thought midnight, but no, they said that the magics fed off the symbolism, the death of the sun mirroring his own.

And its resurrection, or so they all hoped.

"It's not too late to back out," Nicholson told him. "This is a choice, you know." He looked at Tomas without the usual laughter in his eyes, his wide, smiling mouth turned down. He hadn't wanted Tomas to do this, had tried to talk him out of it, but Tomas had been quite sure.

"We have to know if it works," Tomas said, fighting to keep his voice steady. "After all this time, we have to find out for sure. And the mission to Warsaw would be impossible for anyone who isn't – who hasn't done this. They've got heat sensors everywhere, electrified fences."

Nicholson didn't look convinced and Tomas managed a smile.

"It has to be done, and I'll only be... gone for three days." Three days underground. He shivered, despite himself.

Nicholson rested a hand on his shoulder and squeezed. "It has to be done, Tomas, but not by you."

For some reason, a line from a poem kept wandering through Tomas's mind. *Had we but world enough and time...* It was something he'd read to Kate once, when he'd asked her to marry him and she'd told him *not yet*, just like she'd told him the last two times he'd asked.

Had we but world enough and time, this coyness, Lady, were no crime. That's what he'd said, and she'd laughed, lying naked and sweating in his arms, and asked him just what his hurry was. He hadn't been able to think of a response back then. Now, when he knew the answer, it was too late.

Your quaint honour turned to dust.

They'd told him yesterday that Kate's MIA had been officially upgraded to a KIA. There were no remains to bring home, but then he hadn't expected any. Kate had been deep behind the Iron Curtain when she'd gone missing, her cover blown and all her contacts already rounded up. They could hardly ask the KGB to send back her body for a decent burial.

There is some corner of a foreign field... But that was a different poem, wasn't it?

Tomas looked at the ground for a long time, then back up into Nicholson's sympathetic eyes. "Everyone else has something to lose," he said. "I don't."

Nicholson nodded, shoulders slumping in defeat. He'd known Tomas long enough to know when his mind was made up.

A man was approaching them now, black robes flapping from his shoulders. Tomas thought he looked absurd, this balding white executive dressed up like some voodoo *houngan*. But the man held his head high, apparently proud of the role he'd been chosen to play.

"You'll need to wear this," he said, holding out a necklace made of human teeth, dried brown blood on their broken roots.

Tomas took it without a word and hung it around his neck. His hands were shaking, but no one commented. When the necklace was on, the *houngan* dipped his fingers into a bag at his belt and pulled them out covered in a greasy white paste. He smeared it over every inch of Tomas's face, the tip of his tongue caught between his teeth as he concentrated on the task.

"Now if you'll..." He gestured at the coffin, lying open and empty beside a freshly dug grave.

Tomas hesitated. "Is there anything... anything at all I need to do, before?"

"No. Your role in the ceremony is mostly passive. The rest is, well..." The man coughed uncomfortably.

No more excuse to delay, Tomas dragged reluctant legs over to the pine box, the cheapest they could buy. No point splashing out on something more fancy.

"If you'll..." The *houngan* gestured again, meaning that Tomas should climb in. Tomas wanted to shout at the man to finish the goddamn sentence – *if I can do it, you can say it!* – but he kept his mouth shut. His colleagues were all watching him, men and women who'd risked their lives to save his on more than one occasion, and he wanted to die with dignity.

The wood of the box pressed hard against his shoulders. He hadn't realised what a tight fit it would be and he had to suppress a semi-hysterical laugh as he wondered what they would have done if he'd been claustrophobic.

He thought they'd put the lid on immediately, but they kept the coffin uncovered as the other agents stepped forward, lifted the ropes attached to the side and began to lower him into his grave.

Around him, the ceremony was beginning; he could hear chanting in Creole and other languages he didn't recognise. He saw that Nicholson had shrugged on his own robes, pulled tight in the front over his paunch. Then Tomas lost sight of him, and all he could focus on was the ground passing by on each side of him, and the rectangle of dying daylight above, shrinking by the second.

He heard the mindless shriek of an animal slaughtered, the

sound muted by the surrounding earth, and a second later he felt the splash of something warm and sticky against his cheek. A chicken, he guessed. Another symbolic death. The bird's blood trickled coppery into his open mouth, and he spat it out in disgust.

He tried to empty his mind of anything but Kate. The affectionate way she'd smiled at him when she thought he wasn't looking, the dimples that appeared in her cheeks when she did.

The poem kept coming back to him though, a couplet he'd forgotten earlier.

The grave's a fine and private place, but none I think do there embrace.

The grave's a fine and private place...

The line was still ringing in his head when they finally lowered the lid on the coffin and began to shovel soil on top of it. The sound of earth against wood rang hollowly inside his sudden darkness, until the lid was completely covered and he couldn't hear anything any more.

What would it feel like to die? It was the question he'd been avoiding all day, and now it was all he could think of. Would he feel his lungs constricting, the ventricles bursting? Would his consciousness remain as his brain shut down, sensing his personality slowly sliding away? Oh god – would it hurt?

He couldn't help himself then. His fingers scrabbled desperately against the lid. But the space was so tight that he couldn't get any leverage, the weight already too great for him to lift.

There was only a little air in the coffin with him and he was already gasping for oxygen. If he'd had more breath, he would have tried to scream at them to let him out.

The grave's a fine and private place...

The sentence lengthened and distorted as he asphyxiated, crumbling into individual words, then dissolving into meaningless sounds. And then there was only silence.

Geraint pushed open the door quietly, hoping he'd be able to get himself ready before she knew he was home. But he heard her call out, "Is that you, *cheri*?" and he grimaced then smiled as he walked through the hallway into the living room.

She was still in her wedding gown, the pure white of the dress startling against her dark skin.

"Sweetheart, I'm so sorry," he said.

"Your work's important, I understand," she told him, and he knew she really meant it.

"Why don't you go to bed? I'll be with you in a moment." He tried to make his voice gentle rather than impatient.

She swallowed, then nodded, a flush high on the ridges of her cheekbones. Then she turned and climbed the stairs that led to their bedroom.

He waited till she was out of sight before he slipped into the kitchen. He felt a moment's panic as he looked under the sink, but the blood was still there, behind the detergent bottles where he'd hidden it early in the morning before they'd left for the church. The coil of coarse rope lay beside it, but that was for later.

He was pleased to find that the anti-coagulant he'd mixed with the blood had kept it liquid. He stripped his shirt off, then his trousers, dragging his briefs down with them. A quick prayer, then he began to daub the symbols on his chest, shoulders and arms. The pentagram he put on his back was crude and crooked but that didn't matter – it was intent that counted. A last trickle of gore on the thickening length of his penis, and he was done.

He left the blood a moment to dry, then pulled a baggy blue t-shirt over his head to cover the pattern. A more worldly woman might have asked why he was coming to his wedding bed clothed, but he thought her inexperience would make her glad of it. That was the advantage of a virgin bride.

Well, one of the advantages.

She smiled nervously when he walked into the bedroom, a sliver of white teeth barely visible in the gloom. She'd turned the lights down and closed the curtains but that was fine. His Lord liked to work under cover of darkness.

He pulled the sheet away from her, then stripped the nightgown over her head in one quick motion. He ignored her gasp, pinning her wrists to the bed above her head as he lowered his bulk on top of her.

Her eyes found his. "Do you love me?" she whispered.

"Of course I love you," he said, and felt the One he served gorging on the lie.

He pushed his way inside her sharply, against resistance and then a sudden release. He felt her blood trickling into his pubic hair and saw a dark stain of it on the sheet beneath her. Good. There had been a small part of him that wondered whether she really could be as pure as his plans required.

She was crying now, but he wasn't really listening, concentrating instead on the bite of his nails into the flesh of her arms as he held her down, the animal motions of his hips, letting his own consciousness drift away so that another, greater, could move in to occupy him.

It only took a few more strokes to finish, thrusting himself as far inside her as he could while his seed left him in a rush. He kept himself still for a few moments, to be sure the task was completed, then pulled out and rolled away.

She curled into a ball as soon as his weight was off her, her breath coming in sobbing hitches. It was a desperate sound, the anguish of someone who'd lost everything they cared about or hoped for, but he wasn't worried. She was a Catholic. She'd keep it, the thing his spells had ensured would come of this night. He walked downstairs and into the kitchen without a backward glance.

The rope was heavier than he'd expected and it took him three tries before he realised he wouldn't be able to throw it over the beam that ran the length of the room. Eventually, he climbed onto a rickety stool and eased the rope over.

He stayed on the stool, swaying precariously, when the rope was tied. The noose felt loose around his neck, scratchy against his late-evening stubble. He tightened it with a quick jerk, another downward to test the strength of the beam. Unnecessary, really – he'd already tried it out with the largest sack of potatoes he could find. He'd put on a pound or two in the last few years, but he didn't think his weight would break the house. He laughed when he thought it – carried on laughing, with the most intense joy he'd ever felt, because after all this time, he'd finally done it. It was all beginning.

Then he kicked the stool away and dropped.

PART ONE

PART ONE

Altered People

CHAPTER ONE

"What we've gotta do is declare war on a temperate country."

Morgan shifted his feet in the sand, feeling sweat squelch unpleasantly between his toes, and did his best to ignore the other man.

"Or maybe even somewhere cold. Just not another fucking desert."

Morgan sighed and rolled onto his back, covering his eyes with his hand to shield them from the punishing midday sun. This place wasn't just hotter than anywhere he'd ever been, it was hotter than anywhere he'd ever imagined.

The second-rate gear they were wearing didn't help: no military-issue equipment allowed on covert ops, in case you got caught or killed. Morgan didn't find it reassuring that their MI6 handlers obviously considered both possibilities likely. Not that he'd share his worries with John. The other man had already made it clear he thought Morgan was too young to be on this mission. No need to give him more ammunition.

"Russia's cold. We used to be at war with them," he said instead, the parched air instantly snatching the moisture out of his mouth. He lifted his hand so that it was shading rather than covering his eyes, and turned them to John. "Also, we're not at war with Yemen."

"Should be," John said. "Fucking uncivilised fucking terrorists."

His pock-marked face twisted in distaste. After two weeks on this job Morgan was sick of the sight of it, but there was nothing else beside sand to look at. They called it the Empty Quarter for a reason.

"It's okay for you, kiddo," John continued after a moment. "You're used to this kind of weather, coming from where you do."

"What, Lambeth?"

"You know what I mean, you black bastard. No offence, but before I was paired with you they used to send me to *classy* locations." John briefly peered through the binocs at the black dots on the horizon, then shifted back onto his side. "Plus, prior to our working partnership, I used to get access to some fanny now and again. I haven't seen a lass's face since we've been in this fucking country, let alone anything north of her Watford Gap."

"What about that girl back at base, the posh bird? She was happy to report for duty, judging by the racket coming out of your basher that night. 'Ooh, Johnny boy, you can land your Apache in my hangar any day!'"

"Fuck off, that was two months ago. I've not had a sniff of action since. My balls are so blue they're heading into the ultraviolet. I'm telling you, put me in a club and I'd be fucking fluorescing."

Morgan laughed and let his mind drift, filled with images of his childhood home, gentle hills smothered in green. Trying to refresh himself with remembered rain. "He can't stay holed up there forever," he said after a minute, more hope than prediction.

"I reckon he was never here in the first place."

"He'd better be, or we've spent a fortnight shitting in a tin can for no reason."

The stench of that, and all their other waste, was all around them. They'd buried everything under two feet of sand, but the smell had seeped free days ago. Their target might not be able to see them, snug beneath their camouflage netting, but get within thirty feet and he'd know they were there.

Of course, getting him within thirty feet was exactly the problem. Morgan thought John might be right – he was seriously beginning to doubt the quality of their intel. There was *someone* in that cluster of mud-brick buildings shivering under the heat haze, no question about it, but whether it was the man they'd been sent to kill... Still, rumour control back at base said this bastard ran a training camp that was sending recruits against the lads in Afghanistan. If that was true, it was worth a bit of discomfort to put something lead somewhere soft inside him.

"Morgan," John hissed suddenly. "Movement!"

Morgan pulled his own binocs out of his bergan and trained them on the building. It sprang into instant, sharp focus. And yeah, movement and a half. There were at least twenty people pouring out of the wooden gates.

"Damn it!" he said. "They told us he'd have five men with him max."

"Too late now," John said. "Time to see if you're more than just a pretty face." He'd already pulled out the segments of Morgan's M85 sniper rifle, carefully wrapped against the corroding sand. John's fingers, more nimble than their width suggested, freed the weapon in moments.

Morgan slotted the pieces together with practised ease. He enjoyed the sound of each segment clicking softly into place, the feel of the well-oiled stock in his hands. This was what he was good at. It was why he was here.

He rested the barrel against the sandbag in front of him and set his eye to the sight. But – "Fuck!"

"Not him?" John asked. They'd looked at the surveillance photos of their target so many times Morgan knew he'd remember the man's face for the rest of his life: the proud arch of his nose, and the eyes wide and black and a little too innocent for someone who'd done what he had. Morgan remembered every face he'd put a bullet through. They haunted his dreams. Civvies thought sniping was impersonal, but they didn't know shit.

"Can't tell," he said to John. All the men had checked cloths wrapped around their faces, leaving only a strip of flesh visible around the eyes.

"Then take 'em all out."

"But what if the target's still inside the building?" Morgan tracked the figures as they milled just outside the main gate. They were all armed, AK-47s and other heavier ordnance. He and John were out of range right now, but a few shots fired, someone with the brains to figure out a trajectory, and the enemy would be swarming all over them. Best to leave it till there were fewer hostiles and a clear target.

And yet... The more Morgan watched them, the more certain he became that that figure there, the one standing just to the left of the main body of men, was the one he was after. It was something about the way he gestured, small forceful movements of his hand that seemed to be commands. The way the others seemed to keep him permanently in the corner of their eye, turning to respond whenever he spoke. He was their leader, Morgan was sure of it.

"Got him," he said tightly.

"You're positive?"

"That's the bastard." He prepared to draw the breath that he'd hold in his lungs as he fired. "There's going to be blow-back when he hits the deck. Get ready."

"Mate, I always am."

But Morgan wasn't listening to him any more. His mind was focused on the weapon in his hand. He felt himself pushing his consciousness out so that it extended from flesh and bone into metal: stock, barrel, trigger, the gun just another more lethal part of his body.

Other snipers would measure wind speed and direction, carefully calculate distance to target, curvature of the earth... Morgan had been taught all that, but he didn't need it. In his mind, he could already see the bullet, curving gently up into the sky and then down again as gravity grabbed it on the long journey to its target. He felt the dry desert breeze against his cheek and automatically shifted just a millimetre to the left to compensate for it. He took one last look at the man he was going to kill, held the breath in his lungs and squeezed the trigger.

The target stayed upright for a second, swaying. Then, one after another, his joints hinged shut, until he was lying crumpled on the ground. Morgan was too far away to hear the shouts, even in the vast silence of the desert, but he could see the sudden flurry of activity, men ducking for cover, then realising that they didn't know which direction they needed cover *from*.

If he and John sat tight under their camouflage, there was a chance they wouldn't be found.

"What are you waiting for?" John asked.

Morgan hesitated a moment, then picked another target. Breath in, hold, and that was another man down. Then another, but now the hostiles were starting to get a bead on their position.

One of them let out a wild burst with his AK-47 – "Spray and pray", they called it. Another of them grabbed his arm and he stopped firing. The cloth had slipped from the shooter's face in the moment of panic, and Morgan could suddenly see how young he was, even younger than Morgan. Morgan shifted his aim and took out the man beside him instead.

But that was it. They had their own binoculars out now, and someone must have caught his muzzle flash because suddenly they were all pointing in his direction. He only had time for one more shot before they'd dived behind a pile of rocks that hid them all.

"Now it gets lively," John said.

"They can sit us out inside the base," Morgan said. "Wait till we run out of water."

"No way, mate. That type don't have the patience."

He was right. A few more minutes, and then the gates of the compound burst open and an armoured vehicle roared out. These guys weren't amateurs. They waited till the thick metal sides of the transport were shielding them from Morgan's position before they climbed on board.

Morgan let the sniper rifle drop and pulled out his standard-issue 5.56mm as the personnel carrier barrelled over the dunes towards them. He waited for the last minute to break cover, circling low and left as John headed right – far enough apart they'd be separate targets for anything that got thrown at them, not so far they'd end up in each other's line of fire.

One man put his head out the back of the carrier, swaying precariously as it bounced over the ground. He'd only raised his gun to waist height by the time John took him out, a nice little headshot he'd be boasting about later.

Five more metres, and the truck skidded to a stop. But no one emerged and Morgan guessed no one wanted to be the first man out.

In the time their hesitation gave him he sprinted round until he had a clear view into the back of the transport. They hadn't been expecting him to move so fast and he had a brief snapshot of their shocked faces before he threw in the grenade and dived for cover.

He'd timed it so they only had a second to escape. Men leapt out, but body parts too and a fine spray of red, vivid against the prevailing gold. One of the survivors let out an undisciplined volley of bullets, maybe the same boy who'd done it earlier. Most thudded harmlessly into the sand until a last burst hit one of his comrades in the leg.

Morgan estimated there were eight men left active, plus the driver. John was on them before they had a chance to regroup, single aimed shots heading straight where they'd do the most damage. They turned to face him and now Morgan had his chance, putting a short, controlled volley into their exposed backs.

This was high-wire stuff. He and John were totally exposed, vulnerable to the one man who got his shit together quick enough to shoot back. Morgan's body was tight with adrenaline and the combat-fear that was hard to distinguish from exhilaration.

He felt a brush of something soft against his leg, a spray of sand. A moment later the noise slammed into his ears and he knew someone was shooting from behind him. The driver.

Morgan spun and dived, low and forward, straight towards and beneath the bullets. The man was grinning madly as he fired, blackened teeth bared and – absurdly – a cigarette still hanging from the corner of his mouth.

Morgan's gun was trapped beneath him. He reached into his boot and pulled out his knife instead. It wasn't weighted for throwing but it was the only thing he had. It spun end-over-end out of his fingers as he rolled again, left this time, like a goalie gambling which way the penalty was going. The gamble paid off, the shots went right and then high into the sky as Morgan's knife entered the man's throat with a meaty thud, so deep and hard the hilt ended up flush against his chin.

The man's finger tightened reflexively on the trigger as he convulsed and died. The bullets kept raining upward into the blank blue sky, curving and falling back to earth in a lethal hail.

Morgan waited till the last bullet was spent, the man's back arched in a final agony, before he turned around to see how John was doing.

There was a stain of scarlet on the leg of John's desert combats, but he was still standing and only two of the enemy were. They were circling, trying to flank him. With John weakened from blood-loss they'd probably succeed.

Morgan ran towards them, drawing his shoulder-harness knife. He couldn't risk a shot with so much motion and John in the middle of it.

John's bullet tunnelled through the first man's shoulder just as Morgan's knife slashed at the chest of the second. But the blade hit a rib, and the knife glanced off and out again, still moving with all the force and momentum of the blow.

John spun round from his kill, knowing a second target was behind him. Morgan could see it was going to happen a second before it did, but he was powerless to stop it. His blade kept on moving and John kept on spinning, and at the exact moment when John's chest was level with the blade, it sank in.

Morgan froze for a second. But this was combat and there was one more hostile still moving, wounded but not out for the count. He pulled the knife out of John's body and slashed it fiercely against the man's throat. It bit deep into the bone and stuck there as blood jetted out around it.

Morgan stood, dazed, for a moment – until John's agonised groan brought him back to reality. Morgan dropped to his knees in the sand beside him and pressed his hand uselessly against the sucking wound in his chest.

John's eyes were glazed, each in-breath a wheeze through the wall of his ruined lung, each out-breath a sob of pain. He had to work his mouth three times before any sound came out of it, and then it was a dry croak. "Jesus Christ, it hurts."

"It's okay. It's okay-" Morgan said, looking at the blood seeping out around his hand.

"No it's fucking not," John choked.

"Just hang in there, I'll..." But what was he going to do? "I'm sorry," Morgan whispered.

John's mouth twisted and Morgan wasn't sure if he was trying to smile or if it was meant to be a sneer. "They warned me about you," he gasped. "Should have listened."

He looked like he wanted to say more, but the only thing coming out of his mouth was blood. It bubbled with his breath for a moment, then slowed to a thin trickle as his heart stopped pumping beneath the fingers Morgan pressed to his chest.

"Come on, man, come on!" Morgan lifted John's shoulders and shook him, shook him so hard that his teeth rattled. But there was no shaking the life back into him.

When Morgan got back to base, the brass couldn't get him out of the country fast enough. He closed himself off to the accusing eyes around him, but he already knew what they thought about any soldier responsible for a blue-on-blue death.

He was on a flight back to the UK before they'd even held John's memorial service. The coffin was empty, of course. Morgan had buried John's body under a few feet of sand. Only the bones of the men they'd killed would mark where he lay.

They put Morgan on a civilian aircraft, cattle class. You

couldn't fly a man with no official status on a military plane, it buggered up the plausible deniability. His legs were cramped in the narrow space between the seats and the man next to him twitched and snored the whole way.

A rangy African man was waiting for him at Heathrow, holding up a hand-written sign that said "Hewitt". Morgan followed him without a word, through the dank underground car park and into his estate car. The rain was lashing down outside, smearing the windscreen with water, which almost made Morgan smile. He'd been knocking around the Middle East for so long he'd stopped believing rain like that actually happened.

He didn't ask where the car was taking him – his MI6 handlers always chose different locations for his debriefings – just stared out of the window at the suburban landscape scrolling by outside, like the backdrop to a bargain-basement racing game. When they drove underneath tunnels or bridges his reflection stared back at him for a brief moment of darkness, but it didn't seem to be thinking about anything in particular.

After an hour they passed into the centre of town and then out again, until they finally stopped somewhere in the joyless no-man's land between Vauxhall and Oval.

The driver jumped out to open the door for Morgan, he nodded his thanks, and the car drove off without giving him a chance to ask where, exactly, he was supposed to go. He'd been dropped off in front of a two-storey Victorian house, so after a second he shrugged and rang the bell.

The door opened before he'd taken his finger off the button. A dark-haired, smooth-faced man stared at him a moment, then stepped aside and gestured vaguely towards the back of the building. The whole place looked like it had been decorated in the fifties and allowed to slowly deteriorate ever since. Paisley wallpaper was peeling in the corners, red and brown like the rest of the décor.

Phillips, the man who'd first recruited him from the army to the agency, was waiting in the long, narrow sitting room, a frown squashing his bulldog face. "You're a bloody liability, you know that, Hewitt?" he barked. He was smoking a Silk Cut, filling the room with a blue, flavourless fog. He took another drag, then stubbed it out on the carpet. The burn mark was instantly lost in the lurid crimson-and-blue floral pattern.

Morgan pulled himself to attention. "Yes, sir."

"You do realise you're supposed to be killing the other side?"

Morgan's shoulders tightened. "I think it might've been in the mission briefing, yeah."

There was a small cough of suppressed laughter. Morgan saw that there was a stranger in the room – a neat little man just the wrong side of middle-age sitting in one of the high-backed wooden chairs.

"Don't get lippy with me, you little shit!" Phillips roared.

"It was an accident," Morgan said, but he couldn't look Phillips in the eye.

"So I hear. Just like that ricochet that went straight through Curtis's heart during basic. Or the supposedly defused IED that took off both of Perry's legs. Or... how did Brown die, I can't remember?"

"A septic cut. We got back to base too late to treat the blood poisoning," Morgan said.

"And how exactly did he get the cut?"

Morgan didn't bother replying. They both knew that a tent peg Morgan was hammering had skidded against a rock and straight into Brown's foot. Morgan still couldn't quite believe Brown had died from it.

"It's remarkable," Phillips said. "You're only twenty, and you've already notched up a British body count that would give any Al Qaeda operative a warm glow of satisfaction."

"Your sister died too, didn't she?" the other man asked suddenly, just when Morgan had begun to forget he was there.

Phillips shot him a look of irritation.

"When you were seven, I gather," the man continued, "and you chased her into a lake. Tragic, really. And you'd already lost both your mother and father, before you were even born. There's an Oscar Wilde quote about that – I can't quite remember how it goes, can you? Something about losing one parent being unfortunate, but losing both smacking of carelessness. What a lonely little boy you must have been."

"What is this, Trisha Goddard?" Morgan said, trying to keep his voice light.

The man smiled a secretive little smile that made Morgan want to punch him.

"Who the hell is he?" Morgan asked Phillips.

"Giles here is your get-out-of-jail-free card. If it was up to me, you'd never see active duty again."

Morgan felt his cheeks flood with a heat that was half shame, half anger.

"I, on the other hand," Giles said, "think you're far too useful to waste. You simply need to be handled with the appropriate caution."

"Like radioactive waste," Phillips muttered.

Giles laughed. "Yes, very much like that. Young Morgan certainly isn't a safe person to be around – it's almost as if he emits mortality, isn't it?"

"That's absurd," Phillips said.

"Isn't it just."

Phillips snorted. "No wonder they closed you lot down."

"Temporarily," Giles said amiably. "We're back in business now – extreme solutions for a dangerous world."

Phillips's lips pursed sourly around a fresh cigarette.

"If you're not MI6, who are you?" Morgan asked.

Giles shrugged. "A recently reformed department of the SIS – they used to call us the Hermetic Division, back in the day. You may consider yourself officially seconded."

Phillips nodded when Morgan looked back at him, though he didn't look happy about it.

Morgan didn't want to work for this smug little bastard, but it didn't look like he had a whole lot of choice. He couldn't go back to the army if the spooks decided they had no more use for him. The cover they'd created for him had seen to that: AWOL squaddies ended up in the Glasshouse in Colchester, not back on the front line.

"If I'm working for you," he said, "what is it you want me to do?"

Giles smiled demurely. "Oh, this and that. But unlike Mr Phillips here, I believe I can supply you with a partner even you can't kill."

A blink of time, and Tomas was back. He was in darkness, but sound had returned, a dull thumping somewhere above him. They were still burying him, then. He must have blacked out temporarily. Panic swelled in his chest, larger than the thing that was trying to contain it.

Don't breathe, don't breathe, you'll use up all the oxygen. It was useless, of course. If he hadn't been gasping so hard he would have been screaming. And the sounds were getting louder.

Louder. That meant nearer, which had to mean they were digging him up, not burying him under. Had something gone wrong with the ceremony? He heard, quite clearly now, the sound of a shovel scraping against the wood of his coffin, and he was suddenly furious.

He'd reached a decision, the hardest one he'd ever made, and they were taking it back from him. He didn't know if he'd have the strength to put himself through this all over again.

He was expecting darkness when they prised off the coffin lid and he winced and shielded his eyes from the sudden, unexpected light. He felt the flap of fabric against his wrist, and there was a pungent smell that wasn't quite unpleasant.

A moment later he squeezed his eyes open. There was something wrong with his shirt. It had been fresh on that morning, but now the cuff looked dark and frayed – almost rotten. When he tore it away in disgust the rip travelled all the way down his arm. The whole thing fell off him in strips of decaying cotton.

He pushed himself to his knees and tried to get to his feet, but his legs had cramped and he stumbled over the lip of the coffin to sprawl on the freshly dug earth. His shoulder shuddered away from the rubbery flesh of a worm as it dived back into the ground.

Finally, he staggered to his feet and looked around. The sun was hot and high overhead, nowhere near the horizon. He frowned, disoriented and not able to make sense of it.

The gravediggers stood in a loose ring around him. He looked at them, but he didn't recognise any of the faces, all of them young men. He understood their expressions, though: shock and revulsion. They backed away when he stepped towards them.

"Shit," one of them said. "I didn't think... shit."

Another one bent over, hands on his knees, and vomited.

Could three days have passed already in that uncounted blink of time? His eyes finally found their focus and he could see that he was exactly where he'd started. The graveyard was tucked behind a long-abandoned church on the Yorkshire Moors. He could see the prickle of heather through the dry stone wall around it and smell the blossom on the warm breeze.

There was a man sitting on the furthest wall, looking out over the moors. Something about the way he held his body was familiar, and Tomas took a step towards him.

The man's head turned, as if he'd been keeping Tomas in the corner of his eye the whole time.

When Tomas saw his face, he felt an instant, wrenching sense of wrongness. He couldn't think why. It was perfectly normal, jowly and a little grooved with age, fringed by thinning brown hair. Only...

"Hello, Tomas," the man said.

Tomas froze. "Giles?"

The man smiled, and Tomas knew that look so well, the slightly supercilious twist to his mouth. "Yes, I thought you recognised me."

Tomas had a hundred memories of Giles: Giles at a desk, researching the operation that Tomas would soon be sent on, eyes smudged with shadows because he'd been working all night. Giles eyeing up Kate's legs when he thought Tomas wasn't looking. Giles stammering over a condolence when the stories about Kate first started to filter through. But in every memory he had, Giles was a young man, younger than Tomas.

"What *happened*?" The question felt too small for the size of all the things he wanted to know.

Giles spread his hands. "I hardly know where to begin. The Berlin Wall fell. The Cold War ended and the Hermetic Division was disbanded before you could be resurrected. I got married, then she left me for a Welsh schoolteacher. The Spice Girls broke up, then reformed, then broke up again."

"What?" Tomas said again. "In *three days*?"

Giles flipped over the newspaper in his lap so Tomas could read it. The headlines meant nothing to him, but after a moment Giles tapped a finger on the top of the page, and he saw the date: 16 June, 2009.

Tomas looked down at himself, and saw for the first time the way his clothes hung in rags from his chest. He touched himself there but felt nothing, not the faintest stirring of a heartbeat. "What happened to me?"

Giles smiled. "You died, Tomas, twenty years ago. Welcome back."

CHAPTER TWO

They'd kept Morgan's flat for him while he was away, a small bedsit in a tower block near the Elephant and Castle. They hadn't bothered to dust it, though, and he woke up with his sinuses clogged and a gritty, unclean feeling in the back of his throat.

The phone had been disconnected about two years ago, so he'd plugged in his mobile to charge last night. When he'd rolled out of bed and showered he picked it up and scrolled through the stored names. He had until five o'clock, Giles had told him.

But there just wasn't anyone he wanted to talk to. He thought about cleaning the flat, then decided he didn't want to do that either.

Daytime television was as mind-numbing as ever. He sat through two hours of it before he reached for the phone again to call headquarters and get a number for John's family. John hadn't been married, but he'd talked about his parents.

Morgan's thumb hovered over the dial button, then flipped the phone shut again. They wouldn't want to hear his apology. The only reason he'd be calling was to make himself feel better, not them. He knew it was true because that's what Perry's sister had said when he called her five months ago, and then she'd screamed down the phone at him for ten solid minutes and he'd felt obliged to keep listening. Maybe it actually had made her feel better, but Morgan couldn't face the same bitter accusations from John's family.

He flung the phone away from him in a jagged spike of rage. "Fuck!"

There was no food in the flat, so at lunchtime he went to the nearest greasy spoon, in the shadow of the squat red shopping centre, and ordered the full English. The traffic dawdled by outside, the people too, and it felt very strange to be home. He found himself looking at the country through foreign eyes. Too cool, too grey, too restrained.

When four-thirty crawled round, he was glad to start the walk down Kennington Park Road towards Oval. It felt good to stretch his legs, even though the air was heavy with traffic fumes and incipient rain. He hadn't thought it would be possible to miss the clean, furiously hot desert air.

This time he was left waiting thirty seconds at the door of the Victorian semi, but it was the same smooth-faced man who let him inside.

There was no Phillips today. Giles had someone else with him. The man was dressed neutrally, in jeans and a green t-shirt, but he looked uncomfortable in his clothes. His face was very serious, a little too bony under thick blond hair. He inclined his head, but didn't offer to shake hands. Warned him to be careful, had they? Morgan immediately bristled.

"My new partner?" he asked Giles.

The little man nodded. "Tomas Len, this is Morgan Hewitt. Tomas has been out of circulation for a little while, Morgan. You may need to bring him up to speed on a few things."

Tomas nodded a curt confirmation. His eyes were a very startling bright green, and Morgan found that he didn't want to spend too much time looking into them. He didn't want to get to know this man. Definitely didn't want to get to like him. He was done with that, it hurt too much every time.

"All right," he said. "Good to be working with you."

"Likewise." But Tomas didn't sound convinced.

"Lovely," Giles said. "Now, your flight leaves in three hours, so you'll have to absorb the briefing materials on the way. We've provided you with a laptop pre-loaded with everything we know.

You'll need to read it and reformat your hard-drive before you land."

"Three hours?" Morgan said. He hadn't imagined they'd be sending him out again so soon.

Tomas looked equally thrown. "I'm sorry, what's a –"

"Morgan will fill you in," Giles said quickly – too quickly. Morgan wondered what it was he hadn't wanted the other man to say.

Tomas hesitated a moment, then nodded. "My – " He laughed suddenly, not a very happy sound. "My passport has expired."

"All taken care of." Giles handed Morgan a briefcase heavy enough to contain the laptop he'd mentioned as well as a pair of passports. He paused for a moment when he caught Morgan's expression. "I'm sorry, were you expecting a longer leave? People to see, things to do?"

Morgan remembered his earlier inability to think of a single person he wanted to talk to and gritted his teeth. "Not a problem."

"Good. Budapest should make a nice change of scene for you, anyway."

Morgan frowned. "Budapest? What the hell are you sending me to Poland for?"

Tomas looked at Morgan in disbelief. "You mean Hungary."

Giles smiled at Tomas as Morgan scowled at him. "Now you see why we're sending you to babysit. It's not a military mission, Morgan, and you can't go armed. Too high a risk of a diplomatic incident. No guns, no knives."

"Then what the hell am I supposed to use? My cutting wit?"

"Thankfully, we shan't be relying on that. I appreciate that you may seem an unusual choice of operative for this mission, but I'm sending you because you're very good at what you do, and if the situation is as we think it might be, we may need to call on you to do it."

Morgan took a second to unravel the sentence. "You want me to kill someone." Giles seemed to be talking about something cold, calculated – not like the missions they'd sent him on before, which might have been off the books, but had still been part of the larger war.

If he did whatever it was they wanted, could he really still call himself a soldier, or would he be something else?

"An assassination?" Tomas said.

"Quite possibly. There's a man – a very wealthy man – who's acquired, and plans to sell, something far too dangerous to fall into foreign hands. We need you to find out who his intended buyer is, and most importantly to get it back. If that requires you to kill him, all we ask is that you do it discreetly."

"Something dangerous?" Tomas asked.

Giles grimaced. "You remember the Ragnarok artefacts, I'm sure. You did spend half your career chasing after them. That's why you were brought back for this mission."

"You're saying this person has found one of them?"

"We think so."

Morgan held up his hand. "Ragnarok artefacts?"

Giles sighed, as if he wasn't sure it was worth the effort. But after a moment, he said, "Ragnarok is the end of the world in Norse mythology – something like the Christian Apocalypse. The Ragnarok artefacts are said to be capable of bringing it about."

"The end of the world?" Morgan said incredulously.

It was Tomas who nodded. "So the stories say. There are three artefacts, and we never found a single one. But that was all right, as long as no one else did. If the Soviets get hold of them..."

"Or Iran," Giles said hurriedly. "Or almost anyone other than us."

Morgan frowned. "So we're talking about nuclear material? A dirty bomb?"

"Close enough." Giles smiled thinly. "Now, you'll be meeting another contact when you get to Budapest – Anya Friedman of the BND. The Germans were the first to give us the heads-up on this, so it's a joint mission, I'm afraid. But Anya's their lead agent on the artefacts. She's been researching them for seven years, and she knows almost as much about them as you do, Tomas. You're due to meet her at 3pm tomorrow – details are in the files."

As he was speaking, he slid a small photo across the table to them. The woman in it was strawberry blonde and very pretty but there was something forbidding about her face. She didn't look like she'd be a whole lot of fun to be around.

"And Richard?" Tomas said.

Giles shook his head. "Unavailable." His tone of voice shut down any further questions on the subject. "Try not to be late for the rendezvous. You know what sticklers the Germans are for punctuality. "

Tomas nodded curtly. "And who is the man we're going after?"

"Viktor Karamov. He made his money from the rape of Russia's energy industries, and he's been spending it with heroic speed ever since. We don't think this transaction is a matter of conviction for him – in fact, I doubt he has many. It's purely about profit."

"Does he even know what the artefacts are?" Tomas asked.

Giles looked completely serious for the first time since Morgan had met him. "Let's hope not."

Tomas was careful not to touch Morgan as they slipped into the back seat of the Ford together. He didn't know what his own flesh would feel like to a normal human and he couldn't bear the thought of Morgan flinching at his touch.

The same rangy African man who'd brought him and Giles down to London was driving. He caught Tomas's eye in the rear-view mirror and quickly looked away, though his face remained politely blank. He'd been there in that graveyard in Yorkshire.

Tomas found himself obsessively curling and uncurling his fingers, clenching and unclenching his toes. He'd never realised before what a noisy, twitchy, restless thing a living body was. His body still moved in the right way. It was completely under his control. But it was – silent. There was no blood surging through his veins, no food stewing in his stomach juices, no sweat pooling in his pores. He realised that the only reason he'd ever need to draw breath was when he needed to speak. He stopped his lungs for a minute, then two, five, and felt... nothing.

He was entirely inert – an object, not a person.

Morgan stirred in the seat beside him, and Tomas jerked a look at him, worried that he'd noticed Tomas's unnatural stillness. Tomas knew Morgan had been told nothing about what he was.

Morgan wasn't looking at him, though. He was still staring down at the miniature silver computer Giles had given him, one small frown line on his handsome, almost delicate face. Just how young were they recruiting them these days, anyway? Morgan couldn't have been far out of his teens.

A few weeks ago – twenty years ago – Tomas would have started a conversation designed to find out everything he could about his new partner. Because Tomas's life would be depending on him and he needed to know his strengths and weaknesses, the idiosyncratic ways his mind worked. Morgan didn't seem to want to talk, though, and that was fine with Tomas.

The way you formed a friendship was finding the point where you met in the middle. He couldn't imagine anywhere that he and this brash young man could meet.

He looked out of his own window instead, just as the car drew level with the River and turned right, heading east for City Airport. He didn't know this area of London well, but he was sure that building hadn't been there before – the overblown, ship-like thing with its prow pointing towards Vauxhall Bridge.

It had passed by before he had a chance to look more closely, but now he kept noticing these little quirks of change. The tower block opposite Battersea Bridge where there used to be a terrace of Edwardian houses. The cars parked outside just a little sleeker and rounder than the ones he remembered.

The Houses of Parliament were next, reassuringly the same. Except, no. Where the stone had once been black and grimy it was now a rich gold. They'd finally cleaned it.

A little further on, and what the hell was that huge silver wheel on the banks of the Thames behind City Hall? A moment later he realised it was a Ferris wheel. There were people high above the city in those round metal pods.

His hand fisted around the door handle as he made himself stop staring at it. He felt untethered from reality, as if he'd slipped into an alternate universe that was only tantalisingly like the one he knew.

For the first time, he felt the full force of all the time that had passed – but not for him.

"You all right?" Morgan asked.

Tomas nodded and dropped his head, drawing a deep, unnecessary breath. He didn't say anything else until half an hour later, when they reached the crook of the River that held the Isle of Dogs.

By then he was expecting it, of course, but it was still a shock to see: Canary Wharf, no longer an incomplete spike towering over a building site but the priapic focal point of a complete city in miniature. The red light on top of the pyramid winked at him.

"And upside down in air were towers," he said as he looked at it. "Tolling reminiscent bells that kept the hours."

Morgan frowned. "You what?"

"*The Waste Land*," Tomas said. Then, at the young man's unimpressed look, "It doesn't matter. It's nothing."

After that he kept his eyes shut, his forehead leaning against the cool glass of the window until they'd drawn into the airport.

As they stepped out of the car, Morgan handed him the briefcase with the miniature silver computer inside it.

"You'd better read it on the plane," he said.

Tomas handed it back to him. "Brief me when we land."

"Suit yourself." Morgan's cupid's bow lips narrowed in irritation, but Tomas could hardly tell him that he didn't have the first idea how to work the machine.

"You'll need this, anyway." Morgan handed him a ticket and a small red booklet that it took Tomas a second to realise was his passport. He flipped it open and frowned when he saw that it was in his own name. But then, who'd be expecting Tomas Len to reappear now?

"I'll see you at the gate," Tomas said, and Morgan froze a moment before nodding his head and stalking off. Tomas had the impression that he'd hurt him, though he couldn't imagine how.

Inside the big, neon-bright space of the terminal building he felt lost again. He'd thought that in the antiseptic no-where, no-when of the airport he'd be able to avoid it, but the dislocation was all around. The people talking into their tiny cellular phones, or – he thought this was what they were doing – taking photographs with them. The *fashions*.

He caught a glimpse of a stack of newspapers, sitting outside Smiths. The picture of the Queen on the front cover showed an old woman. He remembered her still holding on to a dignified middle age, but the whole world was older now. Everyone he knew. Friends' children now adults, friends' parents dead. If Kate had been alive, she would have been fifty-two.

It wasn't as if this future was unexpected. He'd seen the seeds of it in his own time. He just hadn't expected to be getting here so soon.

Morgan ordered himself a Big Mac Meal, then desultorily poked at his burger as he folded a fry in half and put it in his mouth.

It wasn't like he'd been intending to become best mates with Tomas. In fact, he'd been quite happy for Tomas to ignore him entirely. But there was something about the expression on the other man's face when he looked at Morgan that got to him. As if he wasn't really there – as if he wasn't worth knowing.

Tomas's attitude pressed a hot button somewhere in the part of Morgan's head devoted to his childhood. It released a memory, nearly ten years old, that he hadn't taken out and looked at in a long time. It was a maths lesson, something he used to be good at. Aaron got a question wrong and then Morgan got it right – all "me, me, me" with his hand in the air – and when Mr Logan praised Morgan, Aaron said, "It's Morgan's fault, sir. His smell's putting me off."

And what Morgan remembered was the wince in Mr Logan's eye that told him it was true. He remembered the sick lurch of shame. Of course there was no way he'd explain it was because nobody at the care home had the time to make him wash. But he stopped answering questions in class after that.

A tinny voice finally called their flight, and Morgan shrugged the dark mood off as he headed for the gate. He and Tomas had to find some way to work together. This Karamov sounded like a gold-plated shit, and he had the money to pay for high-calibre protection.

It wasn't until the men surrounded him that he realised they were there. There were five of them and he hadn't seen them in nearly two years.

"Oh look, it's Private Friendly Fire. Shot anyone else in the back recently, Hewitt?" said a bulky man with a red face and a brown crew-cut.

"Let you back in the country did they, Nobby?" Morgan said – smiling, because it was easier to pretend they were both joking.

Nobby didn't smile back. Around him, the four soldiers from Morgan's old platoon formed a solid wall of flesh. Morgan knew they'd all been told his cover story, that he'd gone AWOL just after shipping out to Afghanistan.

"Got some leave, did you?" Morgan asked, still trying to keep it friendly.

"Yeah," Nobby said. "Some of us wait till it's official rather than shitting our keks at the first sign of action. Do they know you're here, Hewitt? Can't do, or they'd have you banged up where you belong."

"I did my time," Morgan said, the nearest to an answer he could give.

Nobby seized the collar of his t-shirt with a sudden vicious jerk that half lifted Morgan off his feet. "Like fuck you did!"

Adrenaline rushed and instinct kicked in. Morgan broke Nobby's grip by gouging his knuckle into the soft flesh between his thumb and forefinger, then drove the other man back with a blow to his solar plexus that left him doubled over and gasping.

Instantly the other four were on him, fists raised, necks corded with strain and anger.

"Jesus," Nobby gasped. "Jesus Christ. Leave him." And when the others continued advancing, "Just leave him, I said. The little bastard isn't worth it."

There was a frozen moment of time, then the men dropped their fists. Their eyes still bored into Morgan, despising him utterly.

When Morgan felt the hand land on his shoulder, his keyed-up nerve endings almost twitched a blow out of him before he realised it was Tomas.

Yeah, of course it was Tomas. Because that was exactly the scene he wanted his new partner to see.

"Come on, we're going to miss the plane," Tomas said.

Morgan only looked up at him when they'd put fifty feet between them and Morgan's former comrades. He knew if he saw even a hint of pity in Tomas's eyes, he was going to deck him.

But Tomas just looked grave. "It's the nature of the job," he said. "No one thanks you, and no one else will ever understand."

For some reason, Morgan found that this made him feel a little better.

Tomas settled into his seat on the plane, careful not to catch Morgan's eye. He knew the younger man was ashamed Tomas had seen the confrontation earlier.

Tomas wanted to tell him that he understood. That when he'd been alive, he'd taught himself not to care what other people thought of him. He'd spent his career deceiving people who believed he was their friend, not just telling lies but living them for months at a time. And now...

But he didn't know how to start that conversation, so he didn't say anything. Instead he looked out of the window and wondered what it meant, that they'd woken him after all this time to continue his search for the Ragnarok artefacts.

Out of Morgan's earshot, Giles had told him more, that there had been worrying portents, several over the last year and four more in the previous week alone. An algal bloom had turned the River Severn red as blood. In Stockholm, a child had been born with two heads and the terrified mother claimed that one of them had spoken to her before it died. Crops failed in perfect weather. All the signs Tomas had looked for, in his long and fruitless search, were finally appearing.

The plane was cruising high above the clouds, an endless white field that looked like snow, and Tomas thought about another journey through snow, twenty-five years ago, with another young man who was his newest partner.

He and Richard had crossed the endless barren wastes of Greenland on a sled. The rank smell of the huskies surrounded them and there was nothing to do but talk.

"How long have you been searching for these things, anyway?" Richard had asked. He was American, soft-spoken and sandy-haired.

"A long time," Tomas told him.

"And you're still no closer to finding them?"

Tomas found Richard's open astonishment refreshing. He laughed. "You know how they say life is what happens when you're making other plans? The Hermetic Division seems to be what happens while we're looking for the Ragnarok artefacts."

"But what are they? The briefing didn't say."

Tomas just looked at him.

"You don't know that either? Jesus – then what the hell is the point?"

Tomas had asked himself the same question more than once, and had reached only one conclusion. "It justifies our existence to Whitehall. The things we are finding – the real discoveries – they're astonishing. You know that. But how much of what we know is of any direct use, the kind of use governments want to put it to? The artefacts offer everything the bureaucrats want. They're a reason to keep the Division open, and that's all Nicholson cares about. For that, it's worth sending me on a wild goose chase every now and again."

Richard shook his head, unconvinced. "But these guys we're visiting – they know about the artefacts, right?"

Tomas shrugged. "We'll see, won't we?"

They reached the abbey on the third day, its spires poking up over the horizon like the masts of a ship before the whole huge edifice became visible. It was said the monks built it anew from the ice every year, that they'd been doing it for a thousand years, since the first Norse settlers arrived on the island.

In the pictures Tomas had seen, the building had looked ethereal and beautiful, all long thin lines and graceful arches. But this year the monks seemed to have opted for a more gothic theme. The abbey was squat and powerful and the flying buttresses were carved into leering gargoyle faces, all the more sinister for their near transparency.

The abbot met them at the door. His blunt Inuit face broke into a sudden, unexpectedly broad smile as they approached. "Our travellers from England. Welcome."

He offered them food and rest but when they declined he nodded understandingly and led them through to his study, buried deep in the buildings. Like them he remained bundled in his furs, breath freezing into fog in front of his mouth. Everything in here, every wall and every door, was carved from the same blue-green ice. Even the high-backed chairs he gestured them to sit in were made from it.

"So you've come to ask me about the artefacts," he said.

Tomas couldn't hide his surprise and the abbot smiled. "I heard about your hunt and I knew you'd find me eventually. We're aware of the legends about this place. Our unusual set-up attracts them."

"Is it true you were founded by the Viking settlers?"

The abbot nodded. "Yes. Our records confirm it."

Tomas felt the first stirrings of hope. All the best sources of information about the artefacts were Scandinavian, dating back to the Elder Edda or before. Could this really be a genuine lead? "But the Norsemen left here nearly five hundred years ago," he said. "They were driven out by famine, weren't they?"

"The invaders fled, but they left their traditions behind. Some of my own people chose to continue them."

Richard looked impatient. He hadn't been at this long enough to understand the importance of validation, establishing provenance. When he'd chased as many dead-end leads as Tomas had, he'd learn.

"But what about the artefacts?" Richard said. "Are they here?"

"The artefacts have no place in God's house."

Richard leaned forward. "So you know what they are? And where they are?"

The abbot stood. He was a short man but his body was thick and Tomas suspected the furs hid layers of muscle as well as fat. Richard's mouth snapped closed as the abbot loomed over him.

"You could search the whole world and never find them," the abbot said.

Tomas recognised a non-answer when he heard one. "But do they exist?"

"They *are* real." The abbot leaned against the desk, round face abstracted as he seemed to ponder something. Tomas let him think. He sensed this wasn't a man who could be cajoled or bullied. Eventually the abbot sighed and reached behind him, pulling an ancient leather-bound volume from a shelf above his desk.

"Let me show you something." He flipped through the book, page after page of primitive, blocky woodcuts, until he settled on one near the end. It showed a man reading from a manuscript, while beside him another man plunged a dagger through a bleeding heart. They were dressed in the loose robes of medieval merchants and their faces, crudely drawn, seemed entirely devoid of emotion. It made what they were doing all the more unpleasant.

Richard frowned. "I can't see anything that looks like it might be the artefacts. The knife, maybe."

The abbot's gaze remained fixed on the page, his expression unreadable. "This claims to illustrate the ceremony in which they're used." He looked up suddenly, eyes spearing Tomas. "Knowing this, do you still want to find them?"

They'd stayed the night, but while the monks had been charming and hospitable, it was clear they wouldn't reveal anything more, and the next morning they'd departed, Richard frustrated and Tomas troubled.

"You were right," Richard said, on the long sled ride back to civilization. "It's a shell game with nothing inside."

Had Richard been right, or had this Russian finally found the artefacts that had eluded them for so long? And what would come of it if he had? Tomas realised that, twenty-five years later, he still couldn't answer the abbot's question. All he could do was watch the clouds slide by underneath them, white and innocent, and wonder what they'd find when they landed.

Two and a half hours later they were in Budapest.

The air hit Tomas as soon as they stepped outside the airport, so humid it was like something solid, even near midnight.

"Shit – I thought I was coming somewhere colder," Morgan said, then gave a slight wince and shut his mouth, as if the words had sparked an unpleasant memory.

Tomas drew him towards the taxi queue and didn't reply. There were at least thirty people already waiting, sweating and bored, but it was better than hiring a car. Anything you put your name to left a trail.

The queue crept forward, everyone seeming to move slowly in the sluggish air.

It gave Tomas time to look around, at the big, modern airport and the local people in their Western fashions and their Japanese cars. All these tourists – what would they have made of the Budapest *he* knew? But they wouldn't have been allowed into it.

Finally they were at the front of the line. The taxi driver – a dark-skinned, sour-faced man – didn't bother to get out, so Tomas popped the boot himself, then threw in his small suitcase beside Morgan's rucksack. Morgan kept the briefcase in his hand as they climbed in the back.

"Hotel Gellert," Morgan told the driver.

That beautiful art nouveau relic had been here the last time Tomas visited. The city they drove through was also reassuringly similar. Only the people looked different. They seemed both busier and more relaxed – free, he supposed.

He still couldn't fathom that the war he'd sacrificed so much to fight had been won while he was sleeping.

They were halfway into Pest, the grubbier, more commercial side of the city, before Tomas realised they were going the wrong way. He leaned forward to speak to the driver, and as soon as he saw the man's eyes slide shiftily away from his he knew that it wasn't a mistake.

Furious, he reached through the glass partition to grab the driver's neck. The man pushed himself against the left-hand window, swerving the car as he did. The wheels squealed against the tarmac and the car instantly stank of rubber. A second later, the driver had control again.

Tomas tried to twist himself sideways, but his elbow jammed in the narrow space between the glass panes.

"What the hell –" Morgan said.

"It's a trap," Tomas snapped, still groping uselessly for the driver. "This isn't the way to the hotel."

Morgan's eyes widened. He wrenched at the door handle, but of course the driver had locked it. And now they were in an area Tomas did know: derelict warehouses where anyone could do anything and no one would see.

Tomas pulled his arm back from the partition, then smashed his palm forward with all his strength.

The glass shattered and the driver ducked, spinning the car in an uncontrolled arc. But he'd already been braking. A few more feet and they were stationary.

Tomas drove his shoulder against the door beside him. Then again. There was a shriek of metal and the lock gave, spilling Tomas onto the cracked concrete of the pavement.

He rolled to his feet, while Morgan tumbled onto the ground behind him. The night was dark, only a sliver of stars showing between the walls of the buildings surrounding them. He thought he heard motion, but he couldn't see where it was coming from. Then the cab reversed, leaving another thin layer of rubber on the road, and as it swung away the beam of its headlights swept over Tomas.

Caught in the sudden gold brightness, four men stood facing them, faces hidden behind black rolls of cloth. All of them had guns.

CHAPTER THREE

Morgan froze, prone on the warm concrete, as the men stared silently at them. The blunt pieces of metal in their hands were the only statement they needed.

They knew they had Tomas and Morgan outnumbered and outgunned and they weren't expecting any resistance. When Tomas leapt straight towards them, there was a moment's hesitation before their fingers could tighten on their triggers.

Morgan opened his mouth to shout at Tomas to *stop, for fuck's sake come back* – but it was already too late. The bullet grazed Tomas's arm as he barrelled into the nearest man, tumbling him to the ground and carrying Tomas behind the other three. The sound of the shot echoed very loudly in the silent alley.

Something switched off in Morgan's mind, the rational analytical part of him that was no use in battle. And something more primal switched on. Their assailants had all spun to face Tomas, the immediate threat. They'd eliminated Morgan from their calculations, and he needed to make them regret it.

Keeping himself low and slow-moving, he belly-crawled over the concrete between him and the first of the men, ten yards in front of him. Further back, the one Tomas had knocked down rolled and rose again, fluid as a gymnast. Pros then, Morgan thought, and factored that into his equations.

Tomas was still moving, never still long enough for the bullets to touch him. Morgan saw him wrap both arms around the shoulders of another man and hook an ankle behind his knee. The two of them tumbled to the ground together, but Tomas was on top and at least twenty pounds heavier.

Two more shots ploughed into the pavement inches from where Tomas had just been. In the strobe light of the muzzle flashes, Morgan saw Tomas's hands grasp the neck of the man pinned underneath him. A wrench left and a snap back right and it was broken. The man slumped bonelessly and Tomas released him and rolled away, narrowly avoiding three more bullets.

And as the dead man's comrades watched in shock and disbelief, their attention entirely focused on Tomas, Morgan finally reached them. He grasped the ankles of the nearest and jerked backwards. The man went down too fast to break his fall. His head smashed straight into the pavement and stayed there, a halo of blood spreading around it.

The others heard the muffled gasp and the *crack* of impact as their companion fell. Instinctively, their heads snapped round to face the new enemy. But they were expecting a standing target. The first sweep of their eyes passed over Morgan's head.

He needed a weapon, anything. A gun. The fallen man's gun, trapped underneath his body. As Morgan strained to roll him over, fingers fumbling beneath his chest, he saw the eyes of one of the others, black behind their mask, slide down to him.

Morgan's hand brushed against the cold metal of the gun just as the other man's weapon swung towards him. Morgan's line of sight led straight up the barrel and he knew the shot would take him right between the eyes. He shut them, not wanting to see it coming.

A second of silence later he flicked them open again, and there was Tomas, arms around the assassin's chest. Morgan saw the fabric of the man's black mask shift as his mouth opened beneath it in a scream that was soundless because Tomas was squeezing all the air out of him.

Tomas's face was pale and impassive, no flush of anger or exertion.

Morgan's fingers finally closed around the gun and he raised it to finish off the man Tomas held imprisoned. His line was true, straight to the assassin's head – until the man beneath him gave one final, unexpected shudder. As Morgan's finger tightened on the trigger, his arm jerked sideways and the bullet he'd meant for his enemy found Tomas's heart instead.

Horrified, Morgan waited for Tomas's body to crumple and fall, for the spurt of blood that was always darker than you imagined. But there was only the smallest stain around the bullet hole in Tomas's t-shirt, black in the moonlight. And Tomas was still standing, his arms squeezing tighter and tighter.

The man he held let out a horrible, gurgling gasp as the gore rose up in his throat to spill red and brown through the material of his mask. The hands that had been clawing uselessly at Tomas's arms splayed in a spasm of pain and then slackened for good. And still Tomas kept on squeezing, seemingly oblivious to the fact that he himself was mortally wounded.

"Let him go, man," Morgan gasped. "It's over."

It was. Tomas must have taken down their final attacker while Morgan was grappling with his. Morgan could see the man's body tossed ten feet away, one arm half torn from the socket of his shoulder, and his neck twisted so far round it looked like his head had been put on back to front.

Tomas nodded and let the body in his arms drop. It slumped to the ground and Morgan suddenly smelt the acid of piss. The man must have lost control of his bladder when he knew he was dying.

Then Tomas turned to one side, and Morgan glimpsed the exit wound in his back, as large as a fist. Inside he could see meaty muscle and the white of bone beneath it.

Tomas noticed Morgan staring. His hands drifted up, probing around the lethal hole in his chest.

Except it wasn't lethal, was it? Because Tomas was still standing.

"We need a hospital. I think you're in shock," Morgan said.

Tomas's lashes flicked downwards a moment, as if he was about to pass out, but then he looked back at Morgan and Morgan realised he'd simply been deciding what to say. "I'm absolutely fine."

Morgan laughed in a way that he knew was near hysterical. "You're a long fucking way from being fine."

Tomas glanced down at the man he'd just killed, and Morgan saw a look pass across his face that he couldn't read but didn't like. "You're right," he whispered. When he looked back at Morgan his expression was suddenly savage. "Turn around," he snarled.

Morgan shook his head. "We need to search the bodies. Quick, and then get out of here. Anyone could have heard those shots."

"In a minute." Tomas raised his hands and Morgan saw that they were shaking. "Turn around. *Now*. And don't look back until I tell you."

Morgan didn't understand what was happening. Was Tomas's wound finally catching up with him? Would he turn back to find his partner dead, before the mission had really begun?

"Turn. Around." Tomas said, his voice as chilly and brittle as ice. Morgan caught the look in his eyes and spun round as fast as he could, turning his back on the murderous expression there.

He stared into the distance, through the narrow gap between the warehouses, willing his eyes to penetrate the darkness. There could be more of them out there, a mop-up crew in case the first team failed. The local police could be on their way, and the last thing he and Tomas were supposed to do was get noticed. They needed to get out of there. But he didn't move and didn't look round. There was a sound behind him, very quiet but so familiar he had to exert an effort of will not to notice how much it sounded like somebody eating.

Morgan felt cold, nothing like the usual drained aftershock of battle. He watched his bullet going into Tomas, over and over in his mind, as if replaying the scene enough times might give it a different ending. He attempted explanations that could make any sense of it. Tomas could have been wearing a Kevlar vest. He could have been in league with their attackers – their guns might have been loaded with blanks.

Very clearly, another tape replayed in Morgan's head. He heard Giles saying that they were going to find him a partner even *he* couldn't kill.

"You can turn round now," Tomas said.

Morgan hesitated.

"Come over here. You were right, we need to search them and get out."

Morgan heard Tomas fumbling behind him, still unable to make himself turn back. "Morgan – look at this," Tomas said sharply.

Finally, Morgan turned round. And it was – fine. Tomas was leaning over one of the corpses and had stripped the black cloth from his face. Even in the darkness, Morgan could see that the features weren't European.

"Japanese, I think," Tomas said. "No ID though."

Morgan nodded and walked to another of the bodies, reflexively turning his head away from the one Tomas was crouched over. He didn't want to examine the new wounds on it, the dark stain which spread beneath its legs and arms, even though Tomas had squeezed the man to death and there shouldn't have been any cuts at all.

He looked down at the body in front of him instead. The black cloth was wound round several times and tied off under the chin. He had to lift the head gently by its hair to pull the cloth off. It felt uncomfortably intimate and he was glad this was one of the men Tomas had killed and not the one whose skull Morgan had cracked open.

This man was Japanese too, his hair spiky and dark, the remnants of hair gel still in it. Morgan wondered why he'd bother when he was going out dressed like some kind of ninja assassin. But maybe he'd meant to go to a bar afterwards, pull some birds. Morgan looked at the man's face, a little too round and snub-nosed to be handsome, and had the sudden uncomfortable knowledge that this wasn't just a dead body, it was a dead *person*.

He shivered and looked away as he searched the man's clothes – ordinary black jeans, a plain dark t-shirt – but he wasn't carrying any papers or cards. "Nothing," he told Tomas.

"They knew we were coming," Tomas said.

Morgan couldn't stop staring at the dark marks around his lips. There was a second of silence, then Tomas seemed to realise what Morgan was looking at. He scrubbed a quick hand over his mouth and the marks were gone.

"Yeah, but how did they know which cab we were going to get?" Morgan said after a moment.

"I'm guessing they didn't. They probably bribed all the cabbies in the rank, or offered a reward for whoever brought us to them."

"They've got money to spend, then?"

Tomas nodded.

"But Karamov's Russian, right? And these guys... aren't."

Tomas shrugged – then tilted his head suddenly, at a noise on the humid breeze.

A second later Morgan heard it too. Sirens. "Shit. We've got to get out of here." He looked longingly at the gun he'd picked up, but Giles had been pretty clear: no weapons. He wiped the muzzle and the grip with his t-shirt to clean off any prints, then dropped it next to the hand of the guy he'd killed. With any luck, the authorities might think this lot had taken care of each other.

Tomas pulled Morgan to his feet as soon as he'd finished and they both ran away from the approaching wail of the police cars, into the deep darkness between two of the warehouses.

The place was a warren, filled with collapsed brick walls and abrupt drops into water-filled trenches. There was broken glass everywhere. Tomas took the lead, running without any apparent effort. Morgan couldn't even hear him breathing hard. And Tomas shouldn't have been able to run at all, but Morgan was trying not to think about that.

They fled for about ten minutes, until they could no longer hear the sound of sirens and the warehouse district had begun to merge into a more residential area. Ahead, Morgan could see a pavement with streetlights along it. Their orange glow pierced the darkness where he and Tomas were hiding. It caught bright highlights in Tomas's fair hair, and Tomas would have just run straight out into it, but Morgan grabbed his arm.

Tomas turned to face him, frowning. He tried to pull himself free but Morgan wouldn't release him.

"You can't just walk down the street looking like that."

"Looking like what?"

Morgan lifted his hand to point at the hole in Tomas's chest, the gaping exit wound in his back. His fingers froze in mid air.

There were two holes in Tomas's t-shirt, a small one in front and a larger one behind. But the skin underneath was completely unblemished. Morgan snapped his eyes up to meet Tomas's and there was a second when it looked like the other man might say something. Then he just shrugged and walked into the light.

The hotel stood on the banks of the Danube, floodlit yellow. The lights reflected in the water beside them, broken up and blurred. Tomas paused a moment on the bridge to look at the building, a little too ornate and pretty to be entirely dignified.

Morgan was looking at Tomas rather than the hotel, but he didn't say anything. He hadn't spoken at all on the long walk back from Pest, except to suggest that they get a cab and then nod when Tomas told him it wasn't safe. Tomas knew he was going to have to give Morgan an explanation some time, but he was glad it wasn't now.

Karamov was supposed to be staying in this hotel. When they'd got themselves settled in and slept they'd have to try and find him. There was no point doing it now. Sneaking around worked better in daylight, when even shiftiness seemed honest. Everyone looked at everyone else askance after midnight.

The receptionist behind the grand entrance desk smiled at Tomas when he told her they had a room booked under the name of "Jones". A porter, slightly sheepish in a stiff uniform, led them up to what was probably – if Tomas knew Giles – the cheapest room in the hotel.

He went into the bathroom with his rucksack to get ready for bed. When he was naked he ran his fingers over the place where the bullet had gone in, and where there was now smooth skin. There was no sign of damage, but it *had* hurt – worse than he could have imagined. And he'd thought that it wouldn't hurt at all. That had been the point of dying, hadn't it? Not to feel anything any more.

And as for the way he'd healed himself... They hadn't told him about that. Maybe they hadn't known. But when he'd looked down at the body of the man he'd killed, blank eyes staring up at stars he couldn't see, Tomas knew what he needed to do. His mouth had flooded with saliva and an impulse stronger than disgust or conscience dropped him to his knees beside the corpse.

Human teeth weren't meant for ripping raw meat from the bone. It had taken Tomas two tentative tries before the skin broke and gave him access to the flesh beneath. Steak tartare he'd told himself and shut his eyes so he wouldn't have to see what he was doing.

He closed his eyes now and tried not to remember the rich coppery taste of raw meat in his mouth and, much worse than that, how delicious he'd found it.

He wanted more. The vague uneasiness he'd been feeling since he came back had a name now. It was hunger.

He pulled a clean t-shirt on over his boxers, brushed his teeth to clean the taste of blood out of his mouth, and went back to the other room. Morgan was already asleep, in his clothes on top of the covers. Tomas thought about waking him up and making him get changed, then decided that he wasn't the man's mother.

He flipped off the light switch and climbed into bed, staring up at the ceiling for a moment before shutting his eyes. He knew he didn't need sleep, but he *wanted* it. There was too much going on in his head.

Sleep wouldn't come, though. Morgan's wide eyes when he'd seen the healed wounds on Tomas's chest and thigh brought back older memories – the first time Tomas himself had glimpsed the occluded world.

It had been 1975, he'd only been a few years older than Morgan was now, and *Space Oddity* had been at number one. He remembered that, because he'd been watching Bowie on *Top of the Pops* when the call came to report to headquarters.

He'd been pissed off as he climbed the steps leading to the drab Edwardian mansion where his section chief was based. He'd only just got back from three months in Poland, and it had been a tough job – the extraction of a defector who, when Tomas finally found him, decided he wasn't that keen on defecting after all. Tomas had been lucky to make it out in one piece, and he'd been looking forward to some down-time. Was owed it, in fact.

His expression must have given away how he was feeling, because his old boss, Davenport, grimaced when he walked in the room. "Sorry," the old man said, scratching at the greying beard he insisted on growing, even though it only came through in scrubby, diseased-looking patches.

Tomas shrugged, unwilling to be mollified quite yet.

"Wouldn't have called you, only Nicholson here was rather keen to meet."

Nicholson had only been about thirty then, face unlined and toothy smile charming beneath his shock of wiry ginger hair. "I'm pleased to meet you, Tomas," he said. He had a faint Welsh accent which made it sound like a question.

"Listen," Tomas said, "I've only been back here three days –"

Nicholson held up a hand. "It's okay, we're not sending you straight into the field again."

"Really?"

"Honestly. You're being reassigned. The Hermetic Division."

"Never heard of it."

Nicholson smiled. "No wonder. We only thought up the name yesterday. Do you like it?"

"It's very...Crowleyan," Tomas said.

Nicholson's smile widened. "Precisely. Which is why you are our first recruit."

"Because I like the name?" Tomas asked, baffled.

"No," Nicholson said. "Because you know what it means."

Nicholson drove Tomas to the Hermetic Division headquarters himself. "You've been fascinated by mythology since you were a child," Nicholson told him, as if Tomas might have forgotten.

Tomas shrugged. "I've always liked poetry. Poems are full of myths and I wanted to understand them."

"Very admirable. And you didn't come to enjoy the legends in their own right?"

"Someone once described myths as poetic truth. I suppose I agree with that."

Nicholson pulled on the handbrake, then clapped Tomas on the shoulder. "Or maybe they're just the literal truth." He climbed out of the car before Tomas could reply.

They'd stopped outside a small sixties block even more down-at-heel than the Edwardian mansion they'd come from. It gave Tomas some sense of the status the new Hermetic Division enjoyed. Which meant this was a demotion of sorts – but despite himself, he was intrigued.

Nicholson took him up in a vandalised lift and to the second flat on the left. The paint on its door was flaking leprously. Inside, a short hallway led through to the brown and yellow kitchen. Nicholson gestured Tomas to sit as he set about made him a cup of tea, adding milk and two sugars without needing to ask. Tomas barely noticed – he'd had three years to stop being unnerved by working with people who knew his school nickname and what colour boxers he preferred.

"You'll have heard about what the Yanks have been up to, I bet," Nicholson said as he handed Tomas his mug and took a quick sip from his own.

"What haven't they been up to?" Tomas said.

"The remote viewing experiments, I mean. Using psychics to look inside Russian missile silos."

Tomas snorted, then felt his face fall as he realised the Hermetic

Division might be British intelligence's answer to that.

"Don't worry, we're not planning any of that nonsense," Nicholson said, reading Tomas's expression. "We're going to do something that actually works." He was pulling things out of his bag as he spoke, carefully placing them on the mottled formica of the kitchen table: a knife, a piece of chalk, a fragment of mirror, a small eyeless cloth doll.

Tomas looked at them warily, shifting on his plastic chair. "The Hermetic Division isn't concerned with the paranormal?"

"Was Crowley's Hermetic Order of the Golden Dawn interested in the paranormal?"

"Not really. More the supernatural."

Nicholson's eyes caught Tomas's suddenly, a red-tinted brown that went with his ginger hair. "Exactly."

"The supernatural?" Tomas laughed, as if that could turn it into a joke. He watched Nicholson arrange all the objects at the five corners of a pentagram he'd scribbled on the table with his chalk.

"It's been thirty years of Cold War," Nicholson said. "And no end in sight. I don't need to tell you what Europe will be like if the Soviets win, you've seen it yourself. A boot stamping on a face forever. We've stockpiled missiles that can destroy the world a thousand times over, and so have they. We came minutes away from doing it, back in 1962. I remember sitting in my house, listening to the radio and waiting for the mushroom cloud – don't you? And needs must where the devil drives. We've made alliances with countries whose human rights records would have made the Nazis blush, all to stop the greater menace. Don't you think, in a war like this, an existential war, we should use any help we can find?"

"Yes," Tomas said. "Of course I think that. That's why I took this job. I took it to do something useful, not something *that can't possibly work*!" He realised that he'd shouted the last words, half-rising to his feet. With an effort of will he clenched his fists and sat back down.

Nicholson didn't seem bothered. He just tapped his finger in the centre of the pentagram he'd drawn, a half-rhythm that wasn't quite a beat. "And what if it really did work? What then?"

Tomas found his eyes drawn to the pentagram, where the nail of Nicholson's index finger was tap-tap-tapping against the shard of mirror. Nicholson was saying something else now, but the words were in a language Tomas didn't understand and all his attention was focused on that small piece of silvered glass.

It wasn't really very interesting. There was nothing reflected in it except the pale cream of the ceiling, with a small water stain right in centre. Only, was it really a stain? The longer Tomas stared at it, the more it looked like a face.

"Do you see her?" Nicholson asked.

And yes, Tomas did. She must have been about fifty. Her face was pudgy and white and probably hadn't been pretty even when she was younger and thinner. Tomas looked up, half expecting to see Nicholson holding some kind of photo over the mirror, but his fingers were still tapping away on the edge of the glass, and the reflection seemed to be coming from absolutely nowhere.

"What is this?" Tomas whispered.

"She died here nine years ago. Murdered, actually, which is why this is possible. That kind of violence leaves an... echo of itself."

In the mirror, the woman's reflection seemed to nod in agreement.

"It's a trick," Tomas said, tearing his eyes away from the glass to stare at Nicholson. "I don't know how, but –"

"No trick. How do you think I persuaded them to set up the Hermetic Division?" Nicholson pulled out a yellowed scrap of newspaper from his pocket. HOUSEWIFE SLAUGHTERED IN OWN FLAT said the headline. And even though the picture was grainy, Tomas instantly recognised it as the woman he'd seen in the mirror.

"Death isn't a wall," Nicholson said. "It's a veil, and it can be drawn aside. Do you want to help me figure out how?"

Tomas realised his hands were shaking and carefully clasped them in his lap. "But why?"

"Because we can use this. Because it's our duty to our country to develop every weapon we can. And because if we don't, somebody else will. Aren't those reasons good enough?"

As Tomas stared up at the ceiling of the Hotel Gellert, where the water stain really was just that, he wondered what else he could have said to Nicholson. *Some things are best left unlearnt? Some weapons should never be used?* Instead he'd just said "yes," and now here he was. He closed his eyes, though he guessed that sleep would never come – that it was something he'd sacrificed twenty years ago along with everything else.

CHAPTER FOUR

Morgan woke at dawn, just as he always did. All the questions he hadn't asked had hovered over his dreams and he didn't feel like he'd slept at all. He'd hoped the memory would have faded by morning, or become explicable in a way it hadn't been last night, but instead of the sunlight driving out the darkness, he felt like the nightmares were seeping into the day. He couldn't work like this.

Tomas was still in bed, but he was already awake, the whites of his eyes reflecting the pale morning light streaming through a crack in the curtains. His blond hair was mussed and spiky, making him look younger, almost Morgan's age.

"Who are you?" Morgan said.

Tomas rolled to sit at the edge of the bed, scrubbing sleep from his eyes. He didn't answer.

"All right then. What's the Hermetic Division?"

Tomas looked up at him. "How much did they tell you about it?"

"Nothing."

"Then clearly that's what they want you to know."

Morgan slapped his hand against the wall. "Stop it! I'm not the junior partner here, man. *You* were assigned to work with *me*."

Tomas sighed, and Morgan found himself fuming at his inability to get a rise out of him. It was like Tomas just didn't take him seriously enough.

"It's not my place to tell you," the other man said with infuriating patience.

Morgan jerked back the curtains, spilling more light into the room. Tomas instantly looked his age again, the fine lines around his eyes and mouth placing him somewhere in his late thirties. "What's the Hermetic Division, Tomas? I'm working for them – I've got a right to know."

Tomas shrugged and rose to join Morgan at the window. For a minute they both stared out over the waters of the Danube, five storeys below. Morgan's breath fogged the glass, but in front of Tomas it stayed entirely transparent.

"Hermes was a Greek god," Tomas said eventually.

Morgan frowned at Tomas's faint reflection in the window.

"Hermes – Hermetic. That's the origin of the word. He's regarded as the father of magic in some traditions. Nineteenth-century occultists were particularly keen on him."

"So the Hermetic Division is... what?"

Tomas turned to look at Morgan directly. "Listen to me – you don't need to know this. And you definitely don't want to. Don't ask me to tell you things *I'd* have been happier never knowing."

"Stop patronising me!" Morgan shouted. In a blur of action he didn't fully remember, he had Tomas pressed up against the glass of the window, Morgan's arm crushing his windpipe. "Who are you, Tomas? Who *are* you? Tell me what the fuck you are!"

Tomas narrowed his eyes but didn't fight back. Morgan knew he should let go –without air Tomas would pass out – but the other man's passivity infuriated him. He pressed harder, then harder still. No blood should have been getting through, no oxygen. Thirty seconds passed, a minute, more – and Tomas just stared back at him gravely.

Finally Morgan released Tomas and stepped back with a gasp that was almost a sob. Tomas put a finger to his throat, as if to check for any damage. "Finished yet?" he asked quietly.

Morgan jerked his head in a gesture that might have been a nod. He wasn't sure himself. "Why doesn't that hurt you? Why didn't my bullet kill you?"

Tomas's smiled bitterly. "It did hurt, so did the bullet. I can feel things – they just can't harm me any more."

"But that's…" Morgan wanted to say impossible, but he wasn't stupid. He'd seen enough to know it wasn't.

Tomas shook his head, as if Morgan had voiced the unspoken word. "No, just very difficult."

"How?" Morgan whispered.

"Rituals, old knowledge, forgotten secrets."

"Magic, you mean?"

"World is crazier and more of it than we think," Tomas said, a sing-song quotation.

"Don't quote fucking poetry at me!"

"I'm sorry. Then how's this for an answer? When our bosses realised the occult contained grains of truth in the mythical chaff, they set up the Hermetic Division to research it. And to use it."

"Why?"

Tomas eyes looked blank and distant. "Because we were in a war, and if something was out there to be found, however odd or improbable, we had to find it before the other side did. The Hermetic Division is part of the secret service, Morgan, and I'm just another weapon."

"What kind of weapon, exactly?"

"One who returned from the other side. They buried me twenty years ago, before you were even born. And two days ago, they brought me back from the dead."

Morgan realised he was gasping for breath, as if he was the one who'd been choked, not Tomas. "Back at the briefing, Giles said those artefacts can cause Armageddon. I thought he was just talking that way because he's a twat."

Tomas smiled and looked down.

"But he wasn't, was he?"

"No." Tomas looked up again, green eyes piercing. "Have you read the *Book of Revelation*?"

"That's part of the Bible, right?"

Tomas nodded. "The last book, also known as the Apocalypse of John. It describes God's final judgement on humanity, when

Jesus breaks the seven seals and the four horsemen are unleashed: a rider on a white horse, who brings pestilence; a red rider who ushers in a time of war; the black rider of famine; and a pale rider on a pale horse, who is death himself. One hundred and forty-four thousand people alone are saved, and the rest are left to endure a time of terrible tribulation, fire and earthquakes, a beast with seven heads, and all the green grass of the earth burned."

Morgan slumped back down on the bed. "And that's actually true, is it?"

Tomas shrugged. "Christian evangelicals believe so. They devote their life to ensuring they're among the limited number of the elect, those who'll be saved, and they wait for the Rapture, when they'll be taken up to Heaven to sit at God's side. Others disagree. Historians see John's words as relating to the time in which he lived, when Rome was the greatest threat to Christianity. They claim the seven-headed beast is a metaphor for the Roman Empire. There had been seven Caesars up till then, you see, and Rome itself is built on seven hills. Then there's the number of the beast –"

"I've heard of that – 666, right?"

"Yes. The ancient Jews were very keen on numerology. Every letter in the Hebrew alphabet had a numeric equivalent, and they used it to construct puzzles. The Bible's full of them. If you translate three sixes into letters, you get Nero – the name of the Emperor who'd most persecuted the Christians. Historians believe Revelation is polemic, not prophecy."

"I don't fucking care what they believe. What do *you* think? Is it real, or not?"

"In its details... Probably not. But the Revelation of John isn't the only apocalyptic story in biblical literature. At the First Council of Nicea, held in the year 325 by the Emperor Constantine, the early church leaders gathered to decide which books should be included in the Christian Bible, and which rejected. Some of the decisions were based on sound reasoning, others were arbitrary, political. And all the other apocalyptic books were banished to the Apocrypha – where they've remained, mostly unread, ever since.

"Other religions also have legends of an ultimate end. The Norse Ragnarok, which the artefacts are named after, foretells the death of the gods and the destruction of the world of man. Jewish and Greek legends of the flood are just another apocalypse, imagined into the past rather than the future."

"It's all just the same bullshit, though, isn't it?" Morgan said. "Yeah the earth can be destroyed – someone can press the red button. But this..."

"As above, so below," Tomas told him. "The world of magic is a mirror to the mundane world. If that world includes the power to end itself, it's almost certain the magical realm does too."

He reached out a hand to Morgan, as if in comfort, but Morgan slapped it away. "No. No. Enough. You can't seriously be telling me my latest mission is to stop the end of the world!"

Tomas dropped his hand. "It is. If we can."

Morgan backed away, then stormed out of the room before Tomas could tell him anything else he didn't want to believe.

Morgan wasn't heading anywhere in particular, just away. An image of Tomas, face impassive as Morgan squeezed the breath out of him, hovered behind his eyelids. And there was the sense memory of other things he hadn't registered at the time: the clammy coldness of Tomas's skin; his statue-like stillness; the lack of any pulse in his throat. The way he hadn't been breathing even *before* Morgan had attacked him.

Morgan heard a hollow hubbub, voices in a vaulted space, and realised he'd made his way to the spa in the hotel's basement. The main room was vast and ornate, but peeling, a little faded in its grandeur. A large pool, floral tilework high above it, led through to a series of smaller chambers with thermal baths inside them. Morgan looked at the water longingly and realised that he wanted to wash the feeling of Tomas's cold skin from his body.

There were only a few people in the changing rooms, the early-morning risers. Morgan stripped hurriedly to his boxers, then headed back to the first of the side chambers and immersed himself in the left-hand pool, hissing at the heat. The water had a strangely oily texture to it – the minerals, he guessed. They were supposed to be good for you, but he wasn't sure he liked the feel of them, as if the water wasn't entirely clean. Still, Morgan lay and drifted in it for as long as he could bear, trying to lose himself in a haze of sensation.

It was no good. He stood up, tossing his head to send droplets of water flying from his tightly curled brown hair. Then he walked out of that pool and into the one opposite.

Morgan gasped at the icy-cold water, but the shock of it seemed to pound some sense back into him. He floated on his back, eyes closed, and thought. The mission shouldn't take long. He would get through it, he would spend as little time with Tomas as possible, and then he would go home, resign and forget that Tomas or the Hermetic Division had ever existed. He would go back to living in the normal world, not the crazy one Tomas wanted to drag him into.

Morgan's body rocked suddenly as several others fell into the water beside him. There was loud talk in a foreign language, men and women, even though there were supposed to be no women in this section of the baths.

One of the men shouted something that probably translated as "fuck me, that's cold!" and the others all laughed.

Morgan slid his eyes open, annoyed to have his solitude interrupted. The women around him were barely that – teenagers with soft, unlived-in faces that were harder around the mouths than they should have been. Hookers, Morgan guessed. The men were all at least ten years older, solid and aggressively muscular. In fact, they looked like *somebody*'s muscle, with their square, not-too-bright faces and watchful eyes. Their hands were all over the hookers.

"Natasha," one of the men said to a small dark-haired women.

She shook her head and said, in accented English, "My name is Dita."

The man's hand tightened on her arm until Morgan could see her wince. He half rose out of the water, but Dita smiled the smile of a woman who's been paid to look happy.

"If I want it, you are Natasha," the man said.

The water swirled against Morgan's legs as the thug sculled himself and the girl to the side and he suddenly had a clear view of the man in the centre of it all.

He was huge, a beached white whale in this shallow pool, roll after roll of fat leaving the greying head on top of it looking too small, like a deformity. "You're Natasha," he said, pointing at one of the girls, and then to another, "And you're Natasha. You're all Natasha – saves us the trouble of telling you apart."

Then he turned his face towards Morgan, and as soon as their eyes met Morgan knew him. This was their target – Karamov.

Karamov's bodyguards actually made it easier to follow him. Tomas could hardly miss the great white lumpy body with the tight knot of men around it, glaring untrustingly at everyone they passed.

Tomas ghosted after, far enough behind to give them no reason to notice him. The crowds allowed him anonymity. It was midday now, nearly lunchtime, and the winding, cobbled street they were following into the old quarter of Buda was crammed with tourists. Up ahead, Tomas could see them parting like a wave in front of Karamov, pushed aside or moving voluntarily when they saw the cold expression in the bodyguards' eyes.

They walked very slowly a few hundred yards up a steep incline, Karamov panting like a dog in the heat, then they turned right. Tomas hurried to the turning himself, pulling out the small portable phone Morgan had given him. "Alagut Road," he said, ringing off before Morgan could answer. His partner was another hundred or so yards behind. Karamov *and* all his men had seen Morgan close-up in the thermal baths and they couldn't risk him being recognised.

A couple more turnings, and the men seemed to have reached

their destination, a basement restaurant in a narrow green-plastered house. Eight of Karamov's guards trooped in after him, leaving only two to scowl at the street outside. It seemed their handlers had been right – whatever business Karamov had here, it was important.

Tomas slipped round the corner, out of sight, and called Morgan to join him.

"I'll follow Karamov," Tomas told him, "see what he's up to."

Morgan grimaced, sweat standing out on his smooth brown skin in the muggy air. "Eating," he suggested. "I'm guessing he does that a lot."

Tomas smiled, but Morgan didn't see it because his eyes were very carefully avoiding him.

"I may need to leave in a hurry," Tomas said. "Be ready."

"Yeah," Morgan said dryly. "You never know what might happen."

Tomas turned away without responding. When he walked down the steps into the restaurant he found a space that seemed pitch dark after the sunshine outside. The whole place smelled of roast pork and boiled cabbage. There was a small, crowded bar at one end, the optics catching stray splinters of light from the open door, and only ten tables. Karamov's party had taken five of them. Tomas kept them in the periphery of his vision as he went to the bar and ordered a Budwar.

"Staying for food?" the barman asked.

Tomas shook his head. "It's crowded already." He used the excuse to look round at Karamov. He was seated by himself, his bodyguards squashed onto the surrounding tables. A waiter approached the big Russian but he waved him away impatiently. He must be waiting for someone else to join him, probably the buyer for whatever he was selling. Tomas hadn't imagined the transaction would be taking place so soon, but if Karamov really did have one of the artefacts, he might be glad to offload it.

Would he hand it over now, or arrange a price and a drop-off? Tomas slid to his knees by the bar, as if he was tying a shoelace, and snapped a quick glance under the tables. It looked like Karamov had a small suitcase on his lap. That might be it but Tomas couldn't be sure. In all his years of searching, he'd never found out exactly what the Ragnarok artefacts *were*.

One of the bodyguards said something to Karamov, leaning back on two legs of his chair. As Karamov twisted round to reply, Tomas caught a glint of silver at his wrist, snaking down to the handle of the suitcase. It must be chained to him, which meant whatever was in there was definitely the thing Karamov planned to trade.

Tomas drained his beer in a couple of gulps. He intended to get out and report back to Morgan, but there was another flash of sunlight as the door opened, and someone new walked in. The newcomer paused a moment for his eyes to adjust to the gloom, then crossed to Karamov's table. He was a slight young man with a round, thick-lipped, wheedling face.

The bodyguards slid their chairs away to make room. Almost too fast. Were they afraid of this man? Tomas turned back to the bar and ordered another beer, though he could feel the first swirling unpleasantly in his stomach, indigestible. While he was waiting for the drink to arrive he sidled between the tables towards the toilet, giving himself another chance to study Karamov's party without being obvious.

The bodyguards were all ordering food, none watching their boss and his dinner companion. Either they trusted him, or they'd been told not to pay too much attention. The newcomer had a briefcase with him too, exactly the same size as Karamov's, though this one wasn't chained to his wrist. Tomas heard a faint chink over the clatter of cutlery as the young man put it down at his feet. Payment, probably, diamonds by the sound of it.

That was a lot of money for such a small thing. Tomas felt the first stirrings of excitement. The best thing to do would be leave now and send Morgan to report back to headquarters while Tomas waited outside to trail Karamov's contact when he left.

But there were too many variables in the equation, the solution dangerously in doubt. What if someone on the restaurant staff was in on it? The package could stay here and Tomas would never know. Or what if the deal went sour and the exchange never took place? Better to stay and watch the whole thing play out.

He spent as short a time as he could get away with in the dingy toilet, glad there was no one else in there so he didn't have to make some awkward pretence of pissing. When he came back to the bar, Karamov and the young man were still at their table, an open bottle of red wine between them. Only Karamov was drinking it. As Tomas flicked a glance at him, he drained a full glass in one swallow and hurriedly refilled it, wine slopping over the edge to stain the tablecloth. Tomas wondered if his hand was trembling, and what exactly he had to be so nervous about, surrounded by all his men.

He looked at the young man sitting opposite Karamov, but he seemed as nervous as the Russian, his foot tapping the floor, fingers drumming. His eyes refused to settle anywhere, dark and greedy, like flies hovering over spoiled meat. It was unlikely he was the end buyer – probably just a go-between who was scared of screwing up.

As Tomas watched, the young man leaned forward and said something urgent to Karamov. The words were too faint to hear, but Tomas picked up the high, anxious tone of them. Karamov shrugged. The tempo of the young man's fingers increased, and the pitch of his voice went up. Karamov seemed to be only half-listening, waving a waiter over, maybe after more food, probably more wine. As soon as he'd caught the waiter's eye, Karamov reached inside his jacket pocket, then fiddled at his other wrist.

He was unchaining the briefcase. That meant the handover was going to take place right now.

The young man seemed to be alone. He'd come here with no protection, holding a case full of diamonds, and he was going to walk out of here on his own, carrying whatever they were worth in exchange.

That just couldn't be the plan. The young man must have some guaranteed way of getting the prize to safety. But Tomas didn't know what it was – he had a severe information deficit. If he let the young man walk out of here, the chances were he'd lose both him and the briefcase.

Behind Tomas, the waiter Karamov had summoned flipped open the hatch of the bar to squeeze out into the main restaurant. Tomas didn't pause to think as he snatched the towel from the waiter's shoulder and tossed it over his own. The waiter looked almost comically shocked, his mouth open in a round, cartoon "O". It made it easier to pry the notepad out of his slack fingers.

He was still staring at Tomas's back as Tomas wove through the crowded tables to reach Karamov. In a moment the waiter would start making a fuss, but not quite yet. Tomas knew that if you did anything – however outrageous – with enough confidence, people usually let you get away with it.

The bodyguards glanced at him and away as he walked between their tables, pulling their chairs in tight to their meaty thighs to let him through. That was something else Tomas's career had taught him. Wear a uniform of any kind, even one as simple as a towel and a notebook, and that was all most people saw.

As he drew level with Karamov's table, he let his arm sweep down, knocking against the bottle of wine so casually that it looked like an accident. The bottle rolled off the table and onto the floor, giving Tomas all the excuse he needed. He muttered an apology in the few words of Hungarian he knew and dropped to his knees. His fingers reached for the bottle and he let them touch but not grasp it, so that it rolled right under the table. He dived under the tablecloth after it.

Karamov was cursing him, the young man too, and the bodyguards were beginning to turn around in their seats. In the background he could hear another raised voice. Probably the waiter. Tomas had seconds, if that.

The space under the table was crowded with legs. The bottle had wedged itself between Karamov's, his fleshy calves terminating in improbably delicate winkle pickers. There was one suitcase down there, too, but Tomas couldn't tell which. They were too similar in size and design – no doubt deliberately.

He knocked the case over as he pulled the bottle out and it fell sideways with a musical tinkle. This was the other one, then – the payment and not the prize.

That meant the case he wanted was in Karamov's lap. There was no way he could pull it away discreetly.

Tomas reached up, scrabbling his fingers across Karamov's massive thigh. The big man grunted and swore but he still seemed to be assuming that Tomas was just a clumsy waiter. Do something stupid enough, Tomas thought sourly, and at least no one thought you were a pro.

Not much longer, though. The waiter's voice was getting louder. The chair legs scraped at the other side of the table as the young man rose to his feet and Tomas thought that he, at least, had realised something was wrong.

And then, finally, he felt the leather of the case under his fingers. He clutched and pulled, dragging himself and the case away from the table in one smooth movement.

Karamov let out a cry that was more startled than angry and more chairs scraped as the bodyguards started rising to their feet.

Tomas kept low, crawling on hands and knees underneath the nearest table and out the other side, the case tucked under his arm. A hand grabbed at his ankle but he kicked out as hard as he could. There was a yelp of pain and the pressure released.

It was odd to be so frightened, and feel no physical manifestation of it. No pounding heartbeat, no ragged breath. Only his racing thoughts told him this was one of the stupidest stunts he'd ever tried to pull.

He pulled his knees under him and rose to his feet while he was still half underneath the table, setting his shoulder to the wood. It was much heavier than it looked. Tomas wobbled in a half-crouch for a second, sure that his knees were about to give. He gritted his teeth and heaved, putting his back into it as well as his thighs.

The table rose and then toppled, showering cutlery and crockery all over Karamov's men. The waiter, who'd been reaching for Tomas, paused to gape in shock. Karamov was shouting, the other customers were screaming, and there was cream sauce spattered everywhere.

Tomas turned on his heel and sprinted up the stairs, the outraged cries of the restaurant staff and the enraged bellows of Karamov's men echoing after him. He had five seconds' start on them, if that.

CHAPTER FIVE

Morgan was in a daze of boredom, looking at the narrow-fronted houses around him and idly wondering how much they cost, when Tomas sprinted round the corner and straight into him.

"What -?" he said, but Tomas just grabbed his arm and ran. A moment later Morgan knew what he was running from. Four, five – no, every bloody bodyguard Karamov had came barrelling round the corner towards them. They hadn't drawn their guns, but from thirty feet away Morgan could see them bulging out their trousers at the ankle. Adrenaline surged through him and his own legs started pumping as Tomas released his arm.

The streets were still crowded, and Tomas had to shoulder people aside as he ran. Morgan heard him muttering "Sorry, sorry" to everyone he hit. Karamov's bodyguards didn't bother to apologise and step by step they were gaining.

Morgan leapt up, getting a brief view over the heads of the crowd. It went on forever, clogging the cobbled road all the way down to the main junction.

They'd never evade Karamov's men here. But there was a narrow, darker street snaking off to the left twenty feet ahead. Morgan started curving round towards it. He thought he heard Tomas say something and he felt the brush of fingers against his arm, but there was no time to ask what he wanted. Karamov's men were so close now that he could hear the rasp of their breathing. He put on a burst of speed, forcing energy into muscles that were already protesting the fierce workout. Sweat was sluicing from his face and arms, soaking his green t-shirt.

Ten more feet and he'd managed to cut his way across the crowd to the side street. The instant he was in there, the gloom hit, the street too narrow to let in the sun. It was damp too, as if all the humidity in the air had condensed to water on the decaying brick walls. A welcome cool washed over him.

Morgan suddenly felt a hand, pulling at his shoulder. He'd almost lashed out before he realised it was Tomas.

"We've lost them, for a minute at least," the other man said. He didn't even sound winded.

Morgan bent over, hands on his knees, as he struggled to get his breathing back under control. When he straightened, he noticed for the first time that Tomas was carrying something clasped against his chest, a small briefcase. "That what this is all about?"

Tomas nodded. "I took it from Karamov. I'm fairly sure it's what we were sent here to retrieve."

"And what happened to keeping a low profile?"

"Last-minute change of plan."

Morgan laughed helplessly, punchy with exhaustion. "No shit."

Tomas grinned for just a moment, the smile slipping as he darted a look behind them. "We won't have lost them for long, there are only so many places we could have gone. We need to keep moving."

"Back to the hotel?"

"They've seen you now. If any of them recognised you... it's too big a risk."

"Sorry," Morgan said grudgingly. "It was stupid going down to the baths."

Tomas cocked his head suddenly, and then swore. A moment later Morgan heard the clamour of running footsteps over the background wash of traffic. "They're coming," Tomas said.

Morgan spun round, took two steps – and collided with a small body he hadn't expected to be there. He tripped and fell, desperately trying to roll away from the blonde girl he'd knocked to the ground. His chin connected with the pavement so hard it snapped his teeth shut, and for a moment all the could think about was the bright flare of pain. By the time he'd shaken the confusion from his head, the girl was already on her feet.

She held out a hand to him. He took it, too surprised to refuse – and found himself pulled to his feet with surprising strength.

"Y'all will be wanting to come with me now," she said with a Southern drawl.

"I... what?"

Tomas turned around, realising Morgan was no longer following. Tomas's eyes tracked over Morgan's shoulder and narrowed, and Morgan realised that Karamov's men must be very close.

Morgan tried to pull his hand away from the blonde girl's soft fingers.

They tightened like a steel band around his wrist. "You'll never outrun 'em, you know," she said. Morgan saw that her bright golden hair was caught back in a red bow. She couldn't have been older than ten. He pulled his arm again, harder this time, less worried about hurting her, but she wouldn't let him go.

Tomas took a step back towards them. "Sweetheart, it's not safe for you here," he said to the girl.

She sighed and shook her head. "I'm not the one being chased by a whole parcel of men with guns, Mr Len."

Morgan saw a brief moment of shock on Tomas's face, and then something like recognition.

"Follow me," she said, and this time when she pulled Morgan went with her, bewildered, as Tomas trotted along silently beside. He couldn't imagine where she was taking them. Karamov's men were only fifty feet behind.

"In here," she said, finally releasing Morgan's wrist as she stepped through the door of a shabby, white-fronted building.

Morgan hesitated, looking at Tomas. The other man nodded

impatiently and pressed Morgan forward, a hand against the small of his back.

Tomas followed Morgan through and slammed the door behind him. He turned the mortice lock and the Yale, but Morgan didn't think it would slow Karamov's men for long.

"What now?" he said to the girl.

She smiled happily, as if they were playing a game. "If y'all will follow me..." She turned and led them to the back of the room, dropping to her knees to fumble at the wooden floor.

Morgan flicked a light switch on the wall beside him as he heard the first muffled blow against the outside of the door. In the pale light of the room's one bare bulb, he could see that the building was half derelict. There was a hole in the ceiling above where the cross-hatched floorboards were visible, and most of the paper on the walls had been scraped away to reveal the mouldering plaster beneath. There was only one piece of furniture, a scuffed table, wobbling on three legs.

The girl was kneeling just to the left of it, and Morgan could see what she'd been looking for – a round metal ring embedded in the floor. As another kick landed on the door, hard enough to splinter the wood, her small white fingers closed around the ring and pulled.

Nothing happened.

"Botheration," she said. "It's stuck."

The blows on the door were coming two at a time now. When Morgan snatched a look he could see that one of the hinges was buckling, the wood around it torn away and the screws anchoring it to nothing but air.

"Let me," Tomas said. He knelt beside the girl and replaced her hand with his own. When he heaved, there was a protesting screech and then a three-foot square of floorboards began to rise. There was nothing beneath but darkness.

"Down," Tomas said, already clambering through the opening.

His head quickly disappeared, and the girl followed, frowning as her feet searched for the steps that must have been below.

Morgan crouched beside her, watching the door. He found himself trying to guess whether the wood or the hinges would give out first.

The hinges, it turned out. As the girl's blonde head finally cleared the entrance, there was one final blow, and the door broke away and flew through the air, straight towards Morgan. He dived to the side as the heavy rectangle of wood crashed to the ground, snapping the trapdoor as it landed.

"Shit!" Morgan said. Now they wouldn't be able to close off the route behind them.

An instant later a figure appeared in the doorway, the shadow-puppet outline of a man clutching a gun, silhouetted against the bright sunlight.

Morgan knew he only had a few seconds till the man's eyes adjusted to the gloom inside the house. He used them to swing himself over the lip of the hole. His feet scrabbled beneath him to find purchase, and it took him a second to realise that the thing banging against his leg was the ladder, rope and not wood as he'd expected.

He slithered quickly down it, a hundred cold slogs round assault courses making him nimble. It was long, sixty foot or more, but he reached the bottom before anyone had followed him, the light from the trapdoor above shining uninterrupted into the darkness below. At the bottom, his feet landed in a thin layer of water which splashed up cold and a little slimy against his ankles.

Beyond the small, pale square of light in which he stood was complete darkness. Tomas and the little girl were dim figures on the periphery of it, none of their features visible.

"This way," the girl said. She'd produced a small torch from somewhere, but the beam barely troubled the darkness, only revealing a thin strip of uneven, rocky ground and nothing of what lay ahead.

After a short, stumbling run, they arrived at a rectangular entranceway to a tunnel as clearly man-made as the cavern was natural. Another, faster run through that, and they were at a

T-junction leading off into darkness left and right. The girl led them right without hesitation, then left at the next junction.

Hurrying in her wake, Morgan soon lost count of the turnings. It was an endless, shadowed flight through featureless stone tunnels and wider, echoing caverns. Sometimes the floor was smooth, sometimes pockmarked. On one occasion it was beneath a foot of water. The air was chilly to the point of discomfort, as if they were buried somewhere beneath Siberia, not Budapest sweltering under its midsummer sun.

The ceiling dipped so low at one point that Morgan was forced to his hands and knees, but he scrambled through anyway, trusting the girl to lead them out and not into a fatal dead end.

"Where the hell *are* we, man?" he whispered to Tomas. He'd already given up asking who the girl was. Tomas couldn't, or wouldn't answer him.

"It's called the Labyrinth, I think," Tomas said. "A huge network of tunnels beneath Buda."

"Who built them?" Morgan asked some time later, when they were crossing a big open chamber bisected by a clear stream.

"Some are World War Two bomb shelters. Some are much older than that – hundreds of years. People have always needed a place to hide."

After that, Morgan saved his breath for the flight. They'd lost their pursuers long ago, but the girl didn't seem to want to stop running. Morgan couldn't figure out why he was willing to trust her, except that she was ten years old, and what the hell was she going to do to them? He guessed someone must have been using her as a go-between, and she'd found herself caught up in the action when Tomas had stolen whatever it was that Karamov was trading.

It was when Morgan finally felt safe that Karamov's man found them. He loomed out of the darkness ahead, a solid lump of black until the torch's beam picked out his features, the sharp nose and wide mouth.

It only took the man a moment to recover from his shock, and then he was fumbling for the Glock he'd tucked into the waistband of his trousers.

Tomas grabbed the girl by the shoulders and Morgan thought he meant to shield her with his own invulnerable body. But she skipped forward two steps before Tomas could stop her.

Karamov's man hesitated, then brought his weapon to bear.

The girl didn't even flinch. She kept the beam of her torch trained straight in his eyes and – brighter as she drew closer – it blinded him. The bodyguard cursed and backed away. Morgan knew that any moment he'd give up trying to get a clear view of his target and just start shooting.

"Now, what would your mamma think of you standing here waving a gun at little old me?" the girl said.

The man's gun instantly zeroed in on the source of the voice. "Don't move," he grated in heavily accented English.

The girl flicked back her head to move a lock of long blonde hair out of her eyes. "Marinka brought you up nice, didn't she? Taught you the golden rule?"

Morgan saw the man's mouth working, a dark hole in his face.

"That's right," the girl continued. "She took you to mass every Sunday, I know she did. But you stopped going when you joined the Bratva. Stopped seeing her too – cut yourself off from all your family, just like they told you to. Broke her heart, didn't it? She didn't last but two more years after that. Everyone said she could have pulled through the stroke, if she'd only had the will."

"Who told you this?" the man asked. His voice shook and so did his hand. The barrel of his gun pointed at the ceiling one moment, the cracked stone floor of the tunnel the next.

"I know everything about you, Fiodor. I know that sometimes you cry at night, when you think about the daughter you left behind and the mother who was cursing your name as she died." The girl's voice had taken on a different cadence as she spoke, deeper and darker. But Morgan could still see the same little blonde-haired figure in front of him, face as blank and innocent as a doll's.

"She's in Heaven now, Fiodor, but she's still crying. She's seen what you've done, all the things you've done – that girl you beat and cut before you killed her. She shouldn't have given in so easily, should she? Shouldn't have cried and begged and told you that you could do whatever you wanted, if only you'd let her live. Because that just took the fun right out of it for you, didn't it? Killed your – let's call it your passion – right there. You would have let her live, you meant to – but not after she'd seen your humiliation. What if she'd told anyone else?"

"No," said Fiodor. "No." He was backing away now, one shuffling step at a time.

The girl took a step forward for every one he took back. "Your mother sees it all, Fiodor. And she's weeping up there in Heaven, she's weeping because she knows she'll never see you again. Because when you die, you won't be joining her. When you die, Fiodor, you're going somewhere else."

The bodyguard was crying silently, a thin stream of tears glistening in the torchlight as they flowed down his cheeks. The Glock had dropped to his side, hanging limply from his fingers.

"No," he whispered. "I can repent. It's not too late."

The little girl moved almost too quickly to see, darting forward to pry the gun from his unresisting hand. She had to use both of her own to hold the heavy, black metal weight of it as she shot him between the eyes. A fine spray of red blood splattered her gold hair and pale, freckled face.

"It's too late now," she said.

Morgan was still shivering when, fifteen minutes later, they emerged at last into a lighted section of the tunnels. The walls were smoother here, decorated with crudely faked cave paintings that suggested they'd stumbled on some kind of tourist attraction. A ghost walk, maybe – the place was still very dim, probably designed to scare people.

"This is the part that's open to Joe Public," the girl confirmed. "But it's shut for the day, so we won't be disturbed." Her voice had returned to its earlier, high-pitched lilt. In the pale lighting Morgan could see that she was wearing a lacy white top over a demure blue-green skirt. Her shoes were black patent leather, perfectly polished.

They finally stopped in a small, octagonal chamber covered in fake plastic greenery. In the centre was a fountain with liquid spurting from a tap on each of its four vine-covered sides.

Morgan realised he was parched. He dipped his head to take a drink, then spat it back out again at the unexpectedly vinegary taste.

"It's just wine, silly," the girl said. "It's their little gimmick."

"Listen," Morgan said. "This is – this has... This has got to end."

"What has to end?" the girl said, and Morgan was almost taken in by her soft, innocent face, except there were still droplets of a dead man's blood all over it. He clenched his fists and wasn't entirely sure he wouldn't hit her.

Tomas took a step towards him "Morgan –"

He backed away. "I've had enough of this," he said. "I've had more than I can fucking take, in point of fact. You show me things that make me think I'm going crazy, only I know I'm not because I've seen... Because I've seen them with my own fucking eyes!"

Tomas rested a hand on Morgan's shoulder but he flung it away violently. "Don't touch me, you freak!"

"I understand, I really do," the little girl said. "This is a strange world we live in and it's full of ugly things, but getting all het up about them just isn't going to help."

"Don't," Morgan said. "Don't pretend you're something you're not. I heard what you said. I know you're another – another thing like him." He glared at Tomas, who dropped his eyes, scratching a hand through the back of his blond hair like someone trying to ignore a socially embarrassing faux pas. It enraged Morgan. He had a *right* to lose it, after the day he'd had.

"I'm curious," the girl said, as unruffled by Morgan's outburst as Tomas was distressed by it. "How do you know I didn't just read the files on Karamov's men before I found you?"

"Because I'm not stupid."

"Whatever the other children might have said." And there it was again, the hollow echo in her voice of something else speaking through her.

The words caught on the jagged edge of painful memories, and Morgan flinched, but his anger drained away. At least she wasn't trying to deceive him. "OK," he said. "OK then. Tell me who you are."

She offered her hand for him to shake and he took it without thinking. It felt perfectly normal, just a small, dry, warm little girl's hand. "I'm Jessie-Belle Jordan," she said. "But you can call me Belle. I'm with the CIA."

Morgan laughed.

Belle pouted, her mouth a little rosebud of displeasure.

"She really is," Tomas said. "Belle's pretty famous in the – in the circles you're now moving in."

"But she's..." Morgan realised he didn't know where to start. He settled for, "Ten years old."

"Eleven actually," Belle said. "I was born in 1967, turned eleven in 1978 and I've stayed that age ever since. To be quite honest with you, Mr Hewitt, I'm getting a mite sick of it."

"So it's an illness then," Morgan said. "I don't know, something genetic that makes you look this way.

She shook her head. "I don't look eleven, I *am* eleven."

Even a day ago, Morgan would have smiled and walked away. But not now. "How is that even possible?" he asked her.

She shrugged prettily. "Regular hormone injections. Growth-stunting – illegal but effective. And magic, of course." She pushed up the sleeve of her lacy cotton blouse, and Morgan saw for the first time that the skin beneath was covered in a tracery of tattoos, the black of them obscene against the soft white flesh of her pre-pubescent body. They continued up to her shoulder, and Morgan somehow knew that they covered her all over, a network of runes and arcane symbols.

He felt a sour lump in his stomach at the thought of grown men doing that to this little girl.

She smiled and rested one of her hands against his arm, the

touch as light as a bird's wing. "There's no need to look so sad for me – nobody did this out of spite. It *had* to be done; I begged them to."

Morgan placed his hand over hers, so much larger it swallowed it entirely. "But why?"

"Because when I was but ten, something happened to me and no one my mamma and papa talked to – not the doctor, or the priest, or the exorcist – could do anything about it. The hormones and the tattoos and the magic are the only way to tame the thing that lives inside me."

He didn't want to understand what she meant. Tomas had been right – he was happier not knowing. But he found himself studying her face, her delicate mouth, her button nose, her cornflower-blue eyes. As he looked into those, the black dots of her pupils seemed to lengthen and lighten, till they were narrow red slits. And he could see something through them, beyond the eyes – inside the little girl. Something that was twisting and writhing and *screaming* to get out.

"Enough," Tomas said. "Belle works for the CIA, Morgan, that's all you really need to know. And what," he asked Belle, "is the Agency's interest in this?"

"I just go where I'm sent, but my handlers told me you Brits have stumbled onto something big here."

"And if we have, why do you imagine we'd want to share it with you?"

"I *did* save your life, Mr Len. Whatever you've found, you might at least let me have a quick peek at it."

Tomas looked like he wanted to argue, but after a moment he sighed and nodded.

"And what have we found?" Morgan asked. "What *is* in that case?"

Tomas set it down on the floor, squatting beside it. "I don't know. But I'm pretty sure it's what Karamov was selling."

"Yeah, what with all those bodyguards chasing us when you took it," Morgan said. "Maybe Karamov just really liked that briefcase."

Belle laughed as Tomas fiddled with the clasp.

"Locked," he said. "Hang on." He slipped his fingers into the join and pulled. His muscles corded above the sleeve of his t-shirt for a moment and then there was the shriek of distressed metal and the case split open.

For a moment, Morgan thought it was empty. Then he saw that there was one thing in it: a small, black, leather-bound book, the edges of its pages yellowed with age.

"That's it?" he asked. It looked like it was ready to fall apart. "Is that the Ragdoll artefact?"

"Ragnarok artefact," Tomas said. His expression was strange, half disappointment, half relief. "I don't think it can be. It doesn't look old enough – or powerful enough."

"Knowledge is power," Belle said, darting a hand to grab the book before Tomas could. "The pen is mightier than the sword."

When she flicked through the book's pages, Morgan saw that the whole thing was filled with spidery black runes, broken up every now and again by pen-and-ink illustrations of unrecognisable, multi-angled objects and sometimes what seemed to be tracings of ancient inscriptions. In places someone had gone back and written in the margins, narrow columns of letters perpendicular to the main text. Morgan wasn't sure why, but he had a strong feeling that whoever had written it hadn't been entirely sane.

"I know that handwriting," Tomas said.

"How?" Belle squinted at the close-packed, incomprehensible runes. "Is it even a language?"

Tomas held out a hand, and she reluctantly handed him the book. "I think so," he said after a second. "A cipher, maybe? I don't know – but I think Nicholson wrote this."

Belle's eyebrows arched towards her hairline. "You're sure?"

Tomas nodded as Morgan asked, "Who's Nicholson?"

"Our boss," Tomas said. "The head of the Hermetic Division."

"Ex-boss," Belle said.

"Nicholson retired?"

"Died, a long time ago."

"So why," Morgan asked, "would anybody be interested in some old notebook of his?"

Tomas frowned. "I don't know. Giles seemed pretty convinced this had something to do with the Ragnarok artefacts. Nicholson knew more about them than anyone in the world, but what he knew he told us. We were the ones he sent into the field to hunt for them. Why would he write down anything important in a book no one could read?"

"Maybe these are the things he wanted kept secret even from his own people," Belle said.

Tomas looked troubled, but after a second he nodded. "Maybe."

"If it even *is* Nicholson's," she added.

Tomas flicked to the front of the book. And there, finally, was something written in English: *Geraint Nicholson.*

Belle sighed. "Let's take the I-told-you-so as read."

Morgan was vaguely aware of her and Tomas talking beside him, discussing the book, Nicholson's reasons for writing it and what made it so valuable. But he couldn't concentrate on anything except the name written in the front of that book.

He knew that name, had known it since the day his parents told him the secret they'd been keeping all his life.

He could still see their faces now. His mother had been so angry Morgan thought she might explode with it. His father hadn't seemed angry at all, which was somehow worse. His face was blank and whenever Morgan spoke to him there was a second's delay before he answered, as if the words had to travel a long way to reach him.

"You're not ours," his father had said. "You never were. Not like –" But he hadn't said the name. Her name hadn't been spoken in their house since the day she'd died.

Morgan had thought this was their way of punishing him for what had happened. "Don't say that," he begged. "Please, mum – tell him it isn't true."

"I wish to God we'd never taken you in," his mum had said, her voice so cold and businesslike that Morgan had barely recognised it. "You've been nothing but trouble since the day you arrived."

Even then, Morgan hadn't believed it. He'd shaken his head and sobbed and his dad might have left it at that. Looking back on the memory now, he thought he might have seen the first flush of shame in his father's face. But his mother had been crazy with grief, and the rage that accompanied it had an easy target.

Morgan remembered her fingers clawing into him as she dragged him to the filing cabinet in one corner of the room. She'd pulled the drawers out so quickly that he'd heard the mechanism break, but she didn't seem to notice. File after file fell on the floor as she threw them aside after only a cursory glance. And then, finally, she'd found the one she was looking for.

For the first time, Morgan had seen a crack in the furious mask of her face, something softer and more human beneath it. But she'd still handed him the file. "Here," she said. "You should see this."

He'd taken it hesitantly. It was a plain brown manila folder with a line of type along one side. It only took him a moment to realise that it was his name and date of birth. "What is it, mum?" he asked.

She couldn't look him in the eye. "Just read it, Morgan."

Morgan had squinted closely, trying to make sense of it. But he was too young to understand and he passed it back to her. "It's just names," he said. "What do they mean?"

His mother hesitated a moment as if, for the first time, she was having second thoughts. Then her face hardened and Morgan knew she was remembering what happened three days ago. "This is your birth certificate," she said. "Those are the names of your parents. Your *real* parents."

And Morgan had looked again, at those four words – *Thalia and Geraint Nicholson*– and wondered how he could have spent seven years not knowing the single most important fact about his life.

CHAPTER SIX

Tomas spent a little longer flicking through the book, but it was futile. Whatever code Nicholson had used, it wasn't one Tomas recognised.

"We should skedaddle," Belle said. "Karamov's men are only lost in the maze, they haven't upped and disappeared."

"What about the book?" Morgan asked. His voice sounded shaky and Tomas wasn't surprised. At least when *he'd* first learned about the Hermetic Division and all it stood for, the veil had been drawn back slowly, giving him time to adjust to each new revelation. Morgan must feel as if the foundations of his world had been chipped away and replaced with quicksand.

It all came back to Nicholson – Nicholson, who was apparently dead. He'd always had such a *vital* presence, blazing with a passion nothing seemed able to quench. Tomas realised that he didn't find Nicholson's death upsetting so much as profoundly improbable. Men like Nicholson weren't meant to die.

"There's one gentleman who might be able to tell us why this book is so important," Belle said.

Morgan looked puzzled, but after a moment Tomas nodded. "Karamov."

"We have to do it now, while his goons are out of the picture."

"He'll have kept some with him," Morgan objected.

"Only a couple," Belle said. "We can handle them."

Tomas saw Morgan shiver, and he couldn't say he liked the thought much himself. He hadn't enjoyed watching what the little girl did to Karamov's man – no one saw another man's secrets being ripped out of him without thinking of his own.

"And after we find Karamov?" Morgan asked.

Tomas shrugged. "We take the book back to the Division."

"Shouldn't we find out more about it first, work out what it says?"

"Karamov –"

"But he's not gonna tell us everything, is he?" Morgan cut across him. He was speaking quickly now, almost stumbling over his words. "It's not like we can get him to translate the whole thing for us, is it? And that's assuming he even knows how. How can we take the book back before we know what it really is? We risked our lives for the fucking thing – don't we deserve to know why?"

"We're not here for our own amusement!" Tomas snapped. "We completed the mission, now we take a bow and go home."

"What's the matter, more than your job's worth?" Morgan snarled. "Listen, if it's too much effort –"

"There's always your German contact, this Anya Friedman," Belle interrupted loudly. "She might have some information for you, right?"

Morgan looked suddenly alarmed. "Shit! Weren't we supposed to meet her an hour ago?"

Anya was still waiting for them when they finally entered the huge, rococo interior of the Café Gerbeaud. Her long red hair flamed a beacon across the room as they squeezed between tables filled with lounging tourists.

Tomas smiled as he approached her, but her sour expression didn't soften even slightly.

"What have you morons been playing at?" she said before they'd even sat down. She was quite a beautiful woman, Tomas thought, a few years younger than him, but her anger made her unattractive.

"And it's lovely to meet you too," Morgan said.

She ignored him. "I want an answer – what the hell did you think you were doing this morning?"

"There was a last-minute change of plan," Tomas said.

"No kidding."

Tomas saw Morgan twitch a smile, then quickly drop it when Anya glared at him.

"We had to act," Tomas said. "We were in danger of losing the... the target object."

Morgan's hands folded reflexively over the waistband of his jeans, where he'd tucked Nicholson's book before they left the labyrinth.

Anya saw the telltale rectangular bulge hidden beneath his t-shirt and frowned. "Did it not occur to any of you amateurs that we might already have Karamov under surveillance? That we might, in fact, be perfectly capable of acquiring the *target object* ourselves at a time and place of our choosing? Maybe somewhere a little safer – and a little less bloody conspicuous!"

Tomas shook his head. "We couldn't take the risk."

"Yes, clearly risk-reduction was a very high priority for you. You alerted Karamov to our presence, scared off his buyer and almost got yourselves killed into the bargain. You couldn't have made more of a mess of this if you'd tried!"

"On the plus side," Morgan said, "we got a free tour of Budapest's premiere subterranean tourist attraction."

Anya's face flushed red with suppressed rage. Tomas knew he should be trying to control Morgan, but a part of him was enjoying watching the young man push the German agent's buttons.

Anya clearly sensed that she was getting nowhere with Tomas and Morgan and turned to Belle instead. "And what," she said, "are *you* doing here?"

"I came to help, Miss Friedman." Belle offered her small hand over the table.

Anya rolled her eyes. "I'm sure you did. I'm sure the CIA are involved in an entirely charitable capacity."

"I've confirmed her role with London," Tomas said. "Giles spoke to Washington and it seems the Yanks have been following the same breadcrumbs we have. They've asked us to pool resources, at least until we locate Karamov's buyer."

Anya shook her head. "I don't trust the CIA. They always have their own agenda."

"I agree," Tomas said. "Which is why I'd rather have her where I can keep an eye on her, than running her own operation and potentially compromising ours."

"Don't mind me," Belle said. "Just pretend I'm not here."

"Look," Morgan said to Anya. "We're here now, and we've got the book – it doesn't really matter how. What can you tell us about it?"

"Book?" Anya said, and Morgan's face fell.

"Later," Tomas insisted, glancing casually round the café, too full of people, far too public for this conversation. "We were considering going back to Karamov, seeing if we can get anything out of him about his buyer. What do you have on him?"

Anya's lips, very wide and red, pulled thin with annoyance. Then she sighed and tossed a thick brown folder on the table. "We've been following Karamov for four months now – on another matter entirely, the bribing of some oil-industry officials – but he's not an easy man to pin down. Nothing definite on his buyer, though we've been tapping every phone number that's registered to him or any of his goons. But see for yourself – it's all in there." She nodded down at the file.

Morgan drew it eagerly towards him.

"My local connection followed Karamov after you left him," Anya said. "He's back at the Gellert for now, a few of his bodyguards with him, but chances are he'll be out of the country by the end of the day. If he heads to Russia, we're in trouble – his power base there is very strong."

"Sorry," Morgan interrupted, pushing his chair back with a dry rasp against the tiled floor. "I need a slash."

Anya shook her head at his departing back. "That's great. Perhaps he'll let us know how it went when he gets back. Tell me, Tomas, when did MI6 start recruiting teenagers?"

"He knows what he's doing," Tomas said, defending his partner on a long-ingrained reflex. But the truth was, Morgan *didn't* know what he was doing, not in this area. They'd told Tomas the younger man was there for any wetwork, and no doubt Morgan was very good at that sort of thing, but that wasn't really the point. Hermetic agents were generally recruited because of their interest in the occult. Richard had been conducting his own research long before he'd come on board, but Morgan seemed to have no affinity for their work at all – a positive dislike of it, in fact. Why had Giles picked him?

Tomas kept his worries to himself, chewing the problem over and finding nothing digestible in it, while Belle and Anya ordered *dobostorte* from their apple-cheeked young waiter.

Five minutes later, the cakes arrived, along with two silver teapots and some delicate china cups with the slightly faded picture of a rose on each of them.

A minute after that, Tomas was still staring at one undrunk, slowly cooling cup of tea. "Where's Morgan gone?" he said.

The weather had finally broken its oppressive heat as grey storm clouds moved in to glower over the city, but Morgan was still drenched with sweat. His heart raced, pounding against his chest with every beat.

He had to get a grip. He knew what he'd just done was extremely stupid. Best case scenario he'd be out of a job – worst case he'd become the Division's next target. But there was no way, just no way, that he was letting this book go before he found out what it meant. If it was written by his real father...

After his adopted mother had shown him his birth certificate, and before that day five weeks later when she'd taken him to the care home and told him he wouldn't be coming back, she'd let him ask her about his real parents.

Dead, she'd told him and he'd felt relieved. At least they didn't give him away because they didn't want him. He'd asked his mum to tell him everything she knew about them, these people he'd never heard of who turned out to be the most important people in his life.

"Your dad was an engineer," she'd said. "With BT, I think."

"And my mum?" he'd asked eagerly, but she'd just shrugged.

Had she been lying, or was she lied to herself? Why had no one ever told him what his father really did? Tomas hadn't said anything about Nicholson having any children. But then he hadn't said very much about him at all. Maybe Tomas had known who Morgan was all along.

Morgan couldn't stop snatching glances behind him to see if Tomas or the other two had followed. But he'd twisted and turned through side street after side street, and unless they already knew where he was going, they'd have a hard time catching up.

He took another look at the sheet of paper he'd lifted from Anya's file. It told him Karamov had made three calls to a Professor Raphael in the Faculty of Ancient Languages at Eotvos Lorand University. Morgan could only see one reason for a man like Karamov to be contacting this Raphael: he had hoped the professor would be able to translate Nicholson's book.

Morgan was hoping the same thing. The tourist map he'd bought from a street-corner vendor told him the Faculty of Ancient Languages was located behind Baha Lujza Square. He walked briskly across the wide space through crowds of locals weaving in and out of its tacky shops and smarter department stores. Most of the faces surrounding him bore the distinctive sharp cheekbones of Eastern Europe and all of them were white. He felt unpleasantly conspicuous.

Finally, on a narrow street behind a bank, he found the faculty. It was a marble-fronted building that might have looked grand if it hadn't been caked in grime, the black residue of the square's gridlocked traffic. A red-faced security guard lounging behind a low table stopped him just inside the entrance.

"I'm here to see Professor Raphael," Morgan told him.

The guard grunted something in Hungarian. Morgan mimed incomprehension and the man sighed and pointed up the stairs to his right, then held up three fingers.

Third floor, Morgan guessed, but when he reached it the place was a warren, narrow green-painted corridors snaking off in every direction. He wandered for a full ten minutes before he found Raphael's door, his name written on a small bronze plaque beneath two others.

Morgan froze, staring at the door. Was he really going to do this? But he'd already stolen the book. Tomas was unlikely to be any less pissed off if he backed out now. He took a deep breath, then knocked.

They'd spent a fruitless half hour hunting for Morgan in the busy streets surrounding the café. It had started to rain while they searched, warm, fat drops of it. When Tomas met up with the others again beside the café's elegant façade, Anya's long red hair was plastered to her scalp, two shades darker than it had been before.

"Well, this just gets better and better," she said grimly.

Even Belle was looking less perky, her white blouse almost see-through with moisture and the shine gone from her black patent shoes. "He seemed like such a nice boy," she said. "What the heck does he think he's doing?"

"Taking it back to Karamov?" Anya suggested.

Tomas shook his head. "He's no traitor. I don't know what he's playing at, but it isn't that."

"I don't care about the purity of his motives, we *have* to find him," Anya said. She looked like she was going to say something else, or maybe the same thing again, but then she broke off to reach inside her jacket, which was just the wrong shade of green to match her hair. When she pulled out one of those small portable phones, Tomas realised the grating pop song he'd heard was its ring tone.

"Yes!" she snapped. She listened a moment, then said, "OK, and where's he going?" There was another pause before she clicked the phone closed without saying goodbye.

"Someone's seen Morgan?" Tomas asked.

She shook her head. "Karamov. He's left the hotel, but it doesn't look like he's heading for the airport."

"Could he be going to meet Morgan?" Belle asked.

Anya shrugged. "Or maybe he's meeting the buyer, or just picking up some groceries. There's only one way to find out for sure."

Tomas hesitated. Following Karamov would mean giving up on Morgan. He pictured Morgan's face, soft-eyed and scared, and then the image in his head morphed into a different one, a little older, skin paler, hair a sandy brown. If this had been Richard, what would he have done?

Everyone knows the risks, he could hear Richard saying. *We're not doing this out of the goodness of our hearts. We've all got some reason to be here.*

Tomas found himself smiling, because Richard was the most cynical idealist he'd ever met. But he was also right.

"We go after Karamov," he said to Anya. "Morgan will have to wait."

Professor Raphael was so old, Morgan was afraid to take his offered hand, worried even the softest grip would crush the fragile bones inside it. After a moment's hesitation, he touched it with his fingertips, seeing the way the flesh gave beneath them and didn't spring back, all the elasticity of youth gone.

The man's face was bright with life, though. He had a surprisingly full mop of pure white hair, and his eyes glittered blue beneath the rheum.

He said something in Hungarian and then, when Morgan looked blank, "English, is it?"

Morgan nodded. Raphael spoke with almost no accent, and what there was Morgan didn't think was Hungarian.

"And what can I do for you, young man?" He sat back down at his desk, disappearing behind the stacks of books and paper piled high on top of it. The whole office was almost comically cluttered, every shelf overflowing with junk which had spilled over onto the floor, barely leaving Morgan room to stand. It was hard to imagine what some of the stuff was *for* – the half-finished child's jigsaw puzzle, a set of lace doilies, torn and grimy with age, a jar of what appeared to be rock salt, some of it spilling out onto the desk.

Morgan pulled his attention back to Raphael. "Karamov sent me. About the matter you discussed."

"Did he?" Raphael said, which told Morgan absolutely nothing.

Ignoring the voice inside him – probably Tomas's – hissing at him not to do it, Morgan pulled Nicholson's book from the waistband of his jeans. "He thought you'd be able to help us translate this."

The professor peered at the book for a moment before reaching one of his blue-veined hands to take it. There was a second while they both had hold of it, Morgan suddenly reluctant to let the thing out of his grasp. Then he relinquished it to Raphael.

"So this is the book he spoke of." Raphael riffled slowly through the pages. "It's not as I imagined."

Morgan leaned forward eagerly. "But can you translate it?"

"Hmm." Raphael's head cocked to one side, birdlike. "It is not any currently spoken language, I can tell you that. Not Roman script, either, though it bears similarities."

"Are you saying you can't help?"

"No, no, let us not be hasty. It isn't a modern language, but I believe it has its roots in one. Tell me, what do you know about Hungarian?"

"That I can't speak it?"

Raphael smiled very slightly. "Unsurprising. It is one of Europe's most mysterious tongues, famously without roots in any nearby language."

"So this is a form of Hungarian?"

"A very ancient one, I think, yes – written in a long-forgotten runic alphabet."

"And there's, what, a dictionary for it somewhere?"

Raphael nodded. "With any luck, we should have the relevant texts in the library downstairs. I can take you there, if you'd like. It isn't normally open to non-students, but for a friend of Mr Karamov's I believe we can make an exception." He rose shakily to his feet, leaning a hand on the desk to steady himself.

"Did you know," he said, as Morgan held the door open for him, "there is an ancient Jewish legend which purports to explain the origin of Hungarian? It claims it was the language of Lilith, the demonic first wife of Adam. When God drove her from Eden to make room for Eve, he told her to take her tainted language with her. But to spite the Creator, who had first chosen her and then discarded her, Lilith went to secret corners of the earth, and whispered the language to Adam's children. And some of them, at least, have never forgotten it. It is an amusing story, is it not?"

Morgan smiled politely as he followed the professor down the gloomy corridor.

Margaret Island lay ahead of them, over a bridge that spanned the Danube in a series of squat arcs. It was their best guess for where Karamov was heading – and if they arrived ahead of him, there was less chance he'd notice the tail. Tomas would still have to keep out of sight, but Anya at least could stay in the open.

She mentally cursed the British operative for the thousandth time since she'd heard about his little stunt in the restaurant. Anger came so easily to her these days. She remembered a time when it hadn't been her first response to everything, but she couldn't seem to recapture it.

The bridge was long, the river broad and sluggish at this point, and the walk gave Anya too much time to think. She'd been sickening of the work for a while now, afraid it was changing her in ways she couldn't change back. She could even pinpoint the time when the transformation began, that trip to Japan chasing down a lead who turned out to be a phantom. It had been a trap, though she'd managed to escape it. But she'd come back a different woman – less trusting, and less happy. How would *this* mission change her? How long before she ceased to know herself at all?

"Which way?" Tomas asked when they stood on the shore, the island stretching out verdant in front of them, an oasis in the urban sprawl which lay on both sides of the river.

"No real way of knowing till he gets here," Belle said.

Anya frowned, thinking. "This is Karamov's first trip to Budapest."

"OK," Tomas said. "And..?"

"Do you have a tourist guide to the city?"

He shook his head, but Belle handed over a dog-eared copy of the *Rough Guide*, and Anya flicked through to the section on Margaret Island.

"I hardly think he's come here sightseeing," Tomas said.

Anya sighed, still looking down at the book. "But we think he's here to meet someone, maybe someone local. Karamov has probably never been to the island before. They'll have to pick a rendezvous point that's easy for a visitor to find."

The grim lines of Tomas's face relaxed. "You're right. So what are the options?"

"The Alfred Hajos swimming pool," Anya said, reading from the book.

Tomas and Belle shook their heads simultaneously. "Too busy," he said.

"There are some ruins at one end, an old Franciscan Priory."

Tomas took the book from her and peered at the photo, a small maze of low stone walls. "Maybe. But where exactly would they meet?" Then he spotted something on the facing page. "The water tower. That's in the park, isn't it?"

Anya read the description of the tall octagonal building that lay near the centre of the island. "Yes," she said. "That has to be it."

"But what if we're wrong?" Belle asked. "We could lose Karamov entirely."

Tomas smiled wryly. "What's life without a little risk?"

"Exactly the attitude," Anya said sourly, "which got us in this mess in the first place."

The library seemed to be buried deep in the bowels of the faculty building. Raphael walked more quickly than Morgan would have expected, leading him confidently through the maze of corridors, down four flights of stairs, across two large vaulted rooms and then into another dark warren until he had absolutely no idea where he was.

"It's a confusing place," he said as Raphael took them into another stairwell, dimly lit and dripping with rank-smelling water.

Raphael raised an eyebrow at him. "In a hurry? Don't worry – we've arrived." He unlocked the steel door in front of him with a rusty key, then swung it open onto blackness, stepping aside to beckon Morgan through.

"In there?" Morgan asked dubiously.

Raphael smiled, wrinkling his face into a thousand shallow crevices. "We are very security conscious here – some of our books are worth a great deal of money. After you, Morgan."

It was only when he heard the door slam shut behind him that Morgan remembered he'd never told the professor his name.

CHAPTER SEVEN

The life of the park went on around her: women walking children, men walking dogs, a group of students tossing a Frisbee, languid in the humid heat now that the rain had passed. Anya kept her gaze on them and not on Karamov as the big Russian walked towards her.

Was he – yes, he was going to sit on the bench right beside her, the one she'd deliberately picked because it was nearest to the water tower.

Both Tom and Belle were elsewhere, out of sight of Karamov and the protection he'd brought with him. The bodyguards were keeping their distance – probably part of the agreement with whoever Karamov was meeting – but Anya was crawlingly aware of their presence. The slightest hint that she wasn't just an innocent tourist, and they'd come swarming. Damn Tomas anyway, for landing her in this on her own!

Beside her, she felt Karamov shift then shift again, probably unable to get his bulk comfortable on the wooden bench. Or maybe he was nervous. He'd been sweating like a pig as he approached, dark patches of moisture in the armpits of his ugly blue-and-yellow shirt and in the crotch of his cotton trousers, and a sour cloud of body odour had engulfed her as he sat down. Anya eased herself away from him, so that his flabby, moist thigh was no longer resting against hers.

He shot her an irritated look. She pretended she hadn't seen it, that she was engrossed in the tinny music blaring out of her iPod headphones. It was a nice little device, a recent invention. The music fed *out*, audible only to those around her. It was amazing how easy people found it to ignore someone with a personal stereo, as if they were inhabiting a slightly different world. The headphones' real input, meanwhile, came from the directional mic in one of her blouse's buttons. If Karamov stayed within her sightline, she should be able to hear what he said.

He shifted again, glanced at her one last time, then settled back with a sigh. It looked like he hadn't rumbled her. Typical of his kind of Russian, she'd found. It never occurred to them that a woman might be anything more threatening than arm candy.

Who was he here to meet, though? She leaned back casually and glanced around her.

Coming up the path to the left was a very tall man leading a tiny, fluffy dog with a big blue bow in its tail. He looked absurd, and from his face she could see that he knew it. Probably not him.

Further out, sitting on the grass, a group of three young people sunbathed. One of them was reading, book held over her eyes to shield them from the newly emerged sun. Definitely not them.

From the right this time, a small, pinch-faced young woman approached. She was pretty but pale, and her eyes squinted as if she wasn't used to daylight. Anya looked away – not her either.

Except then she felt a shadow fall across her, and when she allowed herself to glance upwards she saw that the girl had stopped right in front of Karamov.

"Hello, Mr Karamov," she said. Her Russian was heavily accented. Anya's own wasn't good enough to know its origin, but she guessed somewhere rural and remote.

Karamov's eyebrows rose in amused recognition. "Natasha!"

She nodded sharply. "If you like."

Karamov leered, stretching his fleshy jowls wide. "It's lovely to see you, darling, but I really am very busy. Maybe we can have some more fun together later."

"You're busy meeting me," Natasha said. "*I* summoned you here."

Anya could hear in the woman's voice that she liked saying *summoned,* that she enjoyed its suggestion of control.

Karamov seemed too shocked by her words to protest them. "*You?*"

"Me. You've fucked up, Karamov." Natasha's voice was acrid with hatred. Could he hear how much this woman despised him?

"Not here," he hissed. "Walk with me." He levered himself out of the bench, leaving a sweat stain on the wood. Then he grabbed Natasha's arm and pulled her towards the water tower.

Now the voices were only coming to Anya through the headphones. "So our mutual friend has been watching me a while, eh?" Karamov said. "I guess I should have expected it. But this is his fuck-up, not mine. He was the one who arranged the transfer point."

Natasha shrugged, a twitch of her bony shoulders towards her ears. "And it was your bodyguards who were supposed to secure the venue."

"It's gone, that's what matters. We both need to get it back. Does this mean you've got no more idea who's taken it than I have?"

Natasha rocked back on her heels. "Ah, so you don't know. That changes things, of course."

"You thought *I* had something to do with it?"

"Even you wouldn't be stupid enough to double-cross us. But we thought you might know who was responsible. Perhaps some enemy of yours."

"I don't have enemies. No living ones, anyway."

Natasha laughed. It was a horrible sound, a gloating gurgle, and even Karamov seemed to sense the danger in it. Anya saw him take a step back, releasing the woman's arm.

"You've got some enemies *now,*" she said. "You know too much, and you're worth too little."

While he was still gathering himself to respond, she lifted

something to her lips – and a piercing, unbearably high-pitched whistle screeched through Anya's headphones.

Over by the water tower, the woman smiled around the whistle as the note died. "And by the way," she said. "My name is Valeria, not Natasha."

There was a moment's silence, then another sound took the whistle's place – a high, inhuman howl. Anya couldn't find its source until she saw the man she'd noticed earlier, the tall man with the little dog. The animal was pulling so hard at its leash it actually dragged the man a pace or two. Its mouth was open, spittle hanging off its small white fangs, and suddenly it didn't look so funny.

As Anya watched, the little dog gave one final tug and its leash flew out of the man's hands. The moment it was free, the animal flew over the grass towards Karamov.

And behind it, from every corner of the park, a hundred other dogs raced after.

There was a moment of darkness, and then a dull clank as the lights came on, neon strips in the ceiling. It was Raphael who'd thrown the switch, a metal lever on the wall of the large, white-tiled room. The old man was smiling, still looking absent-mindedly amiable. But the hand holding the semi-automatic pointed at Morgan was absolutely steady.

Morgan spun round, knowing the door was right behind him.

So was another gun. A round-faced, thick-lipped young man waved it at him, the universal gesture for "take a step back".

Morgan stumbled a little as he complied, and saw the young man's finger twitch on the trigger, a sheen of nervous sweat glittering on his forehead.

"Easy, Vadim," Raphael snapped. "Morgan isn't going to do anything unwise, are you?"

Morgan shook his head as he backed away, all the while calculating distances and strategies. He was ten feet from Raphael, fifteen from Vadim. The old man was the obvious target, but Morgan knew that he was the real threat. The boy was unsure of himself. He was the one who could be tricked, maybe manoeuvred into a position where he was blocking Raphael's line of fire...

"Stay where you are please, Morgan," Raphael said, as if he'd read his thoughts.

Morgan nodded, holding his hands away from his sides as he let the tension in his body relax. The old man was too dangerous to play games with, at least until he'd got a better sense of what was going on. He took the chance to look around him instead.

The room might once have been a laboratory. Old, grooved benches and rickety stalls lined its walls, but they didn't seem to be serving their original purpose. The entire central area had been cleared to leave twenty square feet of dark wooden floorboards. At first Morgan took the patterns on them for dirt or decay, but after a second his eyes resolved them into elaborate runes written in chalk. The surrounding benches were crowded with junk. He spotted statues, elaborately carved in ivory, one a horned man, another of a heavily pregnant woman. Nearby, an old-fashioned telescope was resting against the skull of something that might have been a monkey or a man. A jar next to it held the pitiful, deformed remains of a human foetus.

Morgan managed a twisted grin at Raphael. "Doesn't look much like a library to me."

"Indeed," Raphael said. "Nor do you look very much like an employee of Karamov's to me."

"*You* were the buyer for the book, weren't you?"

Raphael nodded, smiling almost apologetically. But even when he lowered his head, he kept his eyes trained unblinkingly on Morgan, and his gun hand never wavered.

Morgan didn't need Tomas there to tell him he'd been an idiot.

Anya ran towards Karamov the second he started screaming. There were three dogs on him already, and more were streaming across the grass, howling as they charged.

When Anya was twenty paces away she saw him stamp his foot to crush the head of the smallest dog, the absurd little Pekingese. There was a splatter of gore, skull fragments and cloudy white brain tissue, but the blood on the dog's muzzle was Karamov's.

As Anya watched, ten paces away and closing, she saw an Alsatian leap forward to clamp its jaws around Karamov's knee. She heard the sound of cartilage crunching and a silver bell on the dog's collar swung in time to the shaking of its head.

There were six dogs on him, then seven. A bull terrier worried at his toes then fell back, three of them in its mouth. A small white poodle scratched its way up his calf to tear at his thigh. It must have caught something crucial in its teeth, because Karamov's leg suddenly gave. He fell to his knees, and now the dogs could reach his face and neck.

He wasn't the only one screaming. When Anya finally reached him she had to push her way through a ring of people. The dogs' owners watched, horrified, as their pets ripped a man to shreds.

Karamov's bodyguards had reached him too, but even they hesitated, watching the carnage in mute shock. Anya didn't want to get any closer either. She really didn't want to see the ragged mess the animals had made of Karamov's face, flaps of skin fluttering from his jaw like ribbons.

But he kept on screaming, and something essentially human in her couldn't hear that desperate noise and not respond. She tackled the poodle first, prising its jaws away from the wreckage of his leg with an effort that nearly tore her shoulder. When it was finally free, she took the little creature by its collar and dashed its head on the ground. Somewhere behind her there was a muted gasp of protest and a woman fell to her knees beside the animal's corpse.

Anya grabbed the Alsatian next – but it was much too strong. Even as she pulled at it, its jaws closed, severing Karamov's right leg below the knee.

The big Russian's face was grey and slack. He'd lost too much blood and suffered too much pain. Anya let the Alsatian go, knowing that nothing was going to save Karamov now.

His eyelids flickered, consciousness fading. Then for one brief moment his eyes opened and stared into hers, bright and clear. "Raphael," he gasped. "All the bastards I know – and he's the one to kill me."

Morgan knew he still had one thing Raphael wanted, the only thing that was keeping him safe. The book was tucked into the waistband of his jeans, hidden from the old man's view. Until Raphael had the book in his hands, Morgan didn't think he'd risk harming it by harming him.

Once he had the book, all bets were off.

"Give it to me," Raphael said.

Morgan backed away a step, towards the far side of the room where there was another door leading – who knew where? Out, and that was all that really mattered. "Why should I?" he said.

Raphael looked at his gun.

Morgan shook his head. "I meant, you know, morally."

"*Morally?*" Raphael laughed. "Because I paid for it. Because I know how to use it. I know what it is. Do you?"

"Obviously not. That's why I came to see you."

Vadim was looking between them, perplexed. His semi-automatic had drooped as his attention wandered, the barrel pointing down at the dark wood of the floor. Good. One less threat to worry about.

Raphael's tongue flicked out, pink and pointed, to moisten his lips. "If you give it to me, I will tell you what its purpose is."

"There's a flaw in that arrangement – I'm sure you can see it." Morgan took another step backwards.

Raphael's eyes narrowed. "Then let's return to the fact that I have a gun."

Another step. "If you were going to shoot me, you'd have done it already."

Raphael's pale face flushed with anger, and Morgan instantly knew he was right. The old man didn't mean to kill him.

Morgan's heart was pounding against his ribs as if it wanted to break them, the confrontation too cold and calculated for battle fever to carry him through it. Death seemed real and imminent – but he had to take the one chance he had.

He took a last look at Raphael, making very sure that he'd judged him right, then turned his back and sprinted for the far end of the room.

One shot rang out, deafeningly loud in the confined space. The bullet shattered the white tiles on the wall ahead of him.

That had been Vadim, he was sure. And he could hear the clatter of hard leather heels on the floor behind him but also the old man shouting in a language Morgan didn't know. He could only hope he was saying "Don't fire!"

Maybe he was, but another shot rang out before Morgan could reach the far wall. It was better aimed this time and he felt a tearing at his side that left a searing pain behind. Every instinct told him to curl in and shield the wound. He compromised with a hand pressed against the blood oozing from beneath his ribs and kept on running.

Two more paces and he was at the door. It was made of a thick, silver metal and it opened with a wheel, not a handle. Morgan spun it desperately, working against stiff resistance.

The footsteps were right behind him now. As he felt a hand claw at his shoulder he kicked back and up, viciously hard. There was a whoosh of lost air and a tiny, almost sub-vocal squeak that in other circumstances might have been funny. Morgan felt the hand slide down his shoulder, fisting in his t-shirt for a moment of pain before slackening and falling off.

Two more twists of the wheel and the door was open. He flung himself through, dragging it shut behind him. There was another wheel on the inside, and he twisted that shut with the same frantic haste until it wouldn't turn any more.

Only one problem left – no lock.

The door had opened inward, though. It could be jammed. Morgan saw five metal tables lined up across the width of the room. He braced his shoulder against the nearest, heaving hard. The exertion forced a gush of blood from the wound in his side, and he wasn't sure he had the strength to lift it, but he had to try. He took a gulp of air, then let out a strangled yell as he strained upwards with everything he had.

The table rocked, lifted – and then it had all the momentum it needed as it swung up and toppled over to rest against the door. Gasping for breath now, Morgan forced himself to make one last effort, levering the table up so that it pressed against the door at an angle, the other end jabbing into the floor. A second later there was a clatter against the outside of the door, then the louder bang of something striking it repeatedly – probably Vadim's shoulder.

The door opened an inch as the table skidded across the floor. Then its corner ground to a halt, digging into the grouting between two tiles. Morgan flung himself prone onto the flat silver surface, and his weight pushed the table down, slamming the door shut and holding it fast.

There were more loud bangs against the outside, but this time the door didn't shift at all. Then there was the much louder retort of a gunshot. The metal didn't even shudder, far too thick for the bullets to pierce.

All the air seemed to finally go out of Morgan, and he sagged to the floor like a deflated balloon. His side hurt like hell. The bullet had missed anything vital but gouged out a thick slice of flesh on its journey in and out. Thankfully, the blood was already starting to clot in the profound cold.

The cold. For the first time Morgan actually looked at his surroundings. The air was so frigid he could see his breath in a cloud of white in front of him, floating towards the low, metal ceiling. The far wall was lined with metal too, even tessellations that looked like a honeycomb. After a moment Morgan realised they were drawers. The other two walls were entirely blank – no other doors leading out.

He crawled towards the far wall on his hands and knees, lacking the energy to stand up. His path took him between two of the other silver tables, the ones that were still upright. He felt something brush against his cheek and brushed it irritably away, only to have it swing back down and hit his face with more force.

It was a hand. There was a body on the table, arms and legs the discoloured yellow of elderly custard, the chest cut open and splayed out, the cavity empty of organs. Those were on a low bench at the side of the room, Morgan realised, the heart sitting on a set of electronic scales.

There were two other bodies on neighbouring tables, one of them a teenaged girl and almost whole, the other rendered down to its constituent limbs. Morgan suspected that the drawers at the end of the room held more corpses, if this was a morgue, and what the hell else could it be?

He shivered again and kept on shivering, the cold slowly seeping through his skin and into his bones. He took one last look around and then crawled back to the door, wondering if there was anywhere worse he could possibly have locked himself.

Anya had retreated to the far side of the water tower, away from the police who'd descended on the scene of Karamov's slaughter, and the shell-shocked dog owners who somehow had to explain what their pets had done.

The scene kept replaying in her mind, over and over on an endless loop, the white teeth tearing into the red flesh. But worse than that, worse than the sight of a man ripped to pieces in front of her, was how familiar it had all felt.

She'd seen Karamov torn apart and something inside her had said, *that once happened to me.* But of course it hadn't. How could it have? So why did she feel like there was a memory of pain as intense and brutalising as the Russian's, hidden somewhere in her past?

Her hands were shaking as she leafed through the folder, shoving pages aside impatiently when she failed to find what she was looking for. She could see that she was leaving red stains on the white paper but she managed to concentrate so hard on her search that she didn't have to think about what they were.

After a few minutes a hand rested on hers, stilling it.

It was Tomas, his grave face unusually gentle. "What happened back there?"

"Karamov's dead."

"We saw." That was Belle. The little girl hovered a few paces away, seemingly reluctant to come any closer.

Anya set the folder aside and batted Tomas's hand irritably from hers. "It was the girl, Natasha – or, I can't remember her real name. God, I really should remember her name..."

"Anya," Tomas said softly.

"What? Oh, the girl. She was the one who made it happen. She used some sort of whistle to summon the dogs. Some power in it, I don't know, I've never seen anything like it before. Sumerian, maybe, I've heard that they -"

"Working for Karamov's rivals?" Tomas cut across her. "He must have – have had – a lot of enemies."

"Not a rival. Raphael." She picked up the folder again and started to leaf through it, the pages swimming in and out of focus in front of her eyes. "He's in here somewhere, I know he is. Karamov had been phoning him and we couldn't figure out why. But it didn't occur to us – it just didn't seem probable – that he'd be the buyer."

Tomas tried to catch her eye again. "Why didn't it seem probable?"

"Damn it!" Anya shouted, throwing the folder to the ground. The wind riffled the paper then began to blow it away. "Where the hell has the briefing document gone!?"

Belle knelt to pick up the pages, stacking them into neat piles with her small white hands.

"Listen," Tomas said, more sternly this time. "You can fall apart later. Right now the trail is hot and we have to follow it. As soon as this Raphael hears the job's been done he'll have no more reason to stay here. Tell me what you know about him."

Anya nodded sharply, trying to jolt herself back to rationality. It seemed to work, because her voice was only shaking a little when she said, "He's a visiting professor at the university here.

He specialises in linguistics, ancient languages mostly. Beyond that, we couldn't find out very much. At the time, we couldn't fathom his connection to Karamov. But now –"

"He might want the book because he's the only person who can actually translate it," Belle suggested.

Anya nodded. "Which is why I need to figure out where the hell the briefing notes on him have got to!"

The same thought occurred to all three of them at once, but Tomas was the first to voice it: "Morgan."

Morgan knew the fact he wasn't shivering any more wasn't a good sign. The blood had stopped seeping from the hole in his side, which he'd plugged with scraps of cotton ripped from the bottom of his t-shirt, and he felt okay. Better than okay. He was in an almost euphoric haze.

That probably wasn't a good sign either.

When the pleasant drowsiness threatened to tip over into actual sleep, Morgan forced himself to stagger to his feet. The pain instantly registered again, along with the searing cold, and he was sorry he'd done it. There was no window in the thick metal door, which meant he had no way of knowing what Raphael and his goon were up to. For all he knew, they could have given up and left – but he doubted it.

He shuffled over to the back wall instead, to the honeycomb of drawers. Most of them were empty. The ones that weren't held corpses in greater states of decomposition than the ones on the tables. A stench of formaldehyde oozed out when he opened the last drawer and he hurriedly shut it, hiding away the blank white face and glassy blue eyes of the occupant.

A second after the metallic chink of the drawer closing there was another softer noise behind him. He spun round, a surge of adrenaline instantly washing away the haze blanketing his mind.

The door was still closed, the upended table wedged tight against it. But the sound came again, recognisable now as the soft whisper of fabric against metal, and this time Morgan realised that it was coming from inside the room.

It was the movement which finally drew his eye, the withered hands reaching out to press against the metal of the table as the corpse levered itself upright. There was a waft of cold air which stank of corruption.

The corpse's hands, wizened and claw-like, groped at its chest, sinking deep into the cavity where its organs had once been. After a second, they dropped to its sides.

Morgan's back pressed against the icy metal of the wall, as far away from the body on the table as he could possibly get.

"Don't worry, this thing won't kill you," the corpse said.

"Yeah?" Morgan's teeth started chattering audibly the moment he opened his mouth. If he hadn't met Tomas, he wondered if he would have thought he was hallucinating.

"Yes. In fact, it's the cold that will finish you off."

Morgan realised he knew that voice. Despite the mushy, awkward sound it made working round a half-decayed tongue, it was recognisably Raphael's.

"Is that book really worth dying for?" the old man asked.

"I don't know," Morgan said. "You tell me."

"Come out here, and I will."

"Tell me and I'll think about it."

There was a brief silence, then, "This isn't stalemate, Morgan. In less than two hours you will die, and the book will be mine anyway."

"Yeah? So why are you going to all this trouble to talk to me?"

The corpse shrugged, gaping the cavity of its chest open and shut. "Maybe I'm sentimental. Maybe I don't want to kill my old friend's son."

Morgan wondered if Raphael could see through the corpse's milky eyes. If he could, the old man would be able to read his expression of shock.

"I'm talking about Geraint Nicholson, of course," Raphael said after a moment. "Not whoever it was that raised you."

Morgan knew this must be a trap, a ruse to get him to give in, but he couldn't help asking the question. It was why he'd come here in the first place. "You're saying you knew my dad?"

The cadaver nodded, head flopping loosely on its neck. "I knew him very well." A brief, wet laugh. "Probably better than anyone. Who do you think taught him to control the dead?"

Morgan tried to make sense of it, but he felt like he was being given pieces to two entirely different puzzles. "That means you were part of the Hermetic Division, right?"

"I knew your father before he founded it. Do you want to know what kind of man he was? I expect you do. I don't imagine they've told you much, those people you're working for. Information is currency to them, and they've always been miserly with it."

"There's no way they could have told me about him, is there? Until today I didn't even know he existed." Morgan snapped his mouth shut at the corpse's smile, knowing he'd revealed more than he'd intended.

"So they've been keeping you in the dark, *you* who had more right to the truth than anyone. How very like them."

There was a long silence, and Morgan understood the old man's game. He was waiting for Morgan to ask a question, to admit that he wanted the information. Morgan wanted to resist, but the cold seemed to be closing in on him, squeezing the air out of his chest and freezing the thoughts in his head. Raphael had got it wrong. Morgan doubted he had two hours. Less than one, probably, before he was finished.

Fuck it. He *did* want to know. "All right then, what kind of man *was* he?"

"He was – "

The corpse fell back to the table, arms flopping brokenly against the metal. For a moment Morgan thought it was a trick, maybe a test of how badly Morgan wanted to know. But the seconds stretched on and the body didn't move. Raphael had gone, and the answers with him.

Whoever was inside hadn't locked the door. It burst inward to hit the wall with a muted ring like a cracked bell. The instant it was open Tomas leapt through, Anya and Belle close behind.

There were two men in the room, both holding guns. Tomas recognised the younger. It was Karamov's contact from the restaurant, with his round face and drooping, weak mouth. He kept darting nervous glances at his companion, as if waiting for instructions.

"Raphael?" Tomas guessed.

The old man frowned. "And I imagined the rash Mr Hewitt was on a solo mission."

"Where is he?"

Raphael didn't react, but the young man jerked an involuntary glance behind him, before looking back at Tomas.

Tomas took a careful step forward, watching the men's eyes and not their guns.

"In case you haven't noticed," Raphael said, "we are armed and you are not."

"I'm not afraid of your weapons," Tomas told him.

"Aren't you?"

Tomas shrugged. "Shoot me and see."

Raphael stared at him a second, then moved the angle of his muzzle a fraction. "And what about the ladies? Do they share your indifference to bullets?"

Tomas knew his expression had betrayed him when Raphael smiled.

"Hurt them and I'll kill you."

"Indeed," Raphael said. "And vice versa, naturally."

Tomas kept his eyes trained on Raphael and his underling, but he saw a swirl of movement in his peripheral vision and knew that Anya had moved to stand beside him. Hopeless – he couldn't shield her that way. But then there were two men with two guns; all they had to do was move apart. Raphael had him locked down and he knew it.

Still, stalemate went both ways. Tomas took three more paces forward. He felt the young man twitch the barrel of his gun round to track him, but Raphael never moved, keeping his own trained on Anya as he'd promised.

"That's quite close enough," the old man said.

Would he fire? Could he really kill a woman in cold blood? Tomas had a brief flash of memory: the pack of dogs tearing into Karamov's flesh as the fat Russian screamed and screamed. If Raphael had ordered that, he was capable of anything.

"I don't want to hurt you, I just want to find Morgan," Tomas said. He really did, though he wasn't quite sure why. His partner had been nothing but a pain in the arse since they'd started working together.

Raphael's lizard-thin lips twitched downward. "I have no idea who you're talking about."

Anya stirred beside Tomas and he spoke before she could say the wrong thing. "That's fine. Just let me look in that room behind you, and I'll go." He'd spotted the thick metal door as soon as he'd stepped nearer, and it didn't take a genius to figure out where the young man had been looking when Tomas mentioned Morgan.

It also didn't take a genius to work out that Morgan must still have Nicholson's book. Why else would Raphael be so worried about keeping Tomas away from him?

"I'll even let you have the book," Tomas said, "if you let Morgan go."

This time it was Raphael who couldn't control his reaction. His mask of elderly affability vanished, replaced by something much less wholesome. "The boy is more important to you than the book? I don't think so."

"We've already copied the entire thing," Tomas said. "You getting hold of the original is regrettable, but within mission parameters."

The old man studied him for a long moment. Finally, he shook his head. "No. Morgan said nothing about any copies."

Tomas kept his face impassive, but inside he was smiling. The old man was slipping, admitting that he *had* seen Morgan. "You think we'd tell a green operative like him what we were up to?

Take the book, Raphael, and give me the boy."

"There are only two real choices here," Anya said. "Everyone walks out of here alive, or no one does. I know which I prefer."

Tomas saw it in the young man's face, the sudden realisation that he might die. He hadn't come here expecting a fight, and he wasn't ready for its consequences. For the first time his gun wavered, barrel shaking with his hand.

In that moment of irresolution, while Tomas was debating whether he could risk rushing the young man, and the young man was wavering in the face of his own mortality and Anya was backing carefully away, and everything seemed poised on a knife edge, something none of them had been expecting happened.

The metal door behind Raphael swung inward, letting out a blast of ice-cold air – and Morgan.

Morgan staggered, Raphael spun to face him, and Tomas finally moved. A bullet from the young man's gun took him in the chest, enough power in it to push him back, teetering on his heels, but he didn't fall and he kept advancing.

The young man's eyes widened in horror as his mouth slackened in fear. And then Tomas was on him, bearing the slighter man's body to the ground with his own.

Too hard. The impact tightened his opponent's finger on the trigger, and Tomas felt a second bullet slam into him. The agony was searing, loosening his hands for a crucial second from around the other man's shoulders.

As soon as he was released, the young man rolled and rose. He could have shot Belle then. She was standing to the side of the action, utterly defenceless. But all he seemed to care about was escape. He didn't even look at Raphael as he bolted for the door.

Tomas didn't try to stop him. Raphael was the one he wanted. As he staggered to his feet, groaning at the pain of the bullet holes in his chest and gut, he saw the older man stumble to his knees, the gun falling from his hand.

It was Morgan. Tomas's partner looked dead on his feet, but his mouth was twisted in a snarl and his fist was still clenched from the blow he'd delivered. Why hadn't Raphael shot him? Slowed by age, maybe.

But not so slow that he couldn't lash out with his own fist to catch Tomas where the first bullet had gone in. Tomas's body curled helplessly around the pain. In the second that bought him, Raphael pressed a wrinkled hand underneath him and pushed himself unsteadily to his feet. Then he was up and running for the door.

Morgan moved to follow but fell to his knees instead, as if all his strength had suddenly given out. Anya crouched at his side, a steadying hand on his back. Tomas straightened with a yell of pain and ran in the old man's shadow.

Raphael was at the door before Tomas caught him. He grabbed Raphael's arm, his own hand so large it enclosed the frail wrist with a finger joint to spare.

"Leaving so soon?" he gasped, through the pain of wounds that should have been mortal.

"Don't worry, it's only a temporary parting." Improbably, Raphael smiled. He was still smiling as the knife he'd hidden in his other hand flashed up, and then down. The blade was surgically sharp, cutting clean through skin and muscle and tendons and finally bone.

The moment the tendon was severed Tomas's fingers loosened. He watched, helplessly, as his hand released Raphael's wrist and fell to the floor. He looked at it there, swimming in a pool of his own blood, like a fleshy pink spider drowning.

With an effort of will, he forced his attention back up to Raphael – and for just a second their gazes locked.

The old man's eyes were bright blue beneath the gumminess of age, and a light shone out of them which froze Tomas where he stood. He felt like something rank had touched him, something he'd never be able to wash away.

Then the door opened and shut, and Raphael was gone.

PART TWO

Things Fall Apart

CHAPTER EIGHT

Tomas felt Anya watching him as Belle sewed his hand to his wrist with precise, neat little stitches. The end of the girl's tongue poked between her teeth as she worked, a tiny pink point like a pimple in the whiteness. They'd booked two sleeper carriages for the four of them, but were crammed into just one of them now, a musty, leather-smelling space that jammed Belle's elbow against Morgan's stomach as she stitched, while Tomas bent his head to sit on the lower bed and Anya perched cross-legged on the top bunk above them.

Every stitch hurt as it went in, joining a deeper ache that somehow spread from his arm out towards his fingers, the vanguard of the feeling that returned to them as Belle sewed. He'd sneaked into the morgue after Raphael escaped and did what he had to do to ensure his wounds healed. It troubled Tomas how easy he now found it to accept what he'd become. His lifeless body didn't feel like the inert weight it once had, vibrating with the rhythmic rattling of the train lines beneath them. He felt another note sounding inside him too, a buzzing tension which hadn't dissipated since they'd left Budapest three hours ago.

He would have liked to take a plane, fly straight back to London and ask all the questions that had been curdling in his mind since he'd first seen Nicholson's name on that book. But Anya had said no airport would let him through security looking the way he did, and she was right. Besides, Raphael was still out there. The airport was probably being watched. Instead, this train would take them overnight to Berlin, where Anya's colleagues in the BND had promised to share their files on Karamov and Raphael.

"You should be dead," Anya said suddenly. There was a flat, shell-shocked tone to her voice. "I knew. I mean, I'd been told. But to see it..."

"Join the club," Morgan said. They'd bandaged the flesh wound in his side, but he still looked unwell, a grey tinge to his brown skin.

If Morgan had been hoping to focus Anya's attention on Tomas, he'd made a tactical error. She turned to look at Morgan, eyes blazing. "You've got some explaining to do."

Morgan's full mouth turned down, and though his eyes remained blank Tomas could guess what was going on behind them. Thinking up excuses.

Before Morgan could try one of them, Tomas said, "You hoped Raphael would be able to translate the book for you."

After a moment, Morgan nodded.

Anya frowned. "Or, alternatively, Morgan was working for him all along."

"Don't be absurd!" Tomas snapped. "People don't generally leave their associates to freeze to death in locked morgues. Even Raphael wouldn't do that – or at least not while Morgan still had the book he wanted."

"I'd never even heard of Raphael before I read about him in your file," Morgan said. "And yeah, I wanted to know what the book said."

"Why did you care?" That was Belle, speaking with a slight lisp as she bit through the end of the thread.

Tomas pulled his sleeve down before Anya could see the way his flesh was already beginning to knit together around the tiny black stitches.

Morgan's fingers played around his mouth, as if he wanted to filter his words before they came out. "Because I don't know why the hell I was sent on this mission. And I don't know why..." He looked at Tomas, then away. "Either the world's gone crazy, or I have. This book is the only thing we've got that might have an explanation in it, and you wanted to just give it away."

"I want to know what Nicholson's book was doing in Karamov's hands, too," Tomas said. "And what it's got to do with the Ragnarok artefacts."

"How very democratic the Hermetic Division must be," Anya said. "All its agents questioning their orders all the time." The sun was setting outside the train window, a blood-red glow on the horizon that accentuated the scarlet of her hair and brought a blush of life to her pale cheeks. "You had a mission, and you fucked it up. Both of you. If you want to side with him, Tomas, that's fine, but don't expect me to carry on working with either of you."

"Please don't argue," Belle said. Her small face looked pinched and tired. "When you get angry I can feel *him* inside me, smiling and enjoying it. I think it makes him stronger. What's done is done – can't we leave it behind?"

"Leave behind the fact that Morgan nearly lost us the book? I don't think so. You need to give it to me, then we can all be sure it's safe." She reached an imperious hand to Morgan from her perch on the narrow bunk.

"I didn't give it to Raphael, did I? And I'm sure as hell not giving it to you."

Anya's reaching hand clenched into a fist. "How can we possibly trust you after what you did?"

"Don't trust me! I don't trust you. I don't trust anybody. Nobody's said a straight word to me since I started on this fucking mission!"

Anya frowned and cast a disapproving glance from Morgan to Belle. Morgan clamped his mouth shut, but his expression remained mulish.

Tomas sighed and ran a hand through his hair. "Let Morgan keep it. We can talk about this tomorrow morning when we've all had some sleep."

There wasn't as much to do on a train as Morgan had imagined when he'd watched *Murder on the Orient Express* one Sunday afternoon and thought that travelling this way must be pretty glamorous. The other passengers seemed disappointingly ordinary, a succession of smartly dressed businessmen and one big, blond-haired family with a collection of children so similar they looked like a set of Russian dolls.

Whenever Morgan leaned against the wall to watch them pass, the rectangular lump of his father's book dug into his back. It made him feel itchy and uncomfortable when he remembered how Tomas had defended him earlier. He tried to convince himself that he hadn't actually lied to his partner, but he knew he hadn't told him the whole truth either.

Morgan's stomach gurgled, loud enough for a passing guard to stifle a smile, and he realised he was starving. When had he last eaten, anyway?

The dining car was in the centre of the train, sparkling with glass and polished silver, exactly the kind of place he'd imagined as a child. But they'd stopped serving long ago, and the attendants looked round when Morgan stepped in, faces hardening in disapproval at his blood-stained t-shirt and army boots. He took a moment to stare them down, then backed out and away.

In another carriage there was a small canteen and he bought himself a ham roll and, after a moment's thought, a cheese sandwich for Tomas. After that there wasn't much else to do but head back to the sleeper cabin they were sharing.

It was dark when he pushed open the door, with only the pale light of the moon to illuminate the outlines of the bed and the small washbasin tucked against one wall. There was the humped shape of a body on the bottom bunk, and Morgan assumed Tomas must have drifted off to sleep already. But when he switched on the overhead light, he found the other man's eyes looking straight at him.

Morgan jerked back, breath catching in his throat. "Shit!"

"I don't need to sleep any more," Tomas said. "Not since..."

"Right. I brought you a sandwich, if you want to eat."

Tomas smiled crookedly. "I don't do that either."

Morgan ate both sandwiches in silence, spreading crumbs over the rectangle of old red carpet. When he'd finished, he wiped his mouth clean with his sleeve, then splashed water on his face from the cold tap.

"What haven't you told us?" Tomas said when Morgan turned back to face him.

Morgan stared at him. "About what?"

"I don't know, Morgan – whatever it was you didn't want to say in front of Anya and Belle."

Morgan took a deep breath, then let it out again. "Raphael brought one of the corpses to life, while I was locked in the morgue. Used it to speak to me."

Tomas nodded calmly.

Morgan perched on the end of the bed, beside the messy outline of Tomas's feet. "So that's normal then, is it? That's just run of the mill. Nothing to get too excited about."

Tomas studied him a moment, and seemed to decide there was a genuine question buried in there. "In a way. There's only one real source of magic. We all end up using it in the end."

"Death, you mean?"

"Life. Everything, every molecule on Earth, used to be part of something living once. The secret is finding a way to remind it. That's the source of all magic, 'the force that through the green fuse drives the flower.'"

"You know quoting poetry doesn't make it any less of a heap of shit, right?"

Tomas laughed. "That's all I know. I was just an operative, Morgan. I used the tools they gave me and I found the things they wanted. I left the philosophy to people higher up the food chain."

"People like Nicholson?"

"Yes. Nicholson ran the Hermetic Division. I was his first recruit – his only recruit for two years." He smiled a little, looking for once like he was lost in a pleasant memory. "We'd travel the world together, chasing rumours – a werewolf in Greece, the Ark of the Covenant in Ethiopia. Most of them turned out to be nonsense, of course. The people at MI6 talked about shutting us down all the time, but we discovered just enough to keep them interested. And then Nicholson found out about the Ragnarok artefacts, and suddenly everything changed."

There was a long silence, Tomas staring blankly at the sagging mattress above him. Finally, he said, "They're supposed to be unspeakably powerful. Powerful enough to end the world. It was researching the artefacts that taught Nicholson how to conquer death, to bring someone back from the other side. And once the government knew about that, we got all the funding and all the agents we wanted." Tomas shrugged, as if it was no big deal.

"Raphael said he knew Nicholson," Morgan blurted, startled into confession by Tomas's honesty. "He said they used to be friends."

"Did he? Yes, I suppose that's possible. A contact gone bad – it would explain how he knew about the book."

But not, Morgan thought, how Raphael knew Nicholson was his father. For a second he thought about saying this to Tomas, then the other man carried on talking and the moment was lost.

"Nicholson trusted too much," Tomas said. "He wanted to believe anything was possible, and he listened to anyone who told him it was."

"But bringing people back to life – that *is* possible?"

"Oh yes," Tomas said bitterly, "that turned out to be a walk in the park."

Morgan looked at Tomas, and wondered how it felt to know you were dead. Was he glad they'd brought him back? He didn't seem it. "How did it happen?" he asked. "To you, I mean?"

"How did I die?"

Morgan nodded.

Tomas's expression twisted into outright pain. "I was buried alive."

"Jesus! That's... Fuck, that is not good."

"You don't have to feel sorry for me. It was my choice. It was part of the ritual to turn me into what I am. They put me in the ground while I was still breathing, and I let it happen. Of course, they were supposed to bring me back in three days, not twenty years."

"Giles told me I emit mortality," Morgan said, a non sequitur. Or maybe not.

"And do you?"

"Everyone around me dies, I know that."

"Your former partners," Tomas said, and at Morgan's frown, "They did tell me a little about you before they assigned us to work together."

"So do you think it's possible? Is it my fault they died?"

Tomas shook his head. "I don't know. There is such a thing as plain bad luck."

Morgan swallowed painfully. "But it wasn't just them. When I was twelve I got sent on a summer camp. Troubled kids, countryside, teach them the real meaning of life, some shit like that. It was me and Leon, my best mate, and late one night we were pissing around, climbing trees in the dark. We'd nicked some beer from the local offie, and we were fighting. You know, just having a laugh. I didn't mean to push him that hard, but one second he was sitting on the branch next to me. And then..."

Tomas's eyes glittered in the moonlight. "Were there other deaths?"

Morgan nodded, but his throat closed tight over the next words. He stood up, filled with a sudden restless energy that the small cabin left him no room to pace off. He peered in the mirror instead, at the dim shape of his reflection.

My sister, he wanted to say. And as if the unsaid words had summoned her, he saw a shape coalesce in the glass, her face floating above his right shoulder. If he turned around, he'd be looking right at her.

He was halfway through doing just that when the window burst inward in a shower of razor-sharp glass.

For a split second he thought it was an optical illusion, a fragment of the night that had fallen in with the shards of window. By the time it had resolved itself into a figure, swathed in black, it was already past him. And it was only as the door slammed behind it that Morgan registered the feeling of the figure's hand, light-fingered at the waistband of his trousers.

When Morgan fumbled there himself, he found nothing. The book was gone.

CHAPTER NINE

Tomas was sluggish with exhaustion. He tumbled out of the bed onto his knees, wincing at the jolt to his bones. By the time he'd scrambled to his feet both Morgan and the thief were gone, the door swinging open onto the dim corridor beyond.

Tomas's chest had been bare beneath the sheets but he didn't stop to dress. The door slammed behind him as he flung himself through it.

He had one second to scan the corridor, night-silent and dim – then, suddenly, window after window along its length smashed open and a swarm of black-clothed figures swung through. He recognised them instantly, or at least what they were: the same assassins who'd attacked him and Morgan when they first arrived in Budapest. The same black cloth concealed their faces.

And they moved with the same whip-like speed. By the time Tomas had fully registered their presence, they'd already gone, half of them to the left, half to the right. And he had absolutely no idea which of the identical figures had taken the book.

He saw Morgan dart though the sliding door to his right. All Tomas could do was turn left. One of them might catch the thief. One of them would have to.

He thumped his fist against the door of Belle and Anya's cabin as he passed, but there was no time to stop and see if it had any effect. Two more paces and he was through the door at the end of the corridor, wrenching it open with his hand when the automatic mechanism slid too slowly.

Three of them were waiting for him. They must have heard something of what he was by now, because they didn't bother trying to shoot him. Two of them grabbed his arms while a third clubbed him over the head with something hard and metal, probably the butt of a gun. Tomas's consciousness began to grey at the edges, and everything was slowing down.

It wasn't a good time to discover that dead men could still pass out.

Tomas was slumped on the floor, back against the wall and one of the assassins with a knife against his throat when his thoughts revved back up to normal speed. The man's wrist cracked audibly as he snapped it, and the knife fell to the carpeted floor with a muffled thump.

One of Tomas's arms was free now. He used its elbow to drive his other assailant's nose through the soft grey matter of his brain, and then he was able to stumble to his feet. The last intruder was already running, but Tomas couldn't follow him yet. He needed to check that neither of the two on the floor had the book.

He searched the dead man first, a cursory glance. His black clothes were tight enough to show they held nothing larger than a shuriken and a silenced revolver. Tomas took the shuriken and left the gun, too dangerous to be caught with.

The other man was harder to search, writhing in pain and moaning with his broken wrist cradled against his chest. Tomas hesitated, then struck him hard at the base of his skull – possibly hard enough to kill, but he didn't have the time to be careful. There was no sign of the book on him, either.

Tomas cursed and sprinted down the corridor in pursuit of the last man.

Anya threw the door open, heart pumping with the panic of someone woken suddenly from a deep sleep.

The corridor was entirely empty. She looked to left and right a second time to make sure of it, but there wasn't a soul out there.

It was only when the cold breeze blew into her face that she registered what was wrong. Every single window was broken, the floor littered with fragments of glass. Lights glittered on them from outside the train, an unknown city passing by.

She pushed open Tomas and Morgan's door without knocking, and wasn't surprised to find them gone. It must have been one of them who'd woken her. She had a moment's paralysed indecision, then hurried back into her own cabin and pulled Belle out of bed. "Trouble," she told the little girl curtly.

Belle followed Anya back into the corridor, footsteps padding softly, like a cat's. Anya thought that, if it had been up to the men, they would have left Belle behind. For her own safety, or some nonsense like that. Anya wasn't that stupid – or that sentimental. Belle was the best weapon they had. The *only* weapon Anya had right now.

"Oh my lord," Belle said, when she saw the destruction outside. "What happened here?"

As Anya shrugged a pair of guards ambled into the corridor, stopping to stare in bemusement at the shattered windows. Anya grabbed Belle, pulling her towards the left-hand exit before they could start asking awkward questions.

She almost tripped over the first body. When she'd regained her balance, she saw that there were two black-clothed men on the floor, one curled into a foetal ball, the other propped against the door of the toilet. Blood had pooled around him, a dark stain on the grey carpet.

"Scheisse!" Anya said.

Belle looked around, wide-eyed. "Where are Tomas and Morgan? Do you think they've been caught?"

"Maybe. There must be more of these guys. Every window in that corridor was broken." Anya knelt down to hook her hands under the shoulders of the nearest man. "Open the door and take a look," she said to Belle. "Tell me if the guards are heading our way."

The man was a dead weight, pulling painfully at Anya's back as she heaved him upright, though she could see his chest rising and falling in shallow breaths. He wasn't quite gone yet.

Belle remained where she was, eyeing Anya warily. "What the heck are you doing?"

"Cleaning up. At the moment, as far as anyone knows it's just vandalism. If they find these bodies there'll be all kinds of questions. Go on – I need you to keep watch."

Belle did as Anya asked, and Anya began laboriously dragging the first man to the outer door. It had an old-fashioned lock, thank god, the sort you could open even when the train was moving. Warm air blasted in along with the strangely comforting noise of wheels clattering over sleepers.

Anya braced herself against the doorframe as she hooked a foot under the man's body, looking away when he finally flopped out and down to whatever lay below. There wasn't much chance he'd survive the fall, but she'd been hardened to this work a long time ago.

The next man was already dead. He was nearer to the door and upright so it took less effort to drag him the last few feet. Just as well; she was already panting with exertion. Typical bloody men, she thought, leaving the women to clear up their messes behind them.

"They're coming!" Belle hissed suddenly, and Anya only just had time to kick the black-clothed body into the night before the guards arrived.

They looked at her then at the open door, and she slammed it before they could say anything. One of them, an older, greying man with the spidery red traces of alcohol abuse on his nose, growled something at her in Hungarian. She held her hands outspread in a gesture intended to convey both innocence and incomprehension. The guard shook his head, obviously not buying it, but his companion said something and after a brief, whispered conference, they moved away, towards the back of the train.

Anya sagged with relief.

"What now?" Belle asked.

"See what further trouble Tomas and Morgan have landed themselves in, I suppose." Anya rolled her shoulders, trying to ease the ache in her muscles.

She'd started massaging her bicep when the door to the toilet swung open in front of her. She stared in mute astonishment at the black-clothed figure and the shattered window behind him.

The moment of immobility thawed into action, the figure reaching inside his clothing, almost certainly for a weapon. Anya took a step back, bringing her level with Belle. The little girl slipped her hand inside Anya's as a spike of a knife appeared in the man's hand, reflecting nothing back but the blackness of his clothing.

Even with his face covered, Anya thought she could read his body language. It was dark in the little antechamber between carriages, and he was still disoriented. He wasn't one hundred per cent sure they were his targets. And if they weren't, he'd be killing an innocent woman and a little girl. But they *were* his targets, and Anya didn't think his indecision would last long.

Anya had never been much of a fighter, and she wasn't armed. Belle and her strange abilities were their only hope. She snatched a glance at the girl.

Belle returned it with a look of desperation. "I can't. I can't. I can't do it if I can't see their eyes."

The words seemed to finally end their opponent's indecision. His knife slashed a silver arc through the air. Anya dropped to her knees, feeling the blade pass so close to the top of her head that it must have cut through hair. The weapon reached the apex of its swing and slowed, and Anya used the second's grace it gave her to run for the door, pulling Belle behind her.

Tomas only knew he'd reached the end of the train when he ran straight into it. His body rebounded from the door that wouldn't open and barrelled into the man he'd been pursuing, who'd stopped in time to avoid his own collision with the wall.

There was a brief tussle, fierce and silent, until Tomas used his superior weight to pin his opponent to the floor. The assassin instantly changed tack, scrabbling inside his black robes for a weapon. Tomas had been waiting for that. The knife that came out left a jagged tear in Tomas's chest and then he'd trapped both his opponent's hands in one of his own, bending back on the wrists until the black-clad man cried out and let the weapon drop.

The man's mask shifted, revealing the outline of a smile. "End of the line," he said. His accent was American. More than that, it was startlingly familiar.

Tomas used his free hand to snatch the black cloth from his opponent's head. The face underneath had aged twenty years since he'd last seen it. The sandy hair was flecked with grey and the long, thin face seamed with wrinkles that radiated from his eyes and mouth with geometric precision. He was still recognisable, though, as the man who'd been his partner for the last five years of his life.

"Richard," he said.

The other man wasn't smiling any more. He looked thoughtful and a little sad. Tomas suddenly felt absurd, with Richard's hands and body pinned beneath him. He rolled off and to his feet, stooping to pick up the knife on the way. There was no point searching for the book; it was clear Richard didn't have it. No concealment was possible beneath the tight black clothing.

Richard rose more awkwardly, with an audible popping of joints. "Tomas," he said, "I was hoping to avoid you."

"Jesus, Richard, what are you doing here? What *happened* to you?"

"I wised up."

"What did the Japanese offer you?"

"You think I'd do this for money? You know me better."

"What am I supposed to think? Two days ago your allies tried to kill me. Did they tell you that?"

Richard hesitated, and Tomas realised with a sick jolt that Richard *had* known. How was that possible? He'd been an usher at Richard's wedding. He'd thought they were friends.

"I'm sorry, Tomas, but I didn't have any choice – not while you're working for *him*."

"Giles? He's just a pen-pusher."

"I meant Nicholson."

"Nicholson's dead."

Richard laughed, and after a moment Tomas couldn't help smiling too. He could see the irony. "Actually dead," Tomas said. "Or have I been misinformed?"

"Probably, but not about that. I was there when they cut him down."

"From what?"

"The big oak crossbeam in his kitchen." There was a pause, then Richard added, more uncertainly, "He hung himself hours after they buried you. Did no one tell you?"

Tomas shook his head. He couldn't begin to imagine it. The Nicholson he knew liked life far too much to voluntarily end it. Nicholson had liked *himself* too much. "But what did Nicholson ever do to you?" he asked. "You were his blue-eyed boy!"

The other man shook his head. "I want to tell you. I want to believe you aren't hip deep in this yourself. But I can't take the risk."

"For God's sake, what's this about?"

Richard kept his mouth stubbornly shut.

"Then at least tell me which side you're on," Tomas said. "Don't you owe me that?"

Richard took a moment to consider the question. It was something Tomas had always liked about him, the way he never resorted to an easy answer. "It's pretty simple," he said finally. "I'm on the side of anyone who *won't* use the book."

He'd started moving before he stopped speaking. Tomas had expected him to move away, maybe try a dive through the half-open window. He hadn't expected Richard to run straight for him.

After a startled second Tomas made a grab for him. His fingers grasped nothing but air. Richard had fallen to the floor, a rolling dive that took him between Tomas's braced legs and through the door he'd been guarding.

Tomas flung himself after, but the door was already closing. His arm went through and stuck at the shoulder, wedged tight. On the other side he saw Richard draw back his fist and drive it into the electronic board. It hissed and sparked, and Tomas felt the two halves of the door closing on his bicep like metal jaws.

He wrenched his arm once, twice, and the third time he pulled it free. But the door snapped shut with Tomas on the wrong side of it, and Richard long gone.

Morgan knew there were men behind him as well as in front, the same black-clothed assassins he'd confronted in Budapest and only survived thanks to Tomas. It wasn't entirely clear whether he was fleeing or pursuing, but the adrenaline fuelling him didn't care.

He wove from side to side as he ran, bouncing from one wooden wall to the other. But it slowed him down, and when he didn't hear gunfire after a few seconds he stopped doing it – only for the sharp streak of a throwing knife to graze his cheek as it passed. They did want to kill him, they just wanted to do it quietly.

He could smell blood, an unpleasant counterpoint to his sour sweat. The wound in his side had opened again, oozing wetly. Occasionally people emerged from their cabins, sleepy-eyed in the dead of night. Morgan shouldered them aside, ignoring their grunts of protest.

There were three black-clothed figures in front of him, so identical they could have been clones, but he still knew which of them had the book. It was the way his head bobbed as he ran, the rock of his stride heel to instep, as individual as a fingerprint. Morgan kept his eyes fixed on the thief and tried not to think about anything else.

The assassins did their best to confuse him, swapping sides as they ran, slipping between each other with the grace of dancers.

Find the queen, Morgan thought as his quarry swapped places again, remembering street hustlers near Brixton Market. The trick was to follow the cards and not their hands. It was almost like a game. That figure slipping left then dodging right was the thief, and again when he ran forward only to fall back.

Another switch, one of them dropped back, and this time Morgan's reaching fingers grasped his black t-shirt. It was only the loosest hold but it was enough to make the man lose his rhythm and his footing. He stumbled forward, fell to his knees, half rolled – and then groaned and collapsed, limbs thumping down to the carpet.

His own shuriken was embedded in his forehead, slicing clean between his eyes. There was no way the fall should have done that, and Morgan thought of Giles' words – *you emit mortality* – as he stooped to frisk the motionless body. Nothing, and then Morgan was up and running again, just two men ahead of him now.

Then the rules changed. The thief veered to the left and Morgan kept going straight, sure he'd move to the right again, the card that had to be concealed. But while the other assassin ran on, through the antechamber between carriages, the thief didn't follow.

For a baffled second Morgan thought he'd vanished – a real piece of magic mixed with the trickery. Then he saw a slither of movement outside the train, black against black, and he realised that the window was gaping wide open. The thief had climbed through it.

Morgan knew it was too small a hole for him to fit through. He wrenched the whole door open instead, staggering back as the train swerved and nearly threw him into the night. Then he braced himself against the doorframe and leaned out as far as he dared. Metal rungs led from beside the door to the roof above, and he knew which way the thief must have gone.

His heart lurched as he grasped the handholds. He knew he was going to have to let his feet swing free and pull himself up the first few rungs using his arms. He could do it, just like a bloody assault course. Only those had never been on a moving train and when he was already injured.

No point worrying about it. Either he'd succeed or he'd fall.

He released his hold on the doorframe and there was a second of wobbling uncertainly, then he was hanging limply from the first metal bar above. The pain in his side squeezed a groan out of him, but his arms weren't injured and he forced them to flex and pull. Another groan of mingled pain and effort, and he grabbed the rung above, then the next, the fire in his side burning hotter with each movement. One more and then – finally – his feet found purchase.

He scrambled up the remaining rungs as fast as he could, and tried not to worry about how he was going to get back inside, or whether they were likely to pass under any low bridges before he did.

The wind on top of the train was overwhelming. Morgan fell to his hands and knees, terrified it would sweep him off and onto the ground he could see rushing by below. They were in a city now, its houses dark as residents slept but a scattering of office blocks still lit up in geometric patterns that flickered their reflection on the train.

It was in one of those brief squares of light that he saw the thief, sitting cross-legged on the roof only twenty feet ahead of him. He must have thought he'd be safe, intending to wait out the pursuit up here.

Morgan slid to his stomach, suppressing a hiss of pain as his injured side met the cold metal of the train's roof. This was familiar territory, suddenly – stalking prey that didn't yet know you were there. Morgan's breathing was ragged and loud, but the wind snatched it and carried it away from the thief's ears.

He crawled forward one foot, then another. Three feet, and there was still no sign he'd been spotted. His attention narrowed to nothing but the man ahead of him, sitting as still and calm as a statue of Buddha.

Morgan was only five feet away when the statue finally moved, leaping to its feet and spinning with startling agility. Morgan stood too, much less gracefully. His knees tensed with fear as the rocking of the train threatened to overthrow him.

The thief moved so fast, Morgan almost didn't see it. One second he was empty-handed, the next he had a shuriken in each fist. Morgan flung himself to the roof as the thief flung the stars. They passed harmlessly overhead, but by the time Morgan was on his feet again, the man had a thirty-foot lead on him. He leapt across the gap between carriages as if he barely noticed it was there.

Morgan sprinted in pursuit, every step jarring his side until the blood flowed in a steady stream. *Don't stop, don't stop, don't stop*, he told himself in time to the clattering of the train.

He was so focused on his own progress he didn't immediately register that the figure in front of him had stopped moving. Its outline thickened and shrank against the spatter of stars behind. The thief was kneeling down. Surely not resting?

The outline shrank still further, and Morgan saw that the thief was on his stomach, head hanging over the edge of the train. He must have been looking for something he didn't find, because a moment later he was on his feet and running again. But now Morgan was only ten feet behind.

He was almost within reach when the thief dropped again. It caught Morgan by surprise and he overshot, skidding to a halt and almost overbalancing, arms flailing wildly as he tried to check his momentum.

It was all the time the thief needed. Morgan didn't know what he'd been looking for but he must have found it, because this time he didn't stand back up. His hands gripped the edge of the train. Then, in a move of gymnastic virtuosity, he flipped himself into a backwards handstand, over and round and out of sight.

Morgan dropped to his stomach where the thief had been, bending his neck to look down. There was nothing but an open window below, and how in god's name had the thief got through that? How the hell was *Morgan* going to get through that? But he didn't have a choice. By the time he found any other way into the train, the thief would be long gone.

It was a desperate, inelegant scramble. He didn't attempt the thief's backflip, just hung down from fingers white with strain and swung his legs. They hit metal and then glass before finally moving through the void of the open window.

His fingernails felt like they were breaking off, and the top of the glass pressed the inside of his calves. This couldn't work. If he let go now he wouldn't go through the window, he'd tumble backwards off the train, probably snapping both his legs in the process. And he was about to let go. He couldn't help himself. There was only a thin strip of metal to anchor him to the train's roof, and it was already slick with sweat.

Not giving himself time to think about it, he swung his legs once, twice, fingers loosening their hold a little more each time – and on the third swing they finally let go. He felt himself falling, gravity wanting to pull him away from the train and down to his death. He fought it, pushed his body against the cold metal as he slid down, fingers finding what purchase they could. And somehow, incredibly, he was sliding through the window and down, scraping agonisingly at his wounded side as he went.

He fell to his knees inside the carriage, gasping with mingled exertion and pain.

It was bright, far brighter than he'd expected, and that probably saved his life. He saw the flicker of motion in the corner of his eye, rolled to the side without thinking, and the shuriken embedded itself in the wall where his head had been.

He finished the tumble and let it propel him to his feet. He couldn't afford to look around, but he knew where he was – the dining car. The room's bright halogen lights had been switched on, reflecting starkly from the floor-to-ceiling mirrors and the regimented silver rows of cutlery.

The thief stood immobile beside a table already set for breakfast. His hand was buried somewhere inside his black robes. Morgan braced himself, ready for another shuriken, but when the hand emerged it was empty. Morgan read something in the stiff lines of the thief's body that might have been consternation.

His weapons must have fallen out in his escape from the roof.

Morgan smiled. Unarmed, he had the advantage here – bigger and stronger than his opponent.

"It's all right," a voice said behind him. "Throw it to me and get out."

Morgan spun round, caught a brief glimpse of a tall, sandy-haired man, then realised that he was letting the book out of his sight. He spun back to see it already arcing over his head as the thief sprinted out of the door. Morgan let him go, an irrelevance now that he no longer had the book, and turned back to face the newcomer.

The man's long, thin face darkened when he saw Morgan's. There was something in his expression that suggested recognition, though Morgan was certain they'd never met before. The man's left hand held the book. His right was empty. Improbably, he seemed to be unarmed.

"Give it to me," Morgan said, "and we can both walk out of here."

"Why do you want it?" His American accent was soft and confident, a man who didn't have to raise his voice to be heard.

Morgan took a sidling step nearer. "Why do *you* want it?"

"The people I'm working with," the man said. "think it's too dangerous to fall into enemy hands."

"But it's all right for you to have it? I don't think so."

"The Japanese aren't keen to use weapons of mass destruction. They're too familiar with the consequences."

He was talking about the atomic bomb, Morgan realised. Tomas had said the Ragnarok artefacts were the bomb's mystical equivalent.

"Last time I checked, we weren't at war with the Japanese." Morgan took another step nearer, and the man took one back in response, only to find himself pressed against the wall of the carriage.

"This book's a threat to everyone in the world. I can't let you have it."

"You're gonna have to," Morgan said – and even as he was speaking he pounced, gripping the man's wrist and squeezing the bones until he cried out in pain and the book dropped to the ground. Morgan kicked it behind him, backing up until he could safely stoop to pick it up.

It was a welcome weight in his hand, the mottled leather of its cover a pleasing texture underneath his fingers. "Sorry," he said. "I need that."

"Is that what they've told you, Morgan?"

He startled at the use of his name.

The man saw it and smiled, almost sadly. "I know who you are, probably better than you do. I know everything about you. Your birth, your family. You think you want this book? You don't. It holds nothing but death – and your ghosts are nearer than its pages."

Morgan took an involuntary step back, and felt his gaze grabbed by a flicker of motion in front of him. It was a reflection in the glass wall of the dining car that was neither himself nor the other man. Morgan cursed, stepped aside and spun, triangulating – the threat from the first man to his left, and the threat he'd glimpsed in the mirror to the right.

But there was nothing there, only another reflection in the glass. He moved just his eyes this time, searching for the source of *that* reflection. There was no one. There was nothing in the room but mirrors – and now every one of them was showing the same thing: the reflection of a person who wasn't there.

She was such a little girl, she couldn't have been older than five, her face still soft and unformed, unshaped by the personality which lived inside it.

Morgan tried hard not to recognise her. But although it had been a dozen years since he'd last seen her, hers was the one face he'd never forget.

"Mary?" he said.

Reflected in every mirror in the room, his long-dead sister's face looked back at him.

CHAPTER TEN

The blade of the knife passed over Belle's head, slicing clean through Anya's blue night-shirt and some of the skin beneath. A dark stain spread on the satin and Anya let out a gasp of pain. Only the train's automatic doors saved them, shutting tight on the assassin's weapon as he darted forward for the killing strike.

Belle knew that if she stayed with the German woman they'd both die. Belle's legs were too short. She just couldn't run that fast, and her arm felt like it was on the point of being dislocated, the shoulder wrenched out of its socket by Anya's desperate grasp. They couldn't carry on like this. If they separated, Anya at least would be able to get away while the assassin took care of Belle.

If they separated, the assassin would almost certainly follow Anya, and Belle at least would be safe.

The two thoughts merged in Belle's head into a chord whose separate notes were indistinguishable. One of them came from her, and one of them from *him*, but after all these years she could no longer tell which. It hardly mattered, anyway. They were both telling her to do the same thing.

Her CIA handlers had given her martial arts training – some aikido, a little krav maga – just enough to survive until she could bring her *real* weapon to bear. She used the aikido, twisting her hand to drive the hardest part of her wrist against the point where Anya's fingertips met her thumb. The older woman tried to hold on, but Belle kept pulling and in a second she was free.

She saw a quick flash of shocked betrayal on Anya's face, then she was through the door and she couldn't see the other woman any more.

"What the hell did you do?" Morgan said, backing away. The movement should have been reflected all around them, but in the mirror the little girl just smiled and waved.

"I opened the door," the other man said. "It's a talent I have, thanks to Nicholson."

The girl in the mirror was saying something too. Her mouth moved soundlessly, her whole image wavering slightly like a mirage, or something seen under shallow water. Her dark skin looked washed-out and pale, and the tight ringlets of her hair drooped over her forehead and into her eyes.

Morgan felt a hard, indigestible lump in his stomach. Guilt he'd never been able to swallow. "It wasn't my fault," he said. "I tried to save you."

But he had never accepted the excuse, and Mary didn't seem to either. She frowned. It astonished him how well he had remembered that expression, through all the years since he'd last seen it. It was the way she'd looked when he stole her sweets, then told on her for hitting him. It was the baffled look of a four-year-old girl, who couldn't understand how the older brother she adored had betrayed her so badly.

"Make her go away," he gasped. "Please."

The other man was looking at the mirrors too. "It isn't so easy to banish the spirits that haunt us. Nicholson taught me how to call them up, but not how to send them back. Like all his lessons, it would have been better unlearnt."

For just a second, the image in the mirror seemed to waver. Instead of Mary, Morgan saw a teenage boy, white, pimply and awkward in his own skin. His short hair was gelled into spikes, and his eyes blinked behind thick, wire-rimmed glasses.

Morgan snatched a glance at the other man, to see that his eyes were misted with unshed tears.

"I wanted to see him just one more time," he said thickly. "And now when I look in the mirror I never see anything else."

Then the image was gone, and Morgan could only see Mary. Her mood had darkened still further. She looked angry - furious. It was an expression Morgan couldn't ever remember seeing when she was alive. It spoke of emotions no four-year-old girl should understand.

"She wants the book," the other man said. "Give it to me and I can send her away."

Morgan's hand clutched the thick leather, fingernails denting the spine. He wanted to give it to her. He wanted to do whatever it took to send Mary back to the locked cellar of his past.

But the book was his past, too. It was the part of it that might make everything else make sense. If he gave it up, he'd never know who he was.

"No," he said. Then, more firmly, "This isn't real. You can't scare me with illusions."

The other man shook his head. "The past may be a shadow, but it's real enough to hurt us." He didn't take his eyes from the mirror as he spoke, and Morgan found his drawn back inexorably to the same place, like a scab he couldn't stop picking.

Mary's face was so twisted with hate that he wouldn't have recognised her if he hadn't already known who she was. Her mouth was still moving but now Morgan didn't want to know what she was saying. He backed away, hands raised to ward her off, until he was pressed against the far wall of the carriage.

Something brushed the small of his back where the material of his t-shirt had rucked up out of his trousers. He flinched instinctively at the cold clammy feel of it, but it was only when it touched him again that he turned to see what it was.

She was in that mirror too. Her face looked quite mad. There was a froth of saliva at the corners of her mouth, open wide in a silent scream of rage.

It was her hand which had touched him, reaching out *through* the glass. He stared at her small brown fingers in frozen incomprehension. They fumbled towards him, blind worms seeking the sun. Then she took a step forward.

The tip of her nose broke through first. The mirror rippled around it like pond water. Her eyebrows were next, and when her eyes followed Morgan knew that she could see him. Her fingers clawed and struck out, leaving five thin trails of blood on his abdomen.

Morgan snapped into movement, his fist lashing out to smash the mirror into shards. Mary let out a thin, horrible scream which ended in a sudden silence.

She wasn't gone. He could see her already in the next mirror along. She was moving faster now, both arms already free of it. He smashed that too and ran to the next one before she could reach it. His knuckles were cut to ribbons but he didn't care. He was more terrified than he'd ever been looking down the business end of a gun.

The floor was littered with shards of glass. He smashed another mirror, then another, and then he made the mistake of looking down at them. She was in every single shard. Her eyes blazed up at him, toxic with hatred.

He stamped on the glittering fragments, trying to grind the glass into powder. Mary snarled and moved again – into the mirrors on the other side of the train. Morgan knew there was no way he could reach them in time to stop her. It was already too late. Her arms were in the carriage, groping towards him.

It was too much. He didn't even think about it. A jerk of his elbow against glass, and this time he'd broken a window instead of a mirror.

"Don't!" the other man shouted.

It was only when he felt his shoulder catch and tear against a jagged fragment of glass that Morgan realised what he was intending to do. It didn't matter. He could sense his sister behind him, almost hear her soft tread across the narrow strip of carpet between them. He couldn't face her. He just couldn't.

Morgan clutched his father's book to his chest and jumped.

The assassin only hesitated for a moment before pivoting on his heel and flinging himself after Belle.

There were a few people moving around the train now, passengers stumbling sleepy and bleary-eyed from their cabins. The first she ran past, an old man with grey hair sticking up at a strange angle, took one look at the knife-wielding maniac chasing after her and hurriedly ran back into his room. The next passenger, a kind-faced young woman, did exactly the same.

Next time she saw someone, Belle tried screaming, but that just made them disappear faster. The part of her that wanted to believe better things about human nature hoped they'd gone to get their phones and call for help. She wasn't going to count on it, though.

She wasn't going to get away. That left only one option.

Five paces ahead of her there was another door, opening too slowly to let her through at a run. She kept moving forward anyway, running *up* the door and round in a backflip she'd learnt in junior high, more years ago than she could really remember.

When she twisted back to face the assassin she was still in the air. His knife slashed but her hand moved quicker, grabbing the cloth across his eyes and pulling it free.

His face was younger than she'd been imagining. Round and unlined and with the sort of innocence that often marked a total lack of conscience. There were no worry lines because nothing he could possibly do would worry him.

And then Belle was falling *through* his eyes, diving into what lay inside.

The most recent memories were always nearest the surface. She saw herself as he saw her, a blonde little girl in a red nightdress. Overlaid on the visual there was a layer of something dirtier. His thoughts. This little girl was a danger, a target. This little girl had to die. He'd never killed a child before. He looked forward to trying it.

Somewhere that wasn't where her attention was, Belle felt herself dropping back to the floor. Her knees jarred but her eyes stayed fixed on his.

And now she'd dived deeper, past that first layer to the things he wasn't thinking about right now. She saw the sushi he'd eaten last night. Felt the cold slide of it down his throat, and the shudder of disgust because these damn *gaijin* never knew how to make it fresh.

She saw the face of the Westerner who'd led them, sneaked them onto the roof of the train as it left Budapest, to wait for the cover of deep night. She felt the hot wind as he pressed himself flat to the roof of the accelerating train, forty, fifty, seventy miles an hour, and the burn of exhilaration, because he didn't see why this was necessary, but it was *fun*.

And with the part of her that wasn't buried inside him, Belle saw that his knife was moving again. He was beginning to recover from the shock of her attack. So she moved deeper still, grabbing the coattails of the thing that lived inside her as it hunted out the things it liked best – the twisted, base material that most people's minds hid at their core.

He was shorter now, probably only a child. But he hated like an adult and he didn't have an adult's control over it. She looked out through his wide eyes at the body of his father. He hadn't realised that a body held that much blood. Ten pints. It doesn't sound so much until you see it spilled out on the floor.

The gun felt like an intolerable weight in his hand. But it felt like something he might get used to, if he was given the chance.

Belle felt the thing that lived inside her purring, like a cat in cream, luxuriating in these memories. Belle knew that she was speaking them aloud too, but she couldn't hear her own voice. The things she was finding inside this young man were so much more compelling. There he was now, dragging his father's body to the centre of the room, dousing it in gasoline. Just a little on himself too, because he was only twelve but he knew he had to make this look convincing.

The assassin's knife dropped to the floor of the carriage with a soft thump. Belle's fingers remembered how it had fitted in his, but to her it just felt awkward, almost too heavy to wield. She had to swing her hips to get any kind of force behind the blow.

The memories she was swimming in took a second to evaporate. She scrambled out of them, backwards into her own mind, dragging the beast with her, because she'd never found out what happened if she stayed with someone when they died.

When her eyes were focused on the outside world again she saw the assassin at her feet, curled around the knife that hadn't quite hit his heart. He'd been right, she thought. There really was a lot of blood in one human body.

She didn't stay to watch it pool. People were finally emerging from their cabins now the danger was past. She didn't think anyone would blame a little girl for killing the man who'd been chasing her, but she didn't want to have the conversation. Like Anya had said, they couldn't afford the delay. There was no way she could get the body out of the door on her own, and anyway they'd been seen. She settled for wiping the handle of the knife clean, then trotting off in the opposite direction before anyone associated her with the rapidly cooling corpse.

Morgan hit something that wasn't hard enough to be the ground. He felt a moment of relief, and then he was sinking and he realised that falling into water wasn't necessarily going to save his life.

He'd never liked swimming, not since Mary died. Now he was deep underwater and it should have been obvious which way was up. It was the way he'd just come – how could he forget that?

But he had. He flailed desperately, bubbles of air he couldn't spare popping from his mouth. He thought if he watched them rise he'd know which direction he needed to swim, but he couldn't seem to concentrate. His mind was already greying towards black as the oxygen left it. *Stay calm*, he told himself. *Calm, you useless fucker! What's the matter with you?*

On the edge of consciousness, he felt a brush of something against his leg. He looked down, through the murky, unclean water, the first hint of dawn shading it deep blue. Below him, a hand was clasped around his leg. He shut his eyes, because he didn't want to see any more.

In his head he was seven years old. He'd dived after her, he honestly had, into that weed-choked lake he'd chased her into. Only then she had grasped hold of his leg, and suddenly he felt as though he was drowning too. So instead of reaching down and pulling her to safety, he kicked out frantically. Kicked her away.

He did it again now, but this time the grip on his leg didn't slacken. He felt her fingers clawing into his shin, the nails breaking the skin. She was doing exactly what he'd been afraid of all those years ago. She was pulling him under.

There was a part of him that wanted to let her. It felt like justice, or at least retribution. But then he felt the hard outline of the book in his hand, and he remembered he had a reason to live.

As he opened his eyes he realised the malicious spirit of his sister was doing him one favour. If she was pulling him down, then he finally knew which way was up. He bowed his legs in the beginning of breast stroke and tried to force himself away, against the press of the water and the pull of her fingers.

His lungs were burning. They were running on empty and the urge to breathe in was almost irresistibly strong. Anything, even water, would feel better than that terrible hollow emptiness in his chest.

He fought, against the urge and against the grip – hopelessly. He wasn't sinking any more but he wasn't rising either. And who knew how deep he'd gone, in that first violent plunge from the train?

He opened his mouth to take a fatal gulp of water when he felt a sudden flaring pain in his shoulder to match the ache in his lungs. He fought it violently, but something was trying to surface through the confusion of his thoughts. This new grasp was drawing him in the opposite direction. It was pulling him up.

With an effort of will, Morgan relaxed into it, letting his arms go limp as he kicked out with his legs. This time, they didn't flail uselessly. There was some traction there and the wonderful feeling of water moving past him.

Another tug, another push, and the hand on his calf slipped down to his ankle. One more tug and it released him entirely. He suddenly felt as light as the air he so desperately needed. It was easy now. Another churn with his legs, the hand on his wrist still pulling him steadily upward, and then his head burst through the surface of the water.

His legs trod water beneath him as he sucked air into starved lungs. He'd never realised it had a taste before, or how amazingly good that taste could be. When he opened his eyes all he could see for a moment was the gold of the rising sun refracted through the droplets of water on his eyelashes. He blinked them away and focused on his rescuer.

"Anya," he said. His voice was halfway between a gasp and a croak. "What happened?"

Her red hair looked much darker when it was wet, something like the colour of dried blood. "For some reason, you jumped out of the train. I jumped after you."

She began swimming towards the shore. Now he had his breathing under control, Morgan took a second to look around before he followed her. As he'd suspected, they'd fallen into a river – a broad grey one that seemed to run through a city, to judge by the apartment buildings all around. To his left, the high span of the railway bridge cast its shadow on the water.

The bank was flanked with concrete. Anya pulled herself out without difficulty, but it took Morgan's weakened arms two tries. As soon as he was clear of the water he rolled onto his back and just stared at the sky for a while. The sun wasn't high enough to be hot yet and the water had been cold. He was shivering, but he didn't care. He was alive.

"Would you like to tell me *why* you jumped out of the train?" Anya asked when he had been quiet so long that the sun was finally beginning to warm him.

He rolled onto his side to face her. "Not really." He reached into his waistband and pulled out his father's book. He should have been more surprised to see that it was bone dry. "I got it back."

"Who said you were completely useless?" She smiled for the first time that Morgan could remember. It made her seem like a different person. A nicer one.

"Thanks for saving my life," he said belatedly.

She shrugged, and sat up. After a second, he did the same. "Where are we?" he asked.

"Bratislava," she said. And at his blank expression, "The capital of Slovakia."

"So, not Germany then."

Anya laughed. "Not quite."

"And I think it's fair to say we missed the train."

Anya nodded. "No chance of re-boarding now. And even if we could, those people would still be there. It's safer to make our own way to Berlin. We'll have to catch up with the others there."

If they survived the attack, Morgan thought. But he didn't say it. He was sure Anya was thinking it too.

The train was crawling with people as Tomas walked wearily back towards his cabin, but none of them were the ones he was looking for. He felt a rising panic that he struggled to keep from his face. He was lucky, he supposed, that dead men didn't sweat. Guards were milling around, barking orders into walkie-talkies, and he was sure police would be getting on at the next stop. Someone would want to know what the hell had happened and where all those dead bodies had suddenly appeared from. Tomas had to make sure he looked as unsuspicious as possible.

But he couldn't stop himself studying the faces of everyone he passed. Damn it! Nothing about this mission had gone right from the start. It felt like it was jinxed. In the back of his head he could hear Richard, telling him that he'd been misinformed – maybe about everything.

He felt a surge of relief when he finally found Belle, waiting outside the door of his cabin. It took him a moment to realise that the dark stain on her red dress was blood. He didn't wait to find out if it was hers before he pulled her into the cabin and slammed the door behind them. Too incriminating either way.

"Where's Anya?" he asked her.

She looked down. In the dim light of the cabin her hair looked darker and the shadows under her eyes deeper. "I don't know. We got separated."

Tomas swore. "And I don't suppose you've seen Morgan or the book?"

She shook her head.

He wondered how he could possibly report back to England now. Partner and target lost. They'd be sorry they ever dug him out of the ground. He was sorry, too – sorry for the young man who'd got dragged into all this against his will and now might very well have died for a cause he didn't believe in.

"We should search the rest of the train," Belle said.

Tomas hesitated. He wasn't sure they should be wandering around at the moment. Innocent people would be hiding in their cabins until the trouble was over. On the other hand, Morgan and Anya could be injured somewhere, needing their help.

"You're right," he said eventually, and pulled the door open.

Anya was standing just outside, hand raised ready to knock. She only looked surprised for a moment, then lowered her hand and said briskly, "Good. You both made it."

"And Morgan?" Tomas asked.

Anya shook her head. Tomas felt something clench inside him, until she quickly said, "Still alive, but not on the train."

Belle perched on the end of the bed, her feet swinging above the floor. "What happened?"

"He jumped. Or he was pushed – I don't know. I saw it from the window. But we were over the Danube at the time, he will have landed in the water."

"Can he swim?" Belle asked.

"If the fall didn't knock him unconscious," Tomas said grimly.

"What's the next stop? We can get off there and go back for him."

"Forget it," Anya said. "You won't get there in time to pull him out of the river. Either he made it or he didn't. If he did, the BND has agents in Slovakia we can send for him – he can rejoin us in Berlin. With the book taken, we have to concentrate on tracking down Raphael's contacts there, before we lose him as well."

Tomas didn't like it, but he couldn't argue with the logic. After a moment he nodded. "OK then. I guess Morgan will just have to look after himself."

CHAPTER ELEVEN

Bratislava was like Budapest dialled down a notch. Anya told Morgan it was westernising fast, and he could see the signs of it in the smart restaurants and cheap bars, but it still felt like a place that had only recently remembered how to have a good time. He shouldered his way through a crowd of young men with Bradford accents and ignored them when they swore at him.

Anya followed behind, to a chorus of wolf whistles. Morgan could imagine her scowling. An increase in the noise from the lads suggested she might also have given them the finger.

She'd told him she wanted to get straight out of the city, hire a car and head to Berlin overland. The train wasn't coming through for another few hours and anyway, it was compromised. But she reckoned the journey would be almost as quick by road, and Morgan wasn't going to argue with her. He just didn't want to go *yet*.

Anya said something quietly behind him. When he turned he saw that she was talking into a mobile rather than to him. That, along with her credit card, had made it out of the river intact. Morgan pulled uncomfortably at the dry clothes she'd bought them both and wished she'd let him spend a bit more time shopping. The jeans were just about okay, but the baggy yellow t-shirt made him look like a middle-aged tourist. Her own shorts and muscle t-shirt ensemble was considerably more flattering.

Morgan had to make an effort not to look at the way the material stretched over her breasts.

She spoke a couple more times, too quiet for him to hear over the chatter of the morning crowd, then snapped the phone shut and handed it to him.

Morgan raised an eyebrow.

"I've spoken to my people," she said. "Now you need to call Tomas and let him know you're okay – and that you've got the book."

Morgan nodded, entering the number he knew by heart, but she put her hand over his before he could dial. "Keep it short, and don't use any names. Someone could be listening."

When Tomas answered, Morgan could hear the sound of the train in the background, clacking over the tracks. "Who is this?" he said.

Morgan smiled, surprised at how glad he was to hear the other man had survived. "Its Mor –" He caught Anya's glare. "It's me. I'm fine. The... the thing's fine too."

There was a sound that might have been a sigh of relief. "Where are you?" Morgan looked at Anya, who shook her head. "I'm safe, and I'm on my way back. Expect me in two days." He closed the phone and handed it back to Anya before Tomas could ask anything else.

She stopped, forcing him to do the same. The crowd buffeted them as it passed.

"Two days?"

"There's some research I want to do while we're here."

"Anything you want to find out, we can do it in Berlin," Anya said. "I'll feel safer when that damn book is off our hands."

Exactly. The book. There was no way Morgan was going to let anyone take it away before he'd had a better look at it. He could feel it now, a reassuring hard lump stuffed into the front of his jeans, hidden by the baggy t-shirt. "*I'll* feel safer when I know what the book *is*," Morgan insisted.

He started walking again before she could reply. She caught up with him in an annoyed little half-jog, then grabbed his elbow to force him to face her. "We can't *read* the book. That's another reason we need to get it back to base."

"Yeah?" Morgan said, snatching his arm back. "Haven't you ever heard of the internet?"

He'd found what he was looking for. The café was run-down and overcrowded, but he could see the row of computers at the back, and at least one of them was free. A bell above the door jangled tunelessly as he opened it. "Mine's a tea, milk and three sugars," he told Anya, and went to sit in front of the free terminal.

He glanced back briefly to see her rolling her eyes at him. After a second, she shook her head and went to the small counter to order.

It took him a few goes to figure out the keyboard. Stupid of him to assume it would use the English alphabet. Still, it was close enough, and it didn't take him too long to navigate to Google. He glanced around surreptitiously, then pulled out the book and put it beside the keyboard, open at a random page. A runic Hungarian alphabet, Raphael had said.

By the time Anya came over with his tea, he'd found what he was looking for.

"It's the same alphabet," Anya said, looking between the book and the screen.

Morgan nodded. "Do I or do I not rule?"

Anya huffed what might have been a laugh and pulled across another chair to squeeze in beside him. "Where did you find it?"

"Wikipedia," Morgan admitted.

Anya definitely was laughing this time. "Bet Nicholson didn't imagine *that* would be possible when he wrote the thing."

"Raphael told me the language was almost forgotten," Morgan said. "But as it turns out, he was a lying bastard."

"You'll still need a dictionary to translate it."

"Well yeah, if it's actually Hungarian like Raphael said. But don't you think it's more likely he was just using it as some sort of code – you know, what's it called? A cypher."

For the first time since he'd met her, Anya looked impressed. "You really aren't as stupid as you look."

Morgan grinned. "I know it's not meant that way, but I'm gonna take that as a compliment."

Tomas could feel Anya twitching restlessly in the car seat beside him. He knew she wanted to debrief him, especially now Belle was temporarily out of the way, reporting to her CIA handlers at an undisclosed location. Anya wanted to know more about Morgan, but there was nothing Tomas could tell. The phone the young man used to call hadn't transmitted its number, and there was no way for Tomas to call him back. Morgan could be anywhere, in any sort of trouble, and there was nothing Tomas could do about it.

He pushed the futile worry from his mind, concentrating instead on the view outside the window. Berlin had been Tomas's second home, but it was a city he'd always found easier to admire than to love. Now it sparkled with all the new buildings, the spruced-up parks and smart commuters. It was like coming back from holiday to find that your wife had lost twenty pounds and had a face lift.

The Wall fell. He'd known that intellectually, of course, but seeing the reality of it was still astonishing. It made him realise he'd dedicated his life to a battle he'd never really expected to win.

BND headquarters were in Pullach, but it was their Berlin outpost which had been tracking Karamov, and that was where Anya told him they were heading. The building was on the west side of the city, but their driver had veered across the old border to avoid heavy traffic.

There wasn't even a trace of cement where the Wall had once run, cutting so brutally across streets and sometimes even buildings. Tomas had expected at least the foundations to be left. Some kind of memorial.

Anya saw him looking. "There's some of it still standing at

Checkpoint Charlie," she told him. "It's a museum now."

"A museum," he repeated in wonder.

"You were around then, weren't you?" Anya asked him. "Back when the Cold War was still on."

Tomas nodded. "I spent a lot of time in this place."

"I should thank you then. I grew up in East Germany. It was your generation that bought mine its freedom."

"I suppose so." It had never felt as though they were fighting for actual people, individuals. The war had been both more abstract and more concrete than that. It was about an ideology that had to be defeated, and about getting through the next two hours with the Stasi on your tail and no safe house within fifty miles.

Five minutes later they'd arrived at a narrow office block faced with tinted glass that gave nothing away. Inside it was almost as characterless, several big open-plan rooms divided into worker-ant cubicles by beige screens. Anya led Tomas past them all and down to a basement room with only the corner of an upper window to give it any natural light. She flicked on a neon and took a seat at the small conference table.

Tomas shrugged, and sat opposite her. "Someone else joining us?"

"The agents who've been tracking Karamov for the last month. They tell me they've got some interesting news."

"We've been fucking idiots, that's what the news is!" The speaker was a big barrel of a man, shouldering the door open to let two others through behind him. He had wiry blond hair and the palest skin Tomas had ever seen, almost albino.

"Gunter," Anya said, and hurried round the table to hug him. Tomas blinked in surprise. Anya had never struck him as a person who liked anyone enough to progress beyond a limp handshake.

"Anya, my sweet," Gunter said in German. Then, switching back to English, "And Tomas, of course." He offered his hand. "Well, we've buggered this one up spectacularly, and I don't mind admitting it."

Tomas saw the other two men hiding their smiles as they sat down. He shook his head. "I'd say there's blame enough to go round. We were the ones who lost the book."

"True, though I hear your partner now has it. Barring any further unforeseen cock-ups, it should be in our hands very soon."

Tomas shifted uncomfortably under Gunter's scrutiny, sure the other man could sense his doubts. But Morgan would bring the book back. He must. "So what is this information you have for us?" Tomas asked when the silence had stretched.

Gunter placed a small computer on the table in front of him, the thin silver looking too delicate in his meaty fingers as he flipped the lid open. "That's just what I'm saying. A balls-up of monumental proportions."

The screen came to life as soon as it was open, and Tomas saw that Gunter had brought up a picture of a white-haired old man, thin to the point of angularity. The photo was black and white and taken from a high, oblique angle. Clearly surveillance footage. "That's Raphael," Tomas confirmed. "You've been tracking him?"

Gunter shook his head. "No, but we have been tracking a German businessman by the name of Gabriel. Tracking him for quite a while, as it happens, so you'd think someone in this building might have pulled their brain out of their arse long enough to notice that it was the *same fucking man.*"

Anya leaned over to scroll through a few more photos. "You're saying Gabriel is Raphael? He's been working right here in Germany under a whole other alias?"

"Give the woman a prize. If Raphael hadn't been such a minor figure in the Karamov investigation, we might have made the connection sooner. Especially with the whole archangel thing – no one could accuse the man of being subtle."

"If you were tracking Gabriel independently of Karamov," Tomas asked, "what had he done to put him on your radar?"

"Nothing major," one of the other men said. His voice was whisper quiet, as if he felt the need to compensate for Gunter's hearty bark. "The corporation he runs is in the internet marketing business and squeaky clean. But some of his employees ran up flags, enough of them that we started to take notice."

"Ex-Stasi," Gunter confirmed. "Low-level, mostly, but then we didn't have names for all their higher-level operatives. They destroyed their files when the Wall fell, you know."

Tomas nodded. It didn't surprise him. The old East German secret service would have been afraid of war crimes prosecutions, and rightly so. "Any thoughts on why Raphael might be recruiting from that particular pool?"

"Our best guess?" Gunter said. "It's those damn Ragnarok artefacts again."

Tomas nodded. All the dots were slowly joining up, though the picture still wasn't clear. "Raphael thinks these agents might know something about their whereabouts?"

"We always suspected the Stasi knew more than we did, but we could never get any of the cold-hearted cocksuckers to talk. Maybe Raphael came to the same conclusion – and had a better incentive to offer than immunity from prosecution."

Anya tapped her fingers against the table, long nails clicking on the wood. "And do we have any idea what Raphael wants with the artefacts? Who is he working for?"

Tomas frowned. "It could be any country – or maybe just himself. Nicholson's book might tell us. That might be why Raphael went to so much trouble to acquire it. Nicholson knew all there was to know about the artefacts, including who else was searching for them."

"But did he know how to use them?" Gunter asked. "If indeed they really had a use."

Tomas realised he was tapping his own fingers as he thought. He clenched his hand into a tight fist to still them. "OK. Sometimes the direct approach is the best. I say we bring in the agents Raphael hired and question them."

"Mm," Gunter said. "We thought so too. Unfortunately, it turns out that every single one of them has disappeared off the face of the earth."

"Disappeared?" Tomas said. "You've got to be joking!"

Gunter raised his hands in a mime of apology. "I did tell you this whole op was an epic cluster fuck. We think Raphael must have taken them somewhere discreet to mine them for information."

"Or he's already got the information," Anya said gloomily, "and now he's disposed of the only other people who knew it."

Gunter nodded. "Yes, that is another possibility. The worst case scenario, in fact, because it means we've reached a dead end."

"You've got a list somewhere, haven't you?" Tomas asked. "Of Gabriel's employees, I mean. Let me look at it."

Gunter's big fingers clattered nimbly over the computer keyboard, and a moment later a list was on the screen. Tomas took a second to marvel at this new technology, so far in advance of anything he could have imagined. Then he shook his head and scanned the names. It had only been a small company and it didn't take him long to go through them. "He isn't there," he said with satisfaction.

Anya's head cocked at a questioning angle.

"Heinrich Stumpf," Tomas told her. "He used to be high up in the Stasi. Any information about the artefacts is likely to have gone through him – but it looks like he slipped through Raphael's net."

Gunter studied Tomas. His eyes were such a pale blue they were almost silver. "You believe this man knows the location of the artefacts?"

Tomas shrugged. "He's the only lead we've got. And he's weak. We... we managed to blackmail him once, get him to spill some fairly important secrets."

One of the other men started tapping at his own keyboard. "Looks like Mr Stumpf is still around. He lives on Genter Strasse."

Gunter rubbed his big hands together and smiled hugely. "Wonderful. At last, some news that doesn't make me want to blow my own brains out. Well, Tomas, I don't know about you, but I think you should pay your old friend a visit."

Anya was sulking on the other bed. Morgan ignored her. He'd insisted they book a hotel to give him some time to translate the book, and short of trying to grab it from him and run, there hadn't been much Anya could do about it.

"Don't mind me," she said. "I'll just lie here and entertain myself, shall I?"

Morgan sighed. The book was balanced on his lap, a print-out of the runic alphabet on the plain orange bedspread beside him. "Give me a chance, I've only just started."

It was painstaking work. The runes were very similar, and he kept having to look between the chart and the book to make sure he'd identified the right one. And Nicholson had left no gaps between letters, nothing to indicate where one word ended and another began. But after a few minutes Morgan looked up, eyes blazing with excitement.

Anya caught his expression. "You were right, then – it is in English?"

"Yeah." His voice was husky and he had to cough to clear it. "I think it might be a diary. The first thing it says is *Seventh of August, 1978.*"

She sat up, eyes widening. "That's right back near the start of the Hermetic Division. My god, if that book's a record of his time there, what he discovered... No wonder Raphael wanted it. What does it say?"

"If you shut up a minute, I can tell you."

She glowered but subsided, letting Morgan work on his translation in peace. After a few laborious minutes he found himself speeding up. He was learning to recognise the runic alphabet, but it was more than that. The words in the book began to take on the odd quality of something he already knew, but had temporarily forgotten.

The sun had moved behind a building by the time he'd finished the first entry, leaving the room in gloomy twilight.

"So what does he say?" Anya prompted, when Morgan finally looked up from the paper. "Is there anything there about the Ragnarok artefacts?"

Morgan almost wanted to tell her it was none of her business. His father's diary felt like something extremely private. Of course, he didn't have a choice.

"This is an absurd thing to do," Morgan read, glancing between the sheet of paper and Anya. "If the department had any idea I was keeping a diary, they'd skin me alive. 'Not good for security, old chap'."

"He's right," Anya said. "Especially when the code's so easy to break."

Morgan nodded and kept on reading. "It was the Polish priest who suggested it, when we met in Prague in '74. I don't know what made him say it, that our kind of work should be recorded for posterity. He was probably joking. Anyway, I hadn't thought about it – or about him, really – for a long time. But something today reminded me.

"Tomas and I have been spinning our wheels for far too long. The head honchos are starting to get impatient. The trouble is, my little parlour trick with the mirror and the wandering spirit whetted their appetite, and now they're hungry for tangible results. We've tried, we really have, but so far we've chased nothing but shadows and rumours.

"And that's all it was today, another rumour. We'd uncovered that copy of the *Prose Edda* weeks ago, but we hadn't bothered to read it. After all the fuss of getting it – those damn Norwegians seem to have wised up to what we're doing, and they were after it themselves. Anyway, after all that fuss, it didn't seem to contain anything new. But yesterday it came back from our translators.

"They were almost as excited by it as I was. Ten new lines that aren't in any previous edition. They want to publish it, of course, which can't possibly be allowed. I suspect we're going to have to find some way of silencing them. The lines are in the Gylfaginning, and they're allusive and vague. Well, of course they are. The Norse myths have always been a terrible jumble, mixing up older traditions with Christian eschatology till you hardly know what's original and what's a far later addition. But these lines feel authentic to me, though I can't really explain why. There's no description in them, just a casual mention of something they call the 'Ragnarok artefacts'. That's what made me think of the priest, I suppose. I'm sure he was the first person who ever told me those stories, late at night when we were hiding in some basement hoping the KGB wouldn't track us down. Anyway, it's not clear, but it seems these artefacts will have some role to play in bringing about the final end of things.

"Could it be true? Could these artefacts really exist? It's absurd to believe it, just a myth after all. And yet. And yet. If it is true, if there's even the slightest chance, one thing is very clear. We *have* to find these things."

"That's... that's fascinating," Anya said. Her face was almost glowing with excitement. "Any more translated beyond that?"

"Only the first line," Morgan admitted. "And the date's a week later. There's no more for that entry."

Anya got up to pace, her feet turning the nap of the carpet first one way, then the other. "This is great. But we need more – we need to find out exactly what *he* found out about the artefacts."

"Yes," Morgan said, but that wasn't really what interested him. "Who do you think the Polish priest is?"

"I imagine it's another code, a cipher within a cipher in case the first one was broken. It could be anyone. It might not even be a person."

Morgan nodded, yet he didn't really believe she was right. He knew it was crazy and impossible – the diary had been started nearly ten years before he was born. But Morgan felt certain it had been written for him.

Tomas emerged from the U-Bahn into the unbeautiful expanse of Alexanderplatz. The huge square was busier than he'd ever seen it, full of people who weren't looking over their shoulder to see who might be following them. Tomas hadn't needed to come to the square – there was a stop closer to where Heinrich lived – but he'd wanted a chance to walk through his old hunting ground.

The sun was hidden behind lowering clouds, the atmosphere hot and damp with unshed rain. The city looked grey in this light – but then Tomas thought East Berlin looked grey in pretty much any light. Nobody spared him a glance, and why would they? The person he was about to visit was one of the few who might remember him.

He took a turning off the main road, into a narrower street still noisy with evening rush-hour traffic. He noticed the way that pedestrians' eyes darted away from his own, heads held lower than in the west of the city. The legacy of oppression lingered, like a foul smell.

Genter Strasse was buried in the straggling, ugly suburbs. Tomas remembered coming to the area before, a visit to a low-level source he'd needed to pay off. But he'd never visited Heinrich here, in such a seedy, hopeless part of the city. He paused a moment to study the tower block where the old Stasi agent now lived. It had probably been put up some time in the sixties, but it already looked on the point of collapse. Substandard concrete, crumbling into dust, surrounded broken and boarded-up windows. The whole place felt half empty, but maybe that was because most of its residents preferred to stay hidden.

Tomas travelled up to the seventh floor in a lift that was dark with graffiti and stank of piss. He barely noticed. He was lost in memories, mostly painful ones.

When Tomas had last seen Heinrich, he'd been in an apartment in the heart of the city, only a few blocks from the Volkskammer. Heinrich had been living the highest life the communist state afforded, while those he spied on sank into poverty and despair. Tomas could picture him quite clearly, standing at his window and looking out over the streets he ruled like a king. Most East Berliners lived in constant fear, the nagging accompaniment to their every move. It was men like Heinrich who inspired that fear, and Tomas had known that the German man revelled in it. Tomas had felt a deep, visceral loathing for Heinrich which he'd found very hard to disguise.

The operation that had brought Tomas into contact with Heinrich had been a honey-trap, though Tomas hadn't felt the need to share that with Gunter earlier. Tomas and Kate had worked it together, back in eighty-one. Kate found Heinrich repellent, with his calculating eyes and self-important smirk, but she'd done what was needed to get the goods on him.

Tomas and Kate hadn't been an item then, but he'd hated it all the same. As the lift reached the seventh floor, and Tomas stepped out into a concrete hallway, he remembered how thoughts of her and Heinrich together had tormented him. He'd looked at the man's hands and imagined them on Kate's body, and it was all he could do not to break them.

His mental image of Heinrich was so strong – the slicked-back black hair, the bulbous nose and high slanting cheekbones – that for a moment Tomas stared dumbly at the shuffling old man who answered the door.

Heinrich stared back at him. He had lank grey hair and stooped shoulders, nothing left of the commanding presence he'd once used to intimidate.

"Tomas," he said eventually, stepping back to admit him. "So. Time has not changed you as it has me." His voice quavered with age, but there was still the same arrogant sneer hidden inside it.

Tomas didn't bother to answer, just brushed past the other man into the apartment. It was a study in brown linoleum, peeling at the corners and clashing horribly with the orange formica furniture. In the centre of the main room, a television sat on an old cardboard box. There was only one chair, a battered leather recliner, and it had been pulled round to face the screen. A curdling cup of tea rested on the floor beside it.

Look on my works, ye mighty, and despair, Tomas thought.

Heinrich sank into the chair with a relieved grunt. "So you actually let them do this to you... do you mind if I ask why?"

"I had my reasons."

"Hmm. Well, sit down, sit down. There's a stool in the kitchen if you want it."

The kitchen was little more than a corridor, lined with sagging cupboards on one side. Heinrich was far too old a hand to leave anything incriminating in plain sight, so Tomas just picked up the stool and headed back to the other room. It wobbled when he sat on it, and put his head a good foot below Heinrich's.

The amused twist of Heinrich's lips told him that had been deliberate. "Don't tell me," he said. "There's only one reason you're here – the Ragnarok artefacts. It doesn't surprise me. Quite a few of the usual suspects have been sniffing around them recently."

"Really?"

"Don't act coy with me. I'm far too old to have the patience for it." Heinrich took a sip from his tea, pointedly failing to offer Tomas a drink.

"OK," Tomas said. "Let's pretend it is about the artefacts. What would you be able to tell me?"

"I don't know," Heinrich said. "What would you be able to offer me? What *can* you offer me? Because now that those oh-so-incriminating photos you took are twenty years old, I'm not so interested in buying them back." He shifted uncomfortably in his chair, as if his back was paining him. "As I noticed you noticing, everything I ever had has been taken away from me. What can you possibly threaten me with now?"

Heinrich's voice was stingingly bitter, and Tomas knew his plans to use the soft approach were futile. "How about the loss of your freedom?" he asked. "Your old bosses might no longer be around to care about your indiscretions, but they turned a blind eye to plenty of other things that the new bosses would care about very much."

Heinrich's unhealthily pallid skin flushed red. "I see. And here I thought the years might have mellowed you. But of course they didn't pass for you, did they? No deal, Tomas. There's no evidence of anything. I made sure of it before the Wall fell."

"No physical evidence, maybe," Tomas said. "What about that girl you raped, then framed and shipped off to Schloss Hoheneck. Anna, that was her name. Think I might be able to track her down? I think I could. You and I both know you'd be dead before they let you out of prison."

Heinrich was quiet for a long time. Tomas almost felt sorry for him, this old man who really didn't have much left to lose. But Tomas had met Anna's parents, a long time ago. Heinrich didn't deserve anyone's pity.

"Fine," Heinrich said eventually. He laughed, an unhealthy rattle deep in his chest. "You win, as you always do, ruthlessness hidden behind a smile. The capitalist way."

"I don't need an ethics lecture from you," Tomas said sharply. "Where are the artefacts?"

Heinrich shrugged. "I don't have the first idea."

Tomas stood up, the stool toppling to the floor behind him. "Don't mess me around, Heinrich. I can't begin to tell you how much I'd enjoy seeing you behind bars." He knew he was being cruel, and he couldn't bring himself to care. Even now, he looked at the other man's hands, and he saw them pawing Kate, combing possessively through her chestnut hair.

Heinrich smiled thinly. "Do you really think I'd be living in this shithole if I had information like that to trade? But –" he held up a hand. "I think I may still be of some assistance. Enough to guarantee my freedom, at least." He said *freedom* as if the word scratched his throat on the way out.

Tomas folded his arms, but didn't sit back down. "I'm listening."

"A businessman called Gabriel is searching for the artefacts too. You know that already, I imagine. His agents contacted me a few months back. I told them I couldn't help, and they left contact details, in case I changed my mind. If you liked, I could set up a meet."

Tomas smiled for the first time since he'd entered the apartment. "Yes, Heinrich. That's exactly what I'd like."

Morgan was in a church. He could see the altar and the silver cross above it, hanging from a long wire. The walls were pure white, the ceiling as well. He thought about looking down and suddenly he was, though he didn't recall moving his head.

The floor was white too. It looked grainy, like sand. That couldn't be right. Churches were supposed to be made of grey stone, with stained-glass windows and rows of pews.

There were no windows here to break up the white monotony of the walls. Instead they were lined with statues, kings and queens in long white robes. Morgan studied the face of the nearest, a proud, thin-faced old man. But then his view shifted, turning to the other side of the statue – and he realised that it was horribly deformed. Its eye had melted down its cheek, which in turn drooped down towards the remnants of its chin. Half its nose was gone, leaving nothing but the cavity of its nostril.

Horrified, Morgan tried to take a step back. He didn't move. Feet he couldn't see remained rooted to the gleaming white floor.

And as sometimes happens in dreams, he suddenly recognised it for what it was. The realisation didn't cut through the illusion, but it deadened the terror a little. It wasn't real. It would soon be over.

Not yet, though. There was still something else he needed to see. His eyeless gaze was drawn away from the statue, back to the altar, and now there was something on it. There was no sensation of movement, but suddenly he was nearer, and he could see what it was. A person. A little girl.

There was another figure, bending over her. His face was hidden, the tall, angular body curving like a bracket around the altar. He cast a dark shadow across the little girl. Morgan knew this person, though he couldn't name him. The fear came back, a cloud of dread as formless as Morgan himself.

The little girl's voice echoed through the empty, vaulted church, at once familiar and strange. "The Polish priest," she said.

The man bending over her jerked and straightened. He turned, a slow, almost balletic pirouette, and Morgan felt a surge of terror. Finally he would see the man, know him for who he was. But when the figure had turned to him it was just another statue, white from head to toe. And as Morgan watched, the priest's stony face began to melt and drip.

Morgan jerked awake, gasping for breath. Something slithered from his lap to the floor, and he let out a little moan of fear. His eyes tried desperately to penetrate the darkness, to convince himself that the dream really was over.

After a few seconds he remembered that there was a lamp on his bedside table. His fingers scrabbled for it, knocking it on its side before he finally managed to find the switch.

It didn't make him feel much better. The lamp bathed the room in a flat, pale glow that made it seem as unreal as anything in his dream.

Morgan fought to get his breathing under control, then leant over the side of the bed to retrieve the diary and notebook which had fallen when he woke. He must have dropped off while he was working on the translation. He certainly didn't remember going to bed, and he was still wearing his jeans and yellow t-shirt.

Anya stirred in the bed to his right. "What the hell are you doing? It's –" her hand reached out to fumble at the bedside clock "– four in the morning."

"I had a dream," Morgan said. Though 'Dream' seemed an inadequate word to describe the experience he'd just been through.

Anya looked like she was about to say something cutting. Then she read his face and her own softened. "Bad one?"

"Not great," Morgan said. He was quiet a long time, trying to get his head in order. The dream had been bad, but it had been more than that. "It was important," he said. "I think. It was about the Polish priest."

He could see it took Anya a moment to realise he was talking about something from his father's diary. Then she shrugged. "No surprise if you're dreaming about it. You've been reading it all day."

"No," Morgan said. A vision from the dream flashed across his mind's eye, the tall figure at the altar, stooping over the little girl. And suddenly he knew why the figure had looked so familiar. "No, it's not that. Raphael said he knew my – that he knew Nicholson. I think *Raphael's* the Polish priest."

"Because of a dream?" Anya wasn't scoffing exactly, but she didn't sound convinced.

"It makes sense, doesn't it?"

She shrugged. "It could be true, I suppose. That's a long way from saying it definitely is."

And now Morgan was remembering the little girl, whose face he hadn't been able to see. The terror in her voice when she told him about the priest. "We have to go to Poland," he said.

He expected Anya to fight him. He was prepared to go on his own if he had to. But she just studied him without saying anything. As the silence stretched on, he had time to notice that a lock of hair was stuck to the corner of her mouth, and there were red seams in her cheek where it had pressed too hard against her pillow.

"What?" he said eventually.

Her eyes didn't drop from his face, disconcerting in their seriousness. "Why did the Hermetic Division choose you for this mission, Morgan? I know what Tomas is. What are you?"

"I don't know," Morgan said.

She nodded. "Then I guess we're going to Poland."

CHAPTER TWELVE

Morgan woke as the sun blazed its light through a narrow gap in the curtains and spread warmth across his face. He was amazed that he'd managed to get back to sleep, but as soon as he'd recognised Raphael, the anxiety of his dream had faded into nothing. He'd been left feeling almost peaceful. Purposeful, anyway.

He rolled out of bed, hitching up his boxers where they'd slipped down his hips and scraping the sleep out of his eyes.

Anya was still dozing, curled in on herself like a baby. Morgan shook her shoulder to wake her. Her hand sleepily tried to bat his away, but he kept on shaking till her body unwound, and he saw her eyes open. He ignored her muttered protests and headed into the bathroom.

The taps only yielded a trickle of cold water. Morgan splashed a handful on his face and hissed at the icy sting of it. He tried to remember the last time he'd washed and realised it was probably back in Budapest, when he'd sat in the thermal baths with Karamov. His fingers grated against his cheeks as he rubbed them. He must have a two-day growth of stubble. Lucky Anya had bought him a razor along with the clothes and toothbrush.

One final splash of water on his face, and he looked up to catch his reflection in the mirror over the sink.

A different face stared back at him.

Morgan shut his eyes, his mind desperately trying not to build snapshot impressions of features into a known face. The snub, little-girl nose. The black hair hanging in damp curls around the broad forehead. The feral smile. No, it wasn't real, it wasn't her. But he opened his eyes again and of course it was.

Morgan backed out of the bathroom, stumbling against the door frame. An awkward scramble and he was out, falling to his knees on the bedroom floor. He could hear his own breathing, rapid and harsh.

Anya was fully awake by then, sitting on the one small chair brushing her hair.

She jumped to her feet when she saw Morgan, letting out a startled yelp. "Shit! What's wrong?" The hairbrush fell out of her hand to bounce once against the carpet.

Morgan's eyes tracked it mindlessly, his brain still buzzing with panic.

"Morgan?"

"Nothing," he said, finally looking up at her.

"Don't lie to me," she said. "It's not conducive to a good working relationship."

He shuddered, and wrapped his arms around himself. "On the train," he told her. "There was a man, an American..." He swallowed hard. "He had some kind of power, I don't know. He used mirrors to call them up."

"To call what up?" Anya was darting nervous glances towards the bathroom now.

"Ghosts," Morgan said. "Spirits. It's okay, you can stop fucking looking, I don't think it's there any longer. They're only there when you can see them."

"But you think this 'spirit' followed you from the train? That it somehow came to *this* mirror to find you?"

"I think she's in *every* mirror I look in," Morgan said. He shivered again, because he hadn't realised the truth of that until he said it.

"And what –"

"It doesn't matter. It's dangerous, and that's as much as I know."

"Okay," Anya said. "Take it easy. Do you think it's safe for *me* to go in there?"

Morgan nodded. "She... it doesn't know you. The man, the American man, said he only opened the gate, that I was the one who called the spirit through. It's me who's being haunted, not you."

Anya looked dubious, but after a second she nodded too, and scooped up her toiletry bag from the floor. "So we're still going to Poland."

"Yes, we've got to." Morgan didn't know how to tell her that he thought the spirit of his dead sister wanted him to find the white church he'd seen in his dream. In fact, he was pretty sure he *shouldn't* tell her. "The answers are there," he said instead. "We just have to work out how to find them."

"It's your decision," Anya said reluctantly. "But perhaps you should buy an electric razor. And for god's sake use some deodorant. I'm going to be stuck in a car with you for hours."

Tomas had told Heinrich he'd be the only other person attending the meeting with Raphael's agent, but both men had known it was a lie. Just because Tomas was using Heinrich, didn't mean he trusted him.

Still, Belle wouldn't have been his first choice of back-up. But she and Tomas were wired for sound, button cameras in their lapels. Anya and the van with the audio-visual equipment were parked a few streets away. They should be safe enough. And it was true they didn't want to scare off Raphael's go-between – that a man walking with his young daughter looked a hell of a lot less suspicious than almost any other combination of personnel.

Heinrich had wanted to arrange the meet in a park. Anya had shuddered and refused and Tomas knew she was remembering what had happened to Karamov in that sunny, open green space in Budapest. So instead Tomas had told Heinrich to fix the rendezvous at the Checkpoint Charlie museum. Tomas had sensed the other man's grimace over the phone line and almost smiled.

Now he was regretting his choice. Here, at last, was a piece of the Wall that used to symbolise so much. Multi-coloured, scrawled with graffiti – and locked away behind glass. An exhibit. Tomas stood and stared at it, lost in memory, until Belle squeezed the hand she held clasped in hers.

Tomas looked down at the little girl. Her eyes were darting around the large exhibition room, too watchful for someone her age.

"Heinrich's here," she said.

She was right. He'd just come through the entry gates, feet cautious and stumbling. Tomas saw his eyes squint in anger when he caught sight of the fragment of the Wall, but he made no acknowledgement of Tomas or Belle. No doubt Raphael already had people in the room. They couldn't afford to betray the connection.

Tomas tugged on Belle's arm to draw her over to the other side of the museum and a large glass exhibit case holding photographs of those who'd tried to cross the Wall and failed. If Tomas stood behind it, he'd be able to keep an eye on Heinrich without being too obvious.

"Any sense of who Raphael's man might be?" Tomas asked, peering at Heinrich through the glass. It made the old Stasi agent seem insubstantial, a shadowy remnant of who he used to be.

"No one's leaping out at me." Belle was still scanning the room, a small frown on her forehead.

"You might want to be a bit less obvious about that," Tomas whispered to her.

"Little girls are supposed to be curious, Mr Len. It's in the manual."

A flicker of shifting colour through the glass told Tomas that Heinrich was moving. Not deeper into the museum, but back towards the exit. "Damn him!" he muttered. If that bastard betrayed them now...

"He's following someone," Belle said.

Tomas studied the crowd, but he couldn't see who she meant. Too many people, and Heinrich was looking down at the floor, not at any one of them.

"There," Belle said. "The lady in the red top. Kind of sad looking, with salt and pepper hair."

Tomas let himself drift closer to Heinrich. All the while his eyes catalogued the crowd, and after a minute he saw the woman Belle was talking about. She was behind Heinrich now, with her back to Tomas. No doubt she'd already told the old man where to go. If Raphael's people knew their business, the real talking wouldn't take place at the original meet. They'd be relocating soon, and Belle and Tomas needed to make sure they were close enough to follow.

Heinrich reached the exit, pushing through the small barrier on his way out. The woman lingered a little, obviously not wanting to look like she was with him. Her head turned slightly as her eyes scanned the room.

Tomas automatically dropped his, feigning fascination with a display recounting the history of the Wall's construction.

A second later, his mind processed his brief glimpse of the woman's face, and his head snapped back up again.

The woman had gone by then, but it didn't matter. The image was so clear, so familiar. The round cheeks, sunk a little with age. The chestnut hair, streaked with grey as Belle had said. The eyes, such a unique, deep blue, almost violet. Tomas dropped Belle's hand without thinking, pushing past people to get to the exit, careless now about being noticed. That didn't matter. Nothing did. The only thing he cared about was finding that woman.

Finding out if there was any way she really could be Kate.

The car was ancient and its motor turned with a choking sound, like a terminal cough. They were travelling so slowly down the windy, tree-shaded road that it would probably have been faster to get out and walk. Morgan knew it was his fault. He'd insisted Anya break off both wing mirrors as well as the rear-view mirror before he'd get in. She was driving pretty much blind, but then the roads were almost entirely empty. They'd passed two cars in the last three hours. There was nothing here but the endless gloomy forest, and the strip of clear blue sky above the trees.

It was beautiful, in a way. It was certainly a change from the deserts where Morgan had spent so much of his time. He glanced up at the scenery now and again, but most of his attention was focused on the book in his lap. He barely had to look at the runic alphabet any longer. He wasn't bothering to write it down, either, just translating straight from the page. That way, he didn't have to share what he found with Anya.

She'd been pestering him for more about the Ragnarok artefacts, but after the first few weeks his father hadn't had much to say about them. Maybe the trail had gone cold. Or maybe – as Anya clearly thought – it had heated up, and Nicholson had been afraid to commit his findings to paper. Most of the entries were mundane, descriptions of meetings with secret service bureaucrats who wanted to shut down the Hermetic Division, or the failed missions with Tomas which were the reason for that. It didn't matter to Morgan. It all fascinated him.

At times, he felt as if he didn't even need to look at the diary at all, that the words could somehow float from the page into his head. When he concentrated, he almost thought he could catch his father's voice in the air. The uncanny connection chilled him, yet a part of him yearned for it to deepen.

May 7, 1981. It's hard to believe I've only been away for a week. So much has changed. Who'd have thought the most important moment of my life would take place in Bolivia? And all the trouble I had scaring up the funding to take us there! They even made us fly second-class, which did Tomas's long legs no good at all. He was limping for the whole of the first day we spent in La Paz, ten thousand feet above sea level and the air so thin you wondered if you'd forgotten how to breathe.

The Bolivians are a short, dark bunch. Tomas and I stuck out like the proverbial sore thumbs. People would stop and stare at us, and children ran up just to touch us in the street. It drove me mad, but I don't think Tomas minded. He's always struck me as someone who feels a perpetual stranger, an outsider even in his own country. At least in Bolivia his difference was visible for everyone to see. In an odd way, I think it helped him relax.

Personally, I didn't find the place relaxing at all. Nothing in that city is on the level. I spent two days feeling as if I was walking permanently uphill. We stayed just long enough to make sure we weren't chasing a phantom, then headed out in a borrowed car that looked like it was being held together with duct tape.

The girl we were looking for lived a hundred miles away, in the Amazon. A hundred miles and nearly ten thousand feet straight down. There was snow on the high plains around La Paz, but when Tomas and I travelled down the unpaved, switch-backed road that led to the girl's village, we travelled into summer. The jungle was humid and bright, full of flowers and insects and the desperate screeching of monkeys. It was beautiful, but Tomas, a northern European to his bones, didn't care for it. Bright colours offend him. I think he thought they were vulgar.

We were following a pretty flimsy lead, but we've been getting desperate these last few months. Of course, Tomas doesn't know that I've taken to falsifying my reports, suggesting we found more than we actually did. Hinting at that elusive, practical application lurking just around the next corner. Not very good form, I know, and bound to catch up with me eventually, but needs must.

The village was deep in the jungle, by the banks of a muddy stream, an offshoot of the Amazon that was clogged with creepers and stank to high heaven. It was an Indian village, of course, but some of the men spoke English. The girl's father did, at least a few words, and he'd been told we were coming. They'd informed him we might be able to help his daughter. Highly unlikely, but I hadn't known how else to get us access.

The elders were waiting for us in the centre of the village, a ragtag bunch dressed in a mixture of western clothes and traditional costume. They might have looked rather pitiable, if they hadn't been carrying enough guns to outfit a small army. A not inconsiderable proportion of them were pointed at us. Tomas, of course, acted like he didn't even notice them. I tried to fit myself in his shadow, and hoped they'd shoot him first.

"We're here to help the girl," I said, when it didn't look like anyone else was going to say anything.

Most of the faces surrounding us stared with dumb incomprehension, but one old man gestured towards a small hut, isolated from the others at the edge of the village. He must have had some kind of authority – maybe he was the girl's grandfather, who knows? – because the others let us through. They didn't drop their guns, but they at least stopped pointing them at us.

My heart had been hammering with fear, but as I walked towards that hut it was excitement which kept it racing. Two weeks ago, an Inca mummy had been unearthed in the Andes, a young girl killed in a ritual sacrifice. And a day after that, in this village, a girl of exactly the same age had begun to speak Quechua, the language of the Incas, though she'd never heard a word of it before in her life. She insisted her parents were strangers, and asked where the mountains had gone.

Or so the rumours claimed. It's not that unusual a narrative, of course. It crops up all over the world with alarming regularity, along with stories about statues weeping tears of blood and the Virgin Mary appearing in a potato. Why did we fly halfway across the globe to investigate this particular one? Because nobody here was trying to make any money out of it. In fact, after the initial feeding frenzy, the locals had done their best to keep the press away. They wanted to cure their daughter, not exploit her. That was highly suspicious.

So we told them we wanted the same thing.

When we walked into the hut, the girl was resting on a bed of twigs and reeds, her limbs as frail as the wood she was lying on. We could barely see her, the little hut was so full of smoke. God alone knows what they were burning, but the picture began to warp the moment I walked in there, the colours bending at the edge of my vision.

Her eyes were closed when we came in, and her skin was more grey than brown. She looked at death's door, though the stories *hadn't said anything about physical symptoms. I wondered what they'd been feeding her, to make her so ill. She was wailing, this thin, keening cry that was almost unbearable to hear. I could feel my hands twitching. I wanted to cover her mouth, squeeze her neck, anything to make that awful sound stop.*

Then her head turned and her eyes opened. I still can't say why I was so certain, but I knew it absolutely. For the first time in my life, I saw a dead person's spirit staring out of a living person's eyes.

She said something, and they hadn't been making it up, she was speaking Quechua. She said – it's incredible, my hand's shaking as I write this – she said, "White devil, I know what it is you seek."

I didn't quite believe it, not right away. It's the kind of thing those dreadful mediums say, isn't it? Waiting for you to fill in the blanks yourself. So I asked her, "And what's that, then?" My Quechua was pretty ropey, but she seemed to understand.

"The End of the World Things," she said. That's a direct translation, but there was no doubting what she meant. The Ragnarok artefacts.

If my heart had been racing before, I was on the point of a coronary then. "That's right," I said, and I know my voice was trembling. "Can you help me?"

"Do you want help?" she said. "It's not too late to turn back, if you choose."

"I want the artefacts," I told her. "If you know where they are, I'll give you anything you want in return."

She looked sad. I think the spirit knew its body was dying. "That's not in your power to give," she said. "And the artefacts aren't within mine. They can be yours, but the price is high."

"How high?" I asked.

She closed her eyes. "Everything you love, and everything you are."

Well, obviously that didn't sound good. But I've discovered that when it comes to the world beyond the world, words don't always mean what you think. It's like the Death card in the Tarot, which is really about transformation. She was saying getting the artefacts would change me, and that was okay. The search for them already had.

"Then that's what I'll sacrifice," I told her.

The girl opened her mouth and a sound came out like – I don't know how to describe it. Like a thousand people sighing all at once.

Tomas grabbed my arm and shouted, "For god's sake think about what you're saying!"

I shook him off. There's a time for caution, and a time to be bold. "Tell me everything," I said to the girl. And she grabbed my hand and pulled me down and whispered in my ear.

And she told me, she finally told me, everything I'd wanted to know. I saw how wrong I'd been all along – and how right. I understood exactly why I'd started keeping this diary, why the Polish priest suggested it. And I knew why I'd recruited Tomas, all those years ago. When she'd finished, I straightened and looked at him with a sort of melancholy fondness. It's the way you look at someone you know you're going to lose.

He didn't notice. He was watching the girl. Now she'd stopped speaking she'd started crying, a thin stream of water leaking silently out of her brown eyes, as if she didn't have the energy for anything more.

"Poor mite," Tomas whispered. He looked a thousand-year-old spirit in the face, and that was all he had to say.

He didn't understand what that moment meant. How could he? For all his intelligence, Tomas is basically a simple man. He believes in right and wrong and duty and country and all those things I moved beyond a long time ago. But that's just fine. He won't complain when I send him off on mission after mission to chase artefacts I now know he'll never find. And meanwhile I can continue with the real work, secret and unmolested.

I'll play my part and – at the end – I'll make sure Tomas plays his. And Ragnarok will come, though Tomas won't live to see it.

Morgan shut the book and shut his eyes, suddenly afraid to read more. He'd wanted to know about his father, and now he did. *Be careful what you wish for,* wasn't that what they said? But Morgan hadn't paid any more attention to the warning than his father had.

With the rear-view mirror gone, Anya had to look across at him to read his face. "What is it?" she said. "What have you found out?"

Morgan shook his head. "Nothing important."

Tomas's shoulder ached where he'd flung himself too hard against the glass exit. He could hear someone shouting his name and vaguely registered that it was Belle. There was another voice, tinny and high, in his ear: Anya, asking what the hell he was doing. Tomas ignored them both.

The woman was heading down Fredrichstrasse, head bent low, salt-and-pepper hair covering her face. Strands of it blew in the breeze from the passing traffic, but not enough to reveal the features beneath.

The woman sped up, almost jogging now, and Tomas accelerated too, caring less and less whether she could tell he was following her. She probably could, because now she was running. He saw her elbow collide with a middle-aged businessman walking in the opposite direction, head down over his paper. The man yelled abuse at her retreating back as Tomas started running after.

He heard the screech of brakes and blare of horns before he spotted the woman sprinting across the road, heedless of the heavy traffic. Belle's voice had been left far behind by now, but Anya's was growing louder in his ear. Her yelling was starting to distract him, so he tore out the earpiece and threw it to the ground. He heard the plastic crunch beneath a car's wheels as it swerved to avoid him. Then he was on the pavement again and the woman was only twenty paces in front of him.

She turned at the next junction, then again, and again, veering wildly across the road whenever she needed to. Tomas knew Berlin well, but even he was becoming disorientated.

He caught her beneath the eaves of a small bakery, where the smell of dough battled the traffic fumes. He could feel the pulse at her wrist, the evidence that she wasn't like him, that she really was alive. He wondered whether seeing her would be enough to shock *him* back into life too. But when she finally turned to face him, he felt a stutter in his chest that was more like his heart stopping.

"Oh, Tomas," she said. "I'm so sorry." Her voice was breathy with exertion, one droplet of sweat winding down the side of her nose.

It was Kate. Of course it was. He'd known it from the second he saw her in the museum. Not even twenty years of time, twenty years of life that Tomas hadn't lived, could disguise her from him.

Tomas opened his mouth, but discovered he had nothing to say. And just like that, he wasn't baffled, or joyful, or astonished – he was furious. Kate was the reason he'd let them do this to him. It was because of Kate's death that he'd become a monster.

Shoppers pushed impatiently past, in and out of the bakery. The sun shone through a narrow gap in the clouds, making a rainbow of the light rain. All around them, the world kept turning, even though for him, it had stopped on the day this woman died.

"They told me it happened in Siberia," he said, finding the words at last. "They showed me pictures of your body. I even saw the autopsy report they smuggled out. A bullet to the back of the head. An execution." He laughed bitterly. "I asked them to bury the picture with me, but they told me they needed it for the files."

"I know," she said softly. She wasn't beautiful any more. Middle age had scored deep crows-feet round her violet eyes, and they'd dimmed with time, or maybe they'd just been over-bright in his memory. But her voice was still the same rich, deep contralto.

"Was it all a lie?" he asked her.

She nodded. "But not mine."

"Whose then? Did you know what they told me about you? Did you let them say it, knowing how I'd feel?" He dropped her arm, suddenly unable to bear touching her.

"I was a pawn too, Tomas. You have to believe me. And you need to trust me."

"How can I?" She didn't say anything, and after a moment he added, "So you're working for Raphael now, is that it? You didn't die, you just switched sides?"

Kate's eyes widened, as if she was shocked at the accusation. Tomas had a painful flash of memory. She'd always done this, when they argued. Made him feel bad for even suggesting that she could be in the wrong.

"I didn't leave MI6, they left me."

"Tell me, then. What did happen in Russia, twenty years ago?" He was desperate for an explanation that he could believe.

"I was captured, that much was true. And yes, it was by Raphael, or at least the people he worked for. He was attached to the KGB back then, did you know that?"

Tomas shook his head, but he guessed it made sense. The Russians had run their own equivalent of the Hermetic Division. They'd never had trouble believing in the occult. Living in their unforgiving country, it wasn't hard to believe in an essential darkness at the heart of it all.

"They... questioned me," Kate said. "For weeks. I broke. Everyone does, don't they? Whatever they tell you, the human mind can only take so much. I told them everything I knew and a few things I was only making up, because I thought it was what they wanted to hear. But I didn't turn traitor." There was a long, painful silence, until finally she added, "I didn't do that until they told me what had happened to you." A single tear slipped from her eye to track down her face.

Tomas felt his fingers itching with the need to brush it away. His arms wanted to find their way around her. He folded them instead. "What did they tell you?"

She wiped the tear away herself, a brusque swipe of her thumb against her cheek. "You weren't the only one who was shown photos. They had spies everywhere back then and one of their men was at your funeral. I saw a picture of you being lowered into the grave. And the worst thing, the absolute worst thing was, I could see that your eyes were still open."

"I thought you were gone," Tomas said. He reached out and

took her hand. "Without you... I would never have done it if I'd thought you were still alive."

"And that's why they told you I was dead. That's why they showed you the pictures. It wasn't the KGB who faked those photos – it was Nicholson. That's how Raphael's men found out. They'd been hoping to send me back as a double agent, only they discovered that the British had already declared me dead."

"I can't believe... Nicholson tried to talk me out of it. He said –" Tomas laughed harshly. "That it wasn't worth it to him, losing me just to find out if the magics really worked."

Kate gave his hand a final squeeze, then released it. "He knew you too well, Tomas. He always knew how to manipulate you. When I found out what had happened, I swore I'd find him and make him pay. But he was already dead. He must have come straight home from your burial and hung himself. I'd like to think it was guilt, but we both knew Nicholson too well to believe that."

"So you worked for Raphael instead," Tomas said.

"Yes." There was no hint of apology in her voice. "I couldn't reach Nicholson, but I could make those bastards in the Division pay for what they'd done to you. And what they let happen to me, of course. The KGB were tipped off, that's how they found me. I'm damn sure I know who did the tipping."

Tomas reached for her hand again, but she took a step back, out of the shelter of the baker's eaves. Raindrops instantly spattered her head, wriggling down the corkscrews of her hair to trickle into the open neck of her red blouse.

"But Raphael tortured you," Tomas said.

"He was doing his job, and at least he was honest about it. Wouldn't we all rather be shot in the chest than stabbed in the back? And he promised me that he'd do everything he could to find out why Nicholson betrayed us."

"Did he?" Tomas asked. He took another step forward, and she took another one back. Distantly, he registered a commotion further down the street, a group of people he thought might be Gunter's men.

"Yes," Kate said. "He's going to tell me the truth about what happened twenty years ago." She was at the edge of the road now, and Tomas realised for the first time that a car had drawn to a stop beside her. "There's just one more thing I have to do for him first."

Tomas lunged for her as she flung herself inside the car. It was moving before she was seated, the momentum slamming the door shut behind her.

"Kate!" he shouted, but she was already too far away to hear it.

Morgan was in a church of pure white. White walls, white floor, white altar. He recognised it, though he couldn't say why. He thought perhaps he'd been here before.

It should have been beautiful, but for some reason it wasn't. Maybe it was the statues lining each wall, staring back at him with blank white eyes. Though looking at them made him profoundly uneasy, he didn't want to look away. He was afraid that when he did, they'd start moving.

It took him a second to realise he wasn't alone. But when he saw the figures by the altar, he gave a start of recognition, not surprise. Of course. He'd been expecting them to be here. They belonged in this place.

The young man remained frozen, bending low over the little girl. But no, he wasn't a person, was he? He was just another statue, face moulded in white, glints of light sparkling off his narrow nose. Morgan could only see the right sight of his face, and he was very glad of that, though he wasn't quite sure why. He thought maybe the left side was the real side, and the one he could see was only a mask.

Was the girl a statue as well?

No. Her head was turning towards Morgan.

"Taste it," she said.

Morgan drifted closer, puzzled. He studied her lips. "What?"

"Taste it." Her mouth moved in time with the words, though

they didn't quite seem to be coming out of it. The sound echoed hollowly from the walls, as if it was the church itself which was speaking.

It seemed absurd to obey, but he dropped to his knees anyway, then forward onto his hands.

"Taste it," the girl said again, only this time the words were muffled, and it sounded as if she was saying "taste *me*".

Morgan didn't want to do it, but the girl was so insistent. He sighed, then flicked his tongue out, a quick brush against the white floor of the church. Then he did it again, a longer, wetter swipe this time. Because that couldn't be right, could it? Why would the floor of the church be covered in salt?

He leaned forward to lick for a third time – only to rear back, shocked, as a roar of protest surged through him, so loud the sound felt like a physical force. There were no words in it, just a fierce denial. He looked up, around, searching for the source. In an instant, he'd found it. The altar. The young man. The little girl.

The girl looked calm, almost sad. The young man...

From this angle, Morgan could see his face in its entirety. The perfectly smooth handsome right side. And the left side, scarred and melted, mouth open in a roar of outrage, eyes blazing with malice, and Morgan opened his mouth to scream too –

– only to jerk, sweating and shaking, into the waking world. But even here the sound followed him, the scream of protest. Now it was higher, sharper, and after a second he realised it was Anya. That she was sitting beside him, face turned towards him, terrified.

Morgan couldn't figure out where he was, why she was so frightened. What this thing in his hands was that was trying so hard to twist out of his grip.

"Morgan!" Anya screamed again, and he realised that he was in a car, that the thing in his hand was the steering wheel. The whole vehicle jolted and rattled as it rolled over the narrow strip of gravel at the side of the road and into the deep grass.

Beyond the grass was deep, dense forest. The first tree was only twenty feet from the car's bonnet.

Morgan wrenched the steering wheel round desperately. It fought him, happier to carry on the course he'd already set it. The shadow of the trees fell over them.

"Stop!" Anya yelled, as if Morgan might not have noticed he was about to total the car and them with it. But he knew if he stamped on the brake the wheels would lock and he'd have lost all hope of control. He pumped his foot instead and kept on pulling at the wheel, throwing the whole weight of his body against it.

They missed the first tree by an inch. Morgan heard the screech of wood against metal as a branch buckled Anya's door. She yelled and flung herself away from it, crushing Morgan against his side of the car.

The car jumped and bucked, Anya's weight pushed against him, and for a second Morgan's hands slipped from the wheel. It instantly spun round to the centre, dragging them back towards the trees. Morgan fumbled clumsily to turn it back, but his fingers were sweating and he couldn't get a grip. And now the next tree was looming ahead of them, a massive oak buttressed with thick, knotty roots.

There was no way they were missing it. Morgan gave up on steering, stamping his foot down frantically on the brake instead. The car growled in protest and the wheels locked, and then Morgan didn't have time to do anything except wrap his arms around his head and brace for the impact.

The force of it jarred all the way up his spine. His head thumped against the steering wheel hard enough that he thought he was going to lose consciousness. His vision blacked and then greyed and finally snapped back to a blinding white that jabbed into his brain between his eyes.

Anya let out a pained whimper beside him. Morgan wanted to check that she was okay, but for a long moment all he could do was rest his head against the wheel and wait for the world to stop spinning. When he finally managed to lift his head and turn it to her, he saw that she'd cut her forehead, the blood running down in a sheet towards her eyes. But at least she was still moving. His friendship hadn't killed her yet.

The car was another story. Morgan pulled open his door, stumbling over the wiry, clinging undergrowth as he walked round to inspect the damage. Not good. The tree trunk had sunk a good foot into the crumpled bonnet and steam was hissing out all around it. The chassis might be bent back into shape, but the engine was clearly a write-off. There was no way they'd be driving away from here.

Anya had walked over to the other side of the hood. She looked down at it a moment longer, then up at him. Steam from the car wreathed her blood-streaked face, making her look like a pantomime villain.

"Sorry," Morgan said. "I fell asleep."

She laughed. After a second he joined in, both of them gasping for breath, bent over their knees. He knew it was the shock, but it felt good to let it out.

When it was over he straightened and studied Anya. Her face was still creased in a wide smile as she let out helpless little aftershocks of laughter.

She'd changed, Morgan realised. The dour woman he'd met in Budapest would never have found that funny. Even her body language had been transformed, loose-limbed and relaxed where it had been stiff and careful. "I guess we'll have to hitch-hike," he said.

Anya nodded. "Unless you happen to be a qualified mechanic. With a spare engine in your pocket."

Morgan took one last look at the wreckage of the car, then pulled his bag from the back seat and tramped back towards the road.

He thought they'd have to wait a while, but in the end it was less than an hour before they saw something heading in their direction, a beaten-up brown Lada. Morgan stayed in the undergrowth by the side of the road while Anya stuck out her thumb, a trick she said she'd learned when she was a student.

Sure enough, the car drew to a halt beside her, belching black smoke out of its exhaust. The driver was in his forties, balding and paunchy. He eyed Anya appreciatively, quite blatantly looking at her breasts before he took in her face. Anya smiled sweetly – and beckoned Morgan to join her. The man's face fell, but by then he'd stopped and it was too late to turn them down.

"Thank you," Morgan said as he slid into the backseat, allowing Anya to take the front. It seemed only fair to at least let the man ogle her while he drove. Besides, in the back it was easier to avoid looking in the rear-view mirror.

"You're welcome," the man said grudgingly, in thickly accented English. "So, where is it you are going?"

"A church," Morgan said. Anya turned round to stare at him, but he ignored her. "A church that's made out of salt."

The man nodded. "You mean the cathedral in the salt mines. Yes, a good place to visit – amazing, really. I will drop you in Krakow and you will take a bus from there."

Morgan could sense Anya staring at him incredulously, but he avoided her eyes. Part of him felt relief that his wild guess had been proven right. But a bigger part of him was just scared. Because although he didn't want to believe it, he thought he knew who'd be waiting for him in the church made out of salt.

Anya was fuming when she caught up with Tomas. He'd expected nothing less.

"What the fuck do you think you're doing!" she raged.

Tomas didn't reply. He couldn't stop staring at the road, uselessly hoping that he'd see Kate's car turn round and come back to him.

"I'm talking to you!" Anya grabbed his arm and spun him to face her. Three of Gunter's men were behind her, out of breath and equally pissed off. The little crowd of them blocked the pavement.

"She was supposed to be dead," Tomas said.

Anya frowned. "That woman? You knew her?"

"I worked with her." *I loved her*, he thought, but that was none of Anya's damn business.

"And that was reason enough to fuck up the mission?"

Tomas jerked his arm out of Anya's grasp, but when she turned and stalked down the pavement, he followed. "It was blown anyway. She knew who I was – she must have known it was a set-up. Heinrich sold us down the river."

"Did he?" Anya sounded a little calmer, but no less angry. "Well, you can ask him yourself. That woman might have got away, but they obviously didn't care too much about protecting Heinrich."

A moment later they found the old man, waiting between two beefy agents by the van Gunter's men had parked in a quiet side street. He'd been caught, and he ought to have looked cowed. Instead he smiled victoriously at Tomas.

Tomas grabbed him by his collar and shoved him up against the side of the van. His feet dangled a foot off the ground and he was gasping for breath against the constriction around his throat, but he kept on smiling.

"You set us up," Tomas grated.

Heinrich opened his mouth to speak, but only a choked gasp came out. Tomas reluctantly loosened his hold, allowing him to slide down the side of the van to his feet.

"How much did they pay you?" Tomas asked. "You'll have years in prison to consider whether it was really worth it."

"Years?" Heinrich laughed, a laugh that turned into a hacking cough. "I haven't got years. I've got months. Weeks, if I'm lucky and the end is quick. I'll be dead before they can ever try me."

Tomas ran his hand against his jeans to brush off the feel of the other man's skin. "You're trying to tell me you're sick?"

"Terminal." Heinrich's smile widened, as if this was the biggest joke of them all. "And for your information, Raphael paid me nothing. He didn't need to – I told him I'd happily fuck you over for free." He took a step forward, aggressive suddenly, and Tomas took an involuntary step back from the malice in the old man's grey face.

"Did you enjoy meeting up with your girlfriend, Tomas?" he said. "Was it a tearful reunion? I must say, *I* very much enjoyed seeing her again. It brought back all those lovely memories. I remember how she used to beg for more when I buried myself in that juicy pussy of hers –"

His words cut off in a shower of blood and slivers of enamel. Tomas pulled back to punch him again, aiming for the nose this time. He'd break that too, and then he'd get to work on the kidneys. But a hand grabbed his arm and two more pulled him back, dragging him away from the old man's huddled body.

Tomas fought them for a second, then sagged. His mouth filled with a bitter taste as he realised that Heinrich had enjoyed two victories today, and no doubt the sweeter had been seeing Tomas losing his control. He scrubbed his hands over his face, turning away from the German in a final, contemptuous dismissal. "It's okay, it's okay, I'm done. No point getting worked up over this, anyway. All the old bastard's wasted is our time."

Then he saw Anya's expression and froze. "What? What's happened?"

Anya's face was white with shock, or maybe anger. "It's Belle. She never reported back in. We think they've taken her."

CHAPTER THIRTEEN

The air in the underground office was thick with unspoken recriminations. Gunter was big and loud and smiling as ever, but his eyes were as accusing as everyone else's.

"Belle is definitely gone," he said, as they all took their seats. "Her colleagues in the CIA confirmed it."

"That's what the whole meeting was about," Tomas said bitterly. "Distract me so they could snatch her."

Anya nodded. "We questioned Heinrich, but he didn't have anything helpful to tell us."

Gunter rested his chin on a meaty fist. "What do you think he *could* tell us, if given the right incentive?"

"Nothing," Tomas said. "He was perfectly open about what he did, but he was never part of Raphael's organisation. He just saw an opportunity to screw me over and took it – phoned Raphael's contact after I'd been to visit and then did exactly what they told him. He said he didn't know they were going to take Belle, and I believe him."

"He actually seemed quite upset about it, claimed he wouldn't have helped if he'd known they were after the little girl," Anya added.

She looked disgusted, but Tomas didn't have the energy to be angry with the old man – he was too busy being furious with himself.

"Well," Gunter said. "Well, obviously we need to get her back. We can't let the CIA think we're incapable of organising a piss-up in a brewery. Even though the evidence would suggest that is, in fact, the case."

"The airports have been alerted," Anya said. "There's no way he can get her out of the country by plane."

"If that's what he's trying to do." Tomas didn't want to think of the other uses a man like Raphael might have for Belle. The demon inside her was what he'd care about; the small child who contained it would be no more than an inconvenience.

Tomas shook his head to dispel the ugly thought, and realised that Gunter's eyes were on him, bright blue and troublingly perceptive.

"Who was that woman, Tomas?" the big German asked. "She must have been pretty important, for you to throw the whole operation for her sake."

Tomas didn't address the rebuke in the statement. It was too true to deny. "She was important to *me*," he told Gunter. "But she wasn't important in the great scheme of things, just another agent in the Division. She doesn't know anything about the Ragnarok artefacts, if that's what you're thinking. I'm certain of it."

"Really? Because apparently you were also certain she was dead."

Tomas's hands clenched into tight fists under the table. "You're right. I'm not sure about anything any more."

The two men stared at each other for a long moment, a test of wills, but Tomas didn't intend to tell Gunter any more than he already had. If Raphael had used his past against him, it was the outcome which mattered, not the personal agony of the details.

The silence was broken by a commotion at the door, someone trying to push his way in and those nearby trying to keep him out.

"Not *now*," Tomas heard one of the agents say, but the man at the door barged through anyway, his thin face pinched with worry. He was clutching a phone in his hand, a cordless.

"It's for Mr Len," the newcomer said.

Tomas looked at Gunter and then Anya, but Gunter shrugged and Anya shook her head. It could be headquarters in London, he supposed, but he'd already reported the failure of the operation to them and explained that he'd call back when he knew more. He took the proffered phone.

The buzzing on the other end sounded faint, as if it was coming from quite a distance, and there was a hint of an echo on the line.

"Yes?" Tomas said. "Who is this?"

"You can call me Raphael," a voice on the other end said. "That is, after all, how we were introduced."

Tomas froze. His eyes snapped to Anya and he mouthed the word *Raphael* to her. She gasped, then leaned in to Tomas to press her ear against his on the phone.

Gunter must have understood too, because his arms were waving and he was hissing instructions which silenced the rest of the room. Three men rushed out of it, and Tomas was sure they'd been sent to record the call, and try to put a trace on it. He was equally certain Raphael would have made that impossible.

Still, he knew his role. Keep the old man talking as long as possible, get as much information as he could and give the men time to do their work.

"Hello, Raphael," he said, "I thought we might be hearing from you, though perhaps not quite this soon."

"Did you?" Raphael sounded pleased. "No need for niceties, then. You know what this is about."

Tomas could feel Anya's breath, hot and moist against his ear. "She'd better be okay. At the moment you're just a person of interest to us. Hurt the girl and there won't be a place in the world that you're safe."

Raphael chuckled. "You care about her, then? You're concerned about her continuing good health? That's good. I was worried you might see her as expendable. After all, you left Kate in my hands, and you once claimed to have loved her."

"You want to trade Belle for the book," Tomas said, voice shaking only a little with anger.

Raphael hissed in a breath, which told Tomas he was right. But he'd already known that. The instant he'd heard the old man's voice on the phone, he'd realised what this was all about.

"Indeed," Raphael said after a brief pause. "The book is meaningless to you, and apparently the girl isn't. It should be an easy decision to make."

But there was something mocking in his tone. He knew the decision wasn't easy, and what that said about Tomas and the people he worked with. That they'd weigh up a child's life against an object and find they tipped the scales pretty evenly.

Gunter had a phone pressed to his own ear now, no doubt listening in to the conversation. He waved an arm at Tomas and nodded firmly when he caught his eye. He wanted Tomas to agree. They'd get no more information from Raphael unless he did.

"Fine," Tomas said. "Tell us how to make the exchange, and we'll arrange it."

"As easy as that?" Tomas heard Raphael shifting as if, somewhere across the world, he was leaning back, making himself comfortable. "The details can wait for later. But keep your German friends out of it – too many people involved will lead to unintended consequences. If you must bring a companion, take that boy you're working with."

There was something in Raphael's tone as he said the last, an off-handedness that was a little too studied. Tomas would worry about what that meant later. "And where will we bring the book?" he asked.

"To St Petersburg," Raphael said, ending the call the second the last syllable was out of his mouth.

Anya pulled away, her lips set in a thin line. Tomas listened to the buzzing dial tone for a moment, then handed the phone back to Gunter's man. Across the room, a middle-aged woman looked up from the electronic equipment she was crouched over and shook her head. They hadn't been able to trace the call.

"You couldn't have kept him talking longer?" Gunter asked.

"I didn't need to," Tomas said. "There's only one place his people could be going."

Gunter raised a sceptical eyebrow.

Tomas turned to one of the men clustered around the tracking device. "Get me a map."

At Gunter's nod, the man flipped open his computer, and a few keystrokes later, Germany was up on the screen.

"Bigger," Tomas said. "Something that shows all of Europe."

When it was there in front of him, he tapped his fingers against the screen, first on the blue dot that stood for Berlin, then on the red dot that was St Petersburg, 800 miles to the east. "If you can't fly, and it's too risky and slow to drive, what's the only way to get from here to here?"

Anya's eyes widened then narrowed. She rested her finger on the screen, a little above Tomas's. "Rostock."

Tomas nodded. "They're going by sea."

From the outside, the mines didn't look like much: a jumble of run-down and abandoned buildings, and a deep shaft leading down. The air was sticky with humidity, and after the coach ride from Krakow, some of the tourists around them weren't smelling too fresh.

Anya knew there were two reasons to doubt the wisdom of coming here. Firstly, there was no guarantee this was the place Morgan had dreamed about. And secondly, there was the idiocy of chasing after something from a dream in the first place.

She sighed, and looked across at the young man. The blazing sun brought a bronze sheen to his brown cheeks and flashed white from his teeth as he smiled politely at the tour guide. There was something fake in Morgan's expression, Anya had noticed that from the beginning. Some time in his life, he'd been taught to smile because it was expected, not because he felt it. When he laughed honestly – as he had after he'd crashed their car – he sounded slightly startled, as if he never expected to be happy.

And his smile wasn't the only deceptive thing about him. Anya knew damn well that he was hiding something about the book. It was in the guilty hunch of his body as he'd sat beside her in the car translating it, and only reading out half of what he'd deciphered.

She snorted, knowing there was a certain irony in *her* suspecting *him* of keeping secrets. But she still knew she was right. And her boss had clearly known more about Morgan than he was telling. She'd only ever been privy to half his plan – which was exactly why she was here now, with Morgan.

There was a stirring in the crowd around them as everyone moved towards the head of the mineshaft, ready to descend behind their tour guide, a dark-haired, over-made-up Polish woman. She was saying something about the age of the place – four hundred years? Eight hundred? Anya wasn't really listening – and then they were heading down, out of the daylight and into the darkness below.

Morgan hung back. Anya stayed beside him, allowing the rest of the group to overtake them. It was a long way down, stumbling uncertainly on the uneven surface of the tunnel, the white rock illuminated only by a string of lights running along the floor and the brighter lamp in the tour guide's hard hat. Anya could feel the press of all that earth and rock above, prickling the back of her neck.

Morgan seemed oblivious to it, his body thrumming with excitement beside her.

"This is it," he said. "I'm sure it is."

A hundred feet down, and they'd left the day's heat behind them, the damp in the air chilling rather than stifling. Now they were at the start of the mine workings, defunct but recreated for the benefit of tourists. Ten paces later, Anya saw the first carving – the head and shoulders of an ancient king, half hidden inside a nook in the wall. The king's beard wriggled from his chin in tentacle-like strands, and he was soot-stained and dark. But underneath the accumulated grime, Anya could see the glitter of salt crystals.

A little further on was a nativity scene, detailed and delicate. Morgan reached out a tentative finger to touch the horn of the bull leaning over Jesus's cot. "This is..." He shook his head.

"Amazing?" she suggested.

"You reckon? I think it's creepy. I keep imagining all those miners down here, spending years carving these things. Getting older and older, and never seeing the sun. Everything down here is black and white, have you noticed? They spent their whole lives in a place without any colour."

Anya flashed him a startled glance. He flushed, then shrugged. "I'm just saying, I don't think this is a very happy place."

She decided he was probably right. The air was fresh down here, circulated by some unseen ventilation mechanism, but it still smelled a little musty and over-used. And there was something else... something unclean she couldn't quite name.

They were deep underground now, the sound of their footsteps muffled as the pressure clogged up her ears until they cleared with a sharp *pop*. But now the tunnel was levelling out, and up ahead she could see a brighter light that seemed to come from a more open space. The other tourists were already there. She could hear their excited babble and see the repeated lightning strikes of camera flashes.

Then they were inside the church. The ceiling stretched high overhead, crystal chandeliers suspended from it which sprinkled the whole vast room with light. The walls were carved into a mockery of brickwork, and the floor beneath them into polished hexagonal tiles, but it was all an illusion. Everything – every inch of floor, every statue in every alcove in every wall – was made out of salt.

Beside her, Morgan breathed in sharply. He stopped only a few feet inside, frozen into immobility.

She put a tentative hand on his arm. "It's okay. Dreams are metaphorical. Whatever you saw in yours won't literally come true."

"No, it's not that." He laughed, a bitten-off sound. "This isn't the place. It's not the church I dreamed about."

Tomas and Anya used an unmarked car to carry them the hundred miles to the coast. Anya drove with a fierce frown of concentration on her face as she wove through the heavy mid-morning traffic. From the corner of his eye, Tomas saw a green road sign flash past, telling them they were fifteen kilometres from Rostock.

Tomas couldn't stop scrutinising the passengers of every car they passed, and twitching whenever he spotted a small blonde girl. It was ridiculous. The truth was, Raphael's people had a good hour's lead on them. There was every chance they were already on the water – if they'd even headed to Rostock in the first place. It was all just a toss of the dice.

Another five minutes of Anya's reckless driving and they'd hit the outskirts of the city, still the same dingy, run-down place Tomas remembered from previous visits.

"Do you know the way to the docks?" he asked her.

"I'm guessing they're next to the sea," she said curtly.

Tomas decided that meant yes. And maybe it was more by luck than judgement, but she was heading in the right direction. Drab residential neighbourhoods led to a picturesque, plaster-fronted town centre, which in turn quickly gave way to a zone of industrial warehouses, many of them boarded-up and long disused.

"This looks worse than when I was last here," Tomas said.

Anya nodded. "The trade mostly moved west after reunification. And there were racial problems a few years ago – riots."

The docks were clearly still working, though. Tomas heard a ship's horn as it entered the harbour. He could see its stacks looming over the warehouses and knew they must be close.

"Any idea how we're going to find him once we get there?" Anya asked, swerving so fast into a turn that she left a patina of rubber on the road behind them.

Tomas shrugged. "We ask around. Subtly. Tourists usually take the ferry, not a chartered ship. We have to hope a group like theirs will have drawn attention." He didn't say it, but he was sure that group must include Kate.

He didn't know what he was going to do when he saw her.

"We'll start at the harbourmaster's office, then," Anya said.

"They weren't answering their phones earlier, but there might be someone there."

She slammed on the brakes, throwing Tomas against his seatbelt, and they skidded to a halt on a patch of concrete beside a small, box-like building. The pavement and the building were the same grey colour as the sea, breaking in choppy waves fifty yards away.

Only the sky was blue, cloudless above them as they headed into the building. Inside, a narrow corridor led to a small reception area, cluttered with cheap, production-line furniture that was already starting to fray. There was a low brown desk guarding a single door. The receptionist slouched behind it, a middle-aged woman with a severe haircut and a slack face. She didn't bother to look up as they came in, though she must have heard their footsteps in the cloistered silence.

Anya slapped a hand on the desk, jerking the woman's eyes upwards. "Harbourmaster?" she snapped.

The receptionist shook her head.

"Well, where is he?"

"Holiday," the woman said grudgingly, obviously not appreciating Anya's tone. "What is it you want?"

"We need a manifest of all the ships that have left here in the last three hours."

The woman opened her mouth to protest and Anya flashed ID at her. Tomas thought about reminding her they were supposed to be keeping a low profile, but he supposed it didn't matter.

The receptionist took her time studying the ID, gaze flipping repeatedly between the embossed photo and Anya's face, as if there might be some question it wasn't the same woman. "All our computers are down," she said eventually. "It may be a few hours before I can get the data for you."

Was she lying? Impossible to know and pointless to call her on it. "There must be workers out on the docks," Tomas said. "People who've actually seen the arrivals and departures. Maybe you could call them in to talk to us."

The receptionist sighed and Anya's expression tightened.

Tomas could see she was ready to explode, and then they'd get no help from this woman at all.

"Please," he said. "We're aware it's an inconvenience, and we'll be happy to compensate you or the men for any lost work time." If she didn't respond to that, he'd head through the door behind her and see if he could roust out someone more helpful.

The receptionist must have sensed the direction of his thoughts, because she finally nodded and stood, levering herself up with two hands against the desk as if her knees were giving her trouble.

"Wait here," she said, closing the door firmly behind her.

"Unbelievable," Anya said.

And that, Tomas suddenly thought, was exactly right. Even once the woman had realised who they were, she hadn't seemed impressed – or terribly surprised. She hadn't asked why they were interested in the shipping manifest. It was as if she already knew.

Tomas shot a quick look around to make sure there were no surveillance cameras, then slipped behind the desk.

Nothing was obviously out of place. A handbag, overstuffed and broken-zipped, lay on its side underneath the chair. There was a collection of paperclips by a stack of notepads, and a switchboard with five green lights flashing. A chewed-up pen lid sat by a battered computer keyboard.

It was only as Tomas was heading back round that he noticed the desk itself and the little red mark on it. It was a thumbprint, exactly where the receptionist had rested her hand as she stood.

She didn't have bad knees. She was injured – maybe shot. And that mark was blood, Tomas could smell it now.

"She's with them," he whispered to Anya, indicating the bloodstain. "They probably left her here to make sure they weren't being followed."

Anya nodded, a red flush spreading across her cheeks. Probably angry she hadn't noticed it herself.

He motioned her to one side of the door, then put himself at the other, his back to the wall. The fake receptionist was almost certainly armed. He didn't know what had happened to the real one or to the harbourmaster, but he guessed it wasn't anything good.

He held up three fingers, then two, then one – and as he made a fist with one hand he wrenched the door open with the other.

The corridor behind was empty. There were two doors leading from it, and one of them was half open. Behind it, just sticking through the gap, he could see a motionless, trouser-covered leg. He doubted their quarry was in that room. Only the coldest sort of killer chose to hang around her victims, and she hadn't seemed the sort.

The other door then. He remained perfectly still for a moment, and in that moment of stillness, in his silent, lifeless body, he heard the woman breathing. It was a cautious whisper of breath in and out, the sound of someone trying not to be heard. She knew they were there. She was waiting for them.

Did she know what Tomas was? Probably. He signalled Anya to stay back, then flung himself at the door. There was no distance to get any momentum going, but he was a heavy man and the door was plywood on cheap brass hinges. The whole thing groaned and gave, tearing from the wall and falling into the room beneath Tomas's body.

The woman was trapped underneath him. For one brief moment, Tomas was looking into her eyes. They were wide and grey and very frightened. Then she pulled the trigger on the machine pistol in her hand.

The bullets chewed through the wood and into Tomas's body. The agony was overwhelming. It hollowed out his mind, leaving room for no other thought. The fear receded from the woman's eyes and the gun kept on firing, eating away at him.

Anya shouted his name and he knew he should be moving but he couldn't find the energy. Or maybe it was the will he was lacking. Maybe he wanted to die here, some way he couldn't come back.

Anya's shoe stamped into and past his field of vision. It thudded into the door, and he felt the wood shift beneath him. There was a sharp cry of pain and the gunfire finally stopped with a last, lethal rattle. Then Anya's hands were under his shoulders, trying to drag him away.

He hung in her arms, a limp and useless dead weight.

"Come on, Tomas," she hissed. "You've got to move – that bitch is still alive."

The woman's eyes were open. They were glazed and blank with pain, but she could start firing again at any moment. With a strangled gasp, Tomas levered himself up and away. He landed on his side and lay there, fighting to master the agony in his body while he watched Anya kick the door away. Her own gun never wavered as she kept it centred on the other woman's face.

The woman's arm was broken. Tomas could see white shards of bone poking through the skin near her wrist, and blood was already pooling beneath her. The machine pistol had dropped to the floor, out of reach of her spasming fingers. She whimpered helplessly as Anya motioned her to her feet. Anya grimaced and pressed the barrel of her gun into the sagging greyish flesh of the woman's cheek.

"Up," Anya said. "I won't ask again."

The woman groaned, her arm hanging uselessly at her side as she rose.

If she could get up, Tomas decided, so could he. He staggered as he found his feet.

Anya pressed the woman back against the wall, the muzzle of the gun against her throat now, angled so any shot would travel straight through her brain. It was a dangerous position, too easy to be disarmed if you got distracted, but the woman didn't look in much of a state to restart the fight. Her horrified gaze centred on Tomas's butchered chest as he approached. He could feel the blood trickling down his legs, soaking the fabric of his jeans. He kept a hand pressed against his stomach, where a coil of gut wanted to escape.

"Lord forgive me," the woman said. "I didn't know it was you."

"Should have got yourself something more substantial than a

Stechkin APS if you wanted to stop me." Tomas had to struggle to keep his voice even. The pain was overwhelming, but the hunger was worse. He knew what it would take to heal him.

He thought maybe the woman did too. There was a flinch in her eyes as she said, "It's too late. You'll never catch them now."

"Why don't you tell us where they are and let us decide?" Anya said.

The woman raised her chin. "I'm not afraid of you."

"Yes you are," Tomas told her. He deliberately took his hand away from his stomach, allowing the inside to sag out, and watched as the woman's eyes widened in horror.

But her voice was unyielding as she said, "Your threats are meaningless to me."

"That's right," Anya said. "Because nothing we can do is as bad as what Raphael will do when he discovers you've betrayed him."

"I would never betray him," the woman said.

Tomas took a step nearer. "But you've already failed him. You were supposed to send us away without a clue, and instead here we are, absolutely certain that Belle *did* sail away from here, and not that long ago, either. How happy do you think he'll be when he finds out?"

The woman's tongue flicked against her lips. "I did my best."

Tomas managed a genuine smile at that. "If Raphael was your primary school teacher, he might be impressed. Tell us where Belle is and we'll stop him. Then you won't have to worry about his revenge."

She laughed, an ugly sound. "Stop him? Do you really think you can?"

"Yes. If you help us."

She looked at him, at the hole in his stomach, then back into his eyes. "It's funny, how important you are, and how little you understand."

Anya frowned. "What the hell does that mean?"

"It doesn't matter," the woman said to Tomas. "Your role in this is already written. The boat is called *The Baltic Queen*, a cod fisherman. They left less than an hour ago, heading for St Petersburg. It's as much as I know." Then, before Anya could react, she grabbed her hand and squeezed her finger against the trigger.

The woman's body jerked once, trembled, and then dropped. Only a red stain remained on the wall behind her.

Daylight crept deeper into the mine than Morgan had expected. The salt crystals in the rock glittered around them long before he could see the clear circle of blue marking the exit up ahead.

"Where now?" Anya said, the first words either of them had spoken on the long walk out.

Morgan shrugged. He felt limp with disappointment. He'd been so *certain* he'd find the church here. Now he was wondering if the dream had been anything but that.

Anya touched his arm as they stepped into the open air. "The guide said there were other salt mines. Other churches. We can keep looking."

Morgan shook his head impatiently, unable to explain why he knew that if it wasn't here, it wasn't anywhere. "It was a stupid idea. We ought to be getting the diary back to Germany. Tomas must be pulling his fucking hair out by now."

There was a twitch of emotion on Anya's face, too brief for Morgan to read it. "It's as safe here as anywhere. Safer, maybe. I imagine Raphael thinks the book's in Germany with Tomas and... the BND. That's where he'll be concentrating his efforts."

"And what about the Japanese?" Morgan asked, his voice suddenly tight. He grabbed Anya around the waist, pulling her against him and back into the shadowed entrance of the mine.

A finger to her lips stifled her protest. When he was sure she knew to be quiet he took it away and pointed at the parking lot fifty paces from the mine-head, where a new coach had arrived, spilling a fresh batch of tourists onto the concrete.

"Shit!" Anya said, and he knew she'd seen what he had. The man was keeping himself hidden in the cluster of other tourists, but his face had been engraved on Morgan's memory. It only took one glimpse to be certain. It was him, the thin-faced agent from the train who'd summoned the spirit of his dead sister.

"How the hell did he find us?" Morgan hissed.

"I've got no idea. We should have been safe underground."

"Why?"

She pulled him a little further into the mineshaft as the man's eyes swept the entrance. "Spirits can't travel through the earth, it's impervious to them. Why do you think we bury our dead? And the salt makes doubly certain."

Morgan instinctively clutched a hand to his stomach, where the diary was tucked under the waistband of his jeans. But the crushing fear he felt wasn't at the thought of losing it. He remembered his sister's eyes, venomous with hate as she stared at him through the mirror. And he remembered the feel of her small fingers on his foot, pulling him beneath the waters of the Danube. He couldn't face her again.

"Give me your phone," he said.

Anya kept staring fixedly at the crowd of tourists by the bus. The tour guide was already gathering them together. They'd be heading for the mineshaft any minute.

"The phone!" Morgan snapped. "We need back-up."

Anya shook her head. "They'd never get here in time."

"Got a better suggestion? Just give me the fucking phone, Anya!"

"No," she said quietly. "I can't do that."

Morgan reached out to grab her, but his fingers stuttered to a halt in the air. She was holding a small black Beretta in her right hand, and she was pointing it at him.

CHAPTER FOURTEEN

Morgan kept a hand against the wall as he backed into the mine, the light fading in front of him as he went deeper. Anya held the Beretta centred on his chest. She remained a careful ten paces apart, slowing every time he did. She was a pro and she knew what she was doing. Rushing her was too risky, too likely to get him shot.

"You're working for Raphael," Morgan said, but Anya shook her head. She waved the gun sideways, a signal to get moving, and Morgan speeded up. He knew she could hear the same thing he did: voices at the mouth of the tunnel. The latest tour group was about to descend.

"I could have killed you while you slept if all I wanted was the book. Think, Morgan."

She was right. She couldn't be with Raphael, it didn't make sense. And she didn't seem to be with the Japanese either. "So you want it for yourself."

"Stop," she said. "Go left."

They'd reached a fork in the tunnel, the left-hand turning leading away from the route they'd followed earlier. A 'no entry' sign strung on a metal chain blocked the way, but Morgan stepped over it easily.

"We'll get lost," Morgan said after they'd turned left twice more, and then right.

"Maybe," Anya said, "but so will they."

It was far darker here, the electronic lighting long gone, replaced by the weak illumination of Anya's torch. It swept across a floor that was rough and uneven, beam diffused by the choking cloud of rock dust churned up by their feet. The dust coated Morgan's throat and nostrils, leaving behind the thirsty tang of salt as it dissolved.

He stopped so abruptly that Anya almost stepped within reach before pulling quickly back. She centred the gun's barrel on his chest again, but he ignored it. It occurred to him for the first time that she didn't have a plan. She hadn't expected the Japanese agents to find them and now she had no idea what to do. And something else occurred to him too.

"Why didn't you let me phone Tomas?" he said. "Does he know you're a traitor? But why didn't he tell me before?"

Anya laughed, high and strained. "You want to know why I couldn't let you speak to anyone in Germany? Because there's a chance you'd have spoken to Anya."

Morgan worked the sentence over twice in his mind, but it still came out the same. "So... you're *not* Anya." He studied her face in the reflected glow of her torch, but it still looked exactly like her. And before, when they'd travelled in the car together – no disguise could be that good.

"I *am* Anya," she said. "I'm Anya too."

"You're her twin?" That was possible, he supposed. It explained why she'd behaved so differently since leaving the train. Smiling where previously she'd always been so dour, sympathetic rather than accusing. Except no one called a pair of twins the same name. "No, that's not what you mean, is it?

He could see the bunch of tensed shoulders beneath her t-shirt. "Your partner's a man who died twenty years ago. You're working with a forty-year-old girl of eleven with a demon trapped inside her. What do you think I mean?"

"Exactly what you say. There are two of you, and you're both Anya."

"Yes. We're two halves of a whole person."

"The other half, the other Anya, does she know?"

She shook her head.

"And has it always been that way? Were you born like this?"

She looked amused. "Morgan, if two babies came out, that *would* make us twins."

He punched the wall in a sudden flare of rage. "Don't act like I'm supposed to know this shit! Three days ago I though the world was a totally normal place!"

His voice reverberated in the long tunnels. When the echoes died they left behind the shuffling sound of footsteps, somewhere behind Anya.

Without needing to be asked, Morgan started walking again, almost running. They were well away from the tourist route now. Those footsteps could only be the American man and his Japanese assassins. Morgan had lost count of the turnings about ten minutes ago. He had no idea where they were, only that they were deep in the mine, maybe deeper than they'd been on the first trip down.

Anya was beside him now, Beretta loose in her hand. Careless, but maybe she knew he had no intention of taking it from her. He didn't want to risk stopping the flow of information.

"I'm sorry," she said. "It's probably my fault Richard and his people have found us."

Morgan froze a moment, then kept on walking. "Richard's the man from the train, right? And you know his name because...?"

"I used to work with him."

Morgan flicked her a quick glance, but her expression gave nothing away. "When did you stop?"

"Oh, about thirty hours ago."

Paradoxically, the admission relaxed Morgan. It would have been far easier to lie. "So what changed?"

"You did."

"My charm and good looks won you over?"

"Actually, your brains."

"That's a first." He took a moment to puzzle it out. "OK, you want the diary. You thought you needed what's his name –

Richard – to translate it. And when you realised I could do it..."

"Yes, that pretty much covers it."

"Still doesn't explain what you are. Why there are two of you."

"The Japanese made me."

"*Made* you?"

"They figured out a way to divide a person – to split a personality in two. It's simpler than you might think, though highly exothermic."

He shook his head, baffled.

"Magic is no different from chemistry, Morgan. Nothing is ever destroyed, only transformed. Splitting a personality is like splitting an atom: the two halves are less than the whole. Whatever it is that's lost comes out as heat, a whole lot of it. The explosion when they did it was the size of a small tactical nuke."

"But why? What would be the point of doing it? If you want more people, just make them the old-fashioned way."

"Because of the Ragnarok artefacts."

"Yeah, of course. Because that's all anybody cares about." His teeth were chattering. They were so deep in the mine it was like they'd walked into winter. Icy water dripped from the ceiling into his short hair, drying slowly to leave it stiff with salt.

Anya's hair looked blood-red in the low light, hanging in lank strands around her cheeks. "The Japanese are obsessed with them, with getting hold of them. It isn't just the Japanese, though. Pretty much every country wants them. When Nicholson led the Hermetic Division, tracking down the artefacts was its primary mission. And he got further than anyone else – rumour has it he'd located all three, though that was never confirmed."

"And you're hoping his diary will tell you where they are." Morgan was glad he hadn't told her everything his father wrote.

She nodded. "The Japanese wanted the artefacts and they wanted the diary, and they knew the BND were closing in on both. They tried to turn some of the German agents, but they didn't get anywhere with anyone high enough to be useful."

"So instead of turning you, they copied you." Morgan took a moment to absorb that. It made a demented sort of sense. "They sent the original back, and kept the copy to work for them."

Anya's eyes flared. "There's no copy, no original. We're both Anya. But yes, that's right. I am – was – the BND's top agent assigned to search for the artefacts. When they made me the Japanese got access to all my knowledge – and a chance to infiltrate the German network, too. If I go in to BND headquarters when the other half of me isn't there, or talk to any of her sources, who'd ever suspect I wasn't who I said I was?"

She'd drawn a little ahead of him, but now she suddenly stopped. A moment later Morgan saw why. The tunnel was a dead end, the way ahead blocked by a stout wooden gate fastened with a padlock. Anya shrugged and turned round.

Morgan put a hand on her arm, stilling her. In the silence that followed he could hear their breathing, Anya's a little faster than his, both of them wheezing slightly with all the dust. And beyond that, quite clearly, the sound of approaching footsteps.

The Baltic was never calm, not even in summer. The surface of the water was broken by choppy little waves which juddered the small boat from side to side. Tomas had never been a good sailor, and he was discovering that his dead body was still quite capable of feeling that it wanted to puke.

The coast guards Anya had co-opted were taking care of the steering, leaving Tomas nothing to do but stare over the water. There was no sign of their quarry yet, but theirs was the faster vessel. And thanks to the information Raphael's agent had given them, they'd been able to lock onto the other boat's transponder signal. When they'd set out an hour ago, they'd been twenty miles behind. Now they were only five and closing fast.

Thinking about Raphael's agent brought a different sensation to Tomas's stomach, a hunger profound enough to overpower the nausea. Anya had left him alone in the room with the agent's corpse while she'd gone to find them a boat. He knew why.

He knew what she'd expected him to do. And god knows he'd wanted to.

And yet he hadn't. Every time he imagined eating, he pictured Kate watching him. He saw the horror in her eyes at the monster he'd become and his hunger twisted into self-disgust.

He could see Anya shooting glances at him. While she was out of the room he'd torn strips from the dead woman's clothing to bandage the terrible wound in his gut, unhealed because he hadn't fed. Then he'd hidden it beneath a fresh t-shirt pilfered from one of the woman's victims. But the gnawing pain of it left him weak, so that he staggered with every shift of the boat. He had to repress a groan as they lurched to starboard, jarring him onto his right foot and loosening something in his belly he was glad he couldn't see.

"They're likely to be heavily armed," Anya said, watching the distant horizon. The day was hot but overcast and the grey light that filtered through the clouds made her face look as lifeless as his.

He nodded. "Catching them's only the start of the battle."

"If they've got Belle with them, they can use her as a hostage. Threaten her and they've got us over a barrel."

"Maybe. But if they kill her they lose the only bargaining chip they've got, and they know it." He also wanted to believe that Kate wasn't capable of killing a child, but he wasn't sure enough to say it.

Anya's eyes flicked to him, narrowed under brows squeezed together with tension. "It's a very big risk to take with a little girl's life."

"You think I don't know it?" Tomas found he was too weary to be angry. "We have to try. Once Raphael finds out we don't have the diary, she'll be shark meat anyway."

"Morgan said he was bringing it back. If you trust him, of course." It was clear she didn't.

He had a sudden memory of Morgan smiling one of his rare smiles. Tomas *did* trust him, he always had. Maybe it was because Morgan was untainted by a past which was turning out to be so much more complicated than Tomas had anticipated. But they hadn't heard from him all day, and Tomas had to fight not to imagine the worst.

He turned away from Anya as one of the coast guards rushed out of the boat's small cabin, excitement written on his coarse face. "We've got them hull-up on the horizon!"

The light was too diffuse to see anything clearly, but Tomas thought he could make out a blur that might have been another boat. It looked big, considerably larger than theirs.

"How long till we catch them?" Anya asked.

The coast guard leaned forward, as if he could personally speed the chase. "Half hour, maybe an hour if they see us and put on some speed. They're only making about twelve knots at present, trying not to attract too much attention."

"Do you think they've seen us?" Tomas asked.

The man shrugged, but Anya said, "Their agent was probably supposed to report in at regular intervals. When she didn't... We have to reckon they're expecting us."

Tomas nodded as he kept his eyes on the shape ahead, now recognisably a boat.

Half an hour, maybe an hour, until he saw Kate again.

Morgan hit the padlock with the largest rock he could find. It didn't break, just rang loudly enough to let everyone in a five-hundred-yard radius know they were there.

"Great," Anya said. "So much for stealth."

"It's not like we'd be able to sneak past them," Morgan snapped. "There's only one way out, and they're blocking it. Give me the gun."

She rolled her eyes at him, then lifted the Beretta and shot out the lock herself.

"Jesus!" Morgan jumped away from the shards of shattered metal. "Give a man some warning."

Anya shoved the door with her shoulder, smirking.

As soon as it was open, Morgan pushed past her and ran down

the short tunnel beyond, stooping beneath its low ceiling. At the very end, a stalactite he hadn't seen grazed his forehead. A bead of blood dropped into his eye, but he barely registered it.

The tunnel opened into a far wider area – a cavern that had been carved into another church. The torchlight picked out the glitter of salt crystals everywhere inside.

Anya saw his expression immediately. She stood beside him, studying the high vaulted ceiling, the rotting remains of wooden pews. "Is this it? Is this the one you saw?"

Morgan nodded, throat too tight to speak. He held out his hand, and after a moment's hesitation she put the torch in it. Its light preceded him in a narrow cone as he walked deeper inside. This was smaller than the place the tourist guide had taken them, more of a chapel than a church. But everything in it was just as he'd dreamed.

The walls were lined with statues, as tall as him. Torchlight picked out the nearest, and he couldn't stop himself letting out a cry of alarm. The face was hideous, nose melting into its mouth, and one eye dragged halfway down its cheek.

"The water came in through here," Anya said, a whisper that echoed sibilantly from the other side of the room. "Look."

Morgan swept the beam of the torch across the far wall. Anya was right. It had caved in, the rock curving down in a gentle arc from floor to ceiling where the first gush of water must have come, shallow runnels scoring the soft white floor as it spread. He had a sudden flash of *The Wizard of Oz* – the Wicked Witch melting as she died. He knew why this place made him think of it. There was something evil and unnatural here too.

He studied the wall a moment longer, then walked to the altar in the centre of the room.

At first he assumed the thing lying on it was another statue, smaller than the rest. Even when he was right next to it, he still thought it was man-made, a facsimile of the thing it seemed to be. It was only as he reached out and touched the sharp curve of its ribs and felt bone rather than rock that he knew the skeleton was real.

The skull was thrown back on the jigsaw bones of its neck, as if it had died screaming. The knife which had killed it was still buried where its heart had once been, blade heavy with rust. Every bone glittered in the torchlight, coated in a thin layer of salt. There was a whisper-thin gold chain around its neck. The unblemished crucifix lay against its breastbone.

The skeleton was tiny. The child couldn't have been more than eight years old when it died.

"Christ," Anya said beside him, her breath the only warmth in the place. "What happened here?"

"I don't know." But that wasn't entirely true. Morgan remembered his dream, the figure bending over the altar, the little girl on it. On the back wall of the church, an ornate silver cross still hung. There was something wrong with it, and it took him a second to figure out what. It was upside down.

Anya was on her knees in front of the altar. Morgan thought she was praying, then saw that she was brushing her fingers over the ground. "Look," she said.

Morgan knelt beside her. The white rock of the floor was streaked with something darker. It was blood, though in this light it looked black. Close up the marks seemed random, but when he stepped back he saw the pattern radiating from the altar: a pentagram, and around that other symbols he didn't know.

"I think someone held a black mass here," Anya said.

"That's... summoning the devil, isn't it?"

"Or communing with him."

"Is that – is it the sort of thing the Hermetic Division does?"

She shook her head. "Your people and mine researched those rituals, but we never used them. Most of the magics we work with are outside of Christianity, part of an older faith. This stuff..." Her voice wavered for a moment as she looked around. "This is *anti-*Christian. Pagan beliefs are a denial of the One God. This is a rejection of Him."

Morgan could hear Raphael very clearly, saying that he and Nicholson had once been friends. If Morgan's dream had lasted longer, would he have seen his father here too? "It's *deliberate* evil," he said.

"Yes." She closed her eyes a moment, seeming to steady herself. When she opened them again they were less shocked and more determined. "No wonder this place isn't on the tourist route. But why were you drawn here?"

He'd opened his mouth to reply when he heard the footsteps behind him – and it was only then he remembered they were being pursued.

He spun to face the entrance a moment before Anya. But she was the one with the gun, and by the time she brought it to bear, four were already trained on them. The newcomers had lanterns, and in their brighter light the desecration of the church was even plainer to see. One of the men gasped, and another backed away. Morgan didn't recognise any of them, but all four were Japanese and there was no doubt who they were working for.

The fifth man, the one Anya had called Richard, stepped forward. He holstered his own gun as he approached, holding his hands up in a peaceable gesture undercut by the ordnance still on display behind him. His thin face looked drawn. "You led us a merry chase," he said. "Hello again, Anya."

Morgan almost smiled at the guilty expression on her face. "Richard."

"My colleagues thought I was being unnecessarily cynical, planting that tracking device on you. Thanks for proving them wrong."

Anya shrugged. "You split me in two, and you sent the half which remembered how to feel loyalty back to the BND. What did you expect me to do?"

A network of wrinkles seamed Richard's forehead as he frowned. "The diary won't do you any good. It's a terrible thing. Why do you think I hid it for so long?"

Morgan shifted, drawing Richard's eyes to him. "*You* hid it?"

"Nicholson gave it to me for safekeeping. That's one of the faults of the fanatic – they can't believe anyone would fail to find their cause as compelling as they do."

There was something in his expression when he said Nicholson's name, the way he looked only at Morgan. Morgan had noticed it before, on the train. It was as if Richard knew the relationship between them.

"Why did he give it to you?" Morgan asked. "What were you supposed to do with it?"

Richard studied him intently. "You know, you're not what I expected. I thought... It doesn't matter."

"Tell me about the book," Morgan said, firmer this time. "I have to know."

"Yeah, I think maybe you do. The diary was meant for Raphael – it really is his. He was in Russia when Nicholson died, and that isn't the kind of thing you send through the post. That book... I didn't truly realise what it was until I tried to destroy it. I threw it in a fire hot enough to melt metal, and the flames didn't even singe it. Knives won't touch it. It's indestructible. In the end, all I could do was hide it in a deep vault and pray. But I knew that wouldn't hold it forever. The book *wanted* to be found, and six months ago, it finally was.

"Understand this: Nicholson put more than his words into that book. He poured every ounce of power and magic he had into its pages. That's why he couldn't send it to Raphael until after he'd hung himself. It was born out of his death. Just like you, Morgan."

The words jolted like electricity up Morgan's spine. Richard *did* know. Morgan was both terrified and exhilarated. He could hardly bear to hear the things this man was telling him – but he wanted to know them all the same.

"What's the book *for*?" Morgan asked. "Why does Raphael want it so badly?"

Anya stepped forward suddenly, reaching out to grip Richard's arm. Behind him, four fingers twitched on four triggers, but she didn't seem to notice. "It's the artefacts, isn't it – the Ragnarok artefacts? Their location is hidden somewhere in the book."

Richard placed his own hand on top of hers, an almost comforting gesture. "Is that what you've been told? In a way, you're right – but not the way you think. The artefacts were never something that could be found. They have to be created."

Anya looked almost desperate, and Morgan realised that he hadn't had the chance to ask her why she wanted the book. "Then tell me how to create them!" she said.

Morgan thought Richard would. He wanted them to know, Morgan could see it in his face. That was why he'd come here, to tell Morgan exactly this. Their eyes caught and held, and Morgan's breath stuck in his throat.

Then Richard's eyes flicked aside, and he saw the skeleton on the altar. "You idiot!" he said to Morgan, suddenly furious. "What were you thinking, bringing us here?"

As if in answer, a sound began to grow around them, a low, growling rumble. It seemed to be coming from everywhere – the walls, the ceiling, the rock beneath their feet.

For a disoriented moment, Morgan thought that he was shaking. Then, like an optical illusion snapping into focus, he saw that it was the world which was moving, not him. The whole church was juddering in violent, uneven bursts. Salt shook from the ceilings and walls in a bitter snowfall. And as Morgan watched, horrified, the skeleton on the altar twitched and started to rise.

When they were half a mile away, the other boat caught sight of them. Tomas saw its wake suddenly froth a creamy white as the engine gunned and it began to draw away again.

"Hold on!" the captain shouted from his cabin.

He gave them only a second to grab the railing that circled the open deck, and then their own engine growled and the distance began to close. Tomas could see brown ovals of faces, staring back at them from the deck of the boat ahead.

"What kind of weapons do you see?" Anya asked.

"Can't make out anything from this distance," Tomas told her. "There's more of them, though. They're bound to outgun us."

"Still, we've got you." But the look she shot him was doubtful. He'd caught a glimpse of himself reflected in the cabin's window, and he knew that he was corpse pale, finally looking like exactly what he was.

"They know about me," he said. "They'll be prepared."

"And no sign of Belle..."

"They'll have her below decks, in the living quarters."

They'd be in range soon. Tomas had drawn the Beretta the BND had supplied him, but he couldn't risk firing till he had a clearer target. A stray bullet could penetrate the hull and anyone inside it. A stray bullet could hit Kate.

For the first time, Tomas admitted to himself that talking to her had become his main priority. Nicholson had faked Kate's death. Kate's death had led Tomas to embrace his own. And when she'd learned of that, Kate had gone to work for Raphael. Nicholson and Raphael must have been working together all along. It was the only explanation that made sense – and Tomas hadn't had a clue. The thought that his own naivety had led to this was unbearable. How many other people were going to pay for his stupidity? No more, he promised himself. Not one more.

He could see the faces on the other boat now, staring at him down the barrels of their guns. The woman wasn't Kate. Too young, her features too sharp.

"I know her!" Anya said. The was a discordant note in her voice, out of tune with her earlier mood.

The boat ahead veered suddenly to port, and theirs followed a second after, scything a broad sheet of water to splash back into the grey ocean. Anya staggered and Tomas did too, putting an arm around her waist to steady them both. Her body felt light and thin in his arms, as if there were less of her than there should be.

He grabbed her hands and pushed them against the railing, clinging onto it himself as the boat swerved again, a tighter arc this time that took them back into the choppy waters of their own wake. "How do you know her?" he shouted above the splash of the waves and the roar of the engine. "Who is she?"

Anya's throat worked as she swallowed. "It's the girl from the park in Budapest. The one who... the one who killed Karamov."

The boat was veering every few seconds, as if they were following some invisible slalom course. Tomas dropped to his knees to steady himself and peered through the railing at their quarry. The girl didn't look like anything, barely old enough to be out of school. As he watched, she raised her right hand.

Tomas ducked, dragging Anya down beside him. He expected to hear the whine of a bullet or the blast of its impact. But the noise he heard was longer and shriller.

"Not again," Anya whispered. The skin of her face looked as white and fine as copy paper.

"What does it mean?" Tomas asked, though he had a horrible suspicion. He'd seen what was left of Karamov after the dogs had finished with him.

Anya pushed herself to her feet without replying. She fired her gun twice before Tomas could prevent it. The smell of gunpowder briefly overpowered the briny tang of the ocean.

Tomas grabbed her arm before she could let off a third shot. Over on the other boat, he could see milling confusion. They hadn't expected to be fired on for the same reason Tomas hadn't fired: the danger to Belle. He thought he saw one of them on the deck, clutching an injured arm. But it wasn't the girl. She smiled as she took the whistle out of her mouth.

"Oh god," Anya moaned. "It's too late."

Tomas shook her, hard. "Listen to me – we're faster than them. We need to get alongside and get on board. Then whatever she's summoned will have to get through them to get to us."

"Too late," Anya said again, and for a moment Tomas thought terror had locked her into a fugue state.

Then he followed her gaze through the ship's rail, to the open sea beyond.

All around the boat, the water was churning. For a moment he thought they'd hit a reef, that the white froth was just water breaking over hidden rock. Then he saw that there were bodies inside the foam. Thousands of them, writhing beneath the surface, everywhere he looked.

CHAPTER FIFTEEN

Morgan could feel the earth shaking. They were hundreds of feet underground. If the roof caved in they'd die here, and no one would ever find their bodies.

Anya fell to her knees beside him, toppled by the violent convulsions. Behind her, the Japanese agents were scrabbling on the ground for the guns they'd dropped. Richard grabbed Morgan's shoulder, fingers clawing hard enough to leave bruises.

Morgan didn't remember making the decision to move, but somehow he was standing next to the altar, close enough to touch the body rising from it. It *was* a body now. As cracks appeared in the floor beneath it, flesh grew to cover the bare bones. He saw the white threads of nerve fibres crawling across the red meat of muscles and round globular yellow pockets of fat. The skin came last, tightening to draw everything else within it.

Richard was still clinging to him when Morgan turned and punched him, then grabbed his shoulders and shook. "You're doing this!" he yelled. "Stop it!"

"I can't. I can't. It's too strong." Richard's voice was breathy with fear. "She's wanted to be free for so long. I can open the door but I can't close it. I told you that. I warned you!" Even as Morgan shook him, his eyes remained fixed on the altar and the unspeakable resurrection that was happening there.

When the process had finished, the little girl was naked, but whole. She was petite and blonde with improbably soft white skin. The gold crucifix glittered against the hollow at the base of her neck.

She turned her face towards Morgan, and he saw that her eyes were still empty black sockets. He flinched in horror as they slowly grew back to a bright, crystalline blue.

"It's you," she said. "I saw you watching me as I died." She wasn't speaking English, but somehow he understood her.

He backed away. "I didn't do it. I wasn't here."

"But you're here now." And when the last word left her mouth, everything changed.

The shaking stopped. The church was clean and bright, black candles burning in the sconces lining the walls. In their light, Morgan saw that Richard was still beside him, but everyone else had disappeared. There were only two other people in the church: the little girl trussed to the altar, and Raphael.

Raphael was dressed in a priest's red vestments. His hair was nut-brown and his face was round-cheeked and unlined. He couldn't have been much older than Morgan. He was holding the same knife that Morgan had seen buried in the skeleton's chest.

Morgan staggered forward two steps and reached out to wrench the knife from Raphael's hand.

There was no contact. His arm drifted through the other man's, as insubstantial as mist.

"You can't," Richard said. "Here, we're the ghosts. It's all already happened."

Raphael didn't acknowledge their presence, gazing through them as if they didn't exist. But Morgan saw the little girl's eyes tracking the movement of his arm. She could see them. Maybe the approach of death had opened a window the living couldn't usually see through.

"Help me!" she screamed.

Raphael seemed to think she was talking to him. "It's your own fault, darling," he said. "You shouldn't have told your parents the things we did together. I said there'd be consequences if you blabbed."

She was shaking and terrified, but the look she shot him was almost defiant. "I couldn't help it! They saw the blood on my dress."

"But you told them I forced you, when you know that isn't true. It was a nasty lie, and God hates liars. He sends them all to Hell." Raphael's voice was horribly reasonable. Morgan felt his hands twitching towards the other man's throat, desperate to silence him.

"Don't pretend you didn't want it," Raphael said. "Why did you dress that way? Why did you smile at me? You knew you were leading me on." His hand reached down to touch her between her legs, his face rapt with remembered pleasure. Morgan had to look away, the gorge rising in his throat.

The little girl whimpered and Raphael seemed to come back to himself. "It's too late now. They've roused all the miners against me, and the barricade across the door won't last long. I've got no choice, I have to do this. He told me if I did, he'd save me. And since it's the only form of salvation currently available, I'm planning to take it." On the final word, he raised the knife high.

Morgan's eyes flinched shut – and when he opened them again, Raphael was gone and the church was collapsing around him.

"Did you see?" the little girl asked, sitting on the altar where she died.

"Yes," Morgan said. "I was there."

"When the mass was finished, the mine collapsed – but not on him. I saw my father and mother crushed beneath the rocks. My family survived four years of war, and he killed them all."

"I'm sorry," Morgan whispered.

"He wasn't," she said. "The next day the Red Army came. He gave them information and they gave him his life. They took him away with them, and they never made him pay for what he did."

"I will," Morgan said. "I'll make him pay. I promise."

He could hear screaming behind him. He thought it might be Anya, but when he looked around he saw that it was one of Richard's men, pinned beneath a fallen statue. The deformed stone face was pressed against his, which panic had twisted into an expression almost as hideous. As Morgan watched, another of the men ran to help him. He pulled on his arm and the trapped man screamed.

Morgan realised someone was pulling on his own arm. It was Anya, face drawn with shock. "We have to get out!" she shouted. "This whole place is coming down!" Her eyes swept through the little blonde girl sitting on the altar, and he realised for the first time that Anya couldn't see her.

"Come on!" she screamed, dragging on his arm.

He pulled back, heels digging into the soft salt rock of the floor. He wasn't finished here, and he knew it.

"Tell me your name," he said to the little girl.

She smiled, as if he'd finally got something right. "I'm Marya." Blunt little fingers fiddled at the back of her neck, and then the gold crucifix was in her hand. She held it out to Morgan.

He stared at it. His flesh cringed at the thought of touching hers.

"Take it," she said. "To remember your promise."

He held out his hand, cupped beneath hers. She tipped her fingers and the little cross dropped into his palm.

It burned fiercely. Morgan scrabbled at the pocket of his jeans with his other hand, dropping the crucifix inside as soon as he could. He expected the sensation to be a phantasm, like the girl herself, but when he looked at his right palm it was burned an angry red. He looked back up at Marya, meaning to ask what it meant.

She was gone. Only her skeleton remained, lying pinned to the altar where she'd died.

"Morgan!" Anya shouted. She'd released his arm but remained a few paces away, looking back at him. He could tell she was on the cusp of running. If he didn't follow her now, she'd leave him behind. She wouldn't stay just to die beside him.

And if they stayed, they *would* die. Morgan could see that now. The exit from the church was already choked with rocks, more tumbling down as he watched. Soon it would be blocked entirely.

He took one last look at the altar and the pathetic skeleton huddled on it, then turned and ran.

His feet kicked something solid that rang metallically as it clattered along the floor. A gun. One of the Japanese agents had dropped it. Morgan stooped to pick it up, losing precious seconds in his flight.

He vaguely registered that Richard was running beside him. The other man was panting in wheezing gasps, older and less fit than Morgan. A second later, and still two feet from the door, he stumbled to his knees.

If Morgan had had time to think about it, he would have left him. But instinct took over. He tucked the gun into the waistband of his jeans, hooked an arm round Richard's back and heaved him to his feet.

Richard let out a grunt that might have been gratitude or simply pain. He stumbled a few steps forward, then tripped and would have fallen to his knees again if Morgan hadn't wrenched him up at the cost of a sharp pain in his own back. Richard's ankle was probably sprained, maybe broken. He wasn't the person you wanted with you when you were trying to escape a collapsing mine.

But no one else would help him. There was no sign of the other Japanese agents. Morgan wasn't sure if they'd escaped when the collapse began, or lay crushed beneath one of the growing heaps of rock. Anya was already at the steep pile of scree that now filled the exit.

She paused at the top, reaching back a hand to help drag Morgan over. The rough stone tore through the thin material of his t-shirt and grated the skin beneath. When he looked down, he saw a dark face leering back at him. He cringed back before he realised it was one of the statues which had once lined the walls. Its beard had scraped his skin. Now it was smeared with blood, as if the statue had been chewing on his flesh.

Morgan blinked his eyes shut as a spear-sharp stalactite fell from the ceiling and impaled the debris inches from his nose. When he looked behind him he saw that the altar was already hidden beneath a heap of rock, Marya's body buried at last. Another few seconds and there would be nothing left of the church.

Richard was almost a dead weight beneath Morgan's arm. Morgan set his teeth in a grimace of effort and dragged him doggedly on. The gap at the top of the rock pile was barely shoulder-width now – and narrowing fast. If Morgan wedged himself in he could be stuck for good. A cold sweat stood out on his skin. He'd always hated confined spaces. They reminded him of those terrible moments in the dark water of the lake, when his sister had died and he thought he might too.

"We have to chance it," Richard gasped. He gave Morgan a weak shove towards the gap.

Morgan gulped in a lungful of air, then used his elbows to drag himself in. He had to drop Richard's arm, but he could feel a warm body pressed against his own as he squeezed further into the rock. The Japanese agents' lanterns were long-destroyed and Anya had taken the torch with her. Within seconds Morgan was totally blind, and he felt a moment of sick panic. What if he was going the wrong way, sideways or even backwards? Would he ever find his way out?

"Calm down," Richard hissed, and Morgan realised that his breath was coming in desperate ragged pants. "We're nearly there, I can see light ahead of us."

When he opened his eyes, so could Morgan. The hope of an end gave him extra strength, though the gap was so narrow he could do little beyond clawing himself forward with his fingernails. Grains of rock stuck beneath them and two or three tore off, salt stinging sharply in the wounds.

Five agonising minutes later he was through, tumbling down the shallow incline that led to the mine's floor. Richard fell a moment later. His shoulder thumped into Morgan's ribs as he landed.

Anya knelt beside them, putting a testing hand against Morgan's throat as if she was afraid he might have died. He gently moved it aside and lay on his back, getting his breath under control and enjoying being alive.

After a minute or less he was breathing normally, but the tunnel was no quieter than when he'd arrived. The same low grumble he'd heard in the church was audible here too.

"Shit," he said, pushing himself wearily to his feet.

"It might just be the final collapse inside," Anya said, though there wasn't much conviction in her voice. A moment later it was clear the sound was growing louder. And then the first flecks of rock began to drift down.

"We've got to get out!" Morgan said.

No one argued. The tunnel was barely wide enough for two people to walk abreast. It wouldn't take much to block it completely. It would be far too easy to get trapped here.

Morgan reached out to grasp Richard's arm again, but the other man shrugged him off.

"I'm okay, you'll slow us both down."

That was fine by Morgan. His legs felt like lead, but he forced them to drag him forward, one painful step at a time. Anya was behind him and Richard ahead, each locked in their own grim battle for survival.

At the first junction Richard turned left. Morgan wasn't sure if he really knew the way, but he followed anyway. So did the rumble of falling rock.

No matter how fast they ran, the sound kept pace, and with it needle-sharp splinters of rock and the constant threat of much worse. As Morgan watched, horrified, one black zigzag crack broadened and spread in the floor beneath his feet.

And something else was following them. At first, the sound was buried beneath the deeper rumble of falling rock. But slowly it grew louder, until it couldn't be mistaken for anything but human screams. And then Morgan could see them.

They were running alongside him, ahead and behind. Their clothes were sturdy and dark, faces streaked with sweat and rock dust. Miners, Morgan guessed. They were shouting in a language he didn't understand. But again and again he heard the name "Marya". And then one of the crowd ran *through* him, and he finally knew who they were.

Of course the little girl wouldn't be the only spirit in these caves. Many more people had died here, thanks to Raphael.

"Richard!" Morgan gasped, stumbling to a halt.

"I can see them," the other man said through gritted teeth, still running.

And as he ran, the ghosts ran with him. The ghosts, and the destruction that Morgan could now see they brought with them. The last insubstantial figure marked the outer perimeter of the damage.

Anya pushed against him, trying to get him moving again. He used his left hand to block her. With his right the pulled the gun from the waistband of his jeans.

"Stop! he shouted.

Richard didn't seem to hear him and he was drawing further ahead. Morgan grabbed Anya and began to run after him.

With the other man's injured ankle it didn't take long to catch up. Morgan barrelled past him, dragging Anya along with him. Then he stopped, blocking the path ahead, and raised his gun.

Richard almost ran into it before he realised it was there.

He looked up, bemused. "For god's sake, what?" The ghosts were crowded close around him, and his hair sparkled with the silver fall of salt from above.

"Back away," Morgan said.

"Is this really –"

"Back away!"

Richard frowned and took two steps back, then another two when Morgan fired a shot into the rock at his feet. He held up his hands. "Listen, whatever this is, can't it wait till we're out of here?"

"You're not getting out," Morgan said.

"Morgan." Anya rested a hand against his gun arm. "He's right – we can deal with this later."

He grabbed her hand and used it to pull her back another ten paces, till Richard was at one end of the stretch of tunnel and he and Anya at the other. "There won't be a later if he comes with us," he said. "Look."

She frowned and he remembered that she couldn't see what he and Richard could. The ghosts clustered tight around the other man were invisible to her.

"It's him," Morgan said. "He's causing it."

"Don't be ridiculous – why would he do that?"

"He can't help it." He met Richard's eyes over the distance separating them. "Can you?"

Richard looked at the rock, cracked and splintering above him. At the ghosts, clustered to either side. Then he looked back at Morgan and smiled sadly. "No, it appears I can't."

"I'm sorry," Morgan said. He meant it.

The other man nodded. Then he staggered, as the floor shook beneath his feet. Where Morgan and Anya stood, it was motionless. He saw her eyes widen as she finally began to understand.

"Come on," Morgan said, turning away from the other man. "We can get out of here now."

"Wait!" Richard shouted.

Morgan didn't.

"Morgan!"

He ran another few steps, but his pace slowly dragged to a halt. He couldn't condemn the other man to death and refuse to even watch it.

Richard smiled when Morgan turned back to him. His face was tight and chalky with pain, and Morgan could see a deep gash in his cheek where a rock must have struck him, but he looked almost peaceful. "Do you know why there's evil in the world?" he said.

Morgan shook his head.

"Because God gave us a choice. Remember that, Morgan. You always have a choice."

Morgan would have liked to deny it. He wanted to say that he didn't, that it was all of them die or just Richard. But a choice between two terrible options was still that.

He opened his mouth to explain, and his words were drowned in the rending sound of stone tearing away from its foundations.

Richard didn't scream, just let out a choked gasp as the rocks hit him. Then he was lost to Morgan's sight, hidden behind a cloud of dust and salt.

Tomas couldn't believe the sea held so much life. It was seething with it, brown and green and silver bodies boiling to the surface in a mass of slick wet flesh.

Anya crouched on the deck, shaking with fear.

"They can't hurt us!" Tomas shouted, but he wasn't so sure.

He'd forgotten how *big* the things that lived in the deep ocean grew. And there were so many of them, their bodies were roiling above the surface. They'd drown in air within a few minutes, but it wasn't stopping them. Tomas felt the first pin-sharp bite of teeth in his foot as a wave of the creatures washed over the sides to slither onto the deck.

Tomas stamped on the soft body, killing it instantly. Anya was doing the same, letting out little, desperate gasps every time her foot came down. The deck was red with blood, but there were always more of them.

One leapt up in front of Tomas, jaws snapping shut around his knee. He swore and prised it off, leaving its teeth buried in his flesh. After that, he gave up stamping and started scooping the creatures up, flinging them over the side in great armfuls. Anya stooped to do the same, and he shouted at her to stop. He could take the damage, but she couldn't. Every armful left him with bleeding bite marks in his arms and chest, tearing into muscle and deep beyond where his chest wound still gaped open.

He bent down to gather another armful, and the boat veered sharply to starboard, staggering him. Another swerve back to port and this time it tumbled him to the deck. Now the creatures were within reach of his eyes. He clasped his hands tight over his face to shield them, but it left him no leverage to lift himself up. He could feel the creatures slithering above and below him. The fish stench of them was overpowering. They began to gnaw at his fingers and he could hear the grate of teeth against bone.

He'd have to risk his eyes if he wanted to save anything. He forced his body into a roll, crushing as many of them as he could. Then, before he could think better of it, he got his hands beneath him and levered himself up.

He didn't think he'd make it. The weight of creatures attached to his body by teeth and suckers dragged him down. It took all his strength not to fall straight back to the deck. He stumbled, braced himself, and rose with one final heave.

"Christ, Tomas!" Anya yelled.

He felt her fingers scraping at his face, and a moment later her hand came away with a small, snaggle-toothed creature that looked like it came from the dark depths of the ocean. In the second before she flung it over the side he saw a scrap of what might have been his eyelid clenched between its jaws.

Anya's face was covered in a fine tracery of blood from a jagged gash in her forehead. "The captain's dead," she gasped.

Tomas could see him through the glass wall of the cabin, slumped over the wheel. Without him to steer it, their boat was following a curving course, cutting a broad circle through the sea. The other boat was out of sight. But it had only been a few minutes and theirs was the faster vessel. They could still catch up.

Tomas began to wade through the carnage on deck towards the cabin. Upright, the fish could only slow, not stop him. He was halfway to the door when the first attack came from above.

The bird's dive was too steep for recovery. Its beak gouged a track through his cheek and then it struck the mass of creatures on the deck with a wet thump. The next one came seconds later, hitting his shoulder this time. When Tomas looked up he saw that the sky was dark with them, seagulls with their wickedly curved beaks and hateful black eyes.

He could feel the blood flowing freely from a thousand cuts and he knew even he couldn't survive this long. Behind him, he could hear Anya screaming. It was a horrible sound, but he dreaded still more the moment when it would stop. He reached back to pull her against his chest, curling his body around hers to shield it.

Their progress was agonisingly slow, an inelegant stumble that constantly threatened to spill them both to the deck and the heaving mass of life there. For a moment, Tomas saw the cold eye of an octopus glaring up at him. Its tentacle lashed out to dig suckers into the already exposed skin of his leg. He brought his other foot down on it bulbous body, bursting it. The tentacle tore away, still dangling from his leg as he took another dragging step nearer to the relative safety of the cabin.

By the time they reached it, his legs were a gaping mass of wounds. The floor was awash with creatures, a jumble of them blocking the door. He used his feet to kick them aside, then squashed the few that remained into a bloody pulp as he slammed it shut.

Instantly, a muffled series of bangs detonated above them. The birds were flinging themselves against the glass roof of the cabin, sacrificing themselves mindlessly in their hunger to reach them. As Tomas watched, a spider-web of cracks spread from the last point of impact.

He looked at Anya, and read the same defeat in her eyes. Then he grabbed the wheel and grimly turned it round, taking them back towards Germany.

When Morgan and Anya finally stumbled out of the mine, coated in rock dust and blood, the emergency services had already arrived. Morgan stood numbly compliant as a paramedic tended to his cuts. Once the sterile dressings were in place, the paramedic gestured towards the ambulance, miming that they should get in.

"We're fine," Morgan told him.

The man didn't looked convinced, but when Morgan pushed him gently away he shrugged and went to tend to someone else.

"We need to get out of here," Anya said, "before someone starts asking too many questions."

Morgan nodded, but he only walked as far as the nearest wall before collapsing to the ground at its foot. After a second, Anya sat down beside him.

"What did Richard mean," she said eventually, "that you were born out of Nicholson's death?"

He thought about lying, but he found he wanted to share this. He *needed* to. "I was adopted," he told her. "Never knew my real parents. Didn't know who they were – until we found that book, and I saw my dad's name written in the front."

She shifted to face him, jeans grating along the gravel. "Nicholson's your *father?*"

He nodded. "He died before I was born. I think that's what Richard was talking about."

"Christ. No wonder you were so keen to translate it."

"I wanted to understand why I'd been sent on this mission. Someone must have known about me and Nicholson, whoever got me assigned. It's too much of a coincidence otherwise, isn't it?"

"Probably." Her eyes studied him too keenly. "And you wanted to know your father, as any boy would. Somehow, I don't think you like what you've found."

"No." But that he couldn't bear to talk about. He levered himself to his feet. "We should phone Tomas."

Anya looked like she wanted to ask him more, but something in his face stopped her. She shrugged and handed him the phone.

Morgan let it ring and ring, but when it went to voicemail he snapped it shut.

Anya took the phone back and pressed some keys. "This is Anya's number," she told him. "It's probably better if *you* talk to her."

As she handed it back to him there was a crackle and then a voice saying, "Who is this?"

"Anya?" Morgan said. "It's me. Morgan."

There was a silence on the other end during which he could hear strained breathing and what sounded like the cries of seabirds. Then she said, "So you're alive. Do you have the book?"

"Yes." Morgan looked at *his* Anya, thinking of all the other things he could add to that. He sighed and said, "It's safe."

"Well," she said. "Then it looks like we're all going to St Petersburg."

PART THREE

The Evil Empire

CHAPTER SIXTEEN

Morgan and Anya stopped for lunch in a nowhere town on the road to St Petersburg. They sat inside the one, run-down hotel, picking at a plate of meat and pickles. The food was copious but as brown and bland as the hotel itself. It looked as if it had been decorated on the assumption that no actual guests would ever be staying there.

Anya realised her hand was tugging nervously at her trousers, where her gun no longer sat beneath her waistband. They hadn't been able to take any weapons through the Russian border and she felt exposed without it. Maybe she should have listened to Morgan. He'd wanted to try sneaking past the border guards but she'd vetoed it, unwilling to risk capture and the diary being lost to them.

Morgan had the book on the table in front of him. Anya saw that he was reading it easily now, no longer needing to laboriously write down his translation, but after a while he shook his head wearily, something deeply unhappy lurking in the shadows beneath his eyes. Anya thought she knew what it was.

"You had to do it," she said. "And you saved my life as well as yours."

"I know." He didn't sound like it was much comfort.

"Richard wanted you dead, if it's any consolation." Morgan darted her a sharp look at that, and she added, "Did you never wonder what I was doing on the train, when Richard's people had already stolen the diary?"

His eyes narrowed, calculation replacing misery. "You were meant to kill me."

She nodded. "I was supposed to use the confusion to replace the other me. Then I could wait for an opportune moment to finish you and Tomas off."

"Did Richard say why?"

"No. And I never asked."

He looked at her a long moment, face unreadable. Then he sighed and looked away. She remembered that he'd been black ops before he transferred to the Division. He probably hadn't asked why his targets were marked for death either. "But you didn't do it," he said eventually.

She forced a smile. "Like I said, you won me over with your charm and good looks."

"I thought it was my brains."

"Well, those too."

He nodded down at the book. "Actually, you let me live because you thought I could get you what you wanted. But this isn't going to tell us where the artefacts are."

She tamped down the bitter disappointment. He had to be wrong. "You haven't finished it yet. How can you be sure?"

"Richard said the artefacts are something you make, not something you find. I think Nicholson *did* make them, and he let Tomas hunt for them to throw people off the scent."

"But why would he try to deceive his own side?"

The misery was back in his face. "They weren't his side any more, not to him."

"Then who was he working for?"

"Raphael." He opened the book, somewhere towards the back. "There's something you should hear. It's from 1987:

"Another interminable meeting in Whitehall. That idiot Hickman actually asked me what evidence I had for the existence of the artefacts. If only he knew! But I'm worried they're beginning to suspect me. Not of the things I've actually done – how could they imagine those? – but of being somewhat economical with the truth. I need to be more careful, because I absolutely can't let them shut down the Division. Not now, when we're so close.

"And then after the meeting, I saw Tomas. He's been away for three months, trudging round Jordan with Richard. I thought it was a wild goose chase, which was why I let them go, but they proved me wrong. We've only translated half the scrolls they brought back, and they're quite extraordinary. I've never found End Days prophecies which are so clear before.

"Does Tomas realise what they mean? I rather think not. But his mind works so differently from mine, sometimes I can't figure out what's going on behind his eyes. It's hard to imagine we once used to be friends.

"Does *he* suspect me? I don't think so either, but I can't be sure, and that's worrying. He's the only one who might be able to prevent it, and he would. Tomas doesn't understand the lure of power, or the joy of surrendering to one's baser urges. I loathe him.

"How strange – I didn't realise it until I wrote it down, but it's true. I hate him. He makes me question myself, just when I need my certainty the most.

"I'm glad of the end we have in store for him. I hope it's as dreadful as it sounds."

Morgan swallowed and shut the book.

"Jesus," Anya said. "And Tomas never had any idea."

"Nicholson wasn't always like that," Morgan said, almost defensively. "When he started out he was just curious. He was excited by the stuff he was discovering. But the artefacts changed him somehow, just looking for them. He got obsessed and he stopped caring about anything else. I think Richard was right – it's better if those things stay lost."

"No," she said. "Think about it. If they're so dangerous, what's worse? Getting them and keeping them safe, or leaving them out there for Raphael or someone like him to find?"

"You're saying they'd be safe with us, but I don't think they're safe with anyone. They're not safe *for* anyone. Look at what they did to my father."

Morgan's face was taut with strain, and Anya suddenly pictured the first time she met him, when she'd pulled him dripping and desperate from the Danube. She'd dived into the river to push him under, not pull him out. But the instant she'd touched his arm, she'd realised she wasn't the half of Anya which was capable of murder.

"I have to get the artefacts," she told him. "I *have* to."

"Why?"

There was no point lying, not any more. "Because I want to be whole again. The artefacts are supposed to be a source of tremendous power. And reversing what they did to me will require a huge amount of it – exactly as much as they released when they pulled me apart."

He squinted at her, puzzled. "What does it matter if there are two of you running around? And if you wanted to get rid of her, you could just kill her."

She shook her head. "You don't understand. She's half of me."

"Yeah, I get it. Like clones."

"No, not like that at all. There's only one way to split a person in two – along the fault lines that are already there."

"Fault lines?"

"You know what I mean, Morgan. Everyone does. We're all full of contradictions, impulses pulling in opposite directions. It's in every decision we make. Because if we weren't tempted by more than one option, why would we need to choose between them?"

"So you're saying it's like, I don't know, alternative realities? One of you is the part that wanted to make one decision, and the other you is the one that would've made the other."

"Yes, in a way. When they split me, they got rid of all my inconsistencies, all my second thoughts..." She trailed into silence, remembering the psychic agony of the process. The magic had crawled through her mind, searching for the parts of herself that shamed her, or scared her, all the aspects of herself she secretly hated, and then it had ripped them away.

"Everything inconsistent and every second thought went into the other you," Morgan said.

"Everything I am was divided between us, and now I'm only half a person. I've learned to fake the emotions I'm missing, but I can't feel them. I've forgotten how."

He frowned. For some reason, the expression always made him look younger. "If I could get rid of... There are parts of me, if I got rid of them, I wouldn't want them back."

"I didn't think I did, either. But sometimes the things you don't want, you still need. I remember how much I used to hate getting angry – how out of control it made me feel. But anger's a motivator, I can see that now. Rage gives you the power to stop people hurting you. Without it..." She shrugged.

"Maybe," he said. "Yeah, okay."

She could have left it at that. He would have let her. But the fear was a constant cold presence inside her. If she let it out into the light of day perhaps it would melt away.

"It's more than that, though," she told him. "When you split an atom, the two halves weigh less than the whole. That's where all the energy comes from – that missing matter."

"You told me that," he said.

"Well, when they split *me* it released energy too. Something was lost. And I think... and I wonder if it could be my soul."

Anya drove most of the final hundred miles to St Petersburg in silence. Morgan took the time to read the last of the book. It wasn't that there was any urgency about it, they'd already stopped to photocopy every page, something Raphael must surely have predicted. But through the diary he'd finally begun to know his father. He hated what he'd discovered, but he needed to know it all.

The final entry was dated 24 June, 1988. When he'd read it he sat still, thinking. An idea hovered at the back of his mind, fully formed but not quite visible yet. He caught Anya looking at him out of the side of her eye. She didn't say anything, but after a moment he sighed, then flicked back to the start.

"This is the end, and the beginning," he read. "The Omega and the Alpha."

"God is called the Alpha and the Omega in the Christian Bible," Anya told him. "He's probably referring to that."

"Except he's reversed it." Morgan remembered the upside-down cross in the desecrated church, an inversion of holiness. He read on:

"I made the decision long ago, but today I find out if I have the courage to go through with it. I have to leave soon to go to Tomas's burial – a plan that's finally come to fruition. I was sorry about Kate, but a small price to pay for getting what we want. Tomas is such a fool, such a romantic. He'd die for love – for just one person. The exchange rate for a human life can be so much higher than that. When I die today, it will be in return for everything.

"Like Jesus, in a way. What an absurd thought.

"Anyway, it's all arranged. Our moles have told us about the speech Gorbachev plans to give the Party Conference tomorrow. Another ending, or the beginning of one. Soon the Cold War will be over and the Hermetic Division with it. I've made sure that questions are already being asked – and Tomas's death and mine will be the final straw for those cowards in Whitehall, afraid of what the public will think if it comes out. The Division will be closed and Tomas will stay in the ground. I wonder if he'll sense the time passing, all those years he'll be waiting.

"I, at least, won't return as a monster. The immortality I've bought is of an entirely different kind. I ask myself one final time if it's been worth it. And the answer is still yes, though my reasons for giving it have changed. I serve Him now, whole-heartedly. No excuses any more. No pretence that there's some other agenda, that my service is just temporary, an alliance of convenience.

"I thought I wanted power for the sake of my country, in the interests of knowledge. I was lying to myself. I thought ends justified means. That was a lie, too. He showed me the truth.

That I wanted power for its own sake. That the means are an end in themselves. I thought I could hide from the darkest parts of myself, but He taught me to embrace them.

"Yes, I can do this. And I will. My death will just be the beginning."

When Morgan had finished reading he looked across at Anya, almost afraid of what he'd see. She was scowling at the road ahead, eyes flicking from side to side as if reading a script inside her head. But when she looked at him her face softened. "I'm so sorry, Morgan. But you're not your father's son – not in any way that counts."

Morgan closed the diary and laid it square on his lap. "Then who else am I?"

The last few miles passed by in a blur of green-grey fields and blue sky. They were well inside the sprawling outskirts of the city when Anya steered the car to a halt at the side of the road. She pulled out the pay-as-you-go mobile they'd bought in a shop inside the Russian border and carefully stored a number in the memory.

"Mine," she said. "I'll be staying in the city, so you can get hold of me when you need me."

He nodded. "I'll let you know what's going on. And I won't give you away to the others unless I have to."

She looked momentarily taken aback, as if she hadn't expected his kindness. A strand of red hair had fallen across her cheek and he reached over to brush it away. He almost told her then, the thing he'd realised about the book. But she'd made it clear how much the artefacts meant to her, and if she knew... So instead he made himself smile and say, "It's a shame we didn't get one more night together."

She shook her head, eyes half closed in amusement. "I'm nearly a decade older than you."

His smile widened. "Yeah, but you're still hot, though."

"That wasn't actually the basis of my objection."

He shrugged, then hooked an arm around her neck and pulled her in for a kiss, holding it a bit too long to just be friendly.

"Take care of yourself," he said, sliding across to the driver's seat as she climbed out of the car.

"I'll do my best. And you take care of me too."

Tomas had chosen the Monument to the Heroic Defenders of Leningrad as their meeting point on one of the main roads into the city. At the heart of the vast, bleak Victory Square, its central obelisk towered over a concrete plaza busy enough that their group wouldn't attract attention, but not so crowded that they'd never find each other.

Looking at the monument as they waited for Morgan, Tomas thought about something his father used to say. *The Russians are lions led by monsters.* There was something monstrous about the monument. The square-jawed, heroic steel statues at its base seemed to remember the million and more people who had died here as symbols of something colder and more abstract than individual human lives.

"Where is he?" Anya grumbled irritably, her back to the statues as she scanned the network of roads which surrounded the square. "The exchange is supposed to take place in three hours, we can't risk being late."

Tomas shrugged. "It's a long drive."

"He'd better not lose the damn book before he gets here!"

"He knows how important it is." Tomas forbore to point out they wouldn't have the book at all if it weren't for Morgan. A sudden wave of lethargy swept over him, and he allowed himself to sink onto the steps leading to the monument, leaving Anya to continue impatiently eyeing the roads.

"I think – yes, that's him," she said, jarring Tomas out of a half-waking, formless grey dream.

He nodded and dragged himself to his feet. When they'd had to give up pursuing the boat that held Belle, something else had been lost to him. He thought it might be hope. Richard had abandoned him, Raphael had outmanoeuvred him. Kate had betrayed him, but not before he'd betrayed her. Now he was about give up the only victory they'd won.

But when he looked up and saw Morgan striding towards them, summoned by Anya's waving arm, he managed a smile. He was glad the young man was alive. That, he supposed, was a victory too.

"Bloody hell," Morgan said when he was close enough to see Tomas's face. "What happened to you, man?"

Tomas reached up a reflexive hand to touch his cheek. He knew it was scabbed with unhealed cuts, the legacy of their failed attempt to stop Raphael at sea. The bullet holes in his stomach still gaped open beneath his makeshift bandage. He forced a smile. "Flesh wounds."

"No kidding." Morgan studied him intently a moment more, then shrugged and turned away. "Hi, Anya."

She nodded, less than friendly. Tomas wasn't sure what it was she so disliked about Morgan. Maybe the fact that, with no discernable sense of humour herself, she could never quite tell when he was joking.

"Lovely to see you too," the younger man said. "Mind if I have a private word with Tomas?"

Anya scowled. "Yes."

Morgan sighed. "Why does no one accidentally drop dead when I actually want them to?" Despite Anya's protest, he slung an arm around Tomas's shoulder, pulling them both out of her earshot.

As soon as they were alone, all humour vanished from Morgan's expression. "Listen, there's two things I've got to tell you."

"You do still have the book, don't you?"

"Yeah." He patted his stomach, and Tomas saw the rectangular shape bulging out the thin material of his t-shirt. "But I sussed out how to read it. I *did* read it, all of it. And at the end..."

Tomas didn't like the expression on Morgan's face. It looked almost like pity. "Tell me."

"Nicholson – he planned for you to die. He arranged it somehow, and he also arranged for you not to get brought back."

Maybe if Tomas had felt better, he would have felt more. "And did he say why?"

"Not directly. But there's something else. The Japanese, they had this American bloke working with them."

"Richard. We used to be partners."

"Yeah, that makes sense. He's dead, I'm sorry."

Tomas felt grief twist a knife inside him, but he shook his head. "Don't be. He betrayed us."

"I guess." Morgan's eyes blanked for a moment, looking back into the past. Then they refocused on Tomas's face, a bright black. "Before he died, he told me something about the Ragnarok artefacts. He said you can't find them – that you have to make them."

Tomas froze into a long moment of stillness as he absorbed that. Then he laughed bitterly. "Of course. No wonder Nicholson was happy to let me search for them all those years. He knew I'd never find them."

"Yeah," Morgan said uncomfortably. "That's what he says in the book. It's Nicholson's diary, from the whole time he was running the Division. You should read it. But here's the thing. There was something else Richard said, about why Nicholson couldn't send Raphael the diary till he was dead –"

Tomas twitched and Morgan nodded, as if this was almost an irrelevance. "Oh yeah, they were working together. But what I'm saying is, I think it might be the diary."

"What might be?"

"The artefacts are supposed to be powerful, a big source of energy, right? And a soul is worth – well, it's worth a lot of that, isn't it? I've read the diary all the way through, and there's nothing in there about what the artefacts are or where they are. It's just the story of how Nicholson..." He laughed awkwardly. "It's him describing how he lost his soul."

"I see," Tomas said, and he thought that he finally did. "You're saying it's the diary, the diary itself, which is one of the artefacts."

"Yeah. It explains why Raphael wants it so much, and why it doesn't bother him that we'll have photocopied it. It's not anything *in* the book that matters, it's the actual, physical book."

Tomas nodded. "You're right. I'm sure of it."

"So can we really give it to him? Even to save Belle's life?"

Tomas looked away, but he could feel Morgan's gaze on him, troubled and intent. The young man wanted *him* to make this decision – he didn't want to take responsibility for it. It was a terribly heavy burden, but Tomas supposed he deserved to bear it. For many years, maybe all of the time he'd worked for the Hermetic Division, he'd been fooled and used by Nicholson. He'd allowed it to happen and now it was his job to deal with the consequences.

After a long time, he said, "I think we have to give the diary up, at least for now. It seems to me that Nicholson – and Raphael – have constantly been sacrificing other people for some purpose of their own. If we do the same, what does that make us?"

The Hermitage dominated one end of a wide square, stately and far more elegant than Morgan had expected. Tomas had told him it used to be a palace. It was a monument to a Russia before the revolution, when beauty wasn't seen as something decadent.

It seemed an unlikely place for the exchange, far too public. "Why here?" he asked Anya, as they queued for tickets like ordinary tourists.

"Perhaps when we see them you can ask," she said flatly.

Morgan sighed. He would far rather have come here with the other Anya, the one who actually liked him. And even better, he would have preferred to go with Tomas to collect Belle. They were supposed to exchange phone calls to confirm that Belle had been handed over before the diary was, but Morgan was sure it wouldn't turn out to be as simple as that. Splitting the exchange seemed designed to ensure it got fucked up, which was no doubt why Raphael had arranged it this way.

By the time they were inside, they only had ten minutes to make it to the meeting place, the Hanging Garden on the second floor. All the same, Morgan couldn't help stopping to stare in wonder.

The chequerboard floor seemed to stretch off into infinity, white arches endlessly repeating like reflections in facing mirrors. In an alcove opposite him, a monumental statue of a man and two young boys wrestled armfuls of snakes. It was an image out of a horror film, but something about its antiquity made it seem almost peaceful, a moment preserved for so many hundreds of years that all the dread had drained out of it.

"Come on!" Anya said. She tugged on his arm to drag him away. But as soon as he started to move she dropped it, as if she didn't enjoy touching him very much.

She led him through more tiled corridors, past the relics of Europe's lost civilisations. On the stairs to the first floor, they mingled with a group of Italian school kids, laughing and yelling as they pushed past. One of them elbowed Morgan in the ribs as he chatted to his friends. Morgan turned to shout at them, but when he saw their cheerful, carefree faces, he kept his peace.

At the top of the stairs, Anya stopped suddenly, staring behind her with a startled, almost fearful look.

"What is it?" Morgan said. "One of Raphael's people?"

She shook her head. "Nothing. I saw someone... it was probably just the red hair."

"Probably," Morgan agreed blandly.

She grimaced. "You know, in German mythology, a doppelganger is a harbinger of death."

"Hopefully Raphael's," Morgan said.

They walked in silence down two more broad corridors, and at the end of them was the doorway to the Hanging Gardens. Morgan scanned the few people who were there, loitering in the shade of the neatly trimmed trees beside languid marble statues of reclining women.

"Think you can see them?" Anya asked.

"No one we know. Not that that means anything." A momentary twinge of anxiety made him pat the waistband of his jeans, but the rectangular bulge of the diary was still there.

"Then I guess we wait," Anya said.

The transfer was to take place in the Piskariovskoye Cemetery, to the north of the city centre. When Tomas arrived at its gates he found a group of disgruntled tourists being turned back by an official in a blue uniform. But the man took one look at Tomas's face, and waved him through. Raphael's power clearly ran deep here.

Inside, the cemetery was deserted, no gardeners to tend the close-trimmed lawns and regimented trees. Tomas walked down the central avenue, wondering why Raphael had chosen this place. Beneath grass-covered mounds on either side of the path lay the unnamed war dead of Leningrad. If they hadn't died, Tomas might never have been born. *Europe's freedom was bought with Russian blood*. That was something else his father used to say.

Tomas felt like he was walking through a dream of greenery and sunshine. His mind wanted to sink into the ground, dust to dust. He knew an end was approaching, but he wasn't quite sure to what. Himself? As he walked past grave after grave, a part of him hoped so.

"Tomas," a voice said behind him.

He'd expected Raphael to bring back-up, but there was only the old man and Belle, the little girl tucked tight against his chest. Tomas felt a bubble of nausea in his stomach, remembering the things Morgan had told him about the church in the salt mine.

How could Nicholson have worked for this man? How could Tomas not have sensed the cancer growing inside his soul which had made it possible?

"The girl's here," Raphael said. "Tell your people to release the book."

"When she's safe with me," Tomas said.

Raphael nudged Belle, and she smiled tremulously at Tomas. "It's okay, Mr Len. If you give him the book, he'll let me go."

"Forgive me for not taking that on trust," Tomas said to Raphael. But he took out the phone Anya had given him, fingers fumbling awkwardly on the small keys. "Morgan?" he said as soon as the ring tone cut out. "Wait there. When Belle's secured, I'll give you the go-ahead."

He hadn't taken his eyes from Raphael the whole time, but the old man didn't seem troubled. He looked supremely calm, his hair glinting white in the clean sunshine.

"Very well," the old man said. He pushed Belle away from him. "You may go."

She took a couple of stumbling steps, as if she was afraid this might be a trick. Raphael smiled gently at her when she glanced back, uncertain, and Tomas ground his teeth. This was all a trap, he could sense it, and yet he couldn't seem to do anything but spring it.

"You really came for me," Belle said, when she was only two paces away. There was a shiny tear track on each of her cheeks.

As soon as she was close enough, Tomas reached his arm out to pull her into a hug. "Yes," he said. "Of course."

She smiled into his eyes. "More fool you."

He felt a small sharp pain at the base of his neck, and then nothing.

CHAPTER SEVENTEEN

Morgan held the phone pressed to his ear, despite the disapproving stare of the blue-uniformed guard. Anya hovered by his elbow, clearly itching to snatch it out of his hands and take control. He ignored her and scanned the room. There was still no sign of the agent who'd carry out the exchange. They'd probably make themselves known when Raphael gave the signal. Tomas should approve the hand-over any second now.

It was only when the silence at the other end of the phone dragged on into minutes that Morgan realised he was listening to dead air.

Anya read his panicked expression. "What's happened?"

"Tomas is gone." His hand went back to the oblong shape of the diary beneath his t-shirt as he scanned the small garden. He was already backing into a corner, giving himself a clear line of sight for any possible attack.

He didn't have to tell Anya what he was doing. She placed herself beside him, hip against his, covering the angles he couldn't. If Tomas had been ambushed, they'd be after the diary next.

Except, after five minutes of frozen waiting, it became clear that they weren't.

"Where *are* they?" Anya hissed.

They'd been still so long they were beginning to attract odd looks from the other tourists. Anya scowled back at them until they looked away and Morgan kept his hand clasped protectively over the diary, though there was no one close enough to see it, let alone steal it.

And then, as vivid as a waking dream, he had a sudden flash of memory: the Italian schoolchildren who'd surrounded them on the stairs as they came up. The elbow in his ribs that had distracted his attention, just when they'd been pressed closest to him and Anya had been furthest away.

His fingers scrabbled at his waist, uncoordinated with haste. Two Japanese girls whispered and giggled behind their hands as they watched him expose the hard muscles of his stomach when he finally managed to wrench the material up.

"What the hell are you doing?" Anya said.

But she didn't need an answer – she could see it for herself. The book he'd been guarding so closely was a copy of the *Lonely Planet Guide to St Petersburg*. The diary had been taken before they even got there.

When Tomas clawed his way back to consciousness, he sensed that only a little while had passed. Just enough time for him to be moved – and bound.

They'd brought him to the centre of the cemetery and his back was pressed against something hard and cold. When he tilted his head, he saw a statue of a woman holding a wreath, dark against the sun.

"Mother Russia," Belle said, "mourning her dead. Hello, Tomas."

The girl sat cross-legged in front of him. Her shadow lay across the concrete behind her. Sometimes it looked small, sometimes so large it stretched to the grass beyond. Two great sweeps of darkness might have been the outline of wings. Tomas wasn't sure if his vision was failing him, or if he was seeing her clearly for the first time.

"How long has the demon been in charge?" he asked her. "All the time you were with us – and how long before that?"

"What makes you think he's in charge?"

He tried to study her face, but the sunlight flattened it into blankness. "You're working for Raphael, aren't you?"

"*With* Raphael," she said. "For the same master."

His mind struggled to encompass that. He knew what she meant, of course. The Hermetic Division had studied Crowley and others like him, but in the end they'd concluded there was little there beyond a desire to find mystical justifications for the unjustifiable. The legends that led to the artefacts were only metaphors, imperfect human transcriptions of truths too large to comprehend. At least, that was what Tomas had concluded. Had Nicholson reached a different understanding and kept it to himself?

"She invited me in," Belle said. "It was her choice. She wanted to stay a child forever. Never aging and never dying. I told her I could make that happen, and she was happy to give me what I wanted in return."

A glint of sunlight caught in Belle's big blue eyes. He'd once thought he could see the demon there, struggling to escape from the spells that bound it. Now he imagined he could see Belle herself, trapped and desperate.

"You were ten years old," he told her. "You didn't know what you were doing. They can't hold you to a deal you were too young to make."

"Some decisions you only get to make once. You should know, Tomas. You made yours twenty years ago."

"I know." He bowed his head. He'd thought there might be salvation for him, but not all mistakes could be undone. "So what do you want with me? You'd already won. We were going to give you the book – the artefact."

"Ah. You figured it out."

"Yes," Tomas said bitterly, "when it was too late to do any good."

"And didn't you wonder about the other two artefacts? About the other things Nicholson created?"

He felt suddenly dizzy, as if the earth was dropping away

beneath him. "What are you telling me?"

"I think you know. A part of you always knew."

He turned his face away, because he didn't want to admit that she was right.

Anya hadn't realised seeing herself would be so disconcerting. She'd shadowed herself on the train, but jumped to follow Morgan before they could meet. Now that one brief glimpse in the museum, the startled look on her own face, and everything inside her had shifted out of alignment. She felt both attracted and repelled, and the conflicting impulses had left her frozen in place while the other her moved on. Morgan had asked her to follow them, hoping her presence would give them an edge. Then she'd seen herself and fled, no use to him at all. She sat on a bench outside the museum, staring at the people streaming out and both hoping and dreading that one of them would be her.

But when she finally saw a face she recognised, it wasn't her own. Round and thick-lipped and not terribly bright, she recognised it from hours of surveillance footage, and from one brief glimpse in Budapest.

It was Vadim, Raphael's go-between.

A group of Italian students had been loitering near the exit, their high-pitched screams and laughter a distraction from the inward spiral of her thoughts. Now, as she watched, Vadim singled out two of them, drawing them aside for an urgent, whispered conversation. Their backs were to her, but the movement of their shoulders told her they were doing more than just talking. Something was changing hands.

Her phone rang just as Vadim peeled away from the students. She answered it as she followed him, hidden by the crowds that filled the square.

"Morgan. I don't know what happened in there, but Raphael's man is here – and I think he has the diary."

Morgan snapped the phone shut. He'd already grabbed Anya's arm, dragging her through the long corridors of the museum as he spoke to the other half of her.

"Jesus Christ!" she said. "Let go of me, will you!"

He released her, barely registering that she continued to follow him. He was jogging now, elbowing the other tourists out of the way. The place was a maze, the occasional exit sign seeming to lead only to more long white rooms. The endless chequerboard pattern of the floor made it seem like they were running in place.

"Was that Tomas?" Anya asked.

Morgan shook his head, then laughed.

"What? Is there something I should know?"

There were a lot of things, but now didn't seem like the time to share them. "A contact," he told her instead. "She's spotted Raphael's man outside and she thinks he has the diary."

"Thank god for that!"

"Yeah," Morgan said. "Now all we have to do is catch him."

When Raphael approached, Belle backed away. "Things to do," she said. "People to see."

Raphael ignored her, his eyes only on Tomas. "I've waited a very long time for this," he said. His voice was almost accentless, but now Tomas was listening for it, he could hear the faint traces of Poland in its sibilants. Nicholson had sometimes talked about a Polish priest, the man who'd first opened his eyes to the world behind the world.

"Nothing to say, Tomas?" Raphael asked. "No questions?"

Tomas's shrug scraped the coarse-fibred rope against his body.

"Nicholson always said you weren't much of a conversationalist."

"I won't help you," Tomas said. "I've been a fool, but I'm not a traitor."

"No," Raphael said, "I don't believe you're either. If you were an idiot, this would all have been a lot simpler. And it still so nearly fell apart. The diary was meant to draw you here, did you realise that? It didn't occur to me you'd manage to steal it before I got my hands on it."

Tomas closed his eyes for a moment as another revelation hit him. "Giles sent me on this mission. Is he working with you too?"

"No. Giles we never managed to turn – too much of a bureaucrat to take any big risks."

"But you got him to reopen the Division, didn't you? To bring me back exactly when you needed me."

Raphael's foot tapped a staccato rhythm against the concrete. He was keyed up in some way. Nervous or excited, it was hard to tell, and his face gave nothing away. "All we needed to do was dangle the artefacts in front of him," he said. "They were the only thing your government was ever interested in. The only reason they allowed the Division to continue. It was never the knowledge they were interested in, only the edge it might give them in their long, pointless war."

"The war wasn't pointless," Tomas said. "And it was won."

Raphael laughed, a dry, creaking sound. "Temporarily. There will always be conflict, Tomas, between those who believe human nature can be perfected, and those who know otherwise."

"I never believed we can be better than we are, only that we can choose to behave better."

"How very moral of you. No wonder Nicholson found you so tiresome."

Tomas sagged with weariness, letting the ropes support him. "Well, he's certainly found an elaborate way to get me out of his hair."

"I have bigger plans for you. But –" Raphael tilted his head, listening. After a moment Tomas heard it too, footsteps approaching down the long avenue.

Raphael smiled. "There's someone who can help me with that."

Tomas wasn't very surprised to see Kate. He could tell that

she'd expected to find him here too, but her eyes still widened at the sight of him.

"Oh god, Tomas." She barely acknowledged Raphael as she rushed to him, hands fluttering over his chest, and then his face and finally his bound hands, but never quite touching any of them. "What happened to you?"

"I tried to stop you taking Belle."

A part of him enjoyed the way she winced away from his bitter smile. "We had to, to get you here."

"I gathered that."

Her hand rested on his face this time. She stroked a finger over the ridge of his brow. "It was worth it. You'll see."

"Worth what? I can understand you going over to the Russians. I don't know, maybe I would have done the same. But *this*, Kate?"

"Just what is it you think we're doing?" Raphael asked. He'd retreated a few paces, watching Kate and Tomas intently.

"I don't know," Tomas admitted. "But I know who... I know what it is you think you're doing it for."

"Do you," Raphael said flatly.

"Morgan told me what happened in your church inside the salt mine, *Father* Raphael."

Raphael's whole body tensed, wasted muscles bunching underneath parchment skin.

"I know about the bargain you made to save yourself," Tomas said.

Raphael moved faster than Tomas would have imagined, until their faces were inches apart. He could smell the old man's sour breath.

"How do you know that?" Raphael hissed.

Kate looked shocked, and with a visible effort the old man reined himself in. "Who told you?" he asked more calmly.

Tomas read the fear in Raphael's eyes. For the first time, Tomas had a measure of power. He could shake Raphael, and Kate's faith in him. But this was a secret Raphael would kill to keep. If Tomas said any more, it would doom Kate. He just shook his head. "It's funny. All the things I saw, but *this* I never believed."

Raphael eased back on his heels, smiling knowingly. "You only ever saw the surface – Nicholson made sure of that. I serve what lies beneath."

Tomas looked at Kate to see if she understood. Could she work for Raphael, knowing this? But she hardly seemed to be paying attention to the old man, her eyes still fixed on Tomas. "None of it matters," she said. "It's all just a... technique. You know that, you used them yourself."

He felt a surge of relief followed by a spike of panic. If Kate wasn't following the same course as Raphael, then she was just another tool to be used and disposed of.

Her hand hadn't left his face. He could feel her fingertips ghosting over his cheek, tracing the lines of the unhealed cuts. "He can save you," she said. "If you help him, he can reverse what they did to you. What you did for me."

He smiled a little, because it meant that, despite everything, she still cared about him. But he'd already seen the gun in Raphael's hand, and a second later Kate saw it too.

"You promised me," she choked, shielding Tomas with her body. "You said that you could bring him back to life."

The old man smiled. "Did I? How dishonest of me."

CHAPTER EIGHTEEN

It took Anya far too long to realise she was being followed. The young, mousy-haired woman was walking on the other side of the road, a few paces behind. She looked like an office worker window-shopping in her lunch hour, and Anya couldn't spare her any attention. Her eyes were focused solely on Vadim.

It was only when she registered the shivery feeling of hidden eyes on her that she knew something was wrong. The young woman wasn't looking *through* the windows. She was following Anya's reflection in the glass.

Anya's footsteps faltered, sending her stumbling over the raised rim of the next paving stone. She righted herself a second later, resisting the impulse to turn and look directly at her shadow. She was safer while the woman following her didn't think she'd been spotted.

Vadim had drawn ahead as her attention shifted. She almost missed the sudden sharp left turn he took into one of the side streets running off Nevsky Prospect. She had ten paces to decide whether to follow him. If she didn't, there was a chance she could make her own escape. They might lose interest in her if she ceased to be a threat.

But if she didn't, the diary would be lost – probably forever.

When the turning came, she took it. The young man was hurrying, footsteps echoing audibly here, away from the crowds.

His new route was taking him north, towards the river. Did he know he was being followed? Her own pursuer had dropped back, trailing her at a distance on this narrower street. The smell of exhaust fumes wafted down from the main road, but no cars followed it. No pedestrians either. The young man didn't turn around. He didn't pause, even though he must have heard her behind him.

She had the phone pressed to her ear before she had time to fully process it. "I've walked into a trap," she said. "Sadovaya Street."

The second she said it the young man was gone, ducked into an alley she'd barely noticed. Two other men appeared out of the shadows to take his place. Anya had never seen them before, but she was sure they were working for Raphael. The taller man on the right smiled, running a hand over his smooth scalp.

Morgan was shouting something into the phone, words she didn't have time to listen to. She spun round. Behind her there was still only the mousey-haired woman. She wasn't carrying a weapon.

Anya knew it was too good to be true. But it looked like a chance and she was desperate enough to take it. "Get the diary," she said into the phone, cutting off Morgan's protest by snapping it shut.

The young woman paused, taking a step back as if she realised what Anya was planning. Then, as Anya sprinted towards her, she raised a whistle to her lips and blew.

"Fuck!" Morgan flung the phone away. It skittered across the pavement to land in the gutter with an audible crack. After a moment, he stooped to pick it up. The screen was broken but it was still working and he supposed that was lucky. It was Anya's only way of getting in touch with him.

Except he'd heard the whistle too. He knew what it meant and he didn't think she'd be calling again any time soon.

The other Anya had gone pale beside him, clawing a hand into his bicep as the high-pitched whistle went on and on, audible even now the phone was off. "We have to get out of here," she said.

He'd never seen that expression on her face before. It made her look vulnerable, far more like her alter ego.

"She needs help," he said.

"It's too late for her. Believe me – I know." Her hand on his arm was holding him back as he pulled against it in the direction of the whistle. But if he'd really wanted to, he could have broken her grip. He knew that. He knew that a big part of him wanted to do as Anya – as both Anyas – had told him.

Tomas was lost, probably dead. Anya would soon be the same. His partners were dying, and he'd almost convinced himself that was over, but it was just like before. The people around him died, and he carried on. But if he had the diary, he might be able to discover why. Raphael knew all the secrets, Morgan was sure of it. He'd sell them for the book, and then Morgan could finally understand.

He hesitated, caught by warring impulses more than by the grip of Anya's hand. Then he saw a figure emerge, blinking in the sudden light as he ran from a side street into the main road. It was Vadim – Raphael's man.

Before Morgan realised he'd made the decision, he set off in pursuit. Anya followed, at first dragged by her grip on his arm and then propelling herself when she saw who his target was.

The young man didn't realise they were following until they were within twenty paces. Morgan saw a brief flash of Vadim's face, sweaty and wide-eyed, and then he ran from the pavement into the centre of the road.

Cars screeched to a halt around him. The drivers screamed at him, lush-sounding Russian swear-words. But one of the cars that had stopped was a taxi, chunky and yellow. Morgan grabbed empty air as he reached for the other man. Another step and Morgan thumped his fist against the closed taxi door. And then the taxi and Vadim were motoring away –

and it was Anya and Morgan that everyone was screaming at as they stood impotently in the middle of the road.

"Here!" Anya said. She ran to another of the stationary cars and pulled the door open. Morgan froze a moment, watching her squeeze into the back seat, before he realised that it, too, was a cab. Then he flung himself after, jeans sticky with sweat against the cheap plastic seats.

The cab was moving before he'd shut the door. Anya leant forward, talking to the driver in urgent Russian. He frowned, then pressed down hard on the accelerator, flinging them back in their seats.

"Let her go," Tomas said. "She's no more use to you."

Raphael's thin white hand looked too frail to be holding the semi-automatic, but it didn't shake as he pointed the gun at Kate's heart. "One more use," he said.

The flick-knife must have been hidden in Raphael's back pocket. It was small enough to fit there, but the blade was wickedly sharp. It made a harsh, rasping sound as he slid it over the concrete to Kate's feet.

She looked down at it, then back at Raphael. "I won't kill him."

"He's already dead. He'd want you to save yourself – wouldn't you, Tomas?"

Tomas had been feeling weak and drained, floating somewhere apart from his thoughts. It was the detachment he'd longed for when he'd chosen to die. Now he fought against it. "Do your own dirty work, Raphael. It's not like you have an aversion to killing."

"And you do, I suppose?"

"I never enjoyed it."

"Does that make it better? The outcome is the same. I'm sure the people you murdered cared not a jot for your reasons."

"It wasn't murder." But Tomas knew there was no conviction in his voice. Since he'd come out of the ground, all his certainties had been dissolving like salt in the rain.

"Cut out his heart," Raphael said, turning back to Kate. "Give it to me, and you may go. Don't, you die and I'll do it anyway."

"Why?" Kate's voice was thick with tears. "Why lure him all this way, just to kill him?"

"Because this is what he was *made* for. This is what it's all about!" He was kneeling as he spoke, gun still trained on Kate with one hand while, with the other, he pulled out a chalk and began to draw a complicated pattern of runes and pentagrams on the concrete.

"He needs me for a spell," Tomas said. "Or my heart, I suppose." He suddenly remembered the illustration in the abbot's book, the one he saw in Greenland all those years ago, which showed the ceremony the artefacts were intended for.

Raphael nodded, still drawing. "The beating heart of a dead man. A dark seed crystal."

"For what?" Kate said. She'd got herself under control, and Tomas could see her gaze sweeping Raphael, waiting for an opening. He didn't think the old man would give her one.

"A crystal can only seed itself," Tomas told her. "I'm dead. All I can bring is more death."

Raphael paused a moment in his drawing to smile at Tomas. The expression looked manic. He must have been preparing for this moment almost half his life. What a remarkable feeling, to see his long-gestating plan finally come to fruition. And none of it would have been possible without Tomas – without his fatal stupidity.

"Just one more thing," Raphael said, and then, "Ah."

Tomas heard them before he could see them, footsteps approaching on the concrete behind him. He wasn't very surprised when the young man appeared, holding Nicholson's diary in one hand and a snub-nosed semi-automatic in the other.

Full circle, Tomas thought. I took it from him in Budapest, and now he has it back again.

Raphael nodded when he saw the book, head wobbling on his fragile neck. "Bring it here, Vadim."

Vadim stared at Tomas as he walked past. Tomas thought his expression wasn't quite fear. More a sort of sick fascination. It was the way you looked at an object or a wild creature, not a man.

"You know what this is, don't you?" Raphael said.

Kate nodded. "Nicholson's diary."

"And the first Ragnarok artefact," Tomas said.

Kate sucked in a startled breath. "That? No. Those things are ancient."

"Tomas is right," Raphael said. "The... formula for the artefacts is old, but they're made anew in each age. This is the first: the total corruption of a soul, recorded in its own hand. And the second is –"

"– is me." Tomas stared at Kate, willing her to understand. "Nicholson made *me* too. A dead man walking, of his own free will."

"Yes," Raphael said. "The broken heart of a dead man. All around the city, at the points of a pentagram, Belle and His other servants are ready to perform the great ceremony. But this, *this* is the heart of it all." He knelt down, placing the diary in the very centre of the pattern he'd drawn, chalk swirls of red and white circling inward towards it, like water heading for the drain.

Kate's gaze blinked between them, unsure.

"The artefacts are reputed to bring about the end of the world," Tomas said. "That's what they're – what we're – for."

The knife still sat at Kate's feet, the sunlight sparking slivers of light from its blade. Raphael stood beside the diary at the centre of the runes, shoulders hunched with age. His semi-automatic still pointed at Kate, and now Tomas could see his finger squeezing the trigger, bringing it to that fine point of balance where only the slightest extra pressure would release the waiting bullet.

"The book," Raphael said. "And your heart. Give it to me, Kate. There's no more time."

"No," she said. "I'm not letting you use me any more."

Her face was full of fear and guilt and Tomas could see the tremors shivering through her body. She wouldn't do it. She couldn't.

He remembered, suddenly, how he'd felt, the third time he'd asked her to marry him, and the third time she'd said, "not yet". The insecurity had eaten away at his confidence in himself, in their feelings for each other, and he'd begun to ask himself if she really did love him. He'd wondered whether all this time he'd been going to bed with a future wife, and she'd been lying beside an over-extended one night stand. He'd made up his mind to ask her for the truth, the day she came back from Russia.

Twenty years later than he'd expected, he didn't need to ask the question, because he could see the answer in her eyes. She did love him. She always had. It was why she would never take that knife and cut out his heart.

But Tomas knew her refusal wouldn't stop anything. Raphael probably expected it. He could see the old man watching her with a gleam of cruel amusement in his eyes. He wanted her to say no, so he could kill her in front of Tomas. He wanted Tomas to be broken-hearted – the ritual required it.

Tomas had died once already. He'd thought it was for something, some big romantic ideal of love. But it had been for nothing. And when he climbed out of his own grave, it had seemed as though he had a second chance at life, but that was never true. Just a part of him had come back, and not the part that could be in the world and change it – or if he could, it was only for the worse.

The second chance he had wasn't at life, it was at death. He had to die again, only this time it could mean something. This time he really *could* die for Kate, in a way that wasn't just a pitiful self-indulgence. And he'd be leaving this job half-finished, but that was what the dead did – they left the world and its problems to the living.

He thought he understood about Morgan now, and why they'd been paired together. The rest of this would be his responsibility, and Tomas didn't know how he'd handle it, but that was Morgan's choice. Tomas only had one more he could make.

"Tell me," he said to Kate. "If you'd come back from Russia. If – if none of this had happened. Would you have married me one day?"

She didn't want to answer, he could tell. She knew he was saying goodbye. But after a second she nodded. "I don't know what I was waiting for. I spent the last twenty years wondering."

He hadn't realised how good it would feel to hear it. He didn't want to let go of the moment, and he held her eyes as he tensed his muscles, pulling against the ropes. They were strong. The people who'd bound him knew what he was, and they'd assumed he'd be at full strength, not weakened after two days of starving himself.

The knife was on the ground in front of him, almost touching his left foot.

He pulled a little harder, dragging the ropes taut across his arms and chest.

"Don't," Kate said. Her fingertips reached out to brush his jaw, and then his cheek.

He shook them off. Everything that was left in him was focused on those ropes. They were digging into his skin as he strained, cutting through it. He was just flesh and blood, but there was magic in him too.

He smiled at Kate. "Had we but world enough, and time..."

He saw the instant Raphael realised what he was doing. The old man's gun swung from Kate to him at the precise moment the first rope snapped.

"I'll shoot her," Raphael said, and turned the gun back round to Kate.

Tomas knew he had seconds before Raphael carried out the threat. He didn't let himself believe that he might fail. The ropes would break, they *would* – and with one last fierce heave they did, tumbling him to the ground beside the knife.

For a second the gun wavered between him and Kate, and a second was all Tomas needed. The knife felt far too small in his big hands. They shook with weakness now, but it didn't matter. There was only one more thing he needed to do.

The pain as he stabbed the knife into his own chest was almost a relief. He wanted to feel something in his last moments. He tore the knife upward, shouting in agony. But it was almost finished. Almost finished. He could see Raphael staring at him, only now understanding what he'd intended. And Kate, looking furious rather than sad, which was so like her he almost laughed. And then he jerked the knife sideways and down, and he felt something fall out of his chest on to the ground. And then there was only silence.

Morgan ran faster than he'd known he could, but by the time he reached them, it was already over. For a long moment, everyone remained frozen in place. A woman, kneeling on the ground in front of Raphael, face buried in her hands. Vadim to one side, staring at his boss in shock. Raphael himself, a gun dangling from his slack hand.

And Tomas, sprawled face first on the ground.

He's dead, Morgan thought. And though he knew that had always been true, this time he could see that it was final. It didn't seem fair Morgan hadn't been there to witness it. It didn't seem right at all.

Then, like a DVD taken off pause, everyone jerked into action.

Raphael must have heard Morgan approaching. He spun to face him, semi-automatic raised and steady.

"Oh god..." Anya said. She was looking at Tomas, lying on the concrete. There was very little blood around him. No heart to pump it. And then Morgan saw it, the thing Raphael had stooped to pick up from the ground. It looked obscenely red against his white skin.

"You vicious fuck!" Morgan snarled.

Raphael dropped the heart in the centre of the sprawl of runes that had been chalked onto the concrete. It sat on top of Nicholson's diary, plump and glistening.

"I wasn't expecting you quite this soon," the old man said, turning to Morgan. "But it may be for the best. You deserve to witness this."

"You don't get to kill Tomas," Morgan said. "That's not something you get to do."

Beside him, Anya muttered what might have been agreement, but he didn't look at her. This was between him and Raphael. In some strange way, he knew that it always had been.

"I'm sorry if you cared for him," Raphael said. "But he chose his death – both times." He pointed at the knife, lying beside Tomas's slack right hand, and Morgan saw that it was caked with blood.

"You made him do it," Morgan said, his voice shaking.

Raphael shrugged, but he didn't deny it.

The woman kneeling beside Tomas's body finally looked up. Her face was streaked with tears but her expression was hard. She didn't take her eyes from Raphael as she backed towards Morgan and Anya. "He's trying to end the world," she said. "The book and… and Tomas, were two of the Ragnarok artefacts. All he needs now is the third."

Raphael smiled, and Morgan instantly knew that he already had it.

"Is that what this whole thing's been about?" Morgan said. He swept his arm around him, a gesture that took in the city and everything that had brought them there. But really he was talking about Tomas. "You want to end the world, you fucked-up freak? You think you can do that?"

Raphael nodded, stooping again to pick up the knife by Tomas's hand. "I can and I will. I know all this is new to you, Morgan, but haven't you seen enough to believe?"

The fear liquidising Morgan's guts told him he had. He looked at the acres of grass around them, a little faded after weeks without rain. At the sky, blue from horizon to horizon except for one small white wisp of cloud in the far distance. He could hear insects and birdsong. It didn't seem like the kind of day when the world would end.

He looked back at the old man. "Why would you do that? Why the hell would you want to?"

"Do you know what Ragnarok is?"

"Yeah, some Norse myth."

"The most important one. The final battle between the gods

and their enemies, a war which both sides lose. When Ragnarok comes, the wolf Fenrir swallows the sun, the seas boil and mankind is reduced to a remnant of a remnant. The old gods die – but something takes their place. Something *better*. The Aesir were tainted by betrayal from the start. The new world will come and it will be better than the old. *That's* why, Morgan. Because my Master promises both an end and a beginning."

"Bullshit," Morgan said. "Don't try and make this into something noble. I saw that church and I saw Marya. You didn't start worshipping Satan because you wanted to make the world a better place. You're a fucking monster and you sold your soul so you wouldn't get caught."

Raphael's face twisted. "And if I do like children, if I love them, who made me this way? It was God who created me as I am – and then told me it was a sin. It's God who fills everyone with desires he forbids us to satisfy. And his Church? The Church that sixty years ago smiled and turned away as his chosen people burned? If you want hypocrisy look at them, not me. They knew what I was and they didn't care. Do you know, Morgan, do you know what my bishop said to me on the day I was ordained?"

Morgan shook his head, speechless in the face of the old man's rage.

Raphael's anger extinguished as quickly as it had taken light. He smiled, a bitter twist of his lips. "He said 'be discreet'. God made my Master too, then cast him out of Heaven for being as he was. *He* doesn't demand anything of us that we're not able to give. And in His name I'll destroy this world of lies and let another take its place – one where everyone can live according to their natures. Even you, Morgan. Especially you."

A spark of sunlight flashed from the knife as he raised it, and another when he brought it down. The blade slid through Tomas's heart without pausing and stuck fast in the pages of the book beneath.

Anya ran forward, shouting something incomprehensible. But Raphael still had the gun, and when he shot a bullet into the concrete at her feet, she skidded to a stop. "Too late," he said.

"It's already begun."

At first, Morgan thought he was the one who was trembling. Then the shaking tumbled him to his knees, and when he put his hands on the ground to push himself back to his feet, he felt the vibration through the skin of his palms.

There was noise, too. Not the growling rumble he'd expected but something high and desperate, an almost animal sound that seemed to be coming from the earth itself.

"What's happening?" Anya said, turning wide, frightened eyes to him.

"I've got no idea." But even as he said the words, Morgan knew they were a lie. Some part of him, unacknowledged and long buried, understood exactly what was going on. The force shaking the ground resonated in his own body, in his chest. Sharp flashes of memory lit up in his mind. His sister's face, slack and pale when they pulled her from the water. John, gasping as Morgan stabbed him in the chest. The compassion in Tomas's voice when he told Morgan that death wasn't the end. Death, which was all Morgan ever seemed to bring to those around him. And there was death here – he felt it with a sense he hadn't even known he possessed.

When the first bodies started to rise out of the ground, Anya screamed, but in a secret corner of his mind, Morgan had been expecting them.

He staggered to his feet. The sky was still the same clear blue and the earth was rich and moist and brown where the fingers scrabbled from beneath it. They were nothing but bone, covered in the ghost flesh of the people they'd once been.

Morgan wanted to run but there was nowhere to run to. The ground was churning with rising corpses all around. Even the concrete beneath his feet was beginning to crack and he saw the white dome of a skull pushing up through the widening gap. He reached for Anya's hand and she didn't pull away. Her fingers biting into his wrist felt like his only anchor to reality.

Raphael smiled. "A million were slaughtered in the siege of Leningrad alone. Twenty million killed in the Soviet Union, an army of the dead to cleanse the world of the living."

There were hundreds, thousands of them now, filling and covering the green spaces of the park. Vadim screamed as they surrounded him. His gun fired a brief burst of bullets into old brown bones, and then he was lost to sight.

Raphael didn't even look at him. His eyes were fixed on Morgan. And then, suddenly, they widened and shifted, moving down towards the ground between them, where Tomas's heart lay impaled on Nicholson's book.

But now the book was burning. Smoke curled up from it, thick and dark and vile smelling, even from ten feet away.

"What -?" Raphael said. And as if it had just been waiting for him to open his mouth, the smoke moved. Faster than any wind could possibly have carried it, it turned and curled and rushed into the old man's throat.

His gagged, fingers clasped to his own neck. Morgan could see that he was trying to shut his mouth, but somehow the smoke wouldn't let him. The book burned on and on, rancid smoke funnelling into Raphael until it was entirely consumed. And then Raphael's face began to change.

His bones seemed to melt beneath his skin, bending and reforming into new shapes. The wrinkled skin sagged and then tightened until not a single line remained. And the fire from the burning book dyed his white hair orange and his blue eyes a curious amber. His stooped shoulders straightened, bringing up an entirely different face to gaze serenely at Morgan.

The man who was no longer Raphael smiled. "Aren't you going to welcome me back, son? I have been gone a while."

"Nicholson?" Morgan said. "How...?"

"Raphael thought he was manipulating me, but he was the one being used. He thought he was setting himself up to rule the new world, when really he was just ushering it in for its true king. Like a modern John the Baptist, I suppose, head lopped off and served on a plate before the good stuff starts."

"Its king?" Morgan said. He looked at the army of the dead, silent around them. "All of that, everything you did, so you can rule this?"

Nicholson rested a hand against Morgan's shoulder. It was warm, and almost comforting. "Not just me. There were three artefacts, Morgan. Three. My book, Tomas's heart – and my son."

"*I'm* the artefact?" Morgan said. And then he smiled in bitter self-knowledge. "Of course I am. I'm the very last thing you made."

Anya released Morgan's hand suddenly, stepping back. Nicholson grinned at her, an absurdly cheerful expression. There seemed nothing of Raphael's darkness about him.

"You're so much more than that," Nicholson told Morgan. His hand was still on his shoulder and now he moved it to lay against his cheek. "Three artefacts for a new world, and a new Trinity to replace the old – Father, Son, and Holy Ghost.

"I passed through death, you see, as all god-kings must, to gain their full power. The ghost of Tomas, his poor sad spirit, occupies and animates these shadow men around us. And you, Morgan, my handsome son. I killed myself on the night of your conception. Raphael arranged for your mother's murder, three days before you were due to be delivered. Thanks to us, you were born out of death, and you've carried it with you all your life. You are death, Morgan, the spirit of death made flesh. And you will ride at the head of my army to conquer the world for us both."

Morgan backed away. Nicholson's hand slipped from his cheek and the dead parted to let him through. He shook his head. "No, I don't want this. I never asked for it."

"It doesn't matter. You were made this way. And all your life, hasn't everyone around you died?"

"That wasn't my fault."

"No it wasn't. It isn't your fault – it's your nature, just as doing all this was in mine. I'm so proud of you, son. Lead my army. It's what you were born to do."

Morgan felt the power blooming inside him, and he knew Nicholson was right. This made sense of him, when nothing else ever had.

"But you worked with that bastard Raphael," Morgan said. "How could you?"

Nicholson's eyes blazed, bright with conviction. "Raphael was a tool, nothing more. A means to an end. But he's gone now – punished for his sins in the worst possible way, trapped impotent inside his own hijacked body. It's just us now, and we can remake the world into whatever we want."

"Don't listen to him!" Anya said. But she sounded afraid, and a part of Morgan liked that.

"Why not?" he asked her. "He's the first person who's ever told me the truth."

"*Him*?" the other woman said. "He's been manipulating everyone from the beginning. Look at what he did to Tomas!"

Morgan's heart jarred. Yes. But Tomas had lied to him too. "Tomas killed himself," he told her. "I saw the knife. Tomas got a choice – unlike me. No one's asked me what I wanted, ever. Not till now."

Anya reached out to him. "You're better than this, Morgan!"

He knocked her arm aside. "Don't give me that! You've never liked me, don't pretend you did. You only care about me now because of what I can do."

He thought, briefly, of the other Anya, who *had* seemed to care about him. But she'd been using him too, hadn't she?

All his life, people had either used or rejected him for being something he didn't choose. And they always would. If he was what Nicholson said, then he'd never have a place in the world. So why not reject them, and it? He'd thought he had no family, but he'd been wrong. Nicholson, his real father, wanted this for him. He was proud of him. Nicholson accepted him for exactly what he was. Who else had ever done that? And what was so great about this world, which had always treated him so badly? What was there here worth saving?

Why *not* wipe the slate clean and start again?

All around, as if they knew the decision he'd made, the risen dead fell to their knees. There were so many that he couldn't see an end to them. Distantly, in the city outside the park, he could hear screams, and he wondered how far the influence of Raphael's spell had spread.

"They're yours," Nicholson said. "Here – take it."

He held something towards Morgan, a silver circlet with a white stone set in its centre.

"Morgan!" a voice said, and he saw that it was the woman who'd been crying over Tomas's body. "Listen to me. Nicholson's already failed. Tomas didn't die broken-hearted, he killed himself to save me. The ritual was flawed – this isn't inevitable."

"Ignore her," Nicholson said. "Be who you're meant to be. Be my son. Take the crown."

The arm Morgan had been reaching towards his father hesitated, hovering in mid air.

The certainty in Nicholson's eyes faded as he stared at Morgan's hand, and Morgan saw doubt there for the first time.

He frowned and pulled his hand back to look at it. He saw immediately what had caught his father's eye. When the pain had faded he'd forgotten it was there, but it stood out, an inflamed red against his brown skin: the imprint of Marya's cross, which had burnt where it touched him.

He guessed what Nicholson must be thinking. The cross was a symbol of the God he'd rejected. Did he think Morgan had somehow got religion, that this was a sign of some sort of pledge?

But when Morgan looked at it, he didn't think about God. He'd never been raised to believe in him, and in the last week he'd seen plenty of evidence for a source of evil in the world, but little enough for the other side. He didn't think about God, he thought about Marya, and what Raphael had done to her.

The dead were all around, and he searched their faces, trying to see hers among them, or any of the other people who'd been lost along the way. He couldn't find them in the throng but it didn't really matter. He thought he knew what they'd say.

Marya would tell him that maybe it *was* in Raphael's nature to want her as men weren't supposed to want little girls. But she had a nature too, and wants, and Raphael had denied them by satisfying his. Nicholson rejected Raphael now, but he hadn't stopped him. How many other little girls had Raphael hurt, in all those years he was doing Nicholson's work?

And Morgan thought that maybe God should have made the world so everybody wanted matching things, and no one had to be hurt getting them. But then he pictured Richard, with his sad half smile as the rocks fell all around him and he accepted an end he hadn't asked for. Richard might tell him to imagine that world, where you were born only desiring one person and that person was born desiring you right back, and everything you wanted from life you got, because you'd been made only to want the things it was possible to have.

Richard would say that was a clockwork world. God would wind it up and set it off and no one in it would mean anything, because no one would decide anything for themselves.

And Tomas had never really spoken to Morgan about big, important things like that. But Tomas had behaved as though the choices he made mattered, and he'd make the right ones even when it was hard. When Tomas cut out his own heart, it was for someone else's sake.

And then there was Morgan's sister. She'd been so angry when he saw her in the mirror, but he wondered now if the anger had really been aimed at him. Had it been for the diary he was carrying, his father's preserved and twisted soul? Morgan had spent years blaming himself for her death. If what Nicholson said was true, it turned out he wasn't responsible. But it wasn't like no one was.

Nicholson had made him this way. All the people who'd died around him – it was Nicholson who'd killed them. Nicholson was his father by blood, but Mary had been his sister in every other way that mattered, and Nicholson had taken her away from him.

Morgan drew his hand back from the crown and clenched it into a fist. "You're right," he said. "None of this is my fault. It's *yours*."

Nicholson didn't pull the crown away. The white gem glistened milky in its centre, like a sightless eye. Nicholson's own eyes sparkled amber and suddenly much colder, much less friendly. "You think God can save you? Do you think he'll welcome you into his kingdom? You'd be no more welcome than I. When I made you, I didn't include a soul."

"I don't know what a soul is," Morgan said.

His father took a step closer. "Then think of the power, Morgan. All yours if you want it."

But Morgan didn't want power. What he wanted was meaning. If he took the crown and accepted this birthright, he would get that – his life would have been *for* something. It wouldn't just be some collection of random shit.

He looked out over his army. Their blank faces were raised to him as they knelt. They were just empty vessels, with nothing of the people they once were left inside them.

Taking the crown would give him meaning, but the meaning would be this: he was nothing but a weapon created by other people, and the only thing he had to give was death. It was better not to know anything than to know that.

He reached into his pocket and pulled out the gold chain holding Marya's small cross. The metal scorched his hand, hotter than ever, but he didn't let go. "Maybe God didn't have much to do with creating me," he said. "But someone gave me a choice about this, and I don't reckon it was you. So no, I won't take it. I won't lead your army. And I won't be your son – not in any way that matters."

Nicholson studied him for a long moment. There was no warmth at all left in his face. For the first time, Morgan could see the man who'd done all those terrible things.

"You're a fool, boy," his father said. "Do you think you can fight me? I've been through death already – and I won't go back. Nothing in the land of the living can hurt me."

"I know," Morgan said. He turned to Anya, who was watching him uncertainly. "Give me your mirror."

The expression turned from unease to puzzlement. "What?"

Nicholson looked baffled too, but that might not last long.

"You're a woman, aren't you?" Morgan said impatiently. "You wear make-up – you've got to have a mirror somewhere."

The look of incredulous affront she gave him almost made him laugh. But she reached into her pocket and pulled out a small silver case.

He snatched it from her and snapped it open before either she or Nicholson could react. Nicholson yelled something, lost beneath the growing clamour of the crowds of dead. Morgan thought his father understood – maybe not what Morgan intended, but certainly that it was a threat. He still had Raphael's semi-automatic in his hand and now he dropped the crown and raised that.

But Nicholson hesitated. Morgan knew he didn't want to do it. He still hoped that Morgan would relent. Morgan slapped the burning golden cross against the glass of the mirror and turned both to face his father.

He saw Anya's face drain of colour and his own hand shook as it held the mirror, even though he'd known what to expect. Because another hand was emerging, small and blunt-fingered, through the silvered glass. It grabbed the cross and kept on moving – and as it emerged, first a wrist, then an elbow, then a shoulder, the glass expanded too. There was a smell like burning plastic, and underneath it a hint of roses.

Morgan released the mirror, which wasn't a mirror any more. It was a gateway, and someone was stepping through it.

"Hello, Marya," he said.

The little girl smiled at him. She was as pretty as he remembered, the shadow of the adult she never became in the soft curves of her cheeks. But there was another face, overlaying or inside hers, brown-skinned and soft eyed. Her smile was his sister's. Nicholson's eyes widened in shock, and suddenly there was another consciousness shining behind them. The blue of Raphael's eyes infected Nicholson's amber and both men looked in horror at the little girls their magic had killed.

The spirit reached out, curling her far smaller hand around Nicholson's. There was a moment of complete stillness – and then she pulled. He stumbled forward a step, then another. She was back inside the mirror now, only the tips of her fingers in the outside world. She shouldn't have been strong enough to compel him, but Nicholson seemed unable to resist. Maybe Raphael's fear paralysed him, locked somewhere inside. Or maybe it was his own – facing a threat from the one realm he couldn't control.

Marya's voice floated out of the mirror, as insubstantial as a cobweb. "Come with me, Father Raphael. That's what *I* want."

Then she gave one final tug. Nicholson fell forward and kept on falling, through the surface of the mirror to whatever lay beyond. Morgan stared after him, and for one second he saw another face. His sister was smiling at him and he smiled helplessly back. Then the gateway blinked out of existence, and Anya's mirror fell to the ground and shattered.

CHAPTER NINTEEN

Anya could scarcely believe Tomas's death, or everything that had followed it. Morgan was standing beside her, glassy-eyed, as if the last few minutes had eaten up every reserve of character and strength he had.

And all around them, the hordes of the dead rose to their feet, blank eyes scanning for a leader who wouldn't come. Naively, she'd believed they'd disappear when Nicholson did. They hadn't, and now they were beginning to move. Their expressionless faces twisted and changed, filling with a mindless, directionless rage.

"Shit!" Morgan said. "I thought..."

"Well they're still here!" Anya snapped.

He looked around him, blinking. "We've got to stop them."

Anya laughed harshly. "Any suggestions?"

"Valeria has something," Kate said. Anya had almost forgotten about the other woman. "A summoning spell tied into an old ivory whistle. I don't know – it's designed for animals – but it might work with these things too."

"Do you know where she is?" Anya shouted. The noise from the dead was fearsome, a unified howl that rose and rose. There was still a clear space ten feet wide around them, the last residue of their deference for Morgan, but Anya didn't think it would last long.

Kate shrugged. "I know where she *was*."

"That's good enough for me," Anya said.

"OK," Morgan said. "OK." He turned to Kate, and whatever power it was that restrained the dead was suddenly broken.

Only the fact that there were so many saved them. There was no single consciousness guiding them now and, released from all constraints, the first target of the dead's savagery was each other.

The living turned and fled. Within ten paces, Anya had lost all sense of direction. The park exit had been behind her, now it could be anywhere. The dead crowded close all around, a strange double vision overlaying them. Sometimes they were nothing but bone, walking skeletons strung with ribbons of clothing or long-mummified flesh. Other times she saw translucent flesh and faces, facsimiles of people. She didn't know which was worse. At least when they were bone she didn't have to pity as well as fear them.

When skeletal fingers brushed her arm she flinched away, but they were all around. They were closing in, and she was losing Morgan and Kate in the crush. At the last minute Morgan's hand groped for hers. She flinched away, convinced in her panic that he was one of the dead. She felt the bones beneath his skin.

"This way!" he shouted, and pulled. She didn't know how he could tell, but she forced herself to grip his hand and trust him. There wasn't any other choice.

Anya wasn't blindfolded. She'd seen the streets they led her through to this place, and she'd be able to find it again if she was asked. That was a bad sign. They'd have hidden it from her if they meant her to survive.

And she'd seen the sacrifice they'd carried out, the girl whose bleeding corpse still lay in the centre of the room, her heart impaled beside her. Anya could see her eyes, staring blank and glassy at the ceiling above her. She'd heard her screams.

But they wanted Anya to live a little longer. Blood was trickling from a hundred scratches on her face and arms, deeper peck-marks oozing a fluid that was almost black. They'd called the birds from the sky to attack her, but then they'd called them off again and brought her here.

She was tied to a solid wooden chair in the living room of a perfectly ordinary apartment. The chandelier that hung from the ceiling was over-ostentatious and just a little dusty, and there were pictures of a family, smiling kids and dour grandparents, on the mantelpiece. This was someone's home. She wondered whose.

Not the woman who sat opposite her, whom the others had called Valeria. Her face could have been pretty – Anya knew a lot of men would have said so – but Anya thought it was too bony, and there was too much anger in her eyes.

Valeria was glaring at Anya as she took apart her gun, carefully oiling each part. The men were elsewhere in the flat. The smell of boiling cabbage suggested they were making themselves something to eat. Nothing like a square meal after a murder.

"Now what?" Anya said.

Valeria carried on oiling her gun.

"What's happened to Tomas? You can at least tell me that."

Valeria sighed, then said, "He's served his purpose in the world."

"And what would that be?"

"Ending it."

The Ragnarok artefacts. The Japanese had known what they could do, it was why they'd tried so hard to prevent them being brought together. But Anya had never quite believed it. Not till now.

At first the growl sounded like it was coming from inside the room. But it built and built and Anya didn't need to see Valeria's expression to understand that something was beginning. Valeria's face was transformed by joy until it wasn't just pretty, but beautiful. She rushed to the far side of the room and flung open the French windows, stepping out onto what Anya saw was a wide balcony.

The sound was even louder with the window open. Anya

had only heard something like it once before, when she'd been trapped in a building in LA during the earthquake of 1994. Was that how the world would end – tearing itself apart?

"Let me up," she called to Valeria. "There's nothing I can do to stop it now."

To her surprise, the other woman came back inside and knelt beside her, pulling at the ropes behind her back. "You're right," she said. "It's too late now. You should see it – everyone should see the birth of the new order."

They went back out to the balcony together. They were ten storeys high and the whole city lay spread out in front of them. The sun shone down on it, bright and clear.

It wasn't an earthquake. At first, Anya couldn't see what it was. She could hear screaming, floating up from the streets below, but she didn't know what was causing it.

Valeria must have sensed her confusion. She pointed to the left, where a green space broke up the gold and grey of the buildings. Anya realised after a second that it was a graveyard. And there, finally, the earth did seem to be moving.

"Our army rises," Valeria said.

Anya thought it was an optical illusion at first, a product of the heat haze hanging over the city. But when she blinked they were still there, the figures clawing themselves out of the ground.

"Jesus," she said. "This can't be real."

They were everywhere. As Anya's eyes scanned the city they found more graveyards, the earth roiling inside them as it was disturbed from below. Elsewhere the dead emerged from beneath pavements and inside buildings and she remembered that this city stood over a mass grave. Just below their balcony she saw one man dragged to the ground, ripped apart by the walking corpses. The stench of blood and shit wafted up.

Anya heard the directionless screaming of sirens and soon policemen and then soldiers appeared. There was gunfire, and in some places the soldiers held their line, firing and firing and firing at the dead because they didn't stop until there was nothing left of them. In other places the soldiers and policemen saw what they'd been called to confront and fled. In the growing chaos, she saw bullets pierce living bodies and soldiers trampled beneath the fleeing feet of the people they were trying to protect.

"This isn't right," Valeria said. She was frowning and chewing on her lip.

"It's too late for regrets now."

"But it shouldn't be like this, so... disordered. They should be an army, not a mob. They're meant to be led."

"By who?"

"By me."

Morgan stood in the open doorway of the apartment, a slender, middle-aged woman on his right side, and the other half of Anya on the left.

Anya saw Kate's shocked expression and knew she hadn't expected this. But Morgan looked relieved. He was smiling at the mirror image of herself, pulling her into a bear hug. He'd known.

The men burst into the room before she'd decided how to react. Kate had Raphael's gun. She'd fired it only once against the dead, before they'd realised it was useless. There were seven rounds left and she shot all of them into the three men. They were down before they'd even drawn their weapons, blood a barely visible red pool soaking into the blue carpet. They lay beside the mutilated corpse of the woman they must have killed.

After the flight through the streets to reach this place, Anya was numb to death. She barely spared them a glance. She looked a moment at Valeria, the woman they'd come to find, but she was cowering away from Kate's gun, no kind of threat. And then she just stared at herself.

The other her stared back, surprised but not amazed, and Anya realised she'd known too.

"Who the hell are you?" she said.

"She's you," Morgan answered. He flushed when she turned to glare at him. "Half of you, I mean – all the things you aren't."

There were a thousand and one questions, but only one that really mattered. "Are you it, then? Are you what's been missing these last four years?"

The other her nodded. Anya could see rope burns around her wrists and she rubbed at them absently as she spoke. "Yes. The Japanese did it to us. They wanted an agent in the BND."

"A real double agent," Anya said. "Morgan, you piece of shit."

She tore her eyes away from the other her. Screams and gunshots drifted through the open French windows, but they were getting quieter. There were fewer people left alive. Soon the dead would leave the city, and then there'd be no stopping them.

"We've come for the whistle," Morgan told Valeria. "It's the only thing that can stop this."

Valeria squared her shoulders, suddenly defiant despite the gun pointed at her. "I don't want to stop it. This is what it was all for."

The other Anya took a step towards her, hand held out half-pleading, half-placating. "But it's gone wrong. You said so yourself."

Morgan stepped forward too, beside Kate. The three of them lined the entrance to the balcony, blocking Valeria's escape. "Raphael's dead," he told her. "It's already over."

"No," Valeria whispered. "It can't be. He promised we'd win. He said we'd make them suffer."

"Who?" Anya asked.

Valeria smiled, baring yellow teeth beneath her pale lips. "Everyone."

She took a step, pressing her back to the balcony railing. The dead continued their terrible work a hundred feet beneath her.

"Give it to us," Morgan said. "Or we'll kill you and take it anyway. Believe me, we don't give a fuck if you live or die."

"I know," Valeria said. "No one ever has."

Anya guessed what she intended a moment before she did it – and a second too late to prevent it. She watched, helpless, as

Valeria's thin hands grabbed the railing behind her, tensing as she vaulted over it. She hung in the air a moment, suspended. Then her fingers slackened, her grip on the rail loosened, and she began to fall.

It seemed to take a very long time for her to hit the pavement. Her body lay there, broken but still twitching, and then the dead swarmed and she was buried beneath them.

Anya saw Morgan slump in defeat. The other her clasped his shoulder and he managed a wan smile, which she returned. Did that Anya actually like him? Had they fucked? The idea both repulsed and intrigued her.

The other Anya turned from Morgan to look at her, and there was an almost physical shock as their eyes connected. The other her looked content. Her mouth wasn't bracketed by the same worry lines that had carved grooves around hers. She smiled as if happiness was easy. Anya found that she was bitterly jealous. Why had that half of her been given all the joy, and she'd been left with the anger, the regret, the crippling sense of duty?

The other her seemed to read the resentment in her eyes. "I've been trying to make us whole again," she said. "That's why I was searching for the artefacts."

Morgan's head jerked up. "And now you've found them."

The other Anya gave him a look of incredulous hope. "You've got them?"

"I *am* one."

"Is that... you're saying you can do it? Reconnect us?"

He shrugged. "I think maybe I've got the power."

"But it needs a huge amount." The hope faded from her face. "Even if you could do it, it would probably kill you."

He laughed. "We're not getting out of here alive. In case you hadn't realised."

"Then what's the point?" Anya asked.

"I want to die a whole person," the other her said. Her face was the same one Anya saw in the mirror every morning, but she hadn't seen that expression on it for a very long time: wistful and yearning.

"No," Morgan said, "that's not why. Think about it, Anya. I was made to lead the army of the dead. That's the point of me. I control that power, even if I don't want to. If I can put it into you, instead of them – maybe I can stop them."

"Maybe, maybe, maybe," Anya said. "Or we know you can command them. You can *tell* them to stop."

"I can't."

"For the love of god –" Anya said.

"No," Kate cut across her. "Don't you see, there's a part of Morgan that wants that? That wants to be what Nicholson made him. He's resisted temptation once, don't make him do it again."

Anya saw that Kate was right. Morgan was tempted, and frightened by it. The other her wanted him to do as he'd suggested and make them whole – but she was afraid that it might kill him. Anya didn't care if it killed him. She could forgive herself for that, now she understood she was the half of herself that *couldn't* care. But she wasn't sure she wanted to be whole again. To stop being who she was now.

There was a silent moment, indecision holding everyone still.

Then, slow and creaking, the door opened.

The three men behind it looked perfectly ordinary. But their old-fashioned clothes hung loosely on them. Their faces were hollow in the cheek and puffy round the eyes, sick and starved. And then the faces faded away and Anya saw the skulls beneath.

Morgan reacted first. He flung himself against the door, slamming it shut. The door bounced against his back and his feet slid two inches along the carpet before he grimaced and forced it closed again. His fingers scrabbled against the lock, trying to turn it, but it needed a key. "Help me," he hissed.

Anya knelt beside the first of Raphael's dead followers, fumbling in his pockets.

"It's no good," the other Anya said bleakly. "Valeria had the key."

The door shuddered as more weight was thrown against it from the outside and there was a deep tearing sound as the wood began to splinter beside Morgan's head.

Morgan dug his heels into the carpet, using the leverage to push back. Then he held out his hands, one towards each half of Anya.

The other Anya reached out and took his hand.

She kept hers behind her back, clenched in a fist.

"For fuck's sake do it!" Morgan yelled as the door slid open another inch.

The Anya holding Morgan's hand was crying. She thought this was going to kill him, and it hurt her. All those soft emotions did hurt, she remembered that now. There was a reason she'd wanted to rid herself of them. That other Anya was all the parts of herself she hadn't been able to live with. Why would she want them back?

"Please," the other her said. "The shadow needs the light."

Anya watched her own hand reaching out to clasp Morgan's. His was hot and sweating and nothing at all happened when it touched hers. Then he brought his hands inwards, joining them all together, Morgan and the two people who were both her.

Something detonated without sound, blinding and deafening her, locking her inside her own head. It was fuller than she remembered, overcrowded. She was awash with contradictions and for a second they were unbearable and she tried to tear herself apart again. But the moment passed and something in her seemed to expand to accommodate these new-old feelings. She was both whole and broken, as everyone always was.

She opened her eyes and found that she was clasping both Morgan's hands in both of her own. His own eyes were blank and as she watched his legs gave and he slid to the floor.

Kate jumped forward, yelling in panic – but the door held. It wasn't moving and behind it there was silence.

Anya knelt down beside Morgan and felt his neck and wrist, searching for a pulse. There was nothing. She felt tears choking her throat, vying with anger that he'd forced her to this and regret that there hadn't been another way. The normal jumble of emotions.

"I think he's gone," she said to Kate.

The other woman held a hand in front of Morgan's mouth to feel his breath. After a moment she shrugged and took it away. "I don't know that he was ever properly alive. But it's too early to give up on him. Things that would kill a normal person, with Morgan..." She shrugged again, then put her hands in his armpits and heaved him aside.

With Morgan gone, the door swung gently inwards. The three men still stood behind it, arms braced to press against a barrier that wasn't there. Anya flinched back, but they didn't move. There was a thin coating of something white and glittering on their faces and clothes.

Anya saw her fingers shake as she reached out to the nearest arm. When she touched it there was a sensation of extreme cold. Then her fingers passed through what had looked like solid flesh. Only now there was nothing there, and she didn't understand how she'd seen anything except bones. They hung in the air for a moment like an anatomy-class skeleton. But nothing was holding them together and with an almost musical clatter, they fell to the tiled floor of the hallway.

Anya released a breath she hadn't known she was holding.

"Look at this," Kate said. She was back inside, by the French doors that led to the balcony.

The light coming from outside was strange, white and diffuse. When Anya joined Kate on the balcony, she saw why. On midsummer's day it was snowing in St Petersburg. She held out her hand and a fat flake landed on it, perfect and beautiful in the moment before it melted.

The snow had already coated the ground, muffling the sound of people running. There were some screams, but far fewer than before. All over the pavement and road, stretching off into the distance, she could see humps of snow where something lay beneath it. Some of them were big enough to be bodies, others just piles of bone.

"When they split me in two," Anya said, "it created an explosion the size of a tactical nuclear bomb. An exothermic reaction."

Kate nodded, still looking out. "And the reverse process needed to draw in an exactly equal amount of energy. It came from the dead through Morgan. It's always the cold, isn't it? It's defeated every army that tried to invade this country, from Napoleon to Hitler."

Anya glanced at Morgan, but he hadn't moved. Only his eyelids had slid shut so that it looked like he was sleeping. "He was right."

Kate looked back at him, and Anya realised she was crying. "Yeah. Tomas would have been proud."

EPILOGUE

EPILOGUE

Morgan had been conscious for two days. They still had a drip in his arm and one of those heart monitors attached to his chest that made him feel like he was in an episode of *Casualty*. He hadn't been able to sleep properly the first night. He kept waiting for the steady *beep-beep-beep* to transmute into the long loud hum that said he was flatlining.

They'd told him Anya was coming to visit, so he wasn't surprised when she poked her head round the door an hour after breakfast. She saw he was awake and moved all of the way in, pulling out an orange plastic chair to sit beside his bed. He smiled when he realised she hadn't brought any flowers. He knew which half of her that came from. There was a long silence as they studied each other.

"How are you feeling?" he asked eventually.

She laughed. "I'm not the one who was in a coma for ten days."

He shrugged.

"I'm fine," she told him. "Apart from the two completely contradictory sets of memories. Someone asks me what I did for Christmas and I've got two answers." She smiled, as if it was all a joke, but she looked strained. Strained, and not quite the woman he knew – either of them.

"Are you happy, though? Is it what you wanted?"

She nodded, but her eyes wouldn't meet his and he thought maybe it was a stupid question. If she was a complete person now she was probably glad and sorry, not just one or the other.

She picked up the book he'd left lying on his bedside table, beside the half-drunk plastic glass of water and the two pills he hadn't yet taken. "Phillip Larkin," she said. "Poetry doesn't seem like your kind of thing."

"Kate brought it – it was Tomas's. She said he'd have wanted me to have it. I don't think he was losing any sleep over my inadequate literary education, but whatever."

She smiled. "Do you like them?"

"He's got one thing right. Your mum and dad definitely do fuck you up." There was a short silence, then he told her, "They've permanently reopened the Hermetic Division, put Kate in charge of it. She wants me to work for them once I'm out of here."

"Has she told them what..."

"What I am?" He grinned at her discomfort. "I doubt it. Did you tell the BND what *you* are?"

She shook her head. "No point."

"Exactly."

"And will you do it – join the Hermetic Division?"

He looked down, toying with the crisp white sheet. "You know, the man who had this room before me died here. He wasn't that old, about forty. His hair had all fallen out, so I guess he had cancer."

She frowned, not understanding.

"I saw him," he told her. "In the bathroom mirror yesterday. Maybe the Division's where I belong."

He glanced up idly when the door opened again, expecting a nurse, come to nag him about his tablets.

"Hello, Morgan," Belle said. "I told the receptionist I'm your goddaughter. I hope you don't mind."

He felt a wave of rage that half lifted him out of the bed, before a wave of exhaustion lowered him back down to it. "You've got a fucking nerve," he hissed. "Get out of here."

She smiled. She wasn't pretending to be just an innocent little girl any more, and it wasn't a pleasant expression. "Or what? You'll call the police?"

"We didn't know if you'd made it," Anya said, as angry as Morgan. "But Kate warned the Hermetic Division about you anyway."

Belle skipped forward, blonde hair swinging, and perched cross-legged on the end of Morgan's bed. "I know," she said. "They'll be here soon, I guess. And when they get here I'll tell them to call the CIA, and the CIA will tell them politely – but firmly – to let me go."

"Then we'll tell the CIA what you are," Anya said.

Belle laughed. "See no evil, hear no evil. They'll choose not to believe you. I'm far too valuable to them to lose."

"Then what are you doing here?" Morgan asked.

She pouted. "I wanted to see if you really were still alive. The Hermetic Division had a news black-out about you. And the Russians are claiming the whole thing was caused by a poison gas attack. Chechnyan terrorists." Her laugh was as light and tinkling as ever. "Fortunately they don't have much in the way of a free press to poke holes in the story. And they're not letting foreign reporters anywhere near St Petersburg."

"Well, thanks for filling me in," Morgan said. "It's been nice seeing you."

She hopped to the floor again, leaving the bed bouncing behind her. "You should have died back there, it would have been easier for everyone. Now you're just a loose cannon, a nuisance to your enemies and a danger to your friends."

"Bullshit," Anya said. "You lost. We won. It's over."

Belle stopped, small white hand on the door handle. "Is that what you think? The other side put all its eggs in one basket once, and looked what happened to him – nailed to a plank in Jerusalem two thousand years ago. We're not so reckless. Or did you really think, Morgan, that you were the only one?"

Her shadow followed behind her as she left the room, the dark outline of wings twitching above its shoulders.

Acknowledgements

Enormous thanks to Matt Jones, Jennifer-Anne Hill, Muriel Levene, Carrie O'Grady and Jon Oliver, without whom this book would either be far worse or nonexistent.

THE INFERNAL GAME

Now read the first chapter of the next exciting novel
in the *Infernal Game* series...

GHOST DANCE

Rebecca Levene

ISBN: 978-1-906735-38-8

£7.99/$9.99

Coming July 2010

WWW.ABADDONBOOKS.COM

PROLOGUE

When he looked in the mirror, George W Bush looked back. The mask was expressionless, blank – the way he felt inside.

He'd laid the guns out on his bed after his mom had left for work. There was the Beretta 391 semi-automatic shotgun which he'd stolen from Joshua Heligman's house, from the gun drawer his dad was supposed to keep locked but never did. Joshua had told him about that once, in home room, pimply face flushed with excitement. Joshua had claimed he used to steal the gun himself, take it out to the woods and use the rabbits for target practice.

The holster for the Beretta fit on his hip. He slung the Browning A-bolt across his back, where it bulged out the leather of his duster. The material creaked protestingly as he moved and released its distinctive smell. Musty – as if the curing hadn't quite halted its decay.

He'd stolen the rifle from a freshman whose name he couldn't remember. His parents had given it him for his fifteenth birthday, a present no one would forget.

The two little pea-shooters in his pockets had come from Christine Dunn's house. They didn't have much stopping power, but he was saving them for her. He wanted to imagine her parents' faces when the cops told them their stuck-up little bitch of a daughter had been shot with their own guns. He enjoyed picturing everyone's faces.

The phone rang, but he ignored it. That would be the school secretary, wanting to find out where he was. She'd know the answer soon enough.

The sun was bright, the sky flat and the air dead as he walked the half mile to school. Old Mrs Corry stared as he passed, probably trying to guess the face behind the mask, but she didn't say anything. She hadn't spoken to him anyway since the day she found her little kitten's guts smeared all over her microwave door. She'd known it was him – known, but not been able to prove it. That made him laugh as he passed her and he heard the clacking of her pumps speed to a half jog as she hurried away behind him.

There was no one at the school gates. He'd waited long enough to ensure that Mr Atkinson was back inside, no longer lurking to pounce on tardy students. No one would stop him. This was really going to happen.

He'd thought he might experience things differently today of all days, but he couldn't see this place through fresh eyes. He felt the same dull ache of hatred as the doors swung open onto the gloom inside.

He squinted, momentarily blind. But the squeak of rubber soles on parquet told him he wasn't alone, and when his eyes cleared he saw Mrs O'Grady striding towards him, red ringlets swaying.

He let her get very close before he pulled out the Beretta and he waited to see the fear in her eyes before he put a bullet between them. The silencer muffled the retort to a dull *thump*, but he still froze, momentarily stunned by what he'd done. The bullet hole in her forehead was surprisingly small. It looked like that mark – he couldn't remember the name – the red dot that some of the Indian students wore.

When she fell to the floor it was with a meaty thump that startled him out of his paralysis. And there was the blood he'd anticipated, spreading in a scarlet halo around her head.

The exit wound must be far larger than the entry and suddenly he wanted to see it. He used his foot to flip her head to the side and the blood leaked on to his shoe, blood and skull fragments and fatty brain matter. There was nothing left of the back of her head.

He expected to feel something. He'd been sure that this, at least, would penetrate the dense fog that softened everything he saw to the same white nothing. But it was... disappointing. Maybe he'd rehearsed it so many times in his mind, he'd already sucked all the marrow from the bones of the experience. Or maybe he hadn't hated Mrs O'Grady enough.

He flipped her back over and saw her face again, slack in death. Back again, and there was the mess and the gore. He could smell it too, along with the shit and piss that stained her dress. He left her like that, exit wound exposed, the truth that was the dead meat, not the lie that had been her face.

He moved deeper inside the building, drawing the rifle from his back to join the Beretta in his hand. Now that he'd notched up his first kill he didn't have much time left and he had to make it count. He removed the silencer from the Beretta's barrel, wanting to make a noise now – wanting to be heard.

Classroom 4B was on the second floor. As he took the stairs two at a time he realised he felt weightless. Was this the elation he'd been waiting for? It hadn't occurred to him that happiness was something so foreign he might not recognise it if he felt it.

A kid scampered towards him as he rounded the second curve of the stairs. No one he recognised, some jock senior with a thick neck and dumb eyes. They widened when the boy caught sight of the semi-automatic in his hand.

He took a moment to savour the raw fear in the jock's face and then he fired. The trigger was lighter than he'd realised and a hail of bullets shattered the silence before he released the pressure. The senior's body danced and jerked, just like in the movies.

When the bullets stopped the screams started. A door to his left opened then quickly slammed and he knew that the cops would be called very soon.

But not soon enough. There was the wooden door to 4B, pitted at the bottom where generations of feet had kicked it open. He added his own toe print, a little memento of his existence that would be lost amidst the bigger legacy he was leaving behind.

It was Mr Skeet's class. He'd planned it that way. Skeet had once taken him aside and told him that he had a real talent for physics. He'd asked if there were problems at home, if there was anything he wanted to talk about.

There were no problems at home, that *was* the problem. There was only the destructive blandness of it all.

Mr Skeet was the first to die. Then ten more in the first wild volley of bullets. He'd read about other school shootings, and the thing that had shocked him was the survival rate. It seemed to him those other guys just hadn't done their research. But he'd read an airport thriller about Navy SEALs once and he knew they never took a kill for granted.

He didn't either. Brittany was bleeding from a wound in her shoulder. It seeped a rich dark blood through the fingers she curled protectively against it. When he took a step towards her she said his name and he wondered how she recognised him behind the mask. But he found it gratifying that she did. He *was* memorable – hell, he was unforgettable. He winked at her as he rested the barrel of the gun against her ear and pulled the trigger.

It became almost mechanical after that, each kill a little less of a high and more of a chore, like the fourth hit of X you took when the pleasure was gone and you were just looking for the energy to go on.

When he'd finished there was blood *everywhere*. He placed himself in the middle of it, feet planted in the deepest pool. He lifted a hand to his mask, considered lifting it. But no, the crime-scene photos would be so much more memorable if he was still wearing it. The media would love it. They'd fucking eat it up.

The barrel of the gun was scalding as he rested it against his temple. All that heat from the bullets, the transformed kinetic energy. That was something he'd learned in Mr Skeet's class. He took a deep, final breath as his eyes slid shut.

They snapped open again when he heard the footstep behind him. His finger tightened on the trigger of his second weapon as he spun, but the chamber clicked empty and the man just smiled.

For a moment he thought this must be his father. The shape of the face was the same, and the wide hazel eyes. But this man was younger, and his father had never worn quite that knowing, cynically amused expression.

The man nodded at the gun in his other hand, the one still pointed at his own temple.

"If you knew where you were going," he said, "you wouldn't be in such a hurry to get there."

The man was waiting for Alex outside the front door of the school. She walked right past him into the bitterly cold Manhattan morning, cellphone pressed to her ear as she made an appointment with her manicurist, only for him to grab her by the wrist and swing her round to face him.

"What the hell do you think you're doing?" she said, jerking her arm futilely in his grasp. "And while we're on the subject, who the hell do you think you are?"

He was tall, dark-haired, Native American, a quality of stillness about him so extreme it was hard to tell if he was even breathing. "I'm an agent of the federal government, Miss Keve," he said. "And to answer your first question, I'm arresting you. I can make it more of a showdown if you like. Miranda rights, handcuffs. Or you could just come quietly."

She was so shocked that she let him pull her unresisting down the broad steps and past the stunted, winter-bald oak trees to the car park out front. It was only when she saw Jenna leaning against her Porsche, eyes unreadable behind dark glasses as she waited for her ride home, that Alex returned to her senses. She dug in her heels, skidding a few inches against the sidewalk before pulling him to a halt.

"Not so fast, Agent Orange," she said. "How about you show me some ID? And how about I get my constitutionally mandated phone call and use to it call my dad? Who, by the way, is a senior 9th circuit judge, in case no one mentioned that to you."

He raised an eyebrow, unperturbed. "Have it your way, kid.

You have the right to remain silent. Anything you say can and will be used against you in a court of law -" He pitched his voice loud enough to carry across the entire car park. Jenna's head jerked up at the sound, expression registering shock when she caught sight of Alex.

"Shut up!" Alex hissed. "I'm coming, OK – just shut the fuck up."

The rest of the walk passed in silence, but he didn't release her wrist and she felt eyes on her, boring into the back of her head. Kids at West Village High didn't get arrested. It just wasn't that sort of school.

Alex waited until she was inside his black Impala before she turned to him again. She'd had the walk over to decide on a new tactic, and it required her to look friendly. Her smile was so stiff it made her jaw ache.

"Look, this has got to be some mistake," she said. "Why don't you drive me home, have a quiet word with my father – I'm sure we can clear this all up." She was sure her father would be furious, but dealing with his anger seemed like the least bad option right now.

"Here's the thing," he said. "Most people, when they're told they're arrested, ask what the hell for."

"I..." she trailed into silence.

"You need to work on your poker face, kid," he said. "Far too many tells."

He was right and he knew it and there was nothing she could do about it. After a second he clicked on the radio to some college station, tapping his finger against the wheel just out of time with the music. She looked at her reflection in the car's tinted window, long blonde hair bleached to ash and pale skin ghost-like. She didn't look like an innocent person taken against her will. She looked like a guilty person who'd been caught.

"I have a problem," she said eventually. "I'll get help. I'll go into rehab. I'm not hurting anybody except myself."

He nodded almost imperceptibly, eyes fixed on the road and finger still tapping.

"What do the FBI care about a little recreational drug use, anyway?"

"They don't," he said. "But thanks for the heads-up. I'll make sure to have local law enforcement search your home and locker."

After that she sat in silence, fists clenched tight and jaw working soundlessly. She'd walked right into it and she only had herself to blame, but that didn't stop her fury. And beneath that, quivering in her belly, her fear. Because she really hadn't done anything other than attend a few pharma parties and maybe score X a few times when they hit the East Village clubs. There was no reason, none at all, why a federal agent should have dragged her out of school and into his unmarked car. And she'd asked for ID, but he'd never shown it.

She thought about screaming, but there was no one to hear except him, and she had the horrible feeling that it would just make him laugh.

She stared out of the window instead, trying to memorise their route, imagining repeating it to a cop, a real one, when she made her escape. The West Village passed by, leafy and quiet, dull Chelsea, the sprawling campus of Colombia and then the shabby-hipness of Harlem. They were on 105th, somewhere between 4th and 5th, when the car finally slowed.

Alex hoped they'd stop on the street where she'd have a chance to call for help, but her captor pressed a button on the dash and the doorway to an underground garage opened onto darkness. She banged against the glass of the window as the car slid down but all it did was bruise her palm, and no one looked round.

"I'm not going to hurt you," the man said mildly as he reversed the car between two others, both identical black Impalas.

Alex took a shaky breath, desperately wishing she could believe him. "You haven't even told me your name."

He shrugged. "You can call me PD. People tend to."

The underground garage was empty, dank and dripping. Her heels caught in the cracked concrete as she walked beside him, but he didn't take her wrist again and she let herself believe that was a good sign.

"PD," she said, "are you really with the FBI?"

"I never said that I was." He turned to stare at her, head cocked to one side, considering. "Listen, kid – you're in trouble, but not the kind you think. You'll be walking out of here alive, I promise you that. Whether you're walking out a free woman or in cuffs is up to you."

He led her to a rusted metal door, punching a number into a keypad lock before swinging it open. The corridor beyond was white painted and strip-lit, clinical and unwelcoming. Her footsteps echoed on the tiled floor but there was no one around to hear them.

The room he brought her to contained nothing but a table and three chairs. PD gestured at one of them and settled himself beside her so that she had to twist her head to see him. She was sure it was deliberate, an interrogation technique. But what the hell did he want to interrogate her about?

She tried to keep calm, not to let the waiting get to her the way it was clearly intended to. She tried to convince herself this was all a trick of her father's, something he'd cooked up with his contacts in the NYPD in an attempt to scare her straight, and it was almost plausible enough that she could buy it.

When the door opened behind her with a whoosh of air she couldn't help her start of surprise. She forced herself not to look around as the newcomer paused behind her. PD's head lifted and she knew the two were exchanging glances.

A few more seconds passed before she heard a soft sound which could have been a laugh, or maybe just a sigh, and the newcomer moved to sit opposite her. He was thin, old and white with a friendly, almost avuncular face and eyes such an odd, pale blue they appeared blind. But the most striking thing about him were his hands. He held them steepled in front of him, slender, desiccated fingers tapering into hooked nails. They were a skeleton's hands covered in only the thinnest parchment layer of skin.

"Miss Keve," he said, "My name is Hammond. You must be wondering why you've been brought here."

She nodded, not trusting her voice.

"The Patriot Act's a marvellous thing, Alexandra. It gives us a freedom we never had before. It allows us to listen in on a populace that once valued its privacy above its safety. And, as the conspiracy theorists have correctly surmised, Al Qaeda operatives aren't the only people we're searching for."

Alex's heart raced as she tried to recall the hundreds of phone conversations she'd held in the last few weeks alone. Had she said anything incriminating? But they already knew about the drugs, and they didn't seem to care about those.

Hammond read her expression and smiled. "No need to rack your brain, young lady. I can tell you exactly what you said that was of such interest to us."

He nodded to PD, and a moment later the sound of her own voice filled the room. It was a little slurred in places, over-enunciated in others. Whatever she was about to say, it was clear she'd been wasted when she said it.

"Hey," her voice said. "Is that the – what's the word? Is that the NBC *complaints division*?" There was a brief pause, but no reply came. She'd probably reached an answering machine and failed to realise it.

"Well, anyway," her voice continued, "I've got a complaint to make. I'm – it's late, I'm a little – I'm watching the news right now, and it's some piece about a high-school football team, and that's supposed to be cheerful, right? I mean boring, but cheerful. But there's *blood everywhere*."

Another brief pause, and in this one you could hear her gasping breath, a whimper buried somewhere in each exhalation. "He killed them all – he shot the whole fucking lot of them. Jesus, I don't know, maybe that's news or whatever, but did you have to show us the bodies? That... that girl with her head blown off, and the guy in the George Bush mask, that's just sick." A shuddering breath, and then her voice was a little steadier. "So yeah, that's what I wanted to say. Just stop showing it, all right. Please stop showing it."

There was the hiss of static, and then a long stretch of silence. Alex had no memory at all of making that call. But she knew when it must have been, 10 days ago exactly after that night at Jenna's place where they'd all tried ketamine and god knows what else and none of them had had a very good time on it, but she'd had the worst. "Down the K-hole," Jenna had said, and after that it was all just a blank till Alex woke up the next morning with a pounding head and a feeling of sick, unfocused dread.

Alex didn't generally follow the news – she didn't give all that much of a shit – but she'd seen the piece about the school shooting in Iowa, where an unknown boy in a George Bush mask had walked into his school and shot down twenty-seven of his classmates before walking calmly back out again. They still hadn't identified the killer, but then it was only *three days* since the shooting.

"I didn't know it was going to happen!" she said. "It was – I don't know, a crazy coincidence or something. You can't possibly think I was involved. I've never even been to Iowa!"

"It was no coincidence," Hammond said blandly.

PD's chair squeaked against the floor as he shifted. When she turned to look at him she saw that he was watching her through narrowed eyes.

"You weren't bullshitting me," she said. "You really work for the government."

Hammond shrugged. "For the... let's say for the CIA."

She'd moved beyond fear into a kind of frozen calm so brittle it might shatter at the slightest pressure. "Look," she said. "I was high. I'd taken... all kinds of stuff and I had no idea what I was saying. I don't even remember saying it."

Hammond nodded, thin lips pressed together. "But you did. You did, Alexandra, and I find that very interesting indeed."

She wondered dully what they would do with her. Were they going to ask her to identify her accomplice, the boy in the George Bush mask? Would they offer her a deal if she did? She considered lying, giving them the first name she could think of. If she made it common enough there'd probably be a boy at the school in Iowa who had it. But that would be like an admission of guilt and she wasn't ready for that. She was innocent, and some part of her that still believed in the pledge of allegiance and America the Brave and all that shit, thought that ought to count for something.

"You want to know what I think happened?" Hammond said. "Those drugs – whatever it was you took – opened a doorway in your mind, and for a brief moment you were in the spirit world, where time has no meaning."

Alex stared at him, dumbstruck. "You think *what*?"

"There really was a broadcast about that school on NBC the night you called. And when you saw it in that state, you saw... well, to say the future would oversimplify things. You saw the psychic scar on the spirit world that the events to come had left."

It would be easier to think that he was crazy, but there was no hint of madness in his pale eyes and when she looked across at PD he nodded encouragement and agreement.

"OK," she said. "Right. So you're saying I *didn't* have anything to do with that shooting. So why the hell have you brought me here?"

Hammond reached across the table, resting his dry, skeletal hand against hers. "You're a spirit traveller, Alexandra, the first of your generation. That makes you very rare and very valuable indeed. In the right hands and with the right training you could be an enormous asset."

PD leaned forward, resting his large, blunt-fingered hand against her other wrist, so that she was caught between the two men. She was suddenly uncomfortably aware of how much larger than her they both were. She felt the quiet strength of their hands and for the first time noticed the bulge of the jacket at PD's hip, the tell-tale shape of a handgun beneath it.

PD followed the direction of her gaze. "I told you I won't hurt you, kid," he said.

"That's the last thing we want," Hammond said. "Our aim today is to recruit you."

She jerked back, pulling her hands from beneath theirs. "*Recruit* me? I'm sixteen!"

"Oh, we'd want you to finish your schooling, of course," Hammond said. "You wouldn't enter active service for a few years yet – though we'd train you in the interim, and perhaps make occasional use of your unusual abilities. What do you say, Miss Keve?"

Her chair scraped shrilly against the tiles as she stood. "No! More no than you can possibly imagine! You're crazy, this is crazy and even if it wasn't there's no way I'm working for the federal fucking government. I've got thirty million dollars in trust – I'm not planning on working at all!"

Hammond leaned back in his chair and she couldn't pinpoint what shifted in his face, but suddenly it didn't look friendly or avuncular at all. "I'm not sure you fully understand the situation here. We have evidence – quite solid evidence, I imagine, since the search warrant on your house was executed a few minutes ago – that you've been engaging in illegal activities. We also have testimony from several of your friends that you have, on more than one occasion, supplied them with controlled substances. I don't have to tell you that's a felony. How do you think you'd enjoy prison, Alexandra – with or without your thirty million dollar trust fund?"

Alex took in a deep, shuddering breath. "You're telling me I don't have a choice."

"There's always a choice," PD said. "You just have to decide if it's worth paying the price for making the tough one."

But Alex couldn't go to prison. She tried to picture it, the shame and the boredom and the fear – every woman in there knowing her father was a judge. Her life would be over, maybe literally, definitely metaphorically. She tried to imagine Jenna standing by her, or Ryan or any of her friends, but she knew that they wouldn't. Their very complicity in her crime would drive them away from her. And her dad would be so stern and cold and disapproving, and her mom would say all the right things to the press and nothing at all to her.

Her knees felt suddenly weak and she let herself sink back into her chair. "You win," she said bitterly. "If you want me, you've got me."

Hammond smiled wide. "I'm pleased to hear it. Welcome to the Bureau of Counter-Rational Warfare, Alexandra."

Visit www.abaddonbooks.com for information on our titles,
interviews, news and exclusive content.

TOMES of the DEAD

DEATH HULK

Matthew Sprange

ISBN: 978-1-905437-03-0
UK £.6.99   US $7.99

Abaddon
Books

Follow us on twitter: www.twitter.com/abaddonbooks

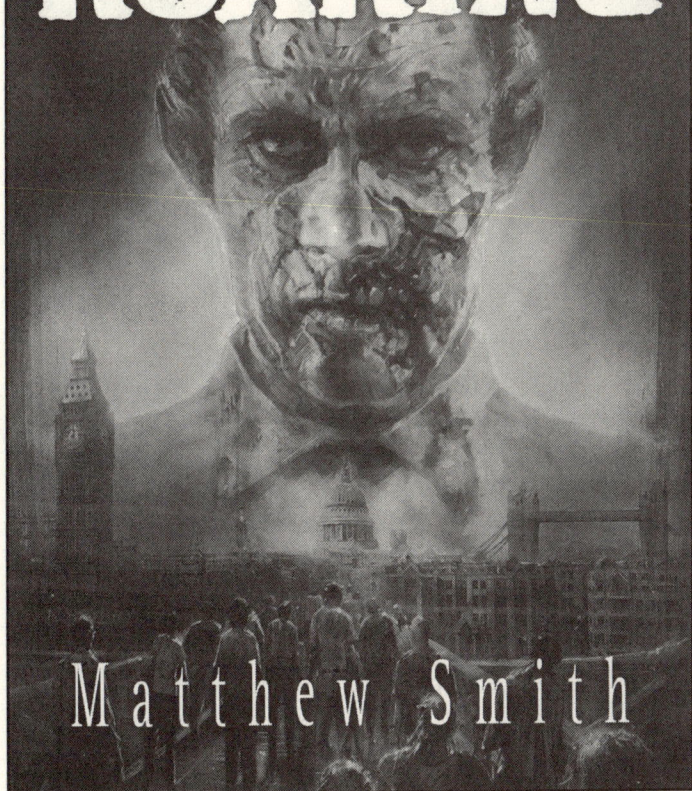

Visit www.abaddonbooks.com for information on our titles,
interviews, news and exclusive content.

TOMES *of the* DEAD

THE **WORDS** OF THEIR **ROARING**

Matthew Smith

ISBN: 978-1-905437-13-9
UK £.6.99   US $7.99

Abaddon
Books

Follow us on twitter: www.twitter.com/abaddonbooks

Visit www.abaddonbooks.com for information on our titles,
interviews, news and exclusive content.

TOMES *of the* DEAD

THE DEVIL'S PLAGUE

Mark Beynon

ISBN: 978-1-905437-41-2

UK £.6.99   US $7.99

Abaddon
Books

Follow us on twitter: www.twitter.com/abaddonbooks

Visit www.abaddonbooks.com for information on our titles,
interviews, news and exclusive content.

TOMES *of the* DEAD

I, Zombie

Al Ewing

ISBN: 978-1-905437-72-6
UK £.6.99   US $7.99

Abaddon
Books

Follow us on twitter: www.twitter.com/abaddonbooks

Visit www.abaddonbooks.com for information on our titles,
interviews, news and exclusive content.

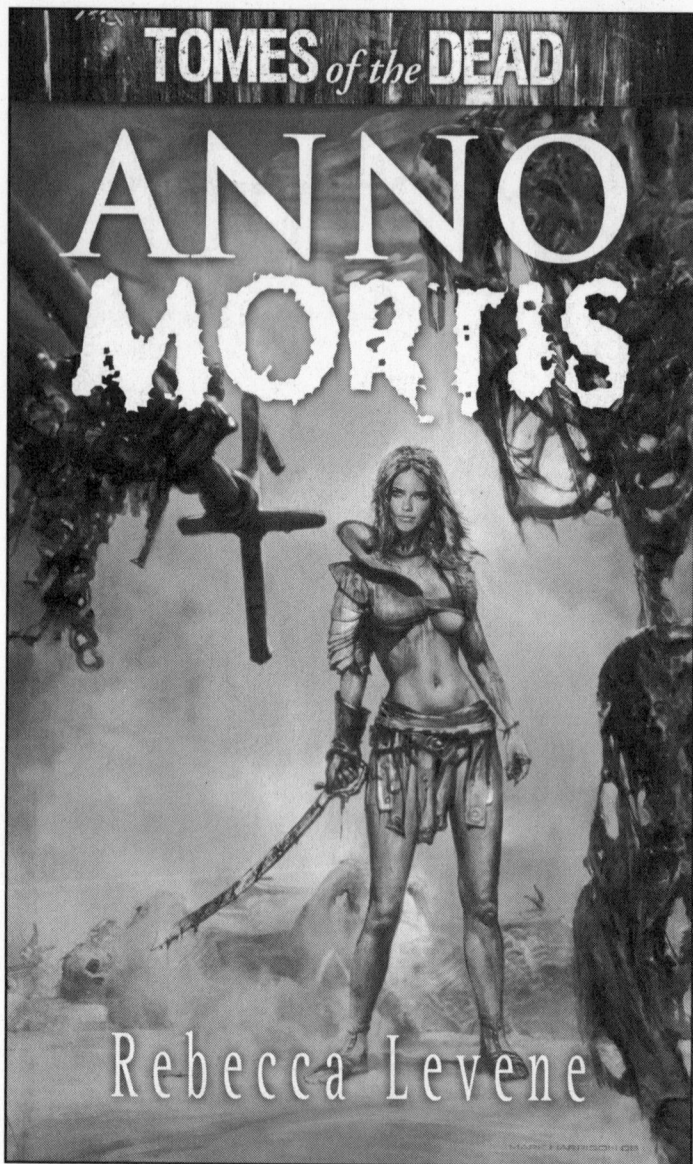

TOMES *of the* DEAD

ANNO MORTIS

Rebecca Levene

ISBN: 978-1-905437-85-6
UK £.6.99   US $7.99

Abaddon
Books

Follow us on twitter: www.twitter.com/abaddonbooks

TOMES *of the* DEAD

Way of The Barefoot ZOMBIE

Jasper Bark

Visit www.abaddonbooks.com for information on our titles,
interviews, news and exclusive content.

ISBN: 978-1-906735-06-7
UK £.6.99   US $7.99

Abaddon
Books

Follow us on twitter: www.twitter.com/abaddonbooks

TOMES *of the* DEAD

TIDE OF SOULS

SIMON BESTWICK

Visit www.abaddonbooks.com for information on our titles,
interviews, news and exclusive content.

ISBN: 978-1-906735-14-2
UK £.6.99   US $7.99

Abaddon
Books

Follow us on twitter: www.twitter.com/abaddonbooks

TOMES *of the* DEAD

Hungry Hearts

GARY McMAHON

Visit www.abaddonbooks.com for information on our titles,
interviews, news and exclusive content.

ISBN: 978-1-906735-26-5
UK £.6.99   US $7.99

Abaddon
Books

Follow us on twitter: www.twitter.com/abaddonbooks

TOMES *of the* DEAD

EMPIRE OF
SALT

WESTON OCHSE

Visit www.abaddonbooks.com for information on our titles,
interviews, news and exclusive content.

ISBN: 978-1-906735-32-6
UK £.6.99   US $7.99

Abaddon
Books

Follow us on twitter: www.twitter.com/abaddonbooks